Ripples in the Surf

Margaret Blanchard

For Colleen, with love,

love Leatherbacks!

Best wishes,

Margaret Blanchard.

Published by

MELROSE BOOKS

An Imprint of Melrose Press Limited
St Thomas Place, Ely
Cambridgeshire
CB7 4GG, UK
www.melrosebooks.com

FIRST EDITION

Copyright © Margaret Blanchard 2009

The Author asserts her moral right to
be identified as the author of this work

Cover designed by Matt Stephens

ISBN 978-1-906561-35-2

FSC
Mixed Sources
Product group from well-managed
forests and other controlled sources
Cert no. SGS-COC-2953
www.fsc.org
© 1996 Forest Stewardship Council

Printed and bound in Great Britain by:
CPI Antony Rowe, Chippenham, Wiltshire

For

My Husband,

Facilitator,

and Family,

Supporters, Fans and Animators.

CONTENTS

PROLOGUE

Screeching banshee winds, drum-rolls of thunder, fork and sheet lightning cracked like gunshots, illuminating the dramatic Cornish coast and cold, steely grey sea. Balanced precariously on the headland, the cottage shuddered and rocked. Inside, Penny watched in awe as massive waves crashed through Razor Rocks onto the small crescent-shaped beach below. She'd never seen the sea like this before, a majestic and frightening force of nature. Her father, David, had 'battened down the hatches' and the family were cosily ensconced indoors. By late afternoon, the storm had blown itself out, the maelstrom quietened and the sun gleamed. Waves lapped innocently onto the beach, its peaceful tranquillity belying its former ferocity.

"Come on Puddin' Face! Let's go for a walk!" enthused her father, grabbing her hand. "It's a beautiful evening and the storm's bound to have thrown up some interesting specimens. Coming, Gemma?" he called to his wife.

"Yes, it's what we need after a stifling day indoors," rejoined her mother.

"Dad – stop calling me 'Puddin' Face'. I'm *ten*, too old for nicknames. Anyhow, my pudding mania's worn off," said Penny untruthfully.

"Sorry," said David, hugging her affectionately and grinning. "So – what specimens are you hoping to see, Professor Penny?"

"Seaweed!" she replied, grinning back. She'd seen great swathes of seaweed slapping past Razor Rocks and could add more exotic stuff to her unexciting 'collection'. This consisted of a bedraggled, smelly strand of 'Fucus Vesiculosis' hanging outside the door (Dad said it was supposed to tell the weather) and a large, dull piece of nondescript 'Laminaria'.

"What about you, Mum? Do you want to come along?" Gemma

asked her mother.

"I think I will, dear. A bit of fresh air before dinner will do us all good," replied Dorothy Fairweather, Penny's gran, removing her floury pinny.

Clad in sensible shoes and jackets, the family set off for the bay, David leading the way with Penny. Gemma and her mother strolled along behind, sniffing the aromatic breeze and delighting in the clarity of sky and sea washed clean by the storm. Pausing on a grassy promontory, they looked at the devastation on the shore below. It was littered with strange seaweeds, shells, dead crabs, big pebbles and all the marine detritus thrown up by the gale. Strange fish floundered in rock pools too small to hold them and slimy jellyfish were scattered thick on the beach, their long transparent tentacles glistening. Rising up from the middle of this pelagic ooze was a strange massive black rock.

"Where did that boulder come from?" asked David. "It wasn't there yesterday. Surely it couldn't have been swept through Razor Rocks?"

"Perhaps it's broken off one of the surrounding cliffs and been washed into the centre of the beach," suggested Gemma. "The waves were enormous and terrifically powerful."

"Yes! It was great …" began Penny but, before she finished, David interrupted, "Gemma, look again at that boulder. Do you see what I do? Come on, quickly, we've got to get down there as fast as possible if we're to be of any use," and he started running down the path like a mad man.

Penny watched, thoroughly puzzled. What was the matter with Dad? She couldn't see anything wrong. Just the big rock.

"Mum! What's Dad up to? What's the rush to reach a rock?" Gemma too was hastening down the path.

"Come on Penny! You'll find out. Your father's usually right about this sort of thing. Mum! Take care, the path's treacherous."

Slipping and sliding in their haste, they followed David onto the beach, picking their way through the strewn seaweed. Penny particularly avoided the jellyfish, knowing that some of these could inflict terrible stings. There seemed to be unusually large ones lying around which she didn't like the look of. Coming closer to the rock they became aware of a low sighing, groaning sound. Someone must be trapped underneath! Penny started to run forwards to help but her mother stopped her.

"Don't run, Penny! It's already frightened and you'll make it worse. Keep quiet and calm. Dad will know what to do. Isn't it a magnificent specimen though! We *must* get it off."

Not understanding, Penny stared at her mother then back at the rock. It moved. She let out a startled scream.

"SHUSH! QUIET!" hissed her father and mother in unison.

Drawing nearer she heard louder sighs from the vast sea monster and saw a great paddle-like arm twitching on the sand. It was longer than Dad – at least eight feet! A giant-sized flipper!

"Mum, Dad," she whispered excitedly, "is it one of those Marine Turtles you were telling me about? It's *enormous*!"

"Yes, it's a Giant Leatherback Turtle and it definitely shouldn't be here. Take a really good look, Penny, because they'll be extinct by the time you're twenty and your children won't *ever* see them," her father replied, sounding grim. "Meanwhile, we've got to get him off this beach – and *soon* or he'll die. What a splendid fellow he is."

"What shall we do?"

"Gemma, get the sledge and shovels from the shed, please, and bring them down. Get Alan to help, he should be around. Dorothy, will you go to the coastguard and say I need plenty of very strong rope. Tell anyone you meet to come down here *at once*, we'll need plenty of muscle. Say it's *very* urgent, a matter of life and death. You stay here with me, Penny, and we'll try to keep the old boy alive and well until help arrives."

No time was wasted on arguing or discussions. The authoritative urgency in David's voice sent everyone scurrying. Anyhow, he was a Professor of Marine Biology and knew about Sea Turtles.

"Follow me, Penny. We've got to keep him calm and wet. You walk towards him, talking quietly and reassuringly, and I'll start digging a channel for water and the sledge."

"Dad …" Penny hesitated, not liking to admit she was a bit afraid. The creature was so big! Twelve feet or more from top to tail and weighing – what? – she wondered.

"Dad – how much does it weigh?"

"About one to two tons at a guess. He's a big lad. I've never seen one as large as him."

"How do you know it's a 'he'?"

David chuckled. "That's easy. Only females come up on the beaches to lay their eggs. That's in tropical countries between certain times. He's far too big for a female, this is not a tropical beach and it's not the right time for laying. Ergo, Puddin' Face Watson, he is a male."

"Dad – *don't* call me Puddin' Face!"

Penny forgot being apprehensive and felt cross instead. Walking slowly towards the Giant Turtle, she kept up a quiet stream of comments.

"I bet your Dad doesn't call *you* Puddin' Face. Your Dad must be massive, even bigger than you! What do you do all day – eat? Or swim about? How far can you swim, miles and miles and miles? You must see some fantastic things! Things we humans know nothing about! Strange fish, giant corals, seaweeds, plants, perhaps flowers even? You must swim the whole of the Atlantic – wow! I bet you swim fast with those colossal flippers."

David listened and smiled. The superb giant watched Penny carefully with large placid eyes, blinking repeatedly to clear them of sea water. Then he nodded slightly and gave a low, approving Leatherback grunt. Penny beamed ecstatically at her father.

"Dad! Dad! Look – it understands! I'm talking to a Turtle!"

David had been scooping out sand to form a trench from the Turtle to the nearest pool so water could flow along it. Pausing, he looked around.

"Penny, fetch me that old bucket, please," he asked, pointing at a rusty-looking affair tossed on a pile of seaweed. Her father turned to the Turtle, patting it gently.

"Hullo there. Got stranded on our beach, have you? Carried in by the storm? But you Giant Leatherbacks are brilliant in water! Chasing something perhaps? I bet I know what it was too!"

Penny came running back. "Here y'are Dad," she gasped. "There's some strange seaweed over there too."

"We'll examine that after we've got this old man of the sea back where he belongs."

Scanning the beach he gave a satisfied smile, nodding as he did so. "Ah, ha! Got it! You *clever* Giant Leatherback! That explains it all!" he chuckled.

"What explains what?" asked Penny curiously.

"*Jellyfish*! Look around. See them? They're stranded, hundreds of them. There's even a Portuguese Man-of-War jellyfish over there. Our Leatherback must have been following a jellyfish bloom and got tumbled through Razor Rocks because of the storm. Now he's stuck unless we get him off – and we *will*," David added determinedly. "He's too unique to die. A real living Dinosaur," he enthused, a besotted look spreading over his face.

There was a scuffling behind Penny and her mother appeared with their friend, Alan, towing a sturdy sledge with three shovels tied to it.

"I brought as many shovels as I could find," said Gemma breathlessly. "Alan and I can dig too."

"Good! Start excavating towards the waterline. We've got to get our friend onto the sledge and tow him out to sea. Can't do that until more help arrives, but if we've dug a shallow trench and water fills it, the sledge'll slide along more easily. That's how the ancient Egyptians did it. Penny, he's taken a liking to you! How about chucking buckets of water over him? Especially his head and eyes, he'll like that."

David, Gemma and Alan began vigorously digging a gully towards the sea. Chattering quietly, Penny ran to and fro, filling the bucket and merrily throwing the cool, salty water over the Giant Leatherback. She was rewarded by grunts of pleasure and approval and much flapping of his magnificent flippers.

"Look Dad, Mum! He's ok! He's moving his flippers about!" she called excitedly.

"Good! Watch out if he starts throwing sand around with them. He's a pretty good shot and powerful too," warned David. "*Ah*! The Relief of Mafeking!" he added, as a strangely assorted group of people came scrambling across the beach towards them.

In the lead was Granny Fairweather and behind her … "I was in luck!" she cried joyfully. "Look who I bumped into!" Six burly leather-clad figures were following her. Carrying sinister black helmets, their jackets covered in spiky studs and spooky insignia, they presented a fearsome sight. David read 'The Gospel Makers' picked out in large letters on a jacket.

"Bikers," announced Dorothy triumphantly. "*Just* what we need. They've got wonderful bikes, Yamahas R1. 1,000 ccs, four cylinder engines! John says the handling round corners is brilliant but stopping power dodgy because the brakes are soft. They've got Cobra aftermarket exhausts and …"

Gemma interrupted, "Mum! Hang on! You can chat about bikes later. Just now we've got to get this Leatherback into the sea again."

"Yes – sorry! Ok, let me introduce them: Matthew, Mark, Luke, John, Peter and Paul. They're lovely bikes, though," she beamed ecstatically.

David, Gemma and Penny grinned – Gran couldn't resist fast machines! Behind them, looking doubtful, came the coastguard, Mr Tregoning, holding a sturdy length of rope, and clambering after him came a motley crew of helpers; Mr Fanshawe, a neighbour, obviously on his way to play golf; two stalwart men in hiking shorts with their wives; a patrol of Boy Scouts out on a nature ramble and a variety of other people.

"Plenty of strong young men, David!" remarked Gemma, "and Mr Tregoning has a rope."

"Migawd Mum! He be a big 'un!" gasped the coastguard. "We've seen them Giant Leatherbacks afore. They follows them jellyfish swarms. Dangerous some of 'em but they Leatherbacks eats they up! Well, zur, what can uz do?"

The increasing crowd gathered around the colossal Turtle exclaiming in delighted wonder and admiration at his size and immense flippers.

"Please don't crowd him, keep back. He never comes out of the sea and he's very frightened." Penny was proprietorial. She felt the Turtle was *hers*.

"What *is* it?" exclaimed one of the burly bikers.

"It's a Giant Leatherback Turtle," explained David. "It'll die if we don't get it off the beach *soon*."

"But it must weigh at least a ton," contributed Mr Fanshawe, carefully laying down his gleaming golf clubs.

"If you come away a little, over here, I'll explain my plan," said David, drawing the astonished but willing helpers to one side.

"First we're going to dig a trench so the sledge can run down to the sea. My wife, our friend, Alan, and I have got started. Next we've got to heave our Turtle onto the sledge. It'll be *very* difficult as we mustn't on any account injure him. Then we've got to get him into the sea until he can swim off."

This straightforward plan caused consternation. People looked at the gargantuan Turtle and back to David, taking in the enormity of the task. He smiled encouragingly.

"If anyone doesn't feel up to it, naturally they can leave," he added, seeing the horrified glances. "But if we all muck in it'll be easy," he continued hopefully.

"If you say so zur!" commented Mr Tregoning with a wry smile. The bikers drew a collective deep breath, looked at the magnificent, stranded creature and started taking their clothes off.

"I say, easy does it old boys. Ladies present," growled Mr Fanshawe.

"S'ok mate. We can't work prop'ly in this lot. We've got jeans and tee shirts on."

"Great! Let's all get down to it then," urged David. "We've got to catch the tide *just* as it begins to ebb so the surge will help carry him through the rocks and out to the sea safely."

"Ay – and that give uz 'bout an hour, if I'm not mistaken," added Mr Tregoning, looking knowledgeably at the softly lapping waves.

Some of the crowd quietly melted away but Mr Fanshawe took off his jacket and rolled up the sleeves of his immaculate, beautifully pressed golfing shirt. The two hikers rummaged around and produced a couple of 'folding' spades from their capacious rucksacks and set to with a will, their wives helping Penny 'water' the Leatherback. Dorothy Fairweather pounced upon a shovel-shaped piece of flotsam whilst another woman gleefully waved a child's spade.

"'Ere," said John, who appeared to be the leader of the 'Gospel Makers', "give us yer spade. Can't stand seeing youse strugglin' with that."

Gemma thankfully handed it over to the young man whose biceps bulged reassuringly beneath his tee shirt.

"An' I'll take that off you, if you'll excuse me," said another biker, unceremoniously relieving Alan of his.

"Here ya are, Miss, I've got an idea." John turned to Penny. "If you run up the path you'll see our bikes. We got bendy spades in the side pockets. Bring 'em 'ere, there's a good girl."

"Keep dousing George or he'll die," she instructed and set off at a run up the path. She liked the big bikers. They reminded her of the Turtle. She was soon back with the spades.

"There. Did you keep George wet?"

"Yus. Why's he called 'George'?" queried the biker called Mark.

"He looked like one. Big, solid, strong and placid natured," replied Penny, "like you."

"'Ere – what makes youse think we're placid? We're very scary we are. Everyone thinks so anyhow."

"But you're not, are you? Not really."

John shook his head, mystified.

"Well, don't let on will youse whack? We've got our reputation to think of."

A muffled snorting came from George. Penny stared at him – did the corners of his long mouth twitch slightly or was she imagining things? Just then David came over to see how the 'lads' were getting on.

"Excellent work! More brawn is just what we need. Well done – er,

xiv

what's your name?"

"John; this 'ere's Mark."

"I'm David, pleased to meet you. Must crack on."

It was quite a crowd, but most people had settled down, admiring the Leatherback and chucking water over him. Mr Tregoning was fashioning an interesting-looking harness out of rope and the muscular bikers, Mr Fanshawe and the two hikers were digging hard. So far, so good, but the difficult part was yet to come.

Sooner than expected, the shallow ditch was complete and rapidly filled with gushing water.

"Marvellous!" enthused David. "Now, Matt, Mark, Luke – round this side of the sledge with Mr Fanshawe and Alan. Try to edge the sledge under him whilst we push him onto it. John, Peter, Paul – round here with me, Simon and Mike. Mr Tregoning, when we've got George – good name Penny! – on, put the ropes round his carapace. Will the women keep throwing plenty of water over him please? It's the best chance we have of keeping him calm. Any questions?"

"Yus – what 'appens if those bloomin' great flippers start moving? They're not to be messed with!"

"Good question. You'll have to keep your eyes open for that. *On no account* must we harm his flippers or he's a dead 'un. Is that understood?"

"Yus, Guv. 'Ere, Matt," John turned to the biggest and hairiest of the Gospel Makers, whose well-muscled arms resembled a mountain range. "You watch out mate and don't go hurtin' the little feller's flippers – understand?"

"Yus," came the laconic reply.

"Everyone ready? One, two, three – PUSH."

Matt pushed the sledge so hard he fell on it and grazed his chin, Mr Fanshawe sat heavily and unexpectedly on the wet sand, his immaculate clothes sodden and the Gospel Makers' distressed jeans became even more distressed. The men pushing George skidded a few feet on the sand but George, unperturbed, didn't budge.

"Dad," said Penny, "let *me* speak to him."

David looked at her. "Now, Penny, Turtles don't *really* understand what you're saying, you know. We've just got to try harder. We'll manage."

"It can't do any harm, David," said Dorothy. "Go on, let the child say her piece."

David nodded. Penny went close up to George and spoke softly but sternly.

"Look here, George. These kind people are trying to get you back to the sea where you belong, ok? They're trying to get you onto a sledge, that wood thing, then they'll slide you down the beach and into the sea. So please will you stop lying there like a rock and *do* something?"

"She sounds just like you, Mum!" Gemma whispered smilingly to her mother.

"That'll do the trick, Miss," chortled Matt.

Penny treated him to a superior look but refrained from replying. "*Now* try," she said confidently. "Dad – what're you doing?"

David had stripped down to his sturdy Calvin Klein underpants. "I'm going in with George. He may need guiding out through Razor Rocks."

"DAVID! You're not going out of the bay? You know the currents can be very strong out there." Gemma was aghast and Dorothy looked on apprehensively.

"No, no! Look at the water. Quiet as a mill pond. Stop fussing, Gemma," he reproved.

"Dad! You *can't* go out there! You're always warning me about Razor Rocks. You want to catch the tide on the ebb when the currents are strong. If you think they'll carry George out they'll carry you too! You CAN'T go in, Dad, you just CAN'T!" Penny shouted.

"Listen – I'll be fine. I'll leave George to find his own way if necessary. I'm not going to take any risks!"

"Tell youse wot Missus. I'm a strong swimmer. I'll go in too," volunteered John.

"What a lot of fuss about nothing!" commented David crossly. "I've swum here for years. Now come on, let's get on with the job."

Penny looked on anxiously. Much as she wanted George to get

back to sea, she wanted her father more.

"Dad – PROMISE you won't take any risks?" she shouted as he walked to George's head.

"I PROMISE Puddin' Face!" he yelled.

"Don't call me Puddin' Face!" she yelled back.

Waving in acknowledgement, David grinned cheerfully and positioned himself by George's head as the men reassembled round the Giant Leatherback and the sledge.

Pushing and pulling, heaving and gasping, the men and women tried to manoeuvre George onto the low sledge. It had sunk into the wet, sandy trench, as David had hoped, and was level with George's soft plastron. At first George looked faintly amused at all the effort but amazingly began to help. Sand flew as he swept it carelessly aside with a magnificent flipper. David and his team ducked hastily then laughed.

"Here ya are Guv! Wotcha think o' that then! He's using his flippers to move himself towards the sledge like!"

It was amazing. Aided and abetted by his helpers, George slid closer and closer to the sledge. Matt's team needed all their strength to hold it steady as two tons of Turtle wriggled cautiously onto it. It was an exhausting task but at last George was ensconced on the sledge, secured with ropes. Raising his large head, he surveyed the assembled sweaty heaving throng like a Roman Emperor on a raised ceremonial dais bedecked with festive ribbons. His long mobile mouth turned up in what looked like a superior, rather smug smile and he draped his flippers elegantly over the sides, flicking them gently, ready to use as paddles once in the water.

David glanced at his watch. Yes, the tide had been coming in and was on the turn. There was not a minute to spare.

"When I say 'Pull' – pull with all your strength. Matt, you and your team push from behind," he instructed. "We've got to get him to the water and FAST!" warned David.

Everyone pulled and pushed with all their might, the sledge gathering speed as it moved along the lubricated tracks down to the sea. David gave a sigh of relief. Everything was going to plan!

A few more minutes and George would be back in his own element. They'd invite all the helpers to the cottage to dry off and enjoy tea and Dorothy's scrumptious homemade scones – and she could enjoy herself talking fast bikes with the boys!

Each new wave refilled the trench and the sledge slid along in grand style. George lowed like a contented cow as he smelt the fresh salty water drawing closer. It was heavy work but the satisfaction of getting this unique creature back to his environment drove the men on. Pausing occasionally they 'pulled' and 'pushed' like a Tug of War but all in the same direction. The sea! At last! But too shallow for massive George to swim in. He'd founder again and although he felt its soothing coolness and tried to use his flippers, he merely grazed the sand.

"Just wait a minute, George, and it'll be deep enough for you. Don't go jumping about, there's a good fellow. You're quite a weight for us humans to drag along!" muttered David. Heavens, he was getting as bad as Penny – talking to Turtles indeed!

"You're all going to get VERY wet shortly," he shouted. "If you want to, turn back now."

No one moved. Mr Fanshawe had long ago given up on his pristine appearance, the bikers' jeans were familiar with water and the hikers wore shorts. Mr Tregoning had discarded his heavy jacket and wore waders up to his chest. If he didn't go out too far he'd be fine. Under David's orders they continued trundling along with the sledge, easier going now as it glided through the water.

"Professor Heffernan zur! I reckons they ropes should be released now. It be up to my waist see, nearly deep enough for 'im to swim."

"Ah yes! Thank you, Petroc."

"You 'old 'em zur. They be attached to the sledge. You can swim back with it."

Releasing the ropes round George, the coastguard returned to shore accompanied by most of the men. David waded on, pulling the now swiftly-moving sledge whilst John pushed from behind. The tide was just on the ebb, brisk waves breaking out through Razor Rocks into a calm sea. Ideal for George!

"Ok, George. Here you go. John!" called David. "Give the sledge a tip, will you, so George gets the idea."

"Right y'are. Eh – we didn't know youse was a Professor! Cor! Wait 'til I tell me Mam ah've bin consortin' with a Professor!"

David laughed. "Y'know – I took my first degree in Marine Biology at Liverpool University. What fun we all had!" he chuckled reminiscently, recalling his student days. "Look John, we'll chat later. You go back now. I'll watch him through Razor Rocks."

"You stayin' here then? Not swimmin' out further? You promised your little girl youse wouldn' – remember?"

"No, I'm staying here. Honest – just see George safe," gurgled David as he struggled to keep hold of the ropes and out of the way of George's frenzied flippers. "Here, John. Our friend's off. Could you tow this thing back? It's Penny's, she'll miss her sledge in winter. We never thought how useful it would be!"

"Right y'are Guv – I mean Professor," John replied saucily with a wink. "Ta ra then."

Taking the ropes he swam swiftly off, towing the sledge through the water as if it were no weight at all. David sighed happily. All's well that ends well, he thought. There was George, heading straight and true for the inlet between Razor Rocks, everyone on the beach was cheering and waving and the sky was a beautiful shade of apricot. A few more feet and George would be out of the bay and away, his powerful flippers projecting him along at enormous speed. David watched, contented and happy, thinking of the glorious celebration tea shortly to come. Thank goodness Dorothy had spent the time indoors during the storm baking!

His foot hit something soft and slimy. Oh yuk! Jellyfish. The reason George was here of course. Well, he shouldn't have any problem stocking up! David could see quite a few surrounding him. Come on, George, get through the Razors, jellyfish are not my favourite marine species, he muttered. Tentacles brushed against his legs and caressed his chest. Oh get off, go away, he breathed, watching George swimming straight through the Razors. Good! Now for home, warm towels, hot scones and good company! A sharp stabbing feeling in his chest – cramp? Relax, he could practically walk to the beach! Another and another. Looking down, David was horrified to recognise the giant jellyfish called a Portuguese Man-of-War attached to his chest. What was it doing here, well out of its usual territorial waters? Of course – the storm! It had taken the jellyfish into the bay and greedy George had followed. Portuguese Men-of-War were a delicacy to George but deadly to humans. David winced as its powerful tentacles, each ending in a deadly sting, tightened round him. He'd been stung. Not once but many times. Unless the antidote was administered very quickly he would die within minutes. There was nothing he could do. "HELP!" he screamed, waving frantically, "HELP!"

Everyone on the beach waved back happily. "Look! Dad's waving. He's so pleased George is alive and back where he belongs! We'll have a smashing evening won't we, Mum? As soon as Dad gets in all our new friends can come to the cottage and get dry and have tea. Gran's already gone up to prepare it and taken Mr Tregoning and poor old Mr Fanshawe with her. He was *drenched*!"

"HELP!" called David again. Already the paralysis was beginning; his arms and legs were losing strength rapidly. "Help," he called more weakly.

"LOOK!" The crowd on the beach watched in bewilderment. George had sailed safe and unscathed through Razor Rocks to a loud cheer from the watching crowd. Suddenly turning, he plunged back through them so abruptly his leathery carapace caught on the sharp jutting rocks.

"What's he *doing*?" wailed Penny. "He was safe in the sea. All he had to do was keep going."

Inside the bay the sea was in turmoil, David nowhere to be seen. Great waves rolled and boiled, pitched and undulated, mists of spume rose high into the sky spattering furiously onto the rocks. It looked as if two giants were fighting under the water.

They were. George had sensed the giant jellyfish as he'd passed through the water but had one thought in his mind – to break free of this confined space and reach the vastness of the ocean, his home. He knew that jellyfish travelled in large colonies. Where there was one Portuguese Man-of-War, there would be others. So he ignored it and swam swiftly on. Safe in the open sea at last he prepared to give the traditional Leatherback 'Thank you and Farewell' to the Humans who had helped him. Half-turning and raising his head above the water to salute them with his flipper, he saw the Man-of-War seize the Chief Human. George thought of jellyfish as his favourite food but sensed the Human's fear and horror. Without hesitation, he turned and swam at top speed back through the Rocks, catching his carapace on the razor-sharp projections. Without pausing to assess the damage or pain, he surged onwards to the helpless Human. Seeing George approaching like an avenging angel, the jellyfish speedily released David and tried to swim for it. No use. George seized him, shook him like the marine rat he was and ate him, flipping the remnants to the smaller fish. That's what you get for touching this friendly helpful Human!

But the Human was looking very strange, floating inert and still, and sinking slowly into deeper water. Air! That's what Humans liked! Fresh air. George could last for hours on one breath but they couldn't. They couldn't last long at all. George carefully slipped a giant flipper under David and gently lifted him to the surface, holding him steady and clear of the water. There! That should do the trick. A few deep breaths and he would swim off.

From the beach, George heard piercing screams and shouting. The Humans were pointing in his direction, at David lying on his flipper. A number of men who'd helped launch him ran wildly into the sea, no longer pleasant and good natured but confused and angry. They were heading straight for him.

"We'll kill ya, ya lousy murdering overgrown tortoise! Wait till we get ya!"

"We'll have ya flippers for soup and ya shell for handbags, ya see if we don't!"

George was deeply upset. What had he done? He'd tried to help David, who lay on his flipper, motionless and quiet. The gang of furious Humans were getting nearer and nearer. He didn't want to hurt any of them. He would have to leave the Chief Human and swim for his life. But would he ever be able to repay these kind and resourceful Humans, and would they ever know what really happened?

Chapter One

THE SECRET ISLE

"We will be landing shortly. Please return to your seats and fasten your seat belts. Passengers on the left of the plane have a good view of the island and sea approach."

Penny, leaning over the wash basin in the toilet, was experimenting with 'Samantha's Special Rehydrating Atomiser for All Skin Types'. At fourteen, she was into all the freebies on offer. Hearing the announcement, she flung open the door and dashed out – WHAM! – straight into a tall, broad-shouldered young man who let out a startled gasp which smelt strongly of peppermint. Tightly frizzled dreadlocks stood out around his head in a dark halo.

"Whoa! Why yo in sich great flurry Missah?" he grinned, "Yo want to watch where yo headin'. Yo sure winded me."

"Sorry! I want to see the island from the air."

"Yo on holi-day?"

"Sort of. My Mum works here. I'm going to join her."

"Yo bin before then?"

"I've been quite a few times. It's a smashing place."

Dreadlocks nodded his head energetically.

"Dis ma island Missah. No other like it. It very spes-hul. Very spes-hul, secret tings on dis island, plants, animals, all sorts," he said proudly.

"I know," agreed Penny, who wanted to get back to her seat and look out of the window without being rude. "It's beautiful."

This pleased Dreadlocks. Breathing more peppermint over her, he smiled broadly, revealing a wide expanse of gleaming white teeth. Drawing himself up to his full height of six feet, six inches and inclining his head slightly he said with enormous dignity, "Welcome to ma island. Yo take care and have great time Missah," and with a courteous nod he drew aside.

Speeding back to her place Penny gathered the bits and pieces from her seat, dropped them into Gran's lap and looked out of the window. *WOW*! What a smashing view of the 'Secret' Island! The plane was banking, wings dipping almost vertically over the water. She could see the low, colourful houses, waving palm trees and mountains. Each crescent-shaped sandy beach sheltered its own village, houses clustered round the beach becoming more scattered on the gently rising surrounding hills. Off the bays, where the clear coastal aquamarine water darkened into deeper indigo, fishing fleets of small boats sped along, their triangular sails snapping in unison like a Calypso dance. Each glittering wake reflected the sun, resembling diamonds scattered randomly on an aqueous canvas.

"Penny, Penny dear, sit back and fasten your seat belt. I'll be glad to land and have a nice cup of tea! It's been a long journey and why the pilot's banking so steeply I don't know. It's quite dangerous. I suppose it's all down to flying by computers on 'automatic pilot'. They think they can get away with anything."

Dear old Gran. She disliked all computers, whatever their uses.

"Bet you didn't have automatic pilots in your day, Gran, when Dinosaurs were still around," teased Penny, grinning.

"We certainly didn't and none the worse for that, more accurate in fact. Oh good, we're landing."

Granny Fairweather was as excited as Penny. It was her first visit to the Secret Island and she was as thrilled as a child. It was such a treat to be travelling with her granddaughter and staying with her daughter. A strong headwind had slowed their long overnight flight to this tiny island in the Caribbean and everyone was keen to get out. Although Penny had been to the island before, she had never visited at this particular time – and for a whole month! It was a miracle the school had given her time off.

There was a catch. Just as Dreadlocks had said, her Secret Island had strange, exotic variations in vegetation which resulted in unique plant, animal and bird life. Similar species had become extinct on the mainland and were found only on the island. Her mother had explained why. Much of the flora and fauna was not native to the island but arrived via a prehistoric land bridge. The bridge flooded, the land drifted away and animals and plants had been marooned on the Secret Island. This year she would help her Mum who studied and tried to preserve species that were becoming extinct. Penny's school had given her time off provided she completed a project on these endangered species. She was expected to make lots of notes from her mother's research work as well as 'observations, deductions and sketches, in colour' of her own. It was a small price to pay for a glorious holiday in the sun.

With a soft bump the aircraft landed and taxied slowly along the shimmering runway towards the new Airport, Customs and Immigration Offices. Simply designed, low and rambling, it fitted perfectly into the island's older buildings. Various uniformed officials lounged about, some men ambled casually towards the plane as it landed, a baggage vehicle rolled out to begin its short journey but paused while the driver greeted a friend to exchange news and views. It was all very leisurely.

"Please remain seated until the aircraft has come to a complete halt and the seat belt sign has been switched off. You are reminded that the no-smoking policy applies until you are in a designated area in the airport buildings. Thank you for flying with us and we hope to see you again soon."

Releasing the seat belt, Granny Fairweather was on her feet with the alacrity of a much younger person. She'd had enough of sitting still and was stiff and thirsty.

"Have you seen my glasses, Penny? I had them just a minute ago, now they've vanished. Perhaps they're under this blanket. No, in my bag, no, oh dear, I'll be forgetting my name next. What I'd give for a nice cup of refreshing tea!"

"Gran, your glasses are on your nose," said Penny, patiently.

"Whaa …? Well, thank you, dear. I expect it's being so tired. But there, what lucky people we are to be in this wonderful place! Well

3

worth the long trip. I've enjoyed travelling with you. Have you enjoyed yourself too?"

"Of course I have, Gran! Thanks for looking after me. It's been great," replied Penny politely. It *had* been interesting, she reflected. Used to her Gran mislaying objects and flapping about, Penny had never before seen her so efficient: flagging down taxis, tipping, producing tickets, passports and visas, chatting and laughing with airport officials who sported lots of gold braid, seemed very respectful and made a terrific fuss of her. Penny had suddenly seen her Gran as a young woman, vivacious, pretty and full of fun. She had seemed like a young girl again. Even the Chief Executive of the airline had emerged from his eyrie to have a word and Gran had slapped him on the back and made a joke! Penny was surprised at the personal attention they received but, after all, that was their job – and her mother was a Professor!

"We're moving!" exclaimed Gran with relief as the long line of people began slowly shuffling down the aisle. After the plane's cool air conditioning the blast of heat at the exit was intense. Penny stood at the top of the steps looking around eagerly. It felt like coming home and somewhere not far away was Mum.

"Come on, Gran! We don't want to keep Mum waiting. You know how busy she is," called Penny, ramming on an old straw hat. "There's no bus. You walk across to Arrivals." And she was down the steps and running across the tarmac, reaching passport control first. Longing to get through the Customs shed and have time to buy some of the nutty toffee crunch sold just outside the airport, she remembered Granny Fairweather had the passports. Just then she appeared, perspiring freely after the short trip from plane to Arrivals.

"Phew! It's hot!" she exclaimed, fanning herself with a magazine.

"It's cooler in here, there's air conditioning now," commented Penny knowledgeably.

"This *is* different from Gatwick!" exclaimed Gran, looking eagerly at the vividly coloured posters showing 'Jump Ups', 'J'Ouvert', 'Chutney Soca Monarch' and other Carnivals. Through the smoked glass windows she could see haphazard clusters of squat buildings, groups of people talking and laughing together under a variety of sunshades. "Much more informal. Quite jolly really, it reminds me of Biggin Hill in…"

"'Lo there Miss Penny! Welcome back," beamed the Immigration Officer cheerfully, "de Professor is waitin' for yo."

As Penny scampered through, she heard him say, "Excuse me Ma'am, you don' seem to have completed your Immigration form. See here? It says 'PURPOSE OF VISIT'. Are you on holiday, business or both?"

"She's my Gran," explained Penny succinctly.

"Yes, and Professor Heffernan is my daughter," said Mrs Fairweather, completing the family tree.

"Gran, I must go and find a trolley, it's urgent," said Penny and tore off into the Baggage Reclaim section. There may be serried ranks of luggage trolleys at Gatwick but at this minor airport they were few and far between. It was a game of hide and seek, first *find* your trolley, then hang onto it. Across the forecourt she flew, round the corner where the taxi drivers had a tumbledown café. Yes! There was an untidy clump of decrepit trolleys looking like a gaggle of bedraggled geese. Triumphantly she disentangled one and about-turned, heading back to Gran. A very large, powerfully-built woman who must have weighed at least twenty stone had other ideas. Wearing the uniform of an airport security guard, she completely blocked the way, towering menacingly over Penny.

"OI! Where yuh takin' that trolley, Missah?"

"To the carousel for my luggage," answered a surprised Penny.

"Do yuh need it tho'? Yuh look young and strong."

"I'm with my Gran, she's a very old lady," responded Penny quickly, hoping Gran wasn't in earshot. "*She* needs one."

"An' where is dis ole lady? I don' see one nowheres."

"She's talking to the Immigration Officer …"

"Ha! Having trouble with clearance is she? Has she got drugs?"

Penny was puzzled. She never normally had this sort of trouble and, come to think of it, there did seem to be a lot of guards about. What was going on?

"No, of course she hasn't! We're *British*," she announced proudly, as if that explained everything.

"Ho yes! We knows dem British. Very rich and rowdy and all on drugs. We don' want none of dey tings *here*." She glowered ferociously at Penny. A loud shout diverted her attention.

"Hey Cora! Dey is over dere! Look, gettem quick!"

The very large lady moved with amazing rapidity towards a small group of men who melted away like frost in sun. Two were left stranded: a small man, his hair clipped short and neat, wearing a smart shiny suit and psychedelic tie and a tall, gangling one with dreadlocks bundled into a multi-coloured woolly hat with a big red bobble. Dreadlocks! Surely that nice man she'd bumped into on the plane wasn't a drug smuggler?

"It's not me, man," shouted Dreadlocks, wriggling like an eel as Cora got him firmly in a half-nelson, "It's 'im," pointing in the direction of the smart man.

"Yuh *both* come quietly wit' me just same. Don't yuh try strugglin' man, I got you good."

Penny almost giggled. She really had got him. With Dreadlocks helpless in her grip and the Smart Man expostulating but firmly held by the second guard, it was clear no one would escape from Cora! Out of the corner of her eye, Penny saw another man with dreadlocks slipping swiftly round the corner near the taxi-drivers' café. Releasing the trolley's handle, she swivelled to get a better view. *He* must be her Dreadlocks and the arrested man someone else! She sighed with relief and turned back to the trolley.

BUMP! SCREECH! came the sound of rubber wheels – someone was running off with her trolley! Oh *no*! They were like gold-dust and Gran really needed one. She must retrieve it and *fast*.

"Stop! Thief!" she shouted, "That trolley's mine!" and set off in hot pursuit. Agile and athletic, she soon gained on the culprit, a neatly dressed boy about her own age. Furiously catching up with him she snatched the trolley back.

"What do you think you're doing? This is *my* trolley. Go and find your own," she yelled.

"How was I to know it was yours? I didn't realise airport luggage trolleys had *names* on them," he replied sneeringly in a muted American accent.

"It's obvious, it was right by me. Haven't you any manners?"

"Haven't you? Watching drug smugglers being arrested! That's real low behaviour!" the boy retorted sharply.

"I was *not*! That big woman was, er, talking to me, that's all. She rushed off and I watched. Anyway, it's none of your business."

Infuriated, the pair stood blocking everyone's way, shouting aggressively at each other, the island people thoroughly enjoying the brisk exchange.

"Yo tell him, Missy! Don' yo let 'im get away wit' it!" encouraged the women.

"What? Yo goin' let a *girl* get de best of yo? Dat no good man!" riposted the men.

Glaring at the boy, Penny tried to grasp the trolley and walk away in a dignified manner but he insisted on keeping hold of the handle.

"LET GO!" she bellowed angrily and gave it a sharp tug. Much to the delight of the watching throng, the boy lost his grip and tumbled inelegantly onto the tiled floor.

"JAMES!" thundered an irate voice. "Stop that at once! Brawling in public with a girl. Leave her. The Chauffeur will sort things out. There's no need for you to get involved. Come along *at once*. The car's waiting."

Crumbs! Penny thought, so the Chauffeur's going to 'sort things out' is he? What did that mean? Well, she didn't care *and* she wasn't going to run either! Squaring her shoulders and drawing herself up to her full height of five feet, four inches, she gripped the trolley firmly and strode unhurriedly towards Gran, who'd got their cases and was looking about for her.

"There you are dear! Some sort of scuffle's been going on. I'm glad you weren't involved. Good, you've got a trolley. Give me a hand with these and we'll be away."

Looking furtively about under cover of loading the cases, Penny couldn't see any large Chauffeur looming and breathed more freely. Her mother would not be pleased if Penny got into trouble as early on in the holiday as this!

"Here you are, Gran! All done and dusted! Let's go," she said hastily and, taking the trolley, steered it quickly through the exit.

The familiar smell of bone dry, dusty heat and soft tarmac hit them as they went through the doors. Waiting families and friends sat on the kerb on the shady side of the road, fanning themselves with small palm leaves. Set back from the road the crunchy nut vendors perched on stools underneath broad shady umbrellas or roofs of bamboo thatch. The car park beyond was higgledy-piggledy, every battered car seeking an inch of shade beneath the sprawling mango and almond trees. In the taxi drivers' shelter a number of men lounged on battered chairs, talking and laughing. From these a burly man dressed in neat jeans and a tee shirt embossed with a cricket motif emerged and headed for Penny and Gran.

"Hi Miss Penny! Is this yo Great Ma? How ya doin' Ma'am? We sho' are honoured an' pleased to meet yo. Yo daughter she be doin' good tings for our hist'ry here, an' yo and Miss Penny is goin' help now!"

"Hi Jomo! It's great to be back! Is Mum about? Has she been waiting long?"

"De Doctor Professor is right over there Missah, buying yo toffee crunch," Jomo grinned expansively, "she know yo like eatin' it in de cyar," and he began stacking luggage neatly in the boot of a nearby car.

Penny grinned. Toffee crunch – her favourite!

"Yuh Miss – yuh been upsetting Mister James?" came a deep, growly voice behind her. Jumping guiltily, she saw a big man dressed in the smart dark green uniform and peaked cap of a Chauffeur.

"No," she replied, unable to keep a slight tremble from her voice, "he stole my trolley."

"Can't see how he 'steal' a trolley when dey belongs to everyone. His father say yuh causin' trouble for 'im."

Penny bit her lip. Causing trouble for a boy her own age – what a sissy he must be! She'd put him right! But Mrs Fairweather stepped quickly in front of Penny, pushing her behind. She may be tired and longing for a cup of tea but she wasn't standing any rudeness or intimidation of her granddaughter!

"Excuse *me*," she began, glowering fearsomely, "I am this young lady's grandmother. If you …" but before she could say any more, Jomo emerged from underneath the boot.

"Is that …" he began, then, seeing the Chauffeur, stopped, grinned and greeted him like a long lost brother. "Hi Orville! Long time no see! What you doin' now? Sure likes yo uniform man!"

To Penny's surprise and Gran's amazement the two men shook hands affably in the characteristic Caribbean manner.

"I'm Private Chauffering now. Pay ok, good tips, reg-lar hours. See here," he continued proudly, "dat my cyar," pointing to a lustrously gleaming vintage Rolls Royce. "Not *mine*," he added hastily, seeing their faces, "de Hotel I works for. Very rich visitors, film stars and suchlike folk. Dey tip me blues man! Better than de taxi rank, ah'm tellin' yuh!"

"Dat cyar's got folk waitin'. What yo doin' over here?"

"Oh dem! He send me. Dey say yuh young lady, she annoy de boy. Why don' he look out for 'imself eh? Forget it Jomo. I'll say she sorry. See yo soon," and with a discreet flick of his hand he was gone, back to the waiting car.

"Phew, thanks Jomo! I thought we were in for trouble," gasped Penny.

"He old fren' o' mine. Used to work in de taxi rank here. He don' well workin' for dat Hotel. It's de new one on de same beach as yours."

"Thank goodness it's a big beach. I don't want to bump into them all the time!"

"No, an' don't yo go makin' no trouble for yo Ma, Miss Penny. Yo knows how … tired she gets and she bin workin' veree hard."

"Ok," replied Penny, exchanging a glance with Jomo.

"Mum! Penny! Sorry I'm late. It's this darn sticky toffee crunch. There was quite a queue."

Mrs Fairweather beamed at her daughter whilst Penny flung herself on her mother. Jomo looked on, flicking away a tear. Families!

Nothing to beat them, he reflected.

"Here's your crunch, Penny. That should glue your jaws together for a bit. Mum! Lovely to see you and none the worse for the long flight! But that's to be expected!" smiled Gemma, whose deep tan, frayed shorts and old sandals belonged to a woman who spent most of her time outdoors.

"Oh darling, I'm not as young as I was, you know! It *was* a very long flight. I could murder a cup of tea."

"Yes, come on Jomo, let's get cracking. It's all laid on back at the hotel. We've got a smashing suite, Mum, three separate bedrooms with big balconies overlooking the bay, two bathrooms, a sitting room and a little cubby hole for my study. Mr MacRobert, the Manager, has been very helpful and the staff are wonderful. I can hardly believe I'll be able to concentrate on my work without having to worry about *anything* else – like housework! Heaven! And now I've got you to help as well. We'll get *lots* done."

Penny glanced at her mother. She would like to help but it would depend on … certain things, she thought censoriously, pursing her lips. After David had died, Gemma had thrown herself into her work, continuing where he had left off. She'd been made a Professor of Marine Biology, specialising in protecting near-extinct Marine Turtles, especially the Giant Leatherback. Years ago Penny remembered her father rescuing a Giant Leatherback when it had been washed ashore. The Leatherback had got safely away but her father had been killed. So why should her mother bother about saving them from extinction? The sooner they all disappeared, the better! She wanted revenge for her father's death and the affection she had felt for George, the benign and placid-looking Turtle, had been replaced with an implacable hatred.

"Come on Miss Penny! Stop dat day dreamin' and hop in. Sit in front wit' me an' yo can view the scene," commanded Jomo.

Beeping his horn and waving cheerfully to his many friends, he careered round the airport roundabout, past a new hotel and out onto the main highway. It was deserted, the heat haze spiralling up from the hot tarmac like ghosts. Weaving expertly, Jomo avoided a party of stray chickens desultorily pecking in the road. Squawking loudly they ran into the parched grass at the side, surprising a brace of tethered goats and kids. With the disapproving air of Dowager Duchesses whose afternoon tea party has been invaded by a rock band, the goats' rhythmic chomping ceased. Lowering their horned heads they regarded the chickens balefully. Without pausing, the chickens ran speedily into the scrubland and disappeared. Quietly and efficiently, the goats recommenced chomping. The taxi passed pretty pastel-painted chattel houses, jalousies shuttered against the heat. Wayside fruit vendors, sheltering under gigantic banana leaves, were the only people around, their stalls bowed under the weight of globe-like melons, mangoes the size of pumpkins, paw-paws bigger than rugby balls, pineapples oozing juice, fresh-picked lemons and limes, none of which bore any resemblance to their imported namesakes in English supermarkets.

"Did yo see de drug smuggler strugglin' wit' Cora?" chuckled Jomo. "Hee, hee, hee! Dat sure was crazy. No one messes with our Cora!"

"Do you know her Jomo? Gosh, she's a big lady," exclaimed Penny.

"She sure is huge an' she got Black Belt Karate. Dere ain't no fat on dat lady, just muscle," commented Jomo admiringly.

Glancing quickly at her mother who was fast asleep in the corner, nodding gently, Gemma asked, "What's that, Jomo? Was there an arrest at the airport?"

"Let's say Cora got her man, hey, hey, hey! Don' know if he be a drug smuggler or not, he gone wit' Cora – *dat* prison enough!"

"Are you sure it was drugs, Jomo, not other forbidden goods? It's illegal trade in threatened animal species that most concerns me. International Police deal with drugs but the Conservation Laws are more difficult to enforce. It's a big problem. I think I'll have to borrow Cora for Turtle Watch," smiled Gemma wryly. "She'd soon put the fear of God into poachers."

"Sure would Prof. She a very God-fearing lady an' attend de Black Rock Gospel Tabernacle reg-lar."

"The egg and Hatchling poaching's got to be stopped. Every year the Turtle count gets lower and lower."

"Our island wouldn't be de same witout dey bootiful creatures. Giant Leatherback Turtles, man, are dey somethin'! Dey be comin' here-ya for millions of y-hear to lay dere eggs. Dey part of our lives, our his-try, livin' Dinosaurs! Mos' of us, we very proud of dey, tho' some still tink dey food. We got to h'edicate folks. Now don' yo go worry no more Ma'am," Jomo said reassuringly. "We look out for yo real good. We kno' which village dey poacher villains come from. Dey wutless lot. We got our eye on dem, yes man!" he smiled menacingly.

"Thanks Jomo! I know I can rely on you and the other Turtle Custodians. You're a great bunch."

Jomo hummed a little tune to cover his confusion at this compliment, then volunteered, "De Turtles due up soon Prof. We best get organised."

"Yes Jomo, any day they'll start arriving. Full moon isn't until the end of next week. That's the most likely time. But we'll keep watch from now on because you never know when they'll decide to arrive. If they *do* arrive that is!"

"Dis dere beach Ma'am; dey won't give up. We soon see de ripples in de surf again."

"If they do give up, Jomo, it'll be the fault of humans. We've *got* to take more care of them."

Listening dozily to the conversation, Penny thought this odd. "Mum – how do you 'take more care of' Marine Turtles? They spend all their time swimming about in vast oceans. You can't keep them as pets!"

"No, you certainly can't. But you *can* show greater respect for their way of life and their habitat. Do y'know, it's estimated that they'll be extinct in ten years. Your generation, Penny, may be the last to see them."

Penny shivered. Without warning, she suddenly remembered her father saying the same thing shortly before he died. She bitterly recalled her last words to him, "Don't call me Puddin' Face!" and his affectionate laughter. She thought of George, the Giant Leatherback her father had

12

rescued. She remembered stroking and talking to him, his muffled grunts as if he were chortling at some inner joke, his enormous size and magnificent flippers. He'd been a wonderful creature. Why, oh why, had he spoilt everything by killing her father? After the horror of seeing her father's body carried ashore she remembered very little. Why had her mother continued his work? She didn't understand. Driving along the coast road Penny stared out to sea. Numbers were dropping. Remembering George and his unique qualities she felt sad then angry. According to her mother and Jomo they were out there now, preparing for the trek up the shore to lay their eggs. That was when they were at their most vulnerable. Penny had an idea – she would avenge her father's death! It would be simple; find out who the egg poachers were, Jomo would tell *her*, keep watch with the Turtle Custodians then tell the poachers where the nests were! Then they would come and steal the eggs. After all, it wasn't the same as killing a Turtle because it wasn't one. Only an egg. She would tell the poachers to take only the eggs, not touch the exhausted females. Dad would approve … he loved the Turtles … no Turtles without eggs … when did eggs become Turtles? … all Turtles began life as eggs … someone was cutting open an egg … two tiny flippers unfolded … trying to slice off the tiny flippers … blood everywhere … she hadn't realised Turtles bled … someone was sobbing, weeping huge golden tears … who was it? … Dad was calling her, telling her … she must listen … listen … her head dropped forward. She slept.

Chapter Two

ENTER GEORGE – GIANT LEATHERBACK PATRIARCH

George was hungry. He had only eaten a light repast of small Pelagia jellyfish found floating aimlessly along in a clump of sea wrack. This was definitely not enough for a fully-grown male Giant Leatherback Turtle, twelve feet long from beak to tail flipper. He had to eat his own body weight every day to survive and as this was two tons he was always on the lookout for a potential meal. Jellyfish was the preferred menu: big, small, round, long, green, pink, purple, it didn't matter. Right now he needed something extra large and juicy, not pathetic Pelagia, and was looking around for a substantial main course. And he spotted it. George's eyes lit up with greedy anticipation. Lying doggo in the water some distance to his right a huge Lion's Mane jellyfish brooded silently. Its three-feet-wide body disc presented a challenge as did its numerous tentacles spread out around it, disappearing into the watery depths to fifty feet. Each one of these bore a sting so deadly it could kill a Human – but not George. At least not if he played it right and he was a dab flipper at catching all kinds of jellyfish. Withdrawing quietly to a position above and behind the coelenterate, George clicked his beak happily, loosening up the numerous serrated eating spines that lined his throat like saws. Surprise was essential. If the Lion's Mane turned quickly its sting might penetrate the Turtle's soft underpart, the plastron. Unprotected by the tough, thick carapace it was the most vulnerable part and George had to keep it well out of reach. Motionless, he waited until the giant Cyanea paralysed a large fish with its sting and drew it slowly into the deceptively pretty frilled lobes of its mouth. Concentrating on digesting the fish, the Lion's Mane was unaware of the massive Marine Turtle closing in at explosive speed, its nine-foot-long flippers making short work of the distance between them. BAM! George's large mouth opened and closed around

14

the mushroom-shaped jellyfish. SSWOOSSSH! Up came the tentacles trying to poison the Turtle's soft plastron. But George was ready. With one mighty flick of a hefty flipper he swept away the Lion's Mane tentacles as if he were swatting a fly and harmlessly they encountered a barrel-shaped, leathery and totally impenetrable carapace, the soft plastron tucked securely away beneath this impregnable shield. Mmmm! Munch, munch, went George as the tentacles loosened. What a toothsome repast! Now he could relax for a while before continuing his journey.

Rejecting the bits he did not want for the flotillas of small fish waiting for leftovers, he folded his enormous flippers over his back and settled down for a restorative snooze. It would be good to meet his friends again: Horace, Godfrey, Archibald and Montague. In the solitary and mysterious life of a Leatherback the time was approaching when they met in force for the Annual Metanoia, Giant Leatherback Scrimmage Fortnight and Egg Laying Ceremony. It was an occasion when the youngest Hatchlings and the most revered Grand Matriarchs and Patriarchs got together for an enjoyable and exciting time. Hatchlings from Turtle Academy rejoined parents and played their part in the Scrimmage Games. Young Nematts (or Newly-Matriculated Turtles) were able to meet and court in the beautiful marinas and older married couples renewed friendships and exchanged gossip. George was looking forward to meeting his chums in mid-ocean. On the way to the Meeting Place they had a happy time chasing jellyfish, getting in some sly practise for the Scrimmage Games and swapping tales of Turtle derring-do – some fact, some fiction – but no one minded provided the story was a good one!

Then there was Laetitia, his beautiful and clever wife. She was a mere eight feet long yet, despite the handicap of short flippers (only six feet), she inevitably won the Chelonian Cup (Females) for Accuracy of Navigation and Speed! Some of his Hatchlings would be there too. How had they fared, how many survived the Terror Run? Were his older Hatchlings coping satisfactorily with the tough syllabus and stiff Matriculation exams of Turtle Academy? Many subjects were essential for survival and the school refused point blank to matriculate any

Turtle who failed even one subject, the risk to life and flipper being too high. What a long time it was since he had been at school with Horace, Godfrey, Archibald and Montague! He sighed happily, reflecting on the fun and mischief they had had – *and* later when they were Nematts too! Now he was a Grand Patriarch and had swum the High Seas for many years without mishap, always remembering what he had been taught by older, more experienced Leatherbacks. Yet, despite his knowledge and common sense, majestic size and strength, there had been *one* very dodgy incident ...

An annoying, insistent buzzing and chirruping interrupted his peaceful reverie. Probably the attendant fish squabbling over leftovers. George shook his head vigorously to disperse them. But it didn't work, the chirruping continued. He shook his head again. *Still* no effect. Perhaps it was his guests complaining or arguing.

"Listen," he said, speaking very clearly, "just be quiet will you? I'm trying to rest and with you lot chattering in my ear that's difficult. If it's a complaint, tell me later." And, so saying, he adjusted his flippers and settled down again. But it didn't stop. On and on it went.

"Now really!" expostulated George, "this is not good enough and not like you *at all*! I thought I had a polite lot of guests but if you're going to keep disturbing me I'll have to ask you to leave."

At this terrible threat the guests – sea anemones and many different molluscs who took refuge on the Leatherback's carapace – set up a twittering of their own.

"I *say* George," tweeted a rare and delicate Mother of Pearl shell, "it's *not* us, *we* wouldn't dream of disturbing you. It's this other lot."

George was intrigued – what 'other lot'? Sleepily opening one eye he saw a remarkable vision. Definitely that Lion's Mane was having a strange effect on him. He closed his eye again but distinctly heard the words: "George! George! Wake up! It's urgent!"

Shaking his head crossly he flapped his flippers a couple of times as a warning sign.

"GEORGE! WAKE UP!" bellowed the voices. Cool waves splashed over him, as if someone was throwing water. Blinking long eyelashes he opened both eyes – and nearly jumped out of his carapace with shock and excitement.

What on sea was this? Clustered in tight formation round his head were a number of small exotically coloured fish, their diaphanous fins fanning the water into miniscule waves. There were tiny brilliant blue Cherubfish, black and yellow Rock Beauties, blue, mauve and lilac Angelfish and one very distinguished-looking Queen Angelfish. Jumping jellyfish! Did Lion's Mane cause hallucinations? Who *were* these stunningly beautiful fish? At the remotest corner of his mind some snippet of information came back to George. But that was *ridiculous*! Could it be?

Casting his mind back to school days when he had been at the top of the Academy and a 'Stroke', George remembered an essay he'd written: 'Comment, with examples, on the Spirit and Purpose of Angel Fish and their relationship with Great Mother Turtle'. Students should consult the following texts:

'Origins and Beliefs of Giant Leatherback Turtles' – Eckert & Scott

'A Brief Compendium on Great Mother Turtle – Dermochelys Deity or Primordial Myth?' – Carr and Pritchard

'A School Turtle's Guide to Theanthropic Philosophy' – Jay and Appleton

He'd been awarded an 'Alpha' and never forgotten the glory of it! If memory served him right, this was a Choir of Angel Fish. These were Messengers of Great Mother Turtle, rarely used and sent only in the direst emergencies. What could they want? How could he be of help? Oh! Oceans deep and shallow – it surely wasn't the Hatchlings? Hastily unfolding his flippers, he adopted a more respectful attitude. True, the Choir wasn't Great Mother Turtle herself but, as her personal messengers, they deserved respect and full attention.

The Choir scrutinised him. "George? Are you fully awake and alert? Are you listening?"

"Oh yes Mesdames. Indeed I am, thank you," he responded politely. "Er … am I right in thinking you are a Choir of Angel Fish?"

Indignantly drawing themselves up to their full size of eight inches, they replied melodiously, singing in the key of F minor to indicate their shock and surprise at not being instantly recognised: "Of *course* we are! *Really*, George!"

"Ah! Pardon my ignorance Mesdames. We've not met and I wasn't sure …" George was about to say he wasn't sure if they existed, fortunately stopping short as he realised it was *not* the most tactful thing to say.

"We have met before, George," they sang in the more moderate major key of G. "We remember you even if you don't remember us! Still, you were only two days old when we guided you to safe water. You were exhausted and out of breath trying to avoid Frigate Birds, too young to stay long under water."

George gasped. So it was true! The Choir *did* help Hatchlings to the Sea of Stillness! What a revelation! He must be sure his Hatchlings knew about this.

"Thank you, Mesdames, thank you. I don't recall that. I remember swimming into a large area of quiet water where there were no huge birds but lots of plankton, jellyfish and other Hatchlings. It was such a relief, so peaceful after the Terror Run. Thank you again."

The Choir preened and smiled happily. They didn't often get thanked; it was part of their job to do good silently, discreetly, invisibly if possible. Many sea creatures didn't believe in them and that too was part of the job. It was no use complaining to Great Mother Turtle. She always smiled serenely, gathered them under her wide golden flippers and said the same thing: "All real good is done anonymously and secretly," and gave them her special look, full of love, understanding and wisdom. But it was gratifying to be acknowledged!

"Thank *you*, George!" they sang mellifluously in a beautiful major diminished 7th in the key of B. "We always enjoy looking after Leatherbacks. They are so courteous and old-fashioned … and endangered." The voices wavered and, for the first time, lost perfect pitch.

"Thinking of danger – come along girls, we have an important message to impart. Pull yourselves together please." The Queen Angelfish Choir mistress spoke authoritatively.

Swiftly sorting themselves out they swam still, their fins hardly moving, waiting for her signal to begin. In response to her bringing down her front fin sharply, the Choir began their message in exquisite contrapuntal harmony. Singing at different pitches, every species of Marine Turtle could hear and understand them. George tingled at the solemn strains of celestial music and admired the crystalline clarity of enunciation.

> *"Patriarch George we're pleased to see you*
>
> *Our trips abroad are far and few.*
>
> *Our Deity, the Turtle Mother Great*
>
> *Is much perturbed and in a state.*
>
> *From tranquil seas we've hastened here*
>
> *To disclose to you a distant fear.*
>
> *Now is the time for your return*
>
> *To Turtle Seas and there you'll learn*
>
> *Of dangers which your friends will face*
>
> *Before they reach the Meeting Place.*
>
> *So go at once – you must not tarry,*
>
> *Your duty's clear, disaster parry.*
>
> *Great Mother speed you on your way,*
>
> *This Choir may no longer stay."*

George goggled, his limpid eyes watering with the stress of trying to remember the Choir's words.

"But, but – *what* do you mean? Is it about Archibald, Horace, Montague and Godfrey? We always join up in mid-ocean, will I meet them? Are they facing danger or others? Is Letty, er, Laetitia, alright?

What about my Hatchlings?"

Here he was interrupted. The Choir's sweet harmony had changed to dark dissonance.

"You must *go – at once*! You will be guided. That is all we know. We've stayed too long, you must *hurry*!" and with a flurry of shot-silk fins the Choir twinkled away and were soon lost to sight.

"Warty sea-urchins!" exclaimed George. He was seriously disturbed. Very few Turtles were visited by Choirs of Angel Fish and many doubted their existence. Salutary stories were told about how they were sent to help guide young Hatchlings after the Terror Run. There was the comforting Leatherback Legend that the Choir guided Hantles of Hatchlings away from busy fishing villages, where massive birds of prey congregated, picking off Hatchlings with ease, towards the isolated Sea of Stillness. George hadn't believed this – until now. Like other baby Turtles he could remember very little after the horrifying ordeal of the Terror Run on that dreadfully arid, scratchy surface called 'land' up which female Leatherbacks had to climb every year to lay their eggs. Phew! He wouldn't be a female if you gave him a year's supply of Lion's Mane!

But Choirs of Angel Fish weren't sent to guide and help mature, educated Leatherbacks who were responsible for their own choices and actions, good or bad, and had to live with the consequences. Yet here he was being told – no, *commanded* – to curtail his present carefree bachelor existence and get back to family obligations ahead of time! Humph! George was not best pleased. He enjoyed his perfectly legitimate freedom, being a good husband and father at the prescribed times as specified in the traditional Chelonian Calendar (Giant Leatherback Edition). He certainly had no intention of wriggling out of his duties. He was very pleased and proud to have his lovely Laetitia and their large family. They had adult, married sons and daughters, young Hatchlings about to attend Turtle Academy, some Senior Strokes about to graduate as well as a number of Nematts. Still, he *was* a Grand Patriarch of the Giant Leatherback genus and was fully entitled to spend a large part of the year on his own. That was Leatherback life. Yet his conscience niggled. Great Mother Turtle had sent him an urgent message to return. He couldn't ignore it, such disgraceful behaviour would not be tolerated by the Leatherbacks especially as he was a member of the Moot, the assembly of Chiefs. This position of responsibility was all the more reason for him to respond speedily.

Shaking his head and flapping his flippers irritably, George decided on a compromise. He would eat a few more jellyfish, have a short kip, *then* set off. Building up reserves for the long journey was vital, he self-righteously reasoned. He couldn't say fairer than that. Muttering crossly he dived and swept a large bundle of luminescent, bright red 'Atolla wyvillei' jellyfish into his capacious mouth. Finding food at 2,000 feet under water was a doddle. The jellies couldn't dim their phosphorescence. Shining like arc lamps in the Stygian gloom they were easily picked off. George chomped casually and consistently as he surged along. It would be a good idea though if he checked his location on the globe. Taking a wrong turn in mid-ocean could have disastrous results. Rising effortlessly to the surface, George took a bracing lungful of air before diving to align his inbuilt compass. Concentrating on the finely-tuned interior navigational sensor possessed by Marine Turtles, he verified the angle and intensity of the Earth's magnetic field. Position: thirty-five degrees west by forty-five degrees north. Jumping jellyfish – too far north! He couldn't understand it. His navigation was always spot on! Legions of Leatherbacks would be on their way to the Spacious Sea Meeting Place swimming further south. As usual he'd followed the jellyfish and plankton bloom floating along on the warm North Atlantic Drift towards that little island called Great Britain. Most of the Leatherback tribe hadn't cottoned on to the abundant food supply around its coastal areas but he had and found the Humans there friendly and *very* helpful. If the deep sea fishermen caught sight of George they stopped fishing, solicitously withdrew their nets and waved energetically at him. He always flapped a dignified giant flipper in return and much was the joy it caused! Smiling and talking excitedly, they pointed him out to other Humans in the boats, who had large black spectacles on their beaks and many were the "ooohs!" and "aaahs!" which ensued. *So* kind and respectful, reflected George happily.

An uncomfortable sensation was slowly but determinedly spreading throughout his mind and body. George shivered, sending three-feet-high waves rippling out into the silent ocean. He recognised the symptoms. Oh dear! His conscience was telling him to stop procrastinating and set off. Something awful may be happening to one of his family or friends and here he was, still lounging around eating despite being warned by the Great Mother! He'd never be able to live with himself if there was an accident. Leatherbacks were a close-knit community used to looking out for each other, which accounted for their continued existence when contemporaries such as Tyrannosaurus Rex – great stupid bully! – had become extinct. He must go.

Adjusting his inborn gyropilot to an accurate direction, George set off like a torpedo, his powerful nine-foot flippers propelling him through the water at incredible speed. Having started he felt better. The uncomfortable feelings dispersed now he was doing the right thing. Flying headlong through dimly lit water, shadowy with weird sea creatures, he was in his element. His massive barrel-shaped body cleaved through Pods of drowsing Dolphins – "Sorry to disturb! Can't stop. In a hurry!" – and Schools of young Whales puffing and blowing, practising aerial leaps, their magnificent fan-shaped tails smacking the surface water with jolly resonance.

"Terrific! Wonderful!" enthused George without pausing to join in the fun. Occasionally, waving walls of tough, black, rubbery sea wrack growing from a wrecked ship or floating island obscured his way but nothing deterred him. Undeviating from his course he hurried ever onwards towards the Meeting Place.

* * *

Some miles to the west in mid-ocean a tidal wave erupted as four joyful Giant Leatherback Patriarchs almost collided on the same spot, their navigation sensors having worked perfectly.

"What ho, old boys!" shouted the irrepressible Montague, "Are we all here?"

"Can't see George yet. Bet he's still in that Great Britain place," replied Archibald.

"Have you ever been there? George thinks it's wonderful. Plenty of food, considerate Humans and warmish water too as it's in the North Atlantic Drift," added Godfrey thoughtfully.

"Sounds promising!" said Horace, his eyes gleaming greedily. It was well known that Horace was a Coelenteconnoiss, or food expert. There was little he did not know about varieties of jellyfish and his girth testified to this. Whilst George was two tons of muscle, Horace was nearly two tons of blubber and nicknamed 'Whale' because of it.

"He'll be along soon. He never lets us down," reassured Godfrey quietly.

"Meanwhile – a little game of Chase the Portuguese Man-of-War?" suggested Horace, naming a large jellyfish popular with Leatherbacks.

"Right you are! First to catch shares. No gulping it down slyly on your own Horace!" commented Archie, as keen on his food as Horace.

Keeping their eyes open for any promisingly large jellyfish the Patriarchs swam and dived, played at 'whales', bringing their flippers down with mighty resounding splashes and behaving like Hatchlings straight out of school. Gurgling with laughter and enjoyment Godfrey suddenly held up his flipper for silence. "Attention please Patriarchs! Females coming through!"

Hastily composing themselves the Patriarchs swam aside to allow a Bale of female Leatherbacks to pass through. As the time for Metanoia had not yet arrived they acknowledged the males with a polite "Thank you" but did not loiter, swimming swiftly on towards the Meeting Place.

"Anyone we know?" enquired Monty cheerfully.

"Mostly Nematts from the look of them," replied Horace. "Striking-looking young females aren't they?"

"Marvellous to see six well-built girls with gleaming leathery carapaces swimming so confidently! Nothing wrong with their navigation! With the terrible decline in our numbers every year it's a worry," sighed Godfrey, shaking his head sadly.

"Oh come on Godfrey!" It can't be as bad as that, surely?" cried Archie impatiently, who took his fun seriously but very little else.

The girls safely on their way, ever-watchful Horace espied the large float of a Man-of-War, its dangerous tentacles trailing succulently. Grunting a warning to the others, he pointed with his flipper.

"Game on!" he whispered and the four stealthily closed in, each taking a different side above their prey.

"Wheee! Surprise, surprise!" shouted a hearty voice and ten male Nematts surged up from the depths chortling with glee. "Hello Uncle Archie! *Fancy* meeting you in the middle of nowhere. The lads and me have been having a great time …"

"And so were we, you young idiot! Now see what you've done!" Showing a surprising turn of speed the Man-of-War had retracted its fishing tentacles and bolted. The four exasperated hunters rounded on the jolly Bale of youthful males who had swum up surreptitiously to surprise them.

"Oh! Gosh! *Sorry* Uncle. We didn't see the jelly. Was it very big?"

"Fortunately for you, no. An immature one, just like you lot. So, you're on your way to the Spacious Sea?"

"Yes, and we've already seen a bunch of corking females about our age. They passed us a little way back but didn't stop of course."

"Corkers indeed!" opined Horace. "We noticed them, did we not Godfrey?"

"Very strong-looking young Turtles. They should make it up the beachheads. Well, good luck lads. Just remember, a mate is for life, not just the Scrimmage Fortnight," Godfrey solemnly reminded them.

"Yes Sir," replied the Nematts. The number of times they'd heard that from their teachers, Madame Louisa and Dr Laurence, to say nothing of their parents! But they wouldn't dream of answering back. Leatherback etiquette regarding the respect due to older, more experienced Turtles was very strict. Anyhow, plenty of time before they needed to settle on a mate and they intended to enjoy every minute of it.

"On your way now. We're waiting for Patriarch George. See you at the Meeting Place."

"Ok Uncle Archie, Patriarch Sirs. See you in the 'Ancestor'," they beamed cheerfully, nudged each other meaningfully, then rocketed off near the surface for an easier swim.

"Humph. Bit full of themselves," tutted Horace.

"Oh, come off it! It'll be their first time in the 'Ancestor' and remember how excited we were! First time drinking Birac Regal with the adults and mixing with lots of females they've never seen before! What red-blooded male wouldn't be excited? Young Ziggy did very well in his matriculation papers. He's earned a bit of fun and frolic."

Sometimes, thought Archie, Horace could be a bit of a misery. Probably because the Man-of-War had escaped!

"Look! Here's more Leatherbacks!" exclaimed Monty.

"Not surprising. We're in Leatherback Lanes, the junction of Latitude and Longitude Leatherbacks use for homing purposes," remarked Godfrey.

"We won't catch any big jellies if we're going to be constantly disturbed," groaned Horace. "Let's move a few degrees north where it's less crowded," he suggested.

"What about George? He'll come here and won't find us. The old boy'll think we've deserted him."

Folding their flippers neatly over their backs, they pondered the problem.

"I don't agree with Horace," said Monty. "We ought to stay here. He'll get anxious if he arrives and we're nowhere to be seen."

"He's no fool. He'll soon hear us. You know how keen his echo location is."

"Maybe, but there's plenty of food here. We've no need to move. What do you think, Godfrey?"

"We always meet at this spot. Some years there are more homing Turtles than others, yet we've never moved our location. It's tradition and shouldn't be broken without good reason. Certainly not for greed. I agree with Monty. We stay."

Archie was now in a fix. He didn't want to leave his friends or cause George worry but he did like the idea of a good, square meal.

"I'm going to move," said Horace decisively. "I'm starving. You three wait here for George. I won't go too far," and without waiting for a reply he swam off. Monty, Godfrey and Archie looked after him doubtfully.

"Oh well," said Archie, trying to make light of it, "I expect he's *really* hungry! We know what Horace is like."

"There's adequate food here. He's no need to go darting off in that inconsiderate way. Let's face it, he's a glutton and getting worse." Godfrey always faced facts, however unpleasant.

Just then Horace's head appeared through the water. "Come on chaps! There's another Man-of-War just a few flippers away. Who's joining me?" and he dashed off again. Archie hesitated and was lost. "See you soon!" he called. "I won't go far," and off he dashed in the wake of Horace.

"*Really!*" snapped Monty, clicking his beak angrily. "That's not what I call consideration. What's got into them?"

"*Food*, Monty, food! Horace will do anything for a gourmet meal and Archie likes his food and drink too. We'll wait here and feed on 'Athorybia rosacea'. Not very exciting but palatable and easy to see with that bright pink colour."

Grazing contentedly and exchanging greetings with other Leatherbacks who swam along, it was some time before Monty and Godfrey realised that Archie and Horace had been away a long time.

"Where *are* those two?" asked an exasperated Monty.

"Yes, they've been gone longer than it takes to catch a Man-of-War," agreed Godfrey. "Monty, I think we'd better go and look for them. Let's hope George doesn't turn up yet."

At the back of their minds was the terrible thought of the gigantic fishing ships that Humans sent out to all sorts of unlikely places. These released long-line fishing nets extending for ninety miles or more, which randomly caught every marine creature in the area. The 'by-catch' of Dolphins, Sharks and Turtles became tangled up in the net and suffocated. All Turtles were warned about them – but who knew where they would turn up next? They were *so* enormous! It was a constant anxiety for the free swimming Turtles who had roamed the world's seas for millions of years. Driven on by these unpleasant thoughts, the two friends set off in the direction that Horace and Archie had taken. Listening carefully they heard various muffled bangings and grunts distinctive to Leatherbacks. Drawing nearer the noises, they stopped, recoiling at the horrific scene before them.

Upended in the sea in a most undignified position hung Archie, one flipper trapped in a wire while the other flailed around frantically, creating an opaque turbulence. His massive carapace twisted and turned as he wriggled and squirmed trying to release the ensnared flipper. Realising a hidden danger, Monty and Godfrey froze. They must remain free to help their friend.

"Archie, Archie! What's the trouble? What's happened to your flipper?"

"*Don't* come any closer, Monty and Godfrey. It's one of those long-line fishing nets my flipper's caught in. I can't loosen it. Every time I move it gets worse. I'm done for. I need air too, can't last much longer. You go home to our lovely Spacious Sea and tell Oneka she's free to choose another mate."

Archie paused, tears welling up as he thought of his pretty wife and their Hatchlings. "*Go on*! It's nearly time for the Metanoia. You mustn't be late or what will *your* wives say!" he added with an attempt at humour.

Poor Archie! To discover a flipper isn't working is death to a Turtle. Swimming is their life and both flippers essential. Instead of surging forward with a powerful swish of his flippers, Archie was stationary. Stationary and surrounded by *food*! Pulling and heaving at the line that snaked nearly invisibly through the water, his considerable strength and one and a half tons of weight had made matters worse. He was well and truly snared.

"Don't be such a pessimist, Archie," shouted Monty as calmly as he could. "We'll think of something, you'll see. How are you fixed for air?"

"Quarter of an hour? Twenty minutes maybe. *Please* don't come closer and get tangled up too. Leave me. There's nothing you can do."

Godfrey had been very cautiously and slowly swimming about to explore possible ways of helping Archie. He saw nothing of Horace and knew the question must be asked.

"Ah! Er, herumph, er, Archie, dear fellow – do you know where Horace is? There's no sign of him."

Archie's eyes filled with tears again as he let out a grunt of anguish. "Oh Godfrey, Monty, he's gone to Great Mother Turtle and the Reef of Righteous Turtles. Horace only had eyes for the Man-of-War giant jellyfish and it swam straight into the net. Horace followed, he didn't even pause. The hooks on the net ripped his plastron open and he bled to death in front of me. That's how I got caught. I was trying to comfort him." Archie broke down completely, the terrible event renewed in his memory.

Barely moving, the three Leatherbacks softly began the keening and soughing sounds of mourning. Horace may have been blinded by greed but what a terrible way to die! It was Godfrey who pulled them up sharply.

"Come along, brace up. We're not Grand Patriarchs of the Giant Leatherback genus for nothing. We will mourn Horace properly when there's time. Right now we've got to try and save Archie. First of all – you *must* keep still, Archie! You're wearing yourself out thrashing about, using up precious energy and air. The water gets cloudy too – more difficult to see what we're doing. So *stay still*."

Godfrey tried to sound authoritative and confident as if these instructions were merely preliminaries to a great escape. Really he had no idea what to do but knew it was important not to panic. How he wished George was here! With his abundant ideas and tremendous strength anything was possible. At least Archie had stopped struggling. Godfrey's words made good common sense and Monty was nodding energetically in agreement.

"Good, that's *much* better! We can see you clearly now. Keep still, we're just popping up for a breath. We'll only be a jiffy."

Archie understood this and wished he could pop up himself. Against his active nature he floated still and supine, allowing the underwater currents to waft him gently to and fro. Seeing how sensible he was being, Monty and Godfrey wasted no time. Keeping well away from Archie they ascended to the surface, took a deep, deep breath as if they were both trying to take one for Archie, and descended again.

"Here we are, back again," they called reassuringly. "We've got all sorts of ideas," enthused Monty, "hang in there!" Said with more hope than conviction, neither Turtle had a clue what to do next apart from remaining with their friend to the last. They cudgelled their brains.

"If only another adult would come this way we *may* be able to do something," whispered Monty. "With only two of us I can't think of anything."

"Trouble is, we've moved from Leatherback Lanes. It's unlikely another Leatherback will pass by here. One of our cousins may pass, the Green or Hawksbill Turtles, but they won't be able to help; too small."

"They could take a message to the nearest Leatherback. They're fast swimmers, especially the Greens."

"Now that is a good idea, Monty! Let's separate, you go that way, I'll go this. Keep our eyes skinned and Archie's spirits up," and raising his voice he shouted confidently, "We're on the right track, Archie! Just relax, save energy and you'll soon be free."

"Thanks boys!" came a weak voice. "I'm doing my best. My flipper's bleeding where it's caught."

Oh no! Thought Monty and Godfrey, that made speed even more essential as Turtles bleed to death quite quickly. "Carry on calmly, Monty! Don't let him feel panic whatever you do," grunted Godfrey in a low voice. Aloud he called, "No problem Archie! We'll release you soon. Keep calm."

As he said these encouraging but untrue words, a flash of bronze and olive appeared in the water beneath him. Diving at incredible speed he called out on the special Chelonian Auditory Wavelength: "Stop! Please stop – Turtle in mortal danger!" waving his flippers to attract the Green Turtle's attention. The Turtle paused at the rapidly approaching Leatherback, his flippers in mid-sweep.

"You startled me, Sir Leatherback! How can I help?"

"Thank you Sir Green, for your prompt courtesy," replied Godfrey, not to be outdone in Chelonian etiquette. "Our friend is in mortal danger, every second counts. We need at least one fully-grown male Leatherback if we are to save him. Would you be so kind as to go to Leatherback Lanes and give an urgent message to the first one you see, sending him here?"

"By all means. Is it a Human danger?"

"It is. You would do well to keep your kin away from this area. There are long-line fishing ships about."

"Ah! I thank you Sir. I'll be on my way to Leatherback Lanes. Rely on me. I have taken the bearing. Goodbye," and so saying he darted away.

Much relieved at his swift understanding and instant cooperation, Godfrey returned to Archie.

"Help is on its way, Archie. A Green's been dispatched with a message and you know how nifty they are!"

"Yes and they don't like being turned into soup any more than we do!" agreed an exhausted, blood-soaked Archie. He was finding it increasingly difficult to stay calm and cheery and his flipper was aching badly with the strain of supporting his weight. Behind him, Monty reappeared from his reconnoitre, his face gloomy.

"I didn't meet anything," he whispered, "not even a jellyfish!"

"I did. I've sent a message via a helpful Green. Someone will be here soon, *very* soon I hope!"

Abruptly a tidal wave of gigantic proportions erupted, the sea frothing, boiling, cascading upon them in torrents. Thrown backwards by the strength and suddenness of the pitching water, Monty and Godfrey were bewildered. What could cause such a disturbance?

"They're winding in the net!" exclaimed a horrified Archie.

Chapter Three

A TEST FOR GEORGE

Foaming water, spumes of plankton, curtains of seaweed and schools of agitated fish obscured the Leatherbacks' vision as they strained to see if Archie was right. But he remained stationary. Something was emerging from the surge and swash, a huge sea monster! Friend or foe? Whale or Shark? Perhaps a Leatherback sent by the quick-witted Green? Half-hoping, half-fearing, alert to further danger, they watched as an unbelievable sight took shape, materialising in the opaque sea. A majestic beak set in determined lines, two titanic nine-foot flippers at full stretch, a magnificent, shining carapace adorned with many rare molluscs – George! George, whom they had all hoped would appear and like magic had.

"George!" the three Leatherbacks gasped in relief and joy.

"Thank Great Mother you're here! How did you find us? We *need* you. Archie's flipper's stuck in a long line fishing net. He hasn't got much breath left. Oh George! *What* are we to do?"

So *this* was why the Choir of Angel Fish had been sent! This was why his navigational sensor kept swinging to the north.

"No time for explanations now. Later. Let's have a look at Archie," replied George and started swimming cautiously towards him. No need to warn George about danger; from his vast experience he knew exactly what to watch out for. He observed Archie's predicament closely. There must be a way of rescuing him or the Angel Fish wouldn't have been sent. It was up to *him*, though, to work it out.

Thinking faster than ever before in his long life, George warily and carefully weighed up the situation. He could see the net extending far away into the distance, Archie, limp and fatigued, hanging from the line wrapped round his bleeding flipper, his life ebbing.

"Hello, old chelone," Archie whispered. "Get away from here.

Don't sacrifice yourselves for me. I'm for Great Mother Turtle. Save yourselves – go now."

George was having none of this. He had swum non-stop to obey Great Mother's command and felt sick as he realised what his delay had caused. Horace was nowhere to be seen. If he'd set off immediately, as the Choir had instructed, would he still be here? Would Archie be nearly dead from loss of blood and lack of air? He thought not. He could no longer save two precious Leatherback lives, that was sadly clear, but he could still save one.

"ARCHIE! ARCHIE!" he bellowed. "Can you hear me?"

"Oh George! The waves keep tightening the line round my flipper. It hurts a lot. Godfrey told me to stay still and I am. But … it's … getting … more … difficult … to … breathe."

"Save your breath Archie, no more talking. You've given me an idea. Try and relax completely. Let the current take you. We'll get you out, never fear."

Archie's words had given George hope. Swimming swiftly to where Monty and Godfrey had remained, he gave his orders.

" … and *please* do *exactly* as I say, *when* I say it or we don't stand a dogfish chance. Ok?"

Nodding vigorously, aware that every second counted, the three Turtles swam gingerly towards Archie.

"Archie, listen to me. Do *not* reply. *Do exactly as I say*. You must keep *perfectly still*. I repeat, *perfectly still*. Don't struggle, let the current take you. When the line slackens around your flipper, I'll shout. *Immediately* you hear me, retreat backwards from the net. Ok?"

"Ok George, I understand," whispered Archie.

"Ready chaps?" asked George of Monty and Godfrey and, receiving affirmative replies, they took up prearranged positions.

Monty swam to Archie's head, Godfrey to Archie's rear and George positioned himself underneath near his middle.

"On my signal boys, not before," commanded George.

He was watching the water lapping around Archie and could see a big wave approaching the line.

"READY, STEADY, HOLD!" shouted George.

The wave concertinaed the stiff line, relaxing it slightly round Archie's flipper. In one smooth, synchronised movement Monty and Godfrey caught and gripped the line firmly between their beaks to stop it tautening again. Using his powerful carapace George attempted to lift Archie to relieve the pressure still further. Archie's flipper relaxed.

"NOW, Archie! NOW! QUICK – glide away!" screamed George. Supporting Archie's dead weight on his carapace was agonising. He couldn't sustain it for long and from his position underneath was unable to see what was happening.

"GO Archie, GO!" he screamed again. But Archie didn't move.

"Sorry George!" gasped Monty's apologetic voice, "the rope slipped at my end. We'll have to try again."

George restrained his wrath with difficulty. It would be a pointless waste of precious energy. Monty hadn't done it deliberately. Easing himself away from Archie and gathering his strength he replied with quiet confidence, "Well done! Stay alert. Keep both eyes on the lines," and began watching the wave pattern again. Here was another promising wave, not as large as the first but the risk must be taken. Archie was weakening visibly.

"Are you ready? HOLD!" repeated George, once again lifting Archie from beneath.

"More support!" said Archie weakly, "More support!"

George braced himself still further, every muscle strained and taut. He could hear his carapace creaking like old timbers on a hot day and thanked Great Mother that a Leatherback's carapace was pliable as well as resilient or Archie's weight would have cracked it wide open. But he hadn't any more strength! George, working blind, called, "What's happened? Is the rope off yet? I can't hold him much longer."

Suddenly the crushing burden lightened. Godfrey's quiet voice called, "It'll be alright now, George. Another two seconds and Archie will be free."

"Stay clear of those ropes you two! We don't want any accidents now!" gasped George.

Suddenly Archie moved, backing away from the treacherous lines of the trawler. Using only one flipper he rose slowly towards the surface. Air was his first priority. As soon as he'd gone up, Monty and Godfrey released the line, backed off cautiously and went to George who was lying in the water gasping with pain.

"Come along George old friend. It's over now. Let's get you to the surface," said Monty, whose beak was cut and bleeding. With flippers entwined, they moved slowly upwards.

Three pairs of large Leatherback jaws opened wide to welcome glorious, restorative air. Archie was still reeling from his narrow escape, incapable of doing anything.

"Archie – how are you? Take it easy while we fetch food and bandages."

George and Monty dived after some easily digestible Rosacea and wide, flexible, Sea Wrack with air pockets to cushion his wound. It wasn't as good as 'Dr Aesculapius's Salubrious Sea Wrack Plaster for Plastron and Flipper Rends' but it would do in an emergency. Once out of Archie's hearing George stopped.

"Monty, your mouth. What happened?" he asked anxiously.

"It's nothing. The line kept sawing back and forth across my beak but I was determined to hold it tight the second time. It'll be fine soon. Drop of fresh sea water and some air will soon mend it up," he remarked cheerfully.

"Well done, Monty," congratulated George, appreciatively clapping him on the carapace with a mighty flipper, "you showed great bravery and determination."

"Thank you George, so did you. What would have happened if you hadn't shown up I dread to think. By the way – what's happened to Godfrey? I haven't seen him at the surface."

"No, nor have I. That's strange. You both came to me but somehow he's got lost. You don't think …"

A terrible idea crossed their minds. Had Godfrey been caught in the net as he was coming up for air? No one had paid much attention to him. He was such a quiet, self-effacing Turtle.

"Quick George, let's get this food to Archie and bandage him up. We must hurry," and they whisked upwards.

"Here's some tasty Rosacea, Archie. Get that inside you and you'll feel better. Here, let me bandage your flipper. You mustn't lose any more blood."

"Amazing, incredible friends, how can I ever thank you enough! Putting your own lives in danger to save me!"

With fresh air in his lungs and pain from the fishing wire easing, Archie was beginning to recover. His flipper, washed clean and sterilised by clear salt water, now tightly bound with sea wrack, stopped bleeding. After a few mouthfuls of sustaining jellyfish he began to feel himself again. What an escape! What loyalty, courage and fortitude his friends had shown! He looked about to thank Godfrey too and saw Monty and George swimming towards another Turtle some distance away. It was moving erratically and slowly, using only one flipper.

"Godfrey!" called George, "Godfrey, is that you? What happened? I heard you speak and everything was alright then. Here, we'll lend a flipper each. Archie's safe and sound, looking quite perky."

Swimming either side of Godfrey the two rejoined Archie.

"Look at Godfrey's flipper! It's sort of squashed. How did you do that?" asked Monty.

"Don't fuss, it'll be ok. Good to see you feeling better, Archie," said Godfrey with a dazed look. "That was a narrow squeak wasn't it?"

"Here, have this jelly. You deserve it after what you did," replied Archie, holding out a flipperful of Rosacea.

George and Monty looked on proudly. Stout fellow, old Godfrey, never moaned or had histrionics, just got on with things.

"Well done, Godfrey, but – how *did* your flipper get flattened? You must tell us!"

"It'll return to normal by and by. Don't fret, let's find ..." But he was interrupted by Archie.

"Godfrey's being modest, I know what happened. When I called for more help he managed to get a front flipper under my tail and supported me until I got free. He held the line steady throughout. I don't how he did it but I'm not surprised his flipper's squashed!"

George and Monty gasped with admiration at this highly dangerous and valorous deed, and clapped Godfrey, not too heavily, on the carapace.

"Well done, well done! Wow Godfrey, that's one for 'Leatherback Lives'," exclaimed George enthusiastically, "and you too Monty," he added, in case Monty felt left out, "you both showed remarkable courage."

"Well," said Monty magnanimously, "the important thing is Archie's alive and flipping. We've saved at least one Leatherback life."

At this Horace sprang to mind.

"What happened to Horace, Archie?" asked George quietly. Archie told George the sad story while Monty fetched fresh supplies of Rosacea.

"And there's nothing to be done?"

"'Fraid not. He would have died of a haemorrhage before he was suffocated. His plastron was ripped open on the fishing net wire."

Archie broke down. The friends remained silent. Poor Horace, what would they tell Cassandra, his wife?

"Er ... listen," said George, "I've been thinking. About Cassandra."

Everyone nodded.

"Perhaps a bit of a white lie is in order? We could say he went into the net and ran out of air immediately? That's bad enough. We would say nothing about his bleeding to death."

"We agree with you. But you know Cassandra, she's bound to think the worst whatever we say."

"Yes, we'll have to stick grimly to our story. Godfrey, do you hear?"

Godfrey was renowned for his complete honesty.

"I agree. Cassandra will be dreadfully upset. Let's not make things worse."

"I've been meaning to ask you, George: when you first arrived and spoke to me, how did I give you an idea? I was in no fit state to have ideas!" asked Archie, puzzled.

"You said the waves kept tightening the line round your flipper. If it tightened, it must have loosened. That's what gave me the idea.

If I watched the waves until the net slackened we may be able to do something – and we did!" he ended triumphantly.

"You're a genius, George!" exclaimed Archie.

"Slippery eels! How did you think of that when Archie was rolling round in agony? My mind was a blank," contributed Monty admiringly.

"Good thinking, and quick too! Well done, George!" Godfrey spoke quietly and sincerely.

Remembering his own greed and slowness in obeying Great Mother Turtle's urgent message, George went a pale shade of mauve at these compliments. If he'd been quicker to obey, Horace might still be alive.

"How did you get *here* when we usually meet in Leatherback Lanes?" queried Monty. "Did a Green Turtle give you a message?"

"A Green Turtle?" George was astounded. "No, I didn't see a Green. I was sent by a Choir of Angel Fish who told me …"

The others were snuffling and making muffled grunting noises, which was Leatherback laughter.

"Oh George! You're a hoot! Choir of Angel Fish indeed! Come off it. We left all that behind at Turtle Academy."

"But there *was* a Choir …"

"Yes – and I'm Archelon! Seriously though, did you meet a Green?"

"I keep telling you, *no* I did not."

Just then the Green Turtle arrived, puffing and blowing, quite worn out with excitement and the exertion of his long swim at best speed.

"Good evening Sir Leatherbacks. *So* pleased to meet again. I hope I was in time? Is everything alright?" he looked around.

"But where's the Leatherback I sent? I can't see him."

"Here he is!" laughed Monty and Godfrey, pushing George forward. "Your tale about Choirs of Angel Fish isn't going to stand up now," they grinned. The Green studied George carefully and shook his head.

"No way. This isn't the Leatherback I met. He was much paler, a sort of yellowy colour, almost *white*."

The Four Leatherbacks exchanged glances.

"Big, was he?" asked George.

"Larger than him, Sir," pointing at Godfrey. "About the same size and weight as yourself, Sir. Funny though, you've lots of guests on your broad carapace, he didn't have any."

"Azazel!" gasped the four, in one horrified breath.

"But surely even he wouldn't leave another Dermochelys to die!" exclaimed Godfrey.

Looking sharply from one to the other the Green reiterated, "Believe me Sirs, I gave your message to the first mature male I met in Leatherback Lanes. Some of your females passed, then this large, yellowish male. I spoke to him, explained how urgent it was and where you were. I gave him the precise latitude and longitude. He promised to veer off to help. Just then another Green arrived, a worried young female. She'd been swept off course by the current like me. Not being as big as you Sirs, we can be swept off course more easily. I reassured her and set her on the right course. Then returned to see if you needed any more help."

"Sir Green, you have been courtesy and helpfulness personified. We cannot thank you enough. You and your kin will be welcomed into our Chelonian Cloister in times of exhaustion, distress or danger. Please make sure your tribe knows this, and that George, Grand Patriarch of the Giant Leatherbacks, invited you."

"I thank you, Sir Leatherback, and will pass on your message. Our kind are as near extinction as yours and it is good to help each other in these dangerous times. And now Sirs, I must be on my way to our Great Sea Grass Grazing Plain."

All the Turtles bowed ceremoniously and with cries of, "Great Mother Turtle protect you!" the Green set off. Once out of hearing the Leatherbacks looked grimly at each other.

"Azazel! How *could* he ignore our Mayday signal?"

"*And* tell a lie!"

"Where is he now?"

"Do we care?"

Archie and Godfrey were so angry they had quite forgotten their injuries. George was planning what he'd say to Azazel when he caught up with him and honourable Monty was amazed any Leatherback could be so treacherous. It just *wasn't done!*

"Time to be moving on. Our wives will be worried about us. But first – we must give Horace our traditional Leatherback Farewell Villanelle."

Nodding their agreement with George, the four Turtles gathered round in an incomplete circle, the tips of their flippers touching. Between George and Archie, who had known Horace the longest, was a gap. With heads bowed they made their Farewell Villanelle to Horace.

VILLANELLE FOR A DERMOCHELYS

"Now you are gone, gone on before –
Horace, our boyhood friend of old.
Yet will you enter through the door

Of Righteous Turtles, we are sure.
There you and others: Hatchlings, Nematts bold;
Together have gone, gone on before.

Far from the ocean's mighty roar,
Shielded from danger, mean and cold,
Many will enter through that door.

But close your eyes in Holy Awe,
Bow down, bow down as flippers Gold
Stretch out to those who've gone before.

Great Mother's nigh to those who keep her Law,

She welcomes them, her wings enfold
Each one who knocks upon this door.

Farewell, dear Horace, our vigil's o'er,
Forever will your kindly deeds be told,
Now you have left and gone before
To enter through that Glorious Door."

After the final words there was a reverent silence as they remembered their friend. The broken circle split up, as one by one the Turtles raised a massive foreflipper in salute, sweeping it deliberately yet gracefully through the water to create a huge wave. As they did so each intoned, "Horace, my friend, my flipper helps waft you to the Reef of Righteous Turtles where no danger exists and jellyfish abound. May it please you to carry my obeisance to our Great Mother Turtle."

There was another pause. The huge heartbreaking sighs of Leatherbacks in distress echoed eerily through the swash. Archie had tears coursing down his wrinkled face.

"Come along. We can do no more for Horace. He's safe in the Righteous Reef. Remember our story for Cassandra," reminded George.

"Yes, it's time we were making waves towards the Spacious Sea. We mustn't be late and cause problems for our wives," added sensible Godfrey.

This was good advice. Late Turtles caused great anxiety. Assuming the worst, females and males occasionally chose another partner. Then their mate turned up! It could be extremely awkward and everyone made a terrific effort to be on time. Surfacing to take a good breath before setting off, the four observed the fiery orange glow of the setting sun in the west. Close by and rising slowly and shyly above the horizon was another sphere. It shone and sparkled like a new and especially brilliant ruby, roseate in the darkening sky. A new Turtle Star! The sign that Horace was safe and at peace! Four large Turtle mouths turned up in wide smiles and four pairs of enormous flippers swept the water aside with renewed vigour.

Chapter Four

ON TURTLE BEACH

A tornado of agitated feathers accompanied by an ear piercing scream caused Jomo to brake suddenly as he drove into the curved drive of the hotel.

"It's dem Cocricos, Prof. Dey likes to take dere dust bath right in front of de hotel. Now *dere's* a specie what's goin' to get h'extinct if he go on doin' dat!"

Gemma laughed.

"Not them, Jomo. They're usually so secretive and their numbers are always rising. Look at that group! Listen to the din they're making now you've disturbed them!"

Settling into the branches of a brilliant red Flamboyant tree a group of large, golden-brown birds were ruffling their feathers angrily and screeching their own name, "Coc ricooo! Coc ricooo! Coc ricooo!"

Beside the Flamboyant tree, overhanging the hotel's entrance, was a Bacanoo tree, its enormous crinkly brown leaves providing welcome shade. Scarlet Firecrackers, Golden Chalice Vine, Hibiscus, Pink Poui, African Tulip trees and rounded clusters of Ixora flowers created a bouquet of tropical colour to welcome visitors as well as screening the buildings.

"Wake up, Mum! Come on, Penny – we've arrived!"

Gemma gently shook her mother and tapped Penny's shoulder.

"No, no!" screamed Penny, "Stop that! Get away, you horrible beast ..."

She awoke with a start to find she was vigorously punching Jomo.

"Hey, hey, hey Missah! Calm down. Yo bin dreamin'. Is all ok. What yo dreamin' 'bout Miss Penny? Yo sure scared me!"

"Oh!" Penny's heart was still thumping. Turning she saw her

41

mother and Gran looking at her anxiously.

"Heavens Penny! What was that about? It must have been bad."

"Yes, sorry. I was dreaming about the Turtles. Someone was trying to cut off their flippers for soup. It was *horrible*!" She shivered at the thought. "Mum, does that really happen?"

"I'm sorry to say it does. That's why Jomo and my other Custodians patrol the beach at night. That's why we could do with Cora! *She* would frighten them off!"

"Oh Mum! That's *terrible*! I thought it was just a dream."

"It was, dear. With Jomo and his friends guarding the nesting sites, that sort of butchery is decreasing. But it did happen a lot." Gemma forbore to say more. "We've arrived at the hotel, look! Here's Mr MacRobert come to greet us."

Penny jumped from the car and took the steps two at a time. She liked the Hotel Manager.

"Hello Mr MacRobert! Phew – isn't it hot? Is Merlyn looking after us? Is Cotoe still cook? Hello Tyrone, hello Ilene. It's good to be back!"

"Welcome back Penny, you look full of beans! This must be your grandmother, Mrs Fairweather, how do ye do. I hope you're not too tired after your long journey? It's very exhausting. Your rooms are ready. I'll send Rousseau with the bags and Merlyn with tea."

Ilene from the bar handed round iced fruit cocktails decorated with juicy pineapple and Penny introduced Gran to the smiling staff. Mr MacRobert turned to Gemma.

"There's a very persistent representative from 'Modern Nature' waiting for you. Turned up not long ago. I told him you were unavailable but he insisted on waiting. I've put him in the lecture room where it's cool and out of the way. Take as long as you want over tea. There are a number of phone messages too."

"Oh dear! I was hoping for a few quiet minutes with my family. I'll take them to our rooms and come straight back. Better to get it out of the way. Come on, Mum, Penny, let's get into the cool of our rooms and have tea."

Mrs Fairweather needed no second bidding and fell into step

with her daughter. They walked briskly down the long winding path bordered by flower beds which led to the rooms.

"Look at the lovely orchids!" enthused Mrs Fairweather.

"Yes, the gardener's very proud of his plants. He's one of my voluntary Custodians, Tyrone. A good man. Here we are." Shielded from the blazing sun by a high wood canopy, they climbed green painted steps to a landing with three doors leading off.

"That's your room and bathroom on the left, Mum. Mine's on the right," she said, and, opening the centre door, went through into a cool, dim lobby.

"This is Penny's bedroom and shower," Gemma indicated a door on the left, "and in here," walking through, "is the main sitting room with a huge balcony." Sweeping aside the sun absorbent curtains, she opened the long tinted windows and ushered her mother through. Mrs Fairweather gasped with pleasure.

"Gemma, how beautiful! I suppose you take it for granted but I've rarely seen anything so lovely."

The spacious balcony had plenty of room for a large round table, chairs and sunbeds. In one corner a thriving rose pink Bougainvillea frothed over the sturdy rails and in the other a Purple Wreath Vine cascaded gracefully to the ground. They provided an ornamental frame for the wonderful view. Cloudless blue sky melted into azure aquamarine of softly lapping sea. A small fishing fleet bobbed quietly, nets neatly stacked. Each boat bore its cargo of statuesque Pelicans. Facing the same way, beaks and pouches lowered and tucked away like furled umbrellas, they resembled dignified Great Aunts sitting in a bus. Small waves flopped onto a long sandy beach which rose inland forming soft friable dunes. Behind the dunes, nearer the hotel, a stretch of grass dotted with Fan Palms, Banana Palms, Coconut Palms, Mango and Almond trees shaded the scattered sunbeds. Craft vendors sat under the trees selling handmade sandals, gaily printed sarongs and coconut juice fresh from the tree. A circuitous path bound by riotous flowers of red Lantana, yellow Canna lilies, scarlet Poinsettia, blue Plumbago and sweet smelling cream Frangipani meandered along the sea-facing rooms linking them with the restaurant and bar area. It was a scene from Paradise, thought Mrs Fairweather, nothing bad or ugly could happen here.

"Isn't it wonderful, Penny?" she exclaimed, but Penny was nowhere to be seen.

"Where's the girl got to?" exclaimed Gemma, surprised. "Last year she clung to me like a limpet. It was quite awkward."

"Why was that, dear? Surely it's to be expected under the circumstances."

"But Mum, I've *so* much work to get through and precious little help."

"Gemma, she hasn't recovered from …"

There was a polite knock on the door and Merlyn the housemaid entered, balancing a large tray, followed by Rousseau with the luggage.

"Ah've put de cases in your rooms, Professor. Here's Miss Penny's."

"Thanks so much, Rousseau. Just pop it in there."

"Where yo want dis, Ma'am?" asked Merlyn. "In de room or out on de balcony?"

"In the room please, Merlyn. It's too hot outside."

Merlyn put the heavy tray down. It was loaded with tea, homemade cakes, scones and almond biscuits, a speciality of the island people. Penny darted into the room and rushed over to her mother.

"Penny!" cried the two women in unison. "Where have you been?" continued Gran quickly, preventing any comment from Gemma.

"Talking to Ilene and Joseph. I saw Merlyn go by with tea and dashed along. Sorry if I'm late."

Merlyn grinned broadly as she poured out the tea.

"Is too hot to-day for running about, Missah. After this, ah go wit' ma family to our bay and swim."

"Ooh, lovely Merlyn! Which bay is that?"

"Pirates Bay, further north on de island."

"Is that the one which can only be reached by sea? It always looks very enticing. Do you go there by boat?" asked Penny.

"No Missah. We people of Caithness Point go down de cliff side. Is de old pirates' path. Very hidden and secret," she chuckled.

"Did they bring rum and gold pieces of eight and precious stones up the path from their galleons?" asked Penny excitedly.

"They did, Missah. There's de caves still where dey stored tings."

Penny eyes were sparkling. She'd never heard this before, only that Pirates Bay was too steep to reach.

"Mum, can we go? Will you take me? Merlyn can show us the way." she exclaimed.

"Merlyn is a busy woman and has other things to do – as I have. It's dangerous too isn't it? I thought there were rock falls there?" queried Gemma.

"Sometime, maybe. But it all safe now. We know where an' when to take care. If that's all yo wantin' Ma'am, I'll be on ma way."

"Yes, thank you so much Merlyn. Hope you have a lovely afternoon."

"An' yo have a nice tea," grinned Merlyn.

Comfortably seated in a large armchair, shoes off and feet up, a cup of tea in her hand and a delicious almond slice in front of her, Mrs Fairweather sighed with contentment.

"I'm well set up if there's anything you want to do," she smiled. "Don't worry about me. I'll unpack and have a kip."

"If you're sure, Mum. I must go and see that journalist and make some phone calls."

"Oh *Mum*! Will you be long? Can I come with you? I'll keep out of the way, honest, and be very quiet."

"I won't be long. You go for a swim."

Penny's face set mutinously.

"But I hardly see you! And even here you're trying to get rid of me!" she said angrily.

"Penny, please! I'll get the work done faster on my own. Gran's here, remember. Go straight out in front of the room and down the beach. She can watch you from the balcony."

"Good idea, Gemma! I'll take my tea out there," agreed Mrs Fairweather quickly.

Sulkily, Penny disappeared into her room to change.

"Don't worry, Gemma," Gran said quietly, "she'll be alright. She's tired."

Gemma nodded and, opening the door, set out for the hotel to see her unwelcome visitor. She was fuming. What a cheek not to make an appointment or leave when he was told she was busy! Some people had no manners. She wouldn't have bothered to see him, but any publicity about conserving wildlife was important and couldn't be ignored. Gemma took the stairs to the lecture room two at a time to confront the unknown journalist.

In her bedroom Penny threw open the case and began rummaging around for a swimsuit. The room faced east with a high ceiling and centre fan creating a refreshing draught. The traditional louvred windows of the island also encouraged a light breeze. The sun was over in the west now, shining into the sea-facing rooms and her room was pleasantly cool. Leading off it was her own shower room. They were both decorated in palest blue with the bedspread and towels dark blue decorated with vivid flowers. On the walls were lively paintings by local artists of more flowers, street scenes, harbour activities and remarkable birds like Collared Trogons and Purple Gallinules. Penny didn't even glance at her delightful little room. Flinging on her swimsuit she called, "Gran! I'm off for a swim. Are you going to watch?"

"Have you unpacked already? That was quick!" remarked Gran.

"Not *quite*, nearly," said Penny.

"I hope you haven't left clothes all over the place," commented Gran, who seemed to have x-ray vision.

"I'll unpack properly after my swim," she cried. "You'll watch, won't you," and without waiting for a reply ran down the steps. Mrs Fairweather looked after her and sighed. Give her time, she thought, give both of them time, and, taking a cup of tea and another biscuit, she reluctantly went out onto the hot balcony.

* * *

"I'm Professor Heffernan. I don't have a great deal of time. As you've been informed, I am officially unavailable this afternoon. Would you state your business quickly please."

Adrian, snoozing gently, shot upright and jumped out of his chair. Wow – this lady didn't mince her words! He looked at her red hair, cut short in a no-nonsense way, the complete lack of make-up and tattered shorts and decided he'd better wake up very fast and get on with the interview.

"Good afternoon Professor. I'm Adrian Kanhai from 'Modern Nature.' Here's my card. I believe you're the expert on Marine Turtles including the Giant Leatherback?"

"That is correct."

"Are you aware that poaching is going on in this area?"

"Yes, of course," replied Gemma briskly. What a silly question! Yet he didn't look stupid. Tall, dusky, with limpid brown eyes, he looked shrewd and intelligent.

"So, what are you doing about it?"

Gemma bridled. The cheek of the man! Anyone would think it was *her* fault the way he said it!

"Can I ask – what are *you* doing about it?" she replied sharply. "I can't wage war against poachers on my own. Everyone must do their bit. If you're writing an article about protecting the Turtles, that's fine. If you're writing an article criticising my efforts, you can leave right now," she said, jabbing a hand towards the door.

Startled by her vehemence, Adrian swiftly back-tracked.

"Sorry, sorry, I didn't mean to be rude. Yes, I do want to protect the Turtles. I want to find out about them and take photos …"

"Oh no you don't! That's out of the question. Far too many people take photos of the Turtles as they come up the beach. The flash frightens them and off they go, straight back into the sea."

"Come now, surely that's an exaggeration? Don't you know about cameras without a flash?" he asked, jet black eyebrows raised sarcastically.

Gemma nearly exploded. What impertinence! What condescension!

"Have you come here to insult me? If not, you're giving a good impression of it. If you're serious about doing a piece on preservation, make an appointment. I haven't time to go into it and I need to check your credentials," replied Gemma, looking meaningfully at the card in her hand. He may be a poacher himself for all she knew, getting inside information.

"I'm not a poacher," he said, as if reading her thoughts, "and I really do want to save the Turtles. But ok, let's make it another day. Perhaps a couple of days?"

"Yes, that would be convenient for *me*," agreed Gemma, with emphasis.

"I'm sorry to be such a nuisance. In this job you don't get anywhere unless you are," smiled Adrian in a conciliatory manner.

Gemma refused to be mollified.

"Be here in two days, same time. I won't hang around so you'd better be punctual."

Shaking hands in a perfunctory way she headed out of the room. Only the phone messages to do and she was free for an evening with her family! But what remained in her mind was Adrian's hair, an amazing mass of soft, woolly dreadlocks.

* * *

Down on the beach Penny viewed the sea dubiously. The softly lapping waves had changed into breakers which appeared to be gaining strength and she didn't feel like braving them. Once before, when the sea had been like this, she'd gone in and been knocked flat. Swallowing a mouthful of sand had stopped her breathing for a short time and when she managed to crawl out on all fours she was sick. Perhaps she'd give it a miss. Waving to Gran on the balcony, she set off for a ramble down the long crescent-shaped bay. There was a new luxury hotel at the far end of the beach with a diving raft. The raft was set in deep water, but as the beach shelved very quickly it was not far out. Their hotel didn't have one; her mother had made sure of that. Anything that obstructed the Turtles' progress towards or up the beach was strictly forbidden. It didn't matter at the far end because it was rocky and the Turtles didn't come up on rocks. Penny suddenly remembered that Cora, the big security guard, lived in the village of Black Rock and smiled, wondering if she'd come across her on the beach looking like a Whale!

Wandering aimlessly along the deserted beach, picking up a shell or watching a crab scuttle sideways out of her path, Penny became aware of a figure stumbling through the softly yielding dunes. His head was bent and he hadn't seen Penny, but she saw and recognised him. It was 'Mister James', the trolley thief! What was he doing in this isolated spot? Why was he wearing a bright orange lifejacket? What a strange boy he was! She was the only person on the vast expanse of sand and had to bump into him of all people! What was it Jomo had said – he was staying in the new hotel at the opposite end of the *same* beach? *Blow*! Could she escape? If she dashed into the scrub and sea grape bordering the sand she could make for a friend's house, the aptly named Pelican Retreat. Trying to run in the deep, shifting sand was impossible, and Penny had just begun to move stealthily up the beach when a loud shout reached her ears.

"HELP! Something's got me! HELP!"

Pausing, she heard it again.

"HELP! HELP! Something's biting my toes off! HELP!"

The stupid boy, thought Penny. He's fallen into one of the rivulets emptying into the sea from Black Rock. He *is* in a panic, she thought.

"HELP!" He sounded quite frightened. Penny chuckled quietly, feeling superior.

"HELP!!!" he screeched again.

"Stop panicking!" she called crossly. "Hold on a mo. I'll soon sort your problem out, *Mister* James."

Trudging steadily through the shifting sand she slid down the river slope to where Jimmy was sitting half-in, half-out of a shallow stream. His welcoming smile disappeared rapidly when he saw who it was.

"*You*!" he greeted her.

"Yes, *me*," she snapped, "do you *still* want help or would you prefer me to go away?"

49

Jimmy's growled response was unintelligible.

"Well?" pursued Penny remorselessly, "what's it to be?"

"OUCH!" yelled Jimmy, "No, don't go. I'm being eaten up."

"Why don't you try bending over and getting hold of whatever it is? It'll soon let go. You won't drown," she added sarcastically. "You've got your life-jacket on."

Jimmy blushed scarlet. Penny was enjoying herself. She had a shrewd idea what the problem was.

"No, no," gasped Jimmy, "It'll get my hand as well. Then I'll have no toes and no fingers."

"No fingers and no toes! Don't be ridiculous. Here, I'll soon save you from that dreadful fate."

Bending down she lifted his foot none too gently out of the water. Clinging to it was a large land crab, far more frightened than Jimmy at having got itself into the alien environment of water and very relieved to have discovered a large rock to attach itself to.

"See? Do you think this crab is going to bite your toes and fingers off?" said Penny sarcastically. "What a coward you are!" she added disdainfully.

Jimmy struggled to his feet, his face resembling the sunset in its brilliant red hue.

"I'm no coward," he stammered angrily. "I've come out on my own. My Pa doesn't know where I am."

"Oh – is that supposed to make you a big brave man then? We have different ideas in England about that!"

"He doesn't like me going off on my own. He reckons it's dangerous."

"Is that why you've got your life-jacket on?" Penny burst out laughing. "Perhaps something will gobble you up, like that little crab? You big sissy!"

"I don't know what he thinks, kidnap I expect – or drowning," he added in a low voice. "Anyways, what's 'sissy' mean?"

"It's someone who's scared to do things. People who get into a funk, lack pluck, milksops, cry-babies, *cowards*! Do you understand now?"

Jimmy glared at her. Penny glared right back.

"Well, aren't you going to thank me for rescuing you from the Monster of the Deep?" she demanded.

Jimmy hesitated. It was what his Pa called 'happenstance' that the one person on the whole beach was Penny! Just when he'd managed to get away on his own too! It was bad luck. But he must get back before his father sent out a search party.

"Thanks," he said perfunctorily.

"Don't put yourself out," exclaimed Penny. "The next Monster you come across I'll leave you to it!" and, turning, she headed back to the hotel, leaving Jimmy to extricate himself from the deep, wet, glutinous sandbank.

Chapter Five

LAETITIA TO THE RESCUE

In the deepest darkest depths of the Continental Slope the water was pitch black. No reflected light from the surface pierced the gloom and the only glow was an eerie phosphorescence which shone from strangely adapted sea creatures. Dark shadows moved silently like spectres gliding sepulchrally through misty churchyards. Perfectly at home and unafraid, Laetitia swam majestically through these mysterious uncharted waters. Gigantura, a fish with weird telescopic eyes out on stalks, moved out of the murk but darted quickly aside when it saw her. An Angler fish, positioned to pounce on an unsuspecting prey, whisked angrily away as she peacefully approached. It travelled with its own larder, able to eat fish much larger than itself, and its monstrous stomach was already stretched to capacity with surplus food.

"Greedy fishy!" called Laetitia, gliding silently past, "If you eat any more you'll burst," she remonstrated.

None of these furtive denizens of the deep were a threat to Laetitia, a Matriarch of the Giant Leatherback tribe. She was too large, too well protected by her leathery carapace and swam too fast. These secluded waters, unknown to Humans, were the preferred choice of Leatherbacks for much of the year. They afforded safety, security, anonymity and a plentiful supply of food. Now she was returning to the Spacious Sea Meeting Place for the annual gathering of Leatherbacks. Consulting her inbuilt magnetic navigational system she sighed with pleasure. The unique senses confirmed that she was spot-on the correct latitude and longitude to reach the Meeting Place. For many miles she had been cruising at a depth of 2,000 feet. Soon she would be entering the relatively shallow, warm water of Leatherback Lanes leading to the Meeting Place. As the sea gradually changed texture and colour her

52

blood system changed too, adapting from cold to warm water. What a wonderful thing the Leatherbacks' circulation was, reflected Laetitia as she swam eagerly onwards. Their unique 'counter current' circulation prevented loss of body heat in cold water and automatically readjusted itself in warmer waters so they could travel almost anywhere in the world. Internal sensors kept their great barrel-shaped bodies at an even temperature, 88.2°F, with flippers and outer skin a pleasant 10° cooler. She remembered asking a 'News Dolphin' why Humans wore 'clothes' which they took off and left behind on beaches. Much to the amusement of the Turtles he said it was to keep them warm or cool because their bodies couldn't adapt to different temperatures. Laetitia had been stunned. Humans, who always seemed to be inventing new and frequently dangerous objects, couldn't work out how to regulate their own body heat? Every Hatchling could do that! What strange creatures Humans were!

Anyhow, it was refreshing to enter warm, cerulean waters near the Meeting Place after nearly a year of solitude in the grey water of the Atlantic. She surged joyfully along thinking of her husband, George, and their large family. Happy, busy days ahead with the Metanoia, Scrimmage Fortnight and Egg Laying Ceremonies and if that scamp, Zozimus, made his mind up, there could be a marriage. He had been eyeing up Isabella last year, one of Horace and Cassandra's Nematts, she must be twenty-two or twenty-three – marriageable age for a Leatherback. A sensible little thing, quite small, only six feet long but with plenty of growing still to do. She could mature into an eight-footer with good strong flippers of six feet. Well able to get up the beach heads and back, thought Laetitia complacently.

Pausing in her matchmaking ploys she began a swift ascent to the surface for a breathe. The water was silky smooth and wafting on the breeze was the wonderfully aromatic, spicy smell of the islands. Yes, she was within miles of the Meeting Place and looked set to win the Chelonian Cup (Females) for Accuracy of Navigation, Speed and Stamina. This would be her third win and Letty was proud of her abilities. It wasn't the Cup that spurred her on, but love of seeing George and her family and the beautiful Meeting Place where

Leatherbacks could relax and enjoy a happy social time in their otherwise solitary lives. Away on her travels she dreamed about it: the marvellous corralline rocks; the frilled Laminaria and winged Alaria seaweed decorations gracefully moving in the gentle current; the enormous, comfortable Meeting Marinas, each one characterised by distinctive colours; the cosy friendliness of the 'Archelon Ancestor' pub and the many other Leatherback haunts. There were innumerable Sea Food Restaurants with magnificent selections of delicious food too. The cafés even managed to get hold of the feathery Gymnangium and Nemertesia jellyfish, only found in the cold Atlantic. Letty supposed they must send out fishing flotillas to bring them back. Voracious George loved these North Sea medusae and frequented the North Atlantic especially to feast on them. Floating along on ocean currents the jellyfish gathered in huge drifts off a little island called Great Britain. George had cleverly realised this and followed the same current, the powerful North Atlantic Drift. It had nearly caused his downfall. Remembering, Letty shuddered; no wonder he loved that country and even changed his name to their Patron Saint. 'George' sounded much more solid and suited an enormous Leatherback Turtle far more than his original name – 'Cecil'.

Drawing a deep satisfying breath, Letty paused to peer about. What was that over to west-nor-west? Another leathery Turtle head was visible in the surf looking at her. Anastasia – her old rival for speed swimming at Turtle Academy! Now she was in trouble! Tasha envied Letty winning the Chelonian Cup and was determined to wrest it from her by fair means or foul. A skilled, swift swimmer, she would certainly be first home if Letty hung around admiring the view. Tasha's navigational skills must have improved, thought Letty. She used to have terrible problems sorting out compass bearings at Turtle Academy and was well known for getting lost. Yet here she was, almost on target and watching Letty very closely to see which way she went. Humph! Diving abruptly, Letty speedily descended to 1,000 feet. It would mean swimming more slowly but Tasha wouldn't be able to follow her easily. Sweeping back her powerful flippers she flew through the water. She wasn't going to let Tasha reach home first! Such a boaster and vain as well! Smiling reminiscently Letty remembered when Tasha had bribed a hermit crab to decorate her carapace. The crab had chosen an unusually curved and exquisitely swirled Voluta shell for its home and was remarkably beautiful. Tasha looked after it well, flattering and feeding it lots of plankton. Perched elegantly on Tasha's gleaming chestnut carapace, she had flaunted her special guest while other female Hatchlings looked on enviously. Decorations of any kind were forbidden at school but as the crab had already taken up residence there was nothing Madame Louisa could do. The crab's decision had to be respected, even if Madame did make some forthright remarks about vanity and using innocent sea creatures as an excuse for breaking school rules. One day when Tasha was asleep, Letty and her friends silently floated up with the idea of removing the crab. They pulled and shoved with their little half-grown flippers to no effect. It resisted furiously, clinging on and lashing out with its razor sharp pincers at their soft plastrons. Ouch! Then they remembered that crabs always move *sideways*. Dr Laurence had instructed them on 'Some Unusual Modes of Locomotion used by Marine Creatures' not long before. The crab favoured movement towards the right so, retreating, they had quietly advanced from the left and pushed the startled crab over Tasha's carapace until it scuttled off complaining loudly about 'orrible 'atchlings. Success! But there had been such a rumpus and Tasha had never forgiven them.

The luminescent sea creatures in the depths beneath Letty faded like ghosts at sunrise as she accelerated into shallower water. Now only Sun fish, Sailfins, Moorish Idols and other common marine creatures accompanied her. On the left she sensed another huge swimmer gliding effortlessly along. It drew level, pausing slightly as if waiting. Letty stretched out her neck to its fullest extent and peered upwards at the vast shadow. It was her friend, Minerva the Manta Ray! What did she want?

"Minnie! What are you doing here? I mustn't stop. I'm racing back to the Meeting Place. Meet you outside once I've checked in."

"Letty! STOP! Your Survivor Hatchlings are in trouble. A freak wave has carried them out of the Sea of Stillness. They're playing tag in the Gulf Stream. You know how dangerous that is! They don't know a *thing* about fishing trawlers or driftnets *or* longline fishing. They'll all be caught and killed, and they *are* the Survivors! I knew you'd be near here and flew to tell you. Letty – you've *got* to save them!"

Letty suppressed a disappointed sigh. If only Minnie had caught up with her *after* she'd checked in! Hatchlings! They always seemed to be up to mischief. Freak wave indeed! Whoever heard of *any* sort of turbulent sea that Giant Leatherbacks couldn't cope with, Hatchlings included! Well, no use crying over what might have been, she'd better get going. There was no time to waste.

"Minnie – can you take me to where they are? Have you time?" This was correct Sea Creature Etiquette. Marine creatures are ruled by nature's clock: the most favourable times to eat, rest and swim, plankton bloom time, seasonal time changes in ocean currents, mating time, hatching time, the phases of the moon which affect tides and so on. It was polite always to enquire if another sea creature, each with their different needs, had 'time'.

"Yes. I've just had a huge mouthful of plankton. I'm in no hurry."

"Come on then. We'll talk as we go," and off flew two of the most powerful and swiftest swimmers in the world.

"Now Minnie, what's all this about a 'freak wave'? Did you mean a tidal wave?"

"No – a *freak wave*. Haven't you seen them?"

"Never. They sound like a good excuse for mischievous Hatchlings to leave the nursery!"

"They're real, Letty. I've seen them and even I get out of the way! You spend most of your time swimming at such depths you don't know what's going on nearer the surface as I do. These waves are great walls of water over one hundred feet high. They just appear from nowhere."

"They'll be due to *Humans*! They're always thinking up new things, good and bad. Sounds like one of their most dangerous inventions."

"I don't know. They snap great liners full of Humans in half and they all drown."

"It'll be one of their 'war' things, trying to kill one another. They're very strange creatures. Some of them try to clean up beaches to benefit marine life and others cut off our flippers and steal our eggs to make 'Turtle Soup'. They consider it a delicacy. Nothing would surprise me about Humans."

"The sunken ships belong to lots of different nations, Letty, but Humans don't seem to understand freak waves."

"We know many mysterious events occur in the deep seas, Minnie, which they know nothing about. Earth tremors which Humans never pick up on their machines, submarine volcanoes erupt spewing out great waves of boiling lava, huge cracks and fissures open overnight, great land masses drift and in the deepest waters of the Ocean's floor, miles beneath land, are vast grotesque chambers so colossal they have their own tides and currents. There are huge, dry caves filled with air, like gigantic bubbles. Humans know nothing of these. Perhaps the origin of freak waves lies in the fathomless Deeps."

"Mmmh," murmured Minnie doubtfully, "you don't see the surface much and I don't see the Deeps. I know all the usual stuff – earth tremors, volcanoes and so on – but nothing about the rest. You could be right. But I wish you could *see* a freak wave. They really are something!"

"Provided they don't hurt me they sound fun," replied Letty, well aware that a Leatherback's carapace, extremely strong yet flexible, could withstand almost anything. "Are we nearing the Survivors? They'd better have a really good reason for this detour, especially as I've just lost the Chelonian Cup," commented Letty sourly.

"Oh, to whom?" enquired Minnie, her magnificent wings spread wide, carrying her effortlessly along.

"Of all Turtles – Tasha!" Letty nearly choked with frustration.

"Tasha? She was wandering round off course as usual. She stopped and asked me for directions."

"There's something seriously out of kilter with that girl's magnetic field," Letty commented crossly, "and to think she's going to take the Chelonian Cup off me all because of my naughty Survivors!"

"Letty!" gasped Minnie, horrified. "You're not putting that trophy above your Survivors surely?"

"No, of course not," replied Letty. "But I *am* annoyed at them. This freak wave sounds very Human to me, and a perfect reason for dangerous larking about. Once the Hatchlings are off the beaches we try to ensure they get to safety in the Sea of Stillness. The Choir of Angel Fish even guides them sometimes. Thousands of miles of quiet, placid water; a dense covering of kelp seaweed for protective camouflage and abundant supplies of plankton and jellyfish. They're safe there until Madame Louisa Leatherback or Dr Laurence Leatherback come for them. If only they'd *stay* put! If they keep popping in and out of the Sea there'll be no peace. We adults will spend the entire year worrying about them and there's nothing we can do."

Once the Hatchlings were relatively safe after the Terror Run the adults had to leave them. Leatherback life was one of non-stop swimming around the world. Ever since Jurassic times when their colossal ancestor 'Archelon' founded the Marine Turtle dynasty it had always been so.

"I can see them, Letty! Change course east-nor'-east. They're not too far out of the Sea of Stillness," added Minnie comfortingly.

Letty, who had been heading due north, immediately swooped in a tight turn. She couldn't see the Hatchlings yet but could smell them. With the scent of the little blighters in her nose and the sound of their excited squeaks and gleeful screams loud and clear in the water, her navigation was flawless. Rising to the surface she spied them a short distance away.

"*Many* thanks, Minnie, for your warning," she cried, as she shot towards them. "Do please go and do your own thing now. We'll be fine."

But Minnie didn't want to go. There were no Manta Ray imperatives that she had to pursue. She was a free agent, curious about the Hatchlings' experience and eager to see how Letty would cope with it.

"It's ok, Letty. I can hang about for a bit," she said, executing a slow forward roll with all the grace of a Prima Ballerina. Oblivious of

Letty hurrying towards them, the Hatchlings continued their frolics, ducking and weaving in and out of the Gulf Stream surge which was carrying them further and further from the safety of the Sea of Stillness. Nearly upon them, Letty gave a piercing high pitched whistle, which only the Hatchlings could interpret.

"That's the Emergency Whistle!" exclaimed a startled Hatchling. "It means we've got to stop whatever we're doing and freeze."

Obediently the little Turtles stopped playing and remained motionless in the water. They were not the Survivors by chance. Instinctively they heeded warnings from their parents, kin and older, more experienced, sea creatures. Their lives often depended on it. They understood the prime technique for survival was to listen and act on warnings. Those who didn't soon disappeared, often into the mouths of voracious Birds and Sharks.

As they lay quietly on the surface Letty was able to round them up rapidly and re-form the compact Hantle.

"Hello Ma!" said one of them cheekily, as she manoeuvred them under her flipper.

"Keep your breath for swimming fast, young man. You're *all* in trouble. Don't make it any worse by impertinence," replied Letty, as she bustled them at full speed back to the Sea of Stillness. Minnie, flapping casually near the surface grinned and accidentally swallowed an entire plankton bloom. How tasty! But 'Ma' indeed! The family abbreviation for Matriarch was only permitted on joyful, informal occasions. This was *not* a joyful occasion – as the baby Turtles would soon learn! Minnie hopefully grinned again, but this time no nearby plankton was drawn into her capacious gape. Not to worry, she was as full as could be and – whee! – turned a lazy somersault to celebrate.

Back in the Sea of Stillness, Letty settled herself on top of an extinct underwater volcano and glared at her Hatchlings.

"Oh, ho! We're in for trouble," whispered Clementine, a strong-looking female. "I think I'll hide behind this kelp trunk!"

"Shush! There'll be worse trouble if we talk," replied another.

"Gather round and take good notice of what I say," commanded

Letty. Towering over her Hatchlings, vast flippers outstretched on a rock, she looked extremely imposing and angry, with her large Turtle mouth turned down disapprovingly.

"You've *all* been *very* silly and naughty Hatchlings. You know that once in the nursery you *stay* there until called for by your teachers, Madame Louisa and Dr Laurence. It is safe here, there is plentiful food and you can practise your swimming hidden in the Kelp Forest. If anything happens, such as *freak waves*," here she paused, looked sceptically around and sniffed derisively, "you take shelter behind the leeward side of a large rock, like this one, wrap your flippers round a stout piece of kelp and hang on. You do *not* leap into the wave and start playing. You're too young and can easily be swept away into hostile water by the current. Sea currents are *extremely* powerful."

Looking down at the Turtles from where she floated a few feet above Minnie nodded her head vigorously in agreement. "Your Ma's right. Even I am careful about currents."

The Hatchlings looked up at her moving easily and majestically as if on air and shuffled their flippers uncomfortably. Greatly daring, one piped up.

"Please Matriarch, we can't stay down *all* the time. We have to surface to breathe. We may have been washed away accidentally," he suggested hopefully.

"You're Sebastian aren't you?" responded Letty, for a Leatherback Matriarch names her Hatchlings as they swim past after the Terror Run on their way to the nursery.

"What do you think the Kelp Forest is for? Just to play in, frightening the girls by pretending to be big Sharks?" The Hatchlings giggled as Sebastian turned a pale mauve with embarrassment.

"It hides and protects when you surface if you cling to it."

Looking sulky he turned away. Where was his friend, Clementine? Funny, she wasn't behind the kelp trunk any more. "You must find her," a voice said quietly but clearly. Who'd said that? He jerked around. Everyone was listening to Letty's lecture and paying no attention to him. "You must find her," came the voice again. Letty was still talking.

"You could have been eaten by Gulls, Frigate Birds, Pelicans, suffocated in fishing lines, choked to death on false foods," Letty paused to look round. She was well-satisfied. The Hatchlings were quivering in horror, their pretty carapaces, still soft, had turned violet with fear and squeaks of alarm issued from their trembling mouths.

"Please Matriarch, we're *very* sorry and won't do anything silly again. Please don't go on, it's *terrifying*," quavered one of the females. "We didn't know about these dreadful dangers."

"*Exactly*!" responded Letty crisply. "Which is why you have so much to learn at Turtle Academy ... What is it this time Sebastian?"

"Matriarch – Clementine's missing! I thought she was behind a kelp trunk but she's not and I can't see her!"

"Is that true or are you trying it on?" Letty replied severely.

"No, *honestly* Matriarch, I can't see her!"

Sebastian's voice quavered, ending on a sob, enough to convince Letty that he was telling the truth.

"Stay here, *all* of you!" she commanded quickly. "*Don't move*! Minnie dear, have you time to help?"

"Certainly, I'll go on ahead!"

And Letty and Minnie shot away to look for the missing Hatchling.

Chapter Six

THE GREAT WHITE SHARK

Prowling restlessly the Great White Shark flicked her forked tail fin irritably. She was pregnant and very hungry. It was not time yet to give birth to her calf but she must keep her body fat at a high level in readiness for that occasion. The sea was empty, marine animals which would have been devoured in one satisfying gulp were nowhere to be seen. The great blooms of plankton and waving fronds of seaweed that stretched out northwards beyond the Sea of Stillness were of no interest to this carnivore. It was meat she wanted, raw, red meat. Rising nearer the surface, she looked about hopefully for a dying or injured fish. No luck, nothing stirred on the barren ocean, not a ship or boat, fishing trawler or merchantman. The quiet sea was undisturbed. What a pity, she thought; boats contain tasty snacks called Humans. It would be a simple matter to ram a little schooner and take her pick for dinner. Other Sharks would soon pick up the scent of blood – but not before she'd had her fill.

Circling slowly, her wide mouth compressed, tight and mean with hunger and frustration, she picked up a promising scent. What was it? Fear – yes, fear! Billowing through the water, crystal clear to her acute senses, she felt fear. Dreadful, panicked fear coming from another sea creature. Good! Dinner of some sort was not far away. But where? Had it been close by she would have seen it. Further south, to the east, informed her sonic signals. Whipping her tail round she headed unerringly towards the frightened creature.

Minnie and Letty were swimming flat out, Minnie flying along near the surface, Letty skimming the water nearby.

"Any sign of her?" Letty called out on the special Chelonian Auditory Wavelength reserved especially for dire emergencies.

"Not yet, but she can't have gone too far. You didn't stay long with

62

the Hatchlings, Letty."

"No, but we're in the North Atlantic Drift now and it's very strong. Clementine would have been pulled into it and whisked away. She's too small to handle it."

"She won't suffocate in a fishing net here. Trawlers don't bother coming. Not enough fish to make it worthwhile."

"Oh Minnie! *Where* is she? We should have spotted her by now."

"I can see spume!" cried Minnie excitedly, "Something is up ahead!" she called and flew even faster towards the disturbed water.

Letty rose doubtfully towards the surface and followed. It wasn't right. She could tell immediately. The smell wasn't right. It wasn't Clementine but a much bigger marine creature, more than one, approaching very fast.

With a sigh of relief she recognised the group hurrying towards them. It was a friendly Pod of Dolphins known to Letty and Minnie. Its Leader, called Jeté because of his incredible balletic skill in leaping high into the air and performing graceful twists of every kind, motioned the Pod to pause.

"Quick, tell me. Have you seen my Hatchling, Clementine?" cried Letty. "She's wandered off. We think she's got into the North Atlantic Drift. You know how powerful that is! Have you seen anything?"

Jeté gasped in horror, then spoke hurriedly, giving Letty an unwelcome message.

"*Hurry*! We spotted a disturbance in the Drift going north. And Letty, a huge Great White Shark is out there. That's why we're heading away. We'll all come with you. We may be able to help," he added without hesitation.

The Pod wheeled and turned as one and, thus augmented and guided, Minnie and Letty followed.

"There she is!" called Jeté, leaping into the air, "Just ahead! She's seen us, she's waving her flipper."

"Clementine, hold on, we're coming. Keep *calm*!" commanded Letty on the Chelonian Auditory Wavelength. Feeling anything but calm herself, she well knew the Shark would pick up panic and move fast towards its source. Bottling her fear she continued confidently,

"We can see you now dear, your problems are over."

Overjoyed to hear Matriarch Laetitia's strong voice and see Minnie and the approaching Dolphins, Clementine relaxed. It had been daring and exhilarating to ride the currents and she'd enjoyed it. Big and strong for a Hatchling, the high waves did not frighten her as they pounded down. When Letty appeared to guide the Hantle back to safety Clementine hadn't wanted to give up her fun and return to the quiet Sea. Defiant and deaf to Letty's ticking-off, she'd decided to slip away and go solo. Unobtrusively edging behind a wide band of kelp, she'd waited for a large wave and launched herself into it. All had gone well and she was highly elated with the success of this daring scheme. She had swum and dived and flapped and jumped with great enthusiasm. How envious the others would be when she told them of the fun she'd had whilst they were obediently listening to boring old Ma droning on! But suddenly Clementine realised she couldn't control her direction any more. The tide was spinning her along like a top away from the sheltering Sea of Stillness. Foaming, crashing waters constantly overturned her and righting herself in seconds made no difference. She was out of control, taken by surprise with the immense strength of the undertow. Little Clementine had no experience of such maelstroms of water and panicked. She was only two feet long but tried to keep in mind that she was a *Giant* Leatherback Marine Turtle who could do *anything* in water, but couldn't help remembering she was only a Hatchling. It might have been more sensible to stay with Ma and the Hantle after all. Still, she had ridden the waves with a bit more confidence. "No water can harm *me*," she desperately repeated again and again, "*I'm* a Giant Leatherback!"

Swept swiftly along on the eager billows she drew comfort from the thought that a friend was bound to turn up and escort her back to the safety of the Sea. Placid, generous-hearted and happy, Leatherbacks were justly popular and had many marine friends. Young and inexperienced, it did not occur to her that the first creature she met could be a deadly foe.

Bouncing along in the dizzy vortex of water she could hear Letty calling on the C.A.W. Every Hatchling had an innate knowledge of the emergency wavelength just as they knew about the special whistle. Turning her head she could see the Dolphins and Minnie. Where was Ma? Of course, underwater where she couldn't be seen. At last Clementine relaxed – and saved her life. The Great White Shark had been swimming straight towards her but suddenly the vibrations given off by a frightened creature ceased. The Shark paused, puzzled, straining her senses to relocate them. Clementine waved cheerfully to her rescuers with one flipper, lost her water balance and pitched over, carapace down, into the surge. Flapping and kicking she righted herself, to look straight into the small cruel eyes of the Great White. Attracted by Clementine's disjointed movements the Shark recognised its original prey. A helpless little Turtle! Not much, but good enough for a snack! The Great White opened her massive jaws and advanced rapidly. Clementine could see the razor sharp triangular teeth ready to seize and tear. Shrieking with terror, she used every ounce of strength to back away.

"Dive! *Dive*!!! As *deeply* as you can!" commanded a strong, insistent voice. Not understanding or knowing where it came from, she hastily obeyed, turning turtle and diving as abruptly and deeply as possible.

Approaching rapidly, Letty, Minnie and the Dolphins heard the shriek and knew the awful reason.

"Battle order – GO!" commanded Jeté, and executed a sublime curvet right over the Shark's head. The Pod knew what it had to do – distract in every way possible. Leaping in all directions, the more experienced close by, the less experienced further out, they splashed and dived, creating a spume screen to shield Clementine. The Shark snapped its ghastly mouth closed to deal with the intruders. Dolphins! Ha! One of these would make a far more satisfactory dinner than a baby Turtle! Turning towards the Dolphins she faced them head on. Thrashing her tail and showing fearsome teeth, she rocketed towards them. The Dolphins faced her, courageously waiting until momentum was built up, then:

"NOW!" whistled Jeté, and off they shot haphazardly in all directions. Jumping, leaping, curvetting, some even nipping her tail fin, the Shark didn't know which Dolphin to pursue. The oldest and most experienced Dolphins even smacked her head and gills with their tails. Instinct told the shark to fight and pick off one or two for vengeance but – her calf. She mustn't upset her unborn calf. Her tail gave one last mighty lash as furiously she turned and swam away.

Minnie and Letty had been trying to find Clementine. In the mêlée of agitated water, furious Shark and leaping Dolphins, she had disappeared.

"She's tried to dive," suggested Minnie. "Go deeper, Letty." Letty dived further into the water where light from the surface was still plentiful. No sign of Clementine. Everyone had seen her wave and heard her scream. With the world's fastest swimmers protecting her she couldn't have gone too far even in the rolling Drift. Surely – *surely* she couldn't have gone into the Shark's mouth? It sometimes happened. Frantic, Letty searched the waters calling continually on C.A.W. Nothing. Rising to the surface she confided her thoughts to Minnie.

"What do you think? Was it possible in the time?"

Minnie was sensible as ever.

"Let's have a word with Jeté and the Pod. They're searching too."

Swimming to where the reassembled Pod was diving in and out of the waves, whistling and calling for Clementine, Letty shouted, "We can't find Clementine. Did you see if … if … she was swallowed by the Shark? Would it be possible?"

At once Jeté leapt up to her.

"Letty, stop worrying. She'll turn up. We'll keep looking," he said calmly.

"What makes you so confident she's alright?"

"She will be. The Shark had her mouth open and was swimming straight at her when we went into action. Clementine didn't swim *away* from her, she *dived under* her. Sharks can't dive abruptly like you or I. They're too big and cumbersome. Then we attacked. Clementine will be hiding in the kelp most likely."

Minnie's excited voice could be heard, "Letty! Letty! There's something floating over there. Look! Look! Let's go and investigate."

Without pausing they set off the short distance, leaving the Pod to continue searching. There, lying on a floating island of weed was Clementine.

"Clementine! Thank Great Mother! Here we are. What happened?" But as Letty anxiously talked she realised all was not well. Clementine neither stirred nor spoke but lay quiescent. They drew nearer and saw red streaks trailing away into the sea. Blood!

"CLEMENTINE!" screamed Letty, "wake up! It's me, your Ma!"

Climbing onto the island she saw what had happened. Her Hatchling's plastron, the soft underside of a Turtle, had a gash in it. She *must* stop it bleeding *at once*. Turtles bleed to death quickly and Clementine was merely a Hatchling. She couldn't afford to lose any more blood. Letty turned to dive for first aid but Minnie was there already holding a large swathe of sea wrack in her mouth.

"Here – quickly Letty. I'll hold this end, you wrap it firmly round her plastron. It'll do for now."

Between them they fastened the soft, bubbly seaweed around Clementine and secured it with a reef knot. The Pod had seen them and swam over to help.

"What can we do? Can she swim? How badly is she injured?" enquired Jeté.

"She's alive and the bleeding has stopped, but she doesn't seem able to speak or swim. I think her body temperature has dropped too," responded the worried Letty.

"We must get her back to the Sea of Stillness. We're drifting further and further away from it and that blood in the water is going to attract more Sharks. We've *got* to move her, *now*," said Jeté anxiously.

"If I tuck her under my flipper I won't be able to swim fast enough using only one flipper. Can you fasten her on my carapace? Then I can dive and move normally."

Everyone helped to ease the Hatchling onto Letty's broad carapace, tying her securely with more of the broad soft sea wrack Minnie had fetched.

"Phew!" said Minnie, floating back to admire their handiwork, "Nothing's going to dislodge *her*! You can swim as fast as you like,

Letty dear."

Firmly bound onto her mother's back like an Indian papoose, Clementine was comfortable and safe. Her mother's body heat acted like a hot water bottle and she began to warm up again. Letty looked around at her friends; Minnie, Jeté and his Pod.

"You've all been wonderful! Thank you *so much* ..."

"We're coming with you," said Jeté, "I've taken a bearing. It's sou'-sou'-west." Whistling his Pod to order, he glanced at Letty and Minnie.

"Right? Let's go!" and leaping straight over Letty and her precious burden he led the way. Letty promptly plummeted into the depths.

Rarely had she swum so swiftly or surely. Jeté's Pod formed a protective shield around her, some above, others below and more on either side. As they sped watchfully along she could hear them talking in their complicated language, squeaks, grunts, clicks and whistles. Sea creatures speak many languages and she understood a good deal of what they said, especially their admiring comments on her speed, which pleased her. Minnie was in her element, watching not only for any sign of danger but also the fascinating curvets and glissades performed by the Pod as they swept along. Always happy to swim with Dolphins, she hoped they would exhibit their beautifully coordinated and athletic leaping on the successful completion of their task to celebrate little Clementine's safe return. Mind you, reflected Minnie complacently, she could show them a turn or two! Because of her size she frequently performed arabesques and pirouettes in slow motion and her flowing, harmonious symmetry was sensational.

The convoy was approaching the Sea of Stillness. Under the water, Letty could hear and see the Hantle huddled together, murmuring anxiously near where she had left them by a large protective rock.

"It's alright dears," she called on the C.A.W. "Clementine's with me, she'll be fine shortly. Swim aside please."

Their squeaks of relief changed to squawks of amazement as Letty swam in accompanied by her posse of Dolphins and Minnie.

"Ma! Are these all friends of ours?" gasped Sebastian, his eyes wide as he gazed at the distinguished company.

"Yes dear," replied Letty, quite forgetting to tell him off for calling her 'Ma'. "Turtles have very many friends and today they saved Clementine's life."

The Hatchlings gasped in horror, relief and wonder and a small female, Decima, ventured to ask,

"What happened Matriarch? Are we allowed to know?"

"Yes, I'll tell you presently. But first let's get Clementine off my carapace and feed her. She's warmed up nicely."

Everyone crowded round to help and Clementine was secured on a large lettuce seaweed. Minnie arrived with her mouth full of jellyfish, far too much for one Hatchling, so it was shared around. Then the Hatchlings were permitted to gently stroke Minnie's wonderful outstretched wings and the Dolphins put on a celebratory exhibition of leaps which had them gasping in wonder and awe.

"We are *lucky* to have such fantastic friends!" exclaimed Winston, a burly young Turtle built like his father, Patriarch George. "We must take care to keep them," he added shrewdly.

"Hatchlings!" called Letty. "Jeté and his Pod must be off now. What do you say to them?"

"*Thank you* Patriarch Jeté and Pod for your wonderful aerial exhibition," chorused the Hatchlings, eyes and faces gleaming with the marvellous memory of many new water gymnastics and tricks they could try out as soon as Letty left them.

"HATCHLINGS!" bellowed a shocked Letty.

"*And* for saving our sister's life!" they added very hastily, with guilty looks.

Minnie turned a slow somersault to hide her expansive grin as the Hatchlings shuffled about uncomfortably.

"Thank you *so much*, Pod, for your truly wonderful help," added Letty. "You know we will help you whenever we can. I'll tell the little 'uns how *very* brave, unselfish and loyal you've been, putting your own lives at risk for Clementine, and I'll make sure the Zamorin, our Chief, George and other Patriarchs know what you've done. Should it be necessary, you are welcome in our Chelonian Cloister."

This invitation was the highest accolade awarded by Leatherbacks to their most valued friends. Only tired, lost or frightened Turtles were able to take refuge and recuperate in this hostelry within the Spacious Sea Meeting Place. Despite being great friends with many sea creatures, other species were not invited into the Cloister. Now, because they had saved a Leatherback life, the Dolphins had been.

Jeté gave a dignified bow in thanks.

"We thank you for your invitation and are deeply honoured. It will not be misused. Farewell and good luck Letty, until we meet again."

So saying he performed a perfect spiralling leap to the front of his Pod and, smiling proudly, led them away. The Hatchlings waved them off, their little flippers working overtime, whilst Letty wiped away a tear.

"Wonderful creatures," she sniffed happily, "no thought for their own safety, only to get Clementine away."

Minnie, watching the Pod swooping through the water, felt it was time to be off too.

"Letty, I must be getting along dear. Clementine's colour has come back and she's eaten a good few jellies. She should be alright now."

"How can I thank *you* for your help? All these naughty Hatchlings would have been lost but for your timely warning! I know it's useless inviting you into the Cloister, but you know where it is in an emergency."

"I do, and thank you, Letty. But size forbids. The last time I visited I couldn't get through the Portal!"

The friends laughed, remembering Minnie's last visit. She was known to everyone and had intended a quick social call to see if Letty had won the Chelonian Cup. It had ended up in chaos. Her enormous wings were too wide to pass through the Portal and Cerberus, the Portal Steward, had demanded she fold them away, like the Leatherbacks, to enter. She couldn't do this, only flap them down slightly before opening them out to their full mighty width again. That was the way she swam, but she tried hard to oblige Cerberus and the resulting tidal waves of water had brought Turtles in the Meeting Place to the Portal to watch the fun and offer useless suggestions. Turtles waiting outside to enter had formed a jovial queue, pushing and shoving, splashing and laughing. Cerberus had danced about waving his flippers ineffectually, bellowing instructions to Minnie as well as the 'inside' and 'outside' Turtles. It had been a hilarious occasion, only ending when Letty went outside the Portal and chatted to Minnie there.

"Time I was getting through the Portal before George starts worrying," commented Letty. "But I can't leave until Clementine's alright. See you soon Minnie, and *many* thanks again."

Minnie dipped one of her wings in salute and floated gracefully away. Letty turned back to the Hatchlings who were making a great deal of excited noise.

"WHEN you're quiet … I'll tell you all I know about Clementine's narrow escape. If it hadn't been for our wonderfully courageous and loyal friends she would have been eaten by a Shark."

The Hatchlings' squeaks and squeals of horror echoed through the sea as they huddled closer to the safety of their big, strong mother.

"The Dolphins and Minnie saved her life. I don't know how she got separated from the Hantle. She will tell you when she's recovered."

There was absolute silence as Letty recounted the story, sparing none of the horror and danger. They needed to know such terrible things if they were to survive. Just as she was finishing there came an excited cry from Sebastian.

"Look! Clementine's up, Matriarch! She's better!"

Sure enough the strong young Hatchling had slipped off the seaweed and swum to join her sisters and brothers.

"Can I take this sea wrack off my plastron please?" she asked.

"No, certainly not! If you start bleeding again the Sharks will arrive very quickly," said Letty firmly. "Leave it until Doctor Aesculapius can see the wound. He'll put his 'Salubrious Sea Wrack Plaster' on if necessary."

Clementine made no objection to this plan.

"Is it tight enough, Ma?" she asked anxiously, "I don't *ever* want to see another Shark after today."

"Yes, it's fine. Now, Clementine, I must get to the Spacious Sea very

71

soon or your father and other Turtles will worry. I'm over the normal time as it is. Tell us quickly dear, how you became separated from the Hantle and nearly ended up as Shark snack."

Clementine went pale mauve. She couldn't admit she'd been bored with her mother's telling off and wanted to get away and play.

"Oh! I don't want to think about it," she quavered, sniffing pathetically.

Letty looked at her severely.

"Well my dear, you'll have to. We *all* need to know about possible dangers. Don't be nervous. You're perfectly safe *here*, no one is going to harm you. Tell us about it."

Clementine bit her lip and turned a darker shade of mauve. Letty correctly interpreted this as embarrassment.

"Come along, Clementine. Don't make a fuss. I need to know what distractions or dangers are about just as much as the Hatchlings. I've got to finish my journey to the Spacious Sea and if there's a problem out there which *you* know about, I need to know too."

Clemmie glanced quickly at Letty's patient but determined face. There was no way she was leaving until she'd heard the whole shameful story. Yet – Ma *was* right. Knowledge and experience had to be shared if they were to survive, and Clemmie had a question she wanted to ask Letty. Turning an even deeper mauve, Clemmie replied, "I was …" she paused, taking a deep breath, "I was very silly. I thought I knew better than you. I'm *very* sorry Matriarch," she added, hanging her head as if inspecting her plastron.

"Clementine," said Letty, "You'll have to tell us more than that. What made you think you knew better than me? What did you do? It very nearly killed you!"

The Hatchlings were listening with bated breath. They knew how close Clemmie had been to death, but what *had* caused her to swim off? Had she been caught in one of the bigger waves? Or perhaps the fierce North Atlantic Drift they'd been warned about had carried her away? Had she seen something strange and swum off to investigate? What *was* she going to say?

But sensible little Clemmie had made her mind up. She'd been thoroughly stupid to disobey Ma. How *could* a one-year-old Hatchling know more than an older, far more experienced, clever and courageous Matriarch? She was going to tell the truth. The other Hatchlings might learn not to be as big-headed and selfish as she'd been – Sebastian for one! Raising her head and looking bravely at her mother she began.

"I was bored with your lecture on safety and not leaving the Sea of Stillness. I wanted to go on playing in the waves. I was enjoying it. So I slipped away."

There was a loud gasp of horror from the Hantle, although one or two gasped with admiration.

"It was great fun to begin with but I soon lost control and was swept further and further out into the North Atlantic Drift."

More gasps from the Hatchlings – the dreaded Drift!

"I was *very* frightened," continued Clemmie in a strong, clear voice (so that Sebastian could hear!), "and the next thing I knew a *huge* Shark was upon me with its mouth wide open and all its great teeth gleaming."

The Hantle were turning various colours of lilac, purple, violet and mauve from fear and started trembling as they heard Clemmie's terrifying tale. It was much more *real* when told by her, not in Letty's mature and measured tones.

"Ooh! What did you *do*?" asked Winston, his eyes round with interest.

"*Screamed* very loudly," replied Clemmie. "Then I heard Matriarch on the special C.A.W. calling to me. The Shark turned away and just as I was righting myself from another big current she came at me again."

"What did you do then?" exclaimed Winston. He was quite envious of Clementine's exciting adventure.

"I heard Matriarch telling me to dive as deeply as I could …"

Letty, who had been listening carefully, interrupted, "No, no dear. I didn't tell you to dive. I couldn't see you or the Shark. Anyhow, it can be dangerous for young Turtles to dive too deeply."

"But Ma," said Clemmie excitedly, "A voice definitely told me to dive. I heard it clearly. It was a *command*. I *had* to obey. I went down until I passed out."

It was Letty's turn to gasp.

"Yes! That's what can happen when you haven't been taught the Physiology, Methodology and Precautions of Deep Sea Diving by Madame Louisa."

"But Ma, if it wasn't you, who was it? I wondered how you could see me from such a distance!"

Here was a mystery! The Hatchlings looked expectantly at Letty who, far from sharing their puzzlement, was nodding her head quietly as she realised what the 'Voice' must have been.

"Did you *really* hear this voice, Clementine?" she asked. "How loud was it? What direction did it come from? Was the message totally clear?"

As one, the Hatchlings' eyes now swivelled towards Clementine.

"Yes Ma, I *definitely* heard a voice. It was quite loud, not shouting but distinct and *very* clear. I don't know the direction. It seemed to come …" she stopped. This was going to sound really silly.

"Yes?" encouraged Letty, "it came from – where?"

"I know it sounds crazy but … well … it *seemed* to come from inside *me*. It didn't have a direction. It just spoke from within."

The Hantle sniggered. Fancy Clemmie hearing voices! She'd always seemed such a sensible Hatchling. It must be shock, they whispered. Letty scrutinised Clemmie. Yes, she was telling the truth. Good!

"HATCHLINGS! Quiet please," she commanded. "Clementine did hear a Voice and it's a *very* special one. Listen to me carefully." She paused to make sure she had their full attention. "It was her Turtle Folk Memory," she continued. "This is instinct and inborn knowledge stored in every Turtle's brain from time immemorial. It goes right back to our Dinosaur ancestor, the Archelon. If you listen to it, and some Turtles don't, it will guide you in difficult and dangerous circumstances. It helped Clementine. She didn't know Sharks prefer prey near the surface. They are more cautious at depth and can't dive as swiftly as we can. So the Voice told her to *dive*. She went into her dive too steeply through fear, but she *obeyed* her instinct and helped save herself."

Clementine and the other Hatchlings, obeying their Matriarch, were listening very carefully, their long mouths dropping open in amazement and interest.

"Has anyone else ever 'heard' the Voice speaking?" asked Letty. She secretly hoped so. Being tuned in to the Voice was of great benefit to Turtles.

The Hantle flapped their flippers and splashed about a bit, casting one another furtive glances under their long lashes.

"Ahem!" said Sebastian at last. "I think I *may* have heard it when Clemmie went missing. I had this urge to look for her but knew I ought to be listening to you. Something kept saying 'You must find Clemmie' until I interrupted you. Would that be the Voice?"

"Yes. It was sending you, her special friend, warning signals. We got on her track faster because of them."

At this the Hatchlings lost their shyness and piped up all round.

"Matriarch, I hear voices all the time telling me to find food!"

"I hear voices telling me to give Winston's carapace a shove when he annoys me."

"My voices tell me to startle Wrasse and make them change colour."

"HANTLE! That's enough." Letty spoke sternly. "*The* Voice does *not* tell you to do selfish, spiteful or silly things. The 'voices' you've been hearing are your own wishes, to be greedy, bad tempered, to bully. The Voice guides you in dangerous situations but cannot *make* you do anything. At Turtle Academy you will be taught more about it. Now, I must be away. I'll see you very soon as Madame Louisa and Dr Laurence will arrive shortly. *Stay here* where you're safe!" instructed Letty ferociously. Submerging, she waved a giant flipper at them and disappeared into the depths with the renowned Leatherback speed and skill.

Chapter Seven

Battle Lines are Drawn

It was boiling hot on the balcony. A pair of brilliant blue Tanager birds landed noisily on the rail, wings whirring like old motorbike engines that needed oiling. Squeaking excitedly to one another, their bulbous eyes bright with anticipation, they edged towards the crumbs left by Dorothy Fairweather's scone. After watching Penny slope off down the beach she had retreated to the air-conditioned bedroom to unpack and have a refreshing shower before dinner. Reading the polite notice in the bathroom requesting economic use of water made her smile. She remembered a time when the maximum permitted for a bath was five inches! To Dorothy's long and capacious memory having a shower remained a treat and she luxuriated in the soothing coolness as it cascaded over her hot sticky face and body. Wrapped in a fluffy and very voluminous towel she padded silently into the bedroom, pausing abruptly. The communicating door to the sitting room was ajar and stealthy noises were coming from beyond it. Dorothy looked round for a weapon. Her tennis racket lay on the bed – just the ticket! At Wimbledon she'd been renowned for her left-handed backhand. It had not deteriorated too much over the many intervening years and remained a useful weapon in Veteran tennis. With racket in hand she fearlessly approached the door and swung it wide.

A broad-shouldered man with his back to her was bending over the table.

"Just *what* do you think you're doing?" she threatened, jabbing the handle of her racket forcefully into the small of his back.

"AAGGHH!" gasped the man, quickly jumping upright. The heavy, carefully piled tea-tray balanced expertly on his hand wobbled dangerously and with an ear-deafening 'CRASH!' smashed onto the floor, fragments of broken china, biscuits, tea and butter flying everywhere.

"Ah'm sorry, Ma'am. Ah didn't know yo were here. Ah've come to collect de tea tings."

"Oh dear!" exclaimed Dorothy, aghast. "I'm so sorry I startled you! I was in the shower. Here, let me give you a hand to clear this mess up."

Advancing into the room, she flung the racket on the settee and held out her hand.

"I'm Mrs Fairweather, Professor Heffernan's mother."

"And ah'm Livingston, Ma'am and veree honoured and pleased to meet yo. Yo daughter's told us a lot 'bout you Ma'am. Please don' you bother wit' dis mess. Ah'll see to it. Yo is on holiday," he beamed.

Livingston towered above Mrs Fairweather as they shook hands amicably. Suddenly she remembered that, vast as it was, she was still only wearing a towel.

"Well, Livingston, if you don't mind, perhaps I'd better get changed," she murmured, embarrassed.

"Yes Ma'am," he replied, his face split in a huge grin. "Ah expect yo ought. But don' yo worry, Mrs Fairweather, Ma'am. Dem bath towels is pretty capacious!"

"And don't *you* worry either Livingston! I'll tell your boss the broken china is all my fault. I don't want you getting into any trouble."

"I sho 'preciate that Ma'am, but is ok. I'm Boss man. Is de staff rest period, so ah stepped in to help out. An' ah'm veree pleased ah did cos ah've met yo."

Dorothy was much cheered. Such irrepressible geniality and good humour, especially after a frustrating accident, was unusual. It was Livingston's off-duty period too, but he made no complaints about the extra work. What an unselfish man! Smiling and chuckling like a pair of conspirators Livingston set about collecting the broken shards of china and mopping up the spillage while Dorothy, all tiredness forgotten, went through into her room to dress. Were all the islanders as kind and considerate as this? If so, no wonder it was the 'Secret' Island!

Mrs Fairweather may have been smiling contentedly but Penny

was grumbling to herself as she left Jimmy combating the glutinous sand. Jimmy – what a *pain*! Still, he was at the south end of the long beach and she was at the north end. Trouble was, it sounded as if he would spend his time trying to give his father the slip, which meant coming northwards up the beach. Funny, she wanted to spend time *with* her mother, whom she didn't see much of, and he wanted to get *away* from his father, whom he saw too much!

And where was Jimmy's mother? She hadn't been seen or mentioned. Perhaps they were divorced and this was Jimmy's holiday with his father. Perhaps Jimmy would prefer to be with his mother. Perhaps his father was bad-tempered and always banging on at him. They had to share a beach and were bound to come across one another. Hmm! Perhaps she ought to make the most of it and try to be a bit more friendly. She didn't want *him* ruining her holiday!

Penny felt very pleased with herself as she reached this magnanimous decision. She'd show him how grown-up she was! As if in reward the waves calmed down as suddenly as they had built up. It was astonishing how quickly storms at sea came and went. Penny threw herself headfirst into the water, yelling with surprise and delight. Yeowwy, owyy, yeowyy! It felt *freezing*! The warm water hitting her scorching body felt cold but within seconds she was happily submerged in its bath-water warmth. Walking out until the water came up to her shoulders, she stood still and waited. Very soon, curious fish came to investigate this pale, wavering shape invading their territory. A flight of luminous flying fish took off and skimmed low over her bowed head. A small school of silver Blackbar Soldierfish arrived, their black gill bar conspicuous in the pellucid water.

Flickering and darting about, they swam round her legs and feet. Watching their antics and trying not to give way to a fit of the giggles they were so tickly, she noticed a disturbance near her feet. Unable to focus properly with the water distorting everything, she couldn't make out what was slowly emerging from the sand. Suddenly – SNAP! – one of the Soldierfish disappeared into its cavernous mouth. A Sand Diver, well known for its needle-sharp teeth. Good thing Jimmy hadn't trodden on one of those! Time to swim back to shore out of reach!

Bursting into the room she exclaimed, "Gran! I've been for a swim and seen some great fish! Flying fish, Soldierfish and I'm almost sure a Sand Diver. Where's Mum? I must tell her."

Dorothy was pleasantly surprised at Penny's gleeful countenance and excited remarks. Amazing how rejuvenating a swim could be!

"Goodness, what a lot you know about fish! She won't be long. Just having a shower before early dinner. I expect you'd better have one too."

"Yes, I'm covered in sand and salt and *starving* hungry! You look posh, Gran!" cried Penny appreciatively and shot off to her bathroom. Dorothy could hear her singing cheerfully as she showered. Well! She *was* a happy bunny!

Closing her eyes against the water Gemma was breathing deeply, trying to calm down. It was not Mum or Penny's fault she'd had such a bad day. That cheeky fellow, what was his name? Oh yes – Adrian Kanhai, from 'Modern Nature' followed by several time-wasting calls had really got to her. Why did people assume *she* had plenty of time when they, by inference, had none? Oh come on, splosh some of that delicious-smelling showergel over yourself and cheer up. Dinner with Mum and Penny, a family evening together after so long apart, lovely! And be patient, she reminded herself, they'd had a very long journey followed by a dramatic change of climate. They needed to recover and acclimatise. She started singing "Underneath de mango tree" in an attractive, rather husky voice.

Dorothy heard and smiled. It was a rare treat to hear daughter *and* granddaughter singing happily. Relaxing in the comfy armchair, Dorothy revelled in the tuneful duo, more beautiful and harmonious to her ears than any world-class opera singers could ever be.

"There, Gran," Penny flounced in, twirling round in a new turquoise cotton dress. "Do you still think it looks nice on me? Seems funny not wearing jeans, tho' a dress *is* a lot cooler."

"Your Mother will love it and yes, I *still* think it looks spiffing. Much better than those perpetual jeans! I'm surprised you don't get fed up with them."

Penny thought about this. Sometimes she did, but *everyone* wore them, same trousers, same trainers, same tee shirts.

"I'd look funny if I didn't, Gran. And anyway, at school I have to wear school uniform so when I'm at home I like to choose what to wear."

"Even if it's another uniform?" smiled Gran. Penny looked puzzled. What did Gran mean? She was wearing what she wanted, no one was making her.

"You are a pretty pair!" exclaimed Gemma, coming through the communicating door from her bedroom. "That dress looks terrific, Penny! Very simple and what a beautiful colour. It's new isn't it?"

"Yes, Gran bought it especially for when we came here. Wow, Mum, what a pong! What is it?"

Gemma laughed at her daughter's frankness.

"Frangipani flower perfume. It's heady stuff! Don't forget it's a poisonous plant!"

"No Mum, you *have* mentioned it once or twice before," sighed Penny.

"Come on," interrupted Dorothy quickly, "I'm hungry and I know you are too, Penny. Let's get down to the dining room bright and early."

As they set off along the winding path the sun was just going down, a brilliant ball of crimson in the indigo sky.

"Breathtaking!" commented Dorothy, pausing to watch. It was halfway down the horizon, now two-thirds down and poof! Gone.

"It never ceases to amaze me how quickly it disappears," said Gemma. "Everything is plunged into darkness so abruptly."

"Only to rise again the next day," reminded Dorothy gently, "throwing fresh new light on everything."

"But when it's night here," chipped in Penny, "it's day somewhere else. So there's always light *somewhere* isn't there? Even if we can't see it."

Dorothy and Gemma raised startled eyebrows at one another and grinned.

"Yes, that's a clever, cheering thought, Penny!" smiled her mother.

Penny blushed and jogged ahead towards the dining room.

"She's hungry, and not surprising," she heard Gran say. But it wasn't hunger that impelled her towards the dining room but her mother's approving words.

"'Ello, 'ello Missah Penny. Howarya doin' Missah Penny? Food 'ere, food 'ere. Who's a clever Chico? Chico! Chico! Food 'ere. Plenny food 'ere."

"Chico! You still around? You must be *ancient!*" commented Penny to the large green, blue and gold Parrot perched watchfully on the veranda rail, shifting from one grey scaly claw to the other. Chico was Mr MacRobert's tame Parrot. Despite being secured to the rail by a long chain his main aim in life was to break into the restaurant and create havoc. The staff knew of his ambition and were careful about closing the wire mesh doors. On rare occasions a guest, innocent of Parrot wiles, would let him off the chain to sit on their hand. Chico would be very well behaved, sitting quietly, preening his feathers and talking ingratiatingly to the unsuspecting person, his quick eyes fixed on the door awaiting his chance. The door would open and with a quick nip to the person's hand as a 'thank you' he was off, a blur of rainbow feathers and chattering beak. All hell was let loose until Chico was captured, cackling triumphantly in between stuffing fruit into his mouth.

"Bitten any innocent people today?" queried Penny, keeping her fingers well out of his reach.

Chico thrust his head towards Penny and ruffled his splendid blue and gold head feathers until they stood on end like a punk.

"Rude girl! Rude girl!" he screeched loudly. "Missah Penny rude, rude girl," he screamed again.

The door of the 'Motmot Restaurant' opened a fraction, a large hand emerged, grabbed Penny and drew her quickly inside. It was Livingston, looking resplendent in white bow tie and evening suit.

"Howarya doin' Missah Penny? We is glad to see yo back Missah. Don' yo trust tha' Chico. Man – he bad mischief but veree clever. He *talk* to Mr MacRobert! Ah makes damn sure he stay outside ma restaurant! Yo bet! Anyhow, yo is hungry ah knows. All is ready for yo and yo Greatma. Ah met that fine lady this evenin'." He smiled even more broadly at the recollection.

"Hello Livingston," grinned Penny, raising her face for his kiss. "Yes, she's come with me this time."

"She sho is a character Missah! We share some amusin' talk." He chuckled benignly.

Before he could say any more, Penny jumped to defend what she considered her grandmother's oddness.

"She's very old you know. You mustn't think she's stupid or deaf if she doesn't understand you. It's because she's used to old-fashioned language. She's terrific, really she is! And she still plays tennis!" Penny's fierce loyalty defied anyone to contradict her.

"Ah knows she sure fine woman!" exclaimed Livingston, surprised.

"Sorry, Livingston. It's just that people at home seem to think old people are stupid."

"We don't here. Old people have big respect. Dey …"

He was interrupted by Mrs Fairweather and Gemma coming in.

"Livingston!" exclaimed Dorothy with a smile. "How lovely to see you again! So this is where you work when you're not being the Good Samaritan and helping others out?"

"Dat veree kind comment Ma'am. Ah 'preciate dat Good Samaritan parable in de Good Book."

"You've met then?" smiled Gemma. "Livingston's our Maître d'Hôtel. You pull your forelock when you speak to him!"

"And ah'm glad to meet yo again Ma'am. Is fine for yo, Doc Prof, to have all yo famibly hereyah."

Livingston's smile stretched from ear to ear. A keen family man himself, he was overjoyed for Gemma to have her mother and daughter with her. He often thought what a sad, lonely woman she was. It did him good to see the three of them together.

"Now, yo all come wit' me. Ah've reserved this hereyah table for yo. Yo say, is OK?"

The group walked through the gaily coloured restaurant which took its decorative scheme from the bird it was named after, the Motmot. Green, red and blue check cloths were spread over the tables, with matching table napkins arranged fanwise on the turquoise placemats. Blue painted tubs containing different coloured bougainvillea were dotted about, the plants growing exuberantly through green and white trellis secured to pillars. Turquoise candles flickered and twinkled on the sparkling glasses and shining cutlery. Restaurant staff putting finishing touches to tables beamed as they passed. It was a pretty and welcoming scene. Livingston led them through the still empty room to the far side, right out onto the veranda overlooking the sea. A secluded corner table had been prepared for three, shielded on one side by a large palm and on another by a white painted balustrade. A refreshing breeze blew gently from the sea. On the centre of the table stood a long, low, elegant arrangement of tropical flowers matching the decor: blue Petrea, red Heliconia, pink Poui, the red / orange / purple Bird of Paradise and white and mauve Orchids. On either side of this stood tall turquoise candles.

"There!" exclaimed Livingston triumphantly, "What yo tink o' dat?"

Dorothy gasped with pleasure. What trouble someone – Livingston? – had gone to, to arrange this beautiful and welcoming table! Such a quiet, secluded spot! They could catch up on family news privately.

"Livingston!" exclaimed Gemma, "Do we have you to thank for all this? It's exquisite!"

"Mr MacRobert, he give me a free hand to welcome yo. De flowers are from he. Do yo like tho'? Is all fine? Not too chill here? Dere's a good draught blowin' from de Doctor's wind. Ah hope not too much for yo Ma'am?" he enquired anxiously of Mrs Fairweather.

"No, it's wonderful, perfect. Thank you Livingston. You've made us *very* welcome."

"Yes, thanks," chimed Penny, "it's smashing. How soon can we eat please?"

Livingston raised his hand and beckoned. One of the most beautiful young women Dorothy had ever seen came shyly from behind a raffia screen. She wore a dress made in the same checked gingham as the tablecloths with a starched white frilled apron. The matching cap formed an aureole around the black curling hair and cinnamon brown of a perfect oval face.

"Dis is Emris an' she is to look after yo. She a good girl. Yo ask she for anytink yo fancies," instructed Livingston.

Emris grinned widely, her almond-shaped brown eyes and flashing white teeth glinting in the candlelight. One of her teeth had a small piece of shaped gold on it. Mrs Fairweather and Gemma smiled and shook hands with her but Penny had been fascinated by the glimpse of gold. She'd never noticed such an ornament on other women staff.

"What have you got on your tooth, Emris?" she asked curiously.

"Sshhh, Penny! Don't ask personal questions," said Gemma.

"Sshhh, Penny! Don't be rude!" admonished Mrs Fairweather simultaneously.

Emris smiled and Livingston tried hard to repress one.

"Is ok Ma'am," Emris replied calmly, "Is all de fashion on dis island. Ma gold is de shape of a heart. Is given by ma man."

Livingston coughed discreetly.

"Yo knows how tings is Doc Prof. De young people, dey must save hard for many years to marry. Dis trinket, it show Emris sort of married."

"Like an engagement ring!" said Penny brightly.

"Oh – dey is too expensive an' risky Missah. Ma gold is safe," explained Emris.

Penny looked puzzled.

"She means she can't lose it, Penny," explained Gemma. "Emris does all kinds of work and it's easy to mislay a ring. She's unlikely to mislay a tooth!"

Everyone smiled and nodded at this practical and sensible explanation.

"Food!" said Livingston, passing each of them a turquoise menu, and there was silence as the family concentrated on perusing it.

"Potato Crusted Red Snapper and Ladera Coco please Livingston," said Penny quickly.

"How did ah guess, Missah Penny!" quipped Livingston. "Yo an' yo Red Snapper! Fresh from out de bay. It was a good haul today."

"That sounds tasty, I think I'll have it too please," ordered Dorothy.

"Now Doc Prof., what yo havin'? Dere's Carapuse Bay lobster an' fresh octopus an' baked Kingfish an' …"

"Mr Livingston Sir! Mr Livingston!" a harassed waiter came bustling up to the table.

"Dere's a man hereyah Sir. He demand de best table. He veree loud Sir and makin' Godalmighty fuss. I tell him wait an' come for yo Sir."

"Yo sure is right there man. Leave 'im a me. Ah'm sorry ladies, ah've got to leave yo. Emris! Pay 'tenshun girl an' vite, vite," and off Livingston went as fast as was dignified.

"Did you hear that, Gemma? He said 'vite, vite,' – quick, quick in French. I suppose he speaks French?"

"Yes, but when you've got used to the dialect you'll pick out quite a bit of French in it. The French were here very early on with the English and the Spanish and the dialect reflects that."

A loud drawling voice could be heard in the restaurant, complaining and criticising. Livingston's voice, soothing and conciliating, followed.

"These tables are far too close together. You're sitting on top of your neighbour! And look at that place setting – there's no dessert knife and fork! And where's the staff? I can't see any around. You run a very inefficient restaurant here. It was recommended to me as excellent and the food delicious. You'd better find me a suitable table and some service FAST!"

A tall, well built man strode purposefully out onto the veranda followed by … it couldn't be! Oh *no!* But it was – Jimmy!

Penny could have wept. Just as she was looking forward to a rare evening together with Mum and Gran *he* had to put in an appearance. Why couldn't they eat at their own hotel? Gemma and Dorothy were casting appraising looks at the man with the loud, hectoring voice when Penny realised she was the only one who knew it must be

Jimmy's father. Seeing their pretty, cosy table the man stopped.

"That is a pleasant table," he announced, and, without bothering to lower his voice, continued, "We'll sit there. Tell those women to move."

'Those women' turned scarlet with anger, Livingston turned an interesting puce colour with embarrassment and even Jimmy went pink and looked away.

"Ah'm veree sorry Sir but that table is occupied," Livingston pointed out in case he'd missed the fact. "Here's a nice table," he gestured to one situated in the opposite corner, "Perhaps you'd like to sit there, Sir?"

"Why can't these women sit there?" the man asked truculently. "I'm sure they'd be just as comfortable."

"In tha' case Sir, so would yo," commented Livingston quietly.

"How dare you answer in that impertinent manner! I'll be reporting you to the Manager."

"Certainly Sir," Livingston was unperturbed. "Would yo like to do so now Sir? I believe he on de premises." He knew Mr MacRobert would understand the situation.

"Later, my son is hungry and we've come here to eat."

Livingston looked on helplessly as he proceeded to walk up to their table and lean over, addressing Mrs Fairweather.

"Excuse me Madam, would you and your family care to move? I would like this table." Seeing their looks of astonishment and horror, he added, "I'll make it worth your while."

Dorothy was totally flabbergasted. She'd never been so insulted in her life! Shaking her head in shock and amazement she opened her mouth to respond, but words failed her. It was not the same with Gemma.

"Are you really as bad-mannered as you seem? Perhaps you have defective vision? Don't you understand – this table is already occupied. We're very happy here and have no intention of moving. Go and find a table somewhere else. There's plenty of empty ones. If you don't like them you can do the other thing. And if you don't leave us AT ONCE, *I'll* complain about harassment."

The man jumped away from the table as if he'd been stung.

"I always knew you English roses were prickly, but this sure is the limit. Come on son, we'll sit over there."

Jimmy had pretended not to know Penny, but as they went and sat down he cast her a look of such mournful desperation she felt sorry for him. Crumbs! No wonder he tried to escape from his father!

"I've never heard you speak like that before dear," whispered Dorothy to her daughter. "Goodness, you told him!"

"I've had to learn to stick up for myself, Mum."

"You did that all right! Oh well, we'll ignore them. No point in getting worked up and spoiling our dinner. I don't like the idea of you having to work with ill-mannered people though, Gemma."

"The Americans I deal with are very courteous. Not at all like him."

"Yes, the G.Is. I met in the war were the same. Very courteous but as tough as old boots with a real no-nonsense frontiersman attitude," she grinned reminiscently.

Gemma smiled at her mother, shaking her head in bewilderment as they watched Livingston settle the pair at the table in the opposite corner. Calling up two of his most experienced waiters from behind the raffia screen where they had been discreetly hidden, he sidled back to Gemma.

"Phew! Ah'm sorry 'bout dat Doc Prof.," he said quietly, "but yo knows how it is! No matter how unappealin' an rude, ah can't turn away custom. Mos' Americans, dey veree courteous. Mebbe he got too much money to care 'bout others!"

"Don't worry, Livingston. It's the same everywhere. Most people are well mannered and know how to behave but there's always a minority, rich, poor or middling, who let their country down and give it a bad name. Look – here's Emris with our drinks and first course! We're going to have a super meal."

Penny could hardly wait for everyone to be served she was so hungry. At last Gran picked up her knife and fork saying, "Bon Appétit!" – the signal she could start. The Red Snapper had never tasted better! Glancing across at Jimmy she was surprised to see him sitting in total silence with downcast eyes. His father was gazing about the dining room and adjacent beach with a speculative look Penny didn't like. Why had they come here the first night of their holiday? Why hadn't they had dinner at their own hotel like most people would after a long journey? She hoped this wasn't going to be a regular event!

* * *

"Well, Jimbo son. I like the look of this set-up. Rather old-fashioned and needs updating of course, but great potential. That beach will take two or three hotels or perhaps holiday condominiums. I'll have it costed out. See which has the greater profit margin."

Gemma stopped chatting with her mother and daughter, her ears pricked to the corner table.

"Great beach, ideal for buggy rides, sand-skiing, water sports, motor boats and so on. It could have a marina built to divide it and moor boats. Yep, I'm going to open up this little backwater of an island and make it a great Vacationland. What do you say to that?"

"Great Pa! Great!" muttered Jimmy, glancing surreptitiously at Penny's table where Gemma was obviously taking a keen interest in the conversation.

"You don't sound very excited, son. Ya know, there's nothing else in life except money and success. You'd better get that straight right now while you're young."

"But Pa, do money and success always go together? Couldn't you be successful and happy without making a stack of dollars?" asked Jimmy tentatively.

"What were you thinking of son? Being an artist? A writer? You won't make serious money that way!" he laughed cynically. "You take my word for it, be a property developer like your old man. That's where the cash is. When I've developed this beach it'll take me into the multi-billionaire bracket!" He gave a satisfied smile and rocked back on his chair. Penny wished it would break.

"You will *not* be developing the beach! You can put that right out of your mind!"

Gemma had jumped out of her chair and was standing over Jimmy's father, authoritative and steely, green eyes flashing.

"Is that so? And who's going to stop me – you, the old lady and that silly little girl?" Jimmy's father turned away dismissively.

"I'm surprised you don't know the beach is protected. There can't be any further development as it would deprive the Giant Leatherback Marine Turtles of their nesting sites. It's developed enough already."

"Looked pretty empty to me when we drove over it this evening. I said …"

"*You drove over the sand*? You *idiot*!!! The Turtles are due up any time and you've just compacted the beach where they lay their eggs! The sand has to be *soft* for them! And Hatchlings are killed if cars drive over the sand."

Gemma was beside herself. Where had the Custodians been? Why hadn't they stopped this stupid, selfish twit of a man driving over the beach?

"Why didn't you take the coast road like any sensible person," she continued, "or walk, if your legs still work? Didn't anyone try to stop you driving across the sand?"

"Yep, two big guys in black thought they could frighten me. They scattered when I drove towards them. I wanted to see how big the beach was, ok? I've got great plans for it."

"So I heard and, as I said, they won't come to anything. This is the only remaining beach where Giant Leatherback Turtles lay their eggs. If you develop this, they'll become extinct."

Jimmy's father rose to his feet. He was a good half foot taller than Gemma but she didn't retreat. Instead, she took a step forward, looking unflinchingly up into his face.

"Who's worried about a few old Turtles? They've been around long enough I reckon. Time for them to become extinct."

"But Pa …" interrupted Jimmy.

"Hold your mouth son. This is between this person and me. By the way," he paused to suppress a yawn, "who are you?"

"Gemma Heffernan. I'm part of 'Save Our Sea-Turtles' or S.O.S. And whom may *you* be?" Gemma queried icily.

"Andrew Saxon, Ma'am, Property Developer. It's an *honour* to meet you." There was an underlying sneer in his voice. "I can see we will be in open and frank discussion over the beach development when we meet more formally. This is just the beginning of my negotiations to buy the beach – and this hotel too. Come along Jimbo, time to go."

This further shock did not prevent Gemma making one last stand.

"Mr Saxon, you can make what plans you like. They won't come to anything. And can I request that you do *not* drive over the sand on your way back? My Turtle Custodians, the men in black, have the full support of the Government and myself in protecting the beach from anything and *anyone* deemed a danger to the Leatherbacks. I would be much obliged if you'd remember that," she stated resolutely.

"Assuredly Ma'am. I wouldn't like to upset you or your Turtles any further – for today," he replied derisively. "Come on son, let's do as the lady asks," and with a mocking bow he made to leave the restaurant. Jimmy got up and followed, head down, not looking at anyone.

"Stay there," whispered Gemma, "I want to know what car he's driving." She slipped out after them.

Penny and her Gran remained thoughtfully in their chairs, the evening ruined. Horrible, rude, greedy man thought Penny.

"Come on dear. Drink your fresh mango juice, it looks delicious," said Dorothy, trying to distract her.

"I will if you order the house special, Passion Fruit Rum Kreole," responded Penny.

Mrs Fairweather hesitated. She enjoyed wine but rum? Still, she was in the Secret Island, she ought to try things out.

"Right – you're on. Emris! A Passion Fruit Rum Kreole please."

Just then Gemma returned, smiling broadly.

"You'll never guess!" she cried gleefully. "That man was *furious*! He parked his car under the palm tree and three huge coconuts fell right on it! There's a massive dent in the roof and he's accusing the staff of doing it deliberately! I told him the Custodians would have warned him not to park there. Serve him right! Oh goody! Here's Emris with a drink – just what I need!" And, whisking the Rum Kreole off the tray, she took an eager swig. Dorothy smiled with relief – saved!

Chapter Eight

THE SPACIOUS SEA MEETING PLACE

Letty made good time to the Spacious Sea. The grey, turgid water of the Sea of Stillness changed to indigo, dark blue and finally sparkling aquamarine. She rose to the surface and looked about, delighted to see small coral atolls dotted about in the crystalline waves. Shoals of multicoloured reef fish darted in and out of the coral. Many of these had service jobs in the Spacious Sea. Yes, the concealed entrance tunnel was very close. She would enter it as soon as she'd had a good breathe. It was great to return to this ancient Triassic place, which the nomadic Turtles thought of as home. Its beauty never failed to thrill and uplift her spirits. Isolated, mysterious, undiscovered by Humans, it was a colossal submarine lake enclosed and protected by hard corralline rock. This secret sea teemed with swarms of rare, weird jellyfish. 'Upside Down' jellyfish abounded, their tentacles reaching up towards the surface. 'Moon' jellyfish emerged only at night and spent the rest of the time secluded on the sea floor. Luminescent lancets of light glinted and flashed through natural gaps in the rock, which also provided breathing apertures for the Turtles. It was here the 'Gardener' jellyfish gathered. The gardens of miniature plants which grew inside their bodies needed light to do so. They were very easy to see, but so colourful and pretty that a 'live and let live' agreement had been reached between them and the Turtles. The Leatherbacks never ate these Gardener jellies but kept them for decorative purposes. Letty dived purposefully, located the camouflaged tunnel and swam slowly down the long, wide, winding gallery that led to the grandiose Portal. This was quite new, only a few million years old, but nevertheless a majestic architectural feat. It comprised soaring pillars, decorated columns and stately statues of antediluvian Leatherback ancestors, the massive 'Archelon' and 'Cotylosauria'. Pausing to admire the brilliant sculptures, she pulled the sonorous bell in the shape of a snake-necked Plesiosauroid and waited for the Portal Steward, Cerberus, to appear.

"Good morning Matriarch Laetitia. I'm very pleased to see you at last. I was getting quite worried. I 'opes as 'ow you are well? Any news of your Hantle?"

"It's good to see you Cerberus! And *so* good to be home at last! I've had a few distractions and excitements on the way but here I am safe and sound. My Hantle caused the delay. They were tossed out of the Sea of Stillness and had to be found and put back in a safe place. Minnie and Jeté's Pod of Dolphins saved Clementine's life and I've awarded them the freedom of the Chelonian Cloister."

"Ah, indeed! Excuse me for one minute Ma'am, if you please," said Cerberus, a solemn look on his large face, and, turning away, entered the Portal Steward's Lodge. The Lodge window shot up and he reappeared, adorned with a pair of glittering square eyeglasses, his flippers covered by thin white seaweed mitts. A finely-honed shellfish pen was grasped in one flipper and the unique Record Book of smooth, shining mica was open on his black basalt desk.

"Now then, Matriarch, if you would please run through the details I'll get them entered up. We don't know when Jeté or his Pod may need our help and I likes to keep the Record straight."

"Of course," responded Laetitia, and gave Cerberus the required details:

Name of species to be allowed in; name of Leader or Chieftain; approximate numbers; deed for which honour has been bestowed; date of said deed; done in the presence of; signed by; witnessed by and finally the date.

Neither could work out how many millions of years it must be since the first entry in the Book, so agreed to put an undecipherable squiggle. Laetitia signed in a neat, clear hand but Cerberus had perfected a dashing flourish for his signature, the capital 'C' curling around the entire name. Laetitia gave a small smile and he blushed slightly, turning pale lilac.

"Well – see Madam, it's like this 'ere. A lot of the year I've not much to do, so I practises calligraphy. Then the Record Book looks properly distinguished when I check in our visitors. We don't want anyone thinking the Leatherbacks lack style, do we Madam?"

"No, that would be a careless bad example for us to give. After all, we *are* the oldest species."

They nodded in agreement, proud of their unique ancestry and ancient lineage.

"I ought to be swimming along Cerberus. You must be very busy now?"

Cerberus smiled happily. He loved this time of year, the Homecoming, when Leatherbacks from all over the world converged on the Meeting Place, jostling and pushing, clapping each other's carapaces with enormous flippers, chortling and joking. He knew them and their families and all the intricate ramifications of the Leatherback world.

"Yes, Matriarch, there's been quite a few in. I wondered where you were, always being so prompt like. But them 'atchlings explains it! You never knows wot they'll do next, bless 'em! Mostly females 'ave been arriving but males are beginning to swarm in now. Oh! tut, tut," he paused, shocked as a noisy group of young Turtles arrived. "Sorry Ma'am, will you excuse me? Here's a batch of male Nematts. They'll need organising, never 'aving been here on their own before. You know how over-excited they get what with being allowed into the 'Archelon' and so on." And he swam purposefully away to remonstrate on their undignified behaviour.

After a year mostly on her own in the High Seas Letty's carapace was in dire need of cleaning and polishing before the Metanoia. Her guests would enjoy a pleasant wash and brush up too. An appointment at the Beauty Parlour would be a good idea and she floated gently through the open Portal towards it. The Great Hall was seething with small fish busy attending to the shops and cafés they ran for the Leatherbacks. She passed the 'Jellyfish Pop-In,' a large rock cavern filled with a huge variety of jellyfish run by 'Stoplight' Parrotfish, the males being green and the females red. In exchange for algae brought by the Turtles the Parrotfish would allow them into sections of the cavern for jellyfish. A large amount of deliciously fresh algae bought the freedom of the cavern, but if a small amount was offered, a small section of it was made available.

Letty passed the 'Perfumery' (Females Only) and 'Gambling Den' (Males Only) and came to the Beauty Parlour situated opposite the Barber's Shop. Pushing aside the shimmering, elegantly draped curtain of black Laminaria seaweed, Letty entered the sumptuously appointed black, pearl and malachite parlour and approached the Receptionist. All the fish who worked in the Beauty Parlour and Barber's Shop were various kinds of Wrasse, or 'Cleaner Fish' as they were sometimes called. The one on Reception today was pale-pink with a short black band down her body.

"Matriarch Laetitia! Welcome home! It is good to see you. How can we help?"

"Is the Sapphire Team available?" asked Letty. She always tried to get this team of brilliant blue Wrasse, whose distinguished long black band from head to tail indicated them to be First Class Cleaner Wrasse.

"Let me see," the Receptionist gazed at the Appointment Book.

"Ah! They're just finishing a client and will be free in about thirty waves. The Green Moon Wrasse Team are available now. Are you straight in from the High Seas?"

"Apart from chasing my Hatchlings back to the Nursery, yes. I'll be so relieved when they're safe at Academy with Madame Louisa and Dr Laurence!"

"Dear me, they're such a worry aren't they?" The Pale Pink Wrasse lowered her voice. "Did you hear about Matriarch Anastasia's *dreadful* experience?"

Tasha! What could have happened to her?

"No – I passed her on the way here. She was fine then."

"She's in there now with the Yellow Head Team," whispered the Receptionist, turning even pinker. "It's *awful!* She's just told us. I'm so relieved it didn't happen to you as well. Of course I've heard about such things before but it seems to be happening more often. I was just saying to …"

Impatient and anxious to know the worst, Letty cut her short.

"What happened?" she asked.

"Well …" hissed the tiny Wrasse, "She was laying her eggs last year and everything was going well when suddenly she realised that a Human had crept up and was *taking* her eggs *as she laid them*!!!"

Letty gasped in horror. What a *terrible* thing to happen!

"Well … being a Matriarch you know that once you start laying you *have* to continue. That's nature. Matriarch Anastasia couldn't stop. She tried flicking sand into the Human's face with her flippers but you know how heavy and ponderous they are on dry land! He just waited until she was exhausted. When she turned round to cover her clutch and lay the false trail – there were *no* eggs *at all*! He'd taken every single one. The Human had a lamp and started going up the beach. She followed the light until they came to very hard ground where there were lots and lots of bright lights whizzing along …"

"A *road*!" gasped Letty in horror.

"Yes, that's what she said. He swung the eggs onto a chariot, and saw she had followed him."

"OH! NO!" Letty nearly screamed. "What did he do?" she asked hesitantly.

"*Laughed*! He laughed at her! She was weeping with sadness, exhaustion and disorientation and he laughed!"

Large round tears sprang from Letty's large round eyes.

"How did she manage to return to the sea?"

"The Human looked in his chariot and when he turned back a machete gleamed in his hand."

"NO! NO! She's not …" Letty couldn't bring herself to say it. But surely …

"YES! He was going to cut her flippers off! They are used for soup as well as eggs. Suddenly there was a terrific rustling in the sea grape and two huge Humans ran towards them. The evil one jumped into his chariot, there was a big bang and a cloud of smoke. When it dispersed, he'd gone."

"Leaving the other two Humans behind? Oh dear! Tasha was even *worse* off!"

"*No*, it's odd because after the evil egg thief had gone, the other two Humans stood in front of Matriarch Anastasia and shielded her from the road. They wore black clothes and gradually Madam's eyes readjusted to nearly normal. Then, very gently, they urged her to turn round. Once she saw the moon reflected on the water she was orientated again and set off down the beach as quickly as possible. The two Humans in black stayed with her until she reached the sea. She was so tired she couldn't give them the Giant Leatherback 'thank you' wave once she was swimming. But they both waved to her. So poor Matriarch Anastasia has no Hatchlings this year and is terrified of going up the beach."

How *evil*! This had never happened to Letty but she knew of such wickedness. The eggs were used for Turtle Soup, considered a great delicacy by some Humans. It was strange because she knew other Humans tried very hard to prevent this malevolent trade. The Humans dressed all in black would belong to that group and must have been trying to catch the egg poacher. How Tasha must have suffered! Letty was truly glad she had won the Chelonian Cup. Minnie had been right, Hatchlings were far more important than the glory of winning a Cup.

"That's a terrible story. You're quite right – better by far to have mischievous Hatchlings that lead you a merry splash than none at all. Poor, *poor* Tasha!"

Tiny Wrasse and Giant Leatherback fell silent. That such evil existed in the Human world was incredible. Humans brought it about and Humans had to solve it. There was nothing they could do to defend themselves on the Arid Land.

"We haven't made your appointment!" tutted the Receptionist. "You'll need a full Carapace Oil Massage, Facial and Flipper Restorative?" she asked, brisk once again.

"Yes please, that sounds lovely. I'll wait for the Sapphire Team."

"In thirty waves then. Perhaps you'd care to have a snack in our Damselfish Café or slip along to the 'Archelon Ancestor' while you wait?"

"I'll go to the 'Archelon' and see if my husband's arrived yet. He'll be swimming in from Great Britain!"

Letty was proud of George's daring exploratory journeys and boasted ever so slightly about them.

"Gracious! How interesting! We never go there. Far too distant and *very* cold I believe. But that doesn't matter to you Leatherbacks. You can explore the world!" the Wrasse exclaimed enviously.

"Not *quite*, but very nearly. You're right – we *are* very unusual creatures," Letty smiled serenely. "See you later then," and wafted out of the Parlour.

The Meeting Place was humming with activity. Giant Leatherbacks from all over the world were swimming in. From Newfoundland in Canada and the Cote d'Ivoire in West Africa; from Malaysia, Argentina, California; from India and the Cape of Good Hope, The Canary Isles and Saint Maarten, in they came, grunting and splashing, greeting and dashing, relieved and happy to be home once again. Many were the wide grins of friendship, jocular comments and resounding flipper claps as they greeted each other. This was their own place, designed millions of years ago by their Dinosaur ancestors solely for the use of Giant Leatherback Turtles. Safe from all danger, everything in it was to their own specification and liking. Abundant food supplies, massive and magnificent Meeting Marinas, informal pubs and cafés run by friendly fish, even a 'Hydrozoa Heaven' for the Hatchlings! What more could any Leatherback ask for!

Letty made her way down the vast hall towards the 'Archelon Ancestor', a smart but informal pub much frequented by the Matriarchs and Patriarchs as they began to relax after their arduous journeys. Progress was slow. Every Turtle she passed stopped to greet her and exchange a few words. Here was young Isabella swimming swiftly towards her looking agitated.

"Matriarch Laetitia! Am I glad to see you!"

"Gracious me dear – whatever's the matter? Is it Zozimus?"

This was one of Laetitia and George's sons. He'd left Turtle Academy a few seasons ago and at last year's Metanoia had made plain his interest in Isabella. Both parents had been delighted. Zozimus had been a right tearaway and it was felt he may never settle down and become a Patriarch. He seemed to prefer a bachelor existence with no responsibilities. With the frightening decrease in Leatherback numbers this worried George and Laetitia a great deal.

"No – well yes. In a way. He hasn't returned yet, which worries me."

"Oh! Don't worry about that. He went over to Great Britain with his father. It's his first excursion so he's probably having a good look around. He'll be back. I'm on my way to see if Patriarch George has returned."

"But can I have a talk with you first please?"

"Certainly. Come along to the 'Archelon' with me. We'll meet everyone there."

"Yes, that's what I don't want, Matriarch. I'd like to have a word in *private*," said Isabella, looking around at the milling throng of joyful Leatherbacks.

"After I've been to see if George is in the 'Archelon' I've an appointment at the Beauty Parlour. Why don't you wait for me there in the Damselfish Café? It's usually very quiet."

"Yes! I will. Thank you," said Isabella breathlessly and with a quick flip of her tail flippers turned and was gone. Laetitia watched this graceful manoeuvre enviously. It was only young, supple females who could manage it. At half a ton Isabella was slim and slight for the tough climb up the beach for egg-laying. She needed to put on weight or she'd get stranded without enough energy to return to the sea. Still, if she was thinking of marrying Zozimus she must be about twenty-two and had not reached her full size. Yes, she'd be a solid three-quarters of a ton by the time she was ready to lay her first clutch. Thus heartened, Letty glided into the prehistoric splendour of the 'Archelon Ancestor'.

Bertie the Barman, quick and observant, saw her easing through the throng.

"Matriarch Laetitia Ma'am! Good to see you safe and sound again.

One of my 'Specials'?"

"Yes *please*, Bertie! How good to be home again where everyone knows you!"

Bertie grinned enthusiastically.

"Nice to be of service, Madam. It's very quiet most of the year. Just a few visitors, usually ill or lost, and some Special Guests in the Cloister. I like things humming!"

He began mixing his 'Special'. A refreshing combination of Pacific Salt Water with Sea Fern and a touch of scarlet algae, still and not too warm, prepared in the Gallon Tankard Laetitia liked. It was carved out of Gabbro in the shape of two Leatherbacks, their flippers forming large sturdy handles. Bertie completed the drink with a flourish of his flipper and handed it to Laetitia.

"Welcome home, Matriarch Laetitia! You're a little later than usual. Is your 'Special' ok?"

"Mmmmm! Lovely, perfect! Thanks so much, Bertie. Is George anywhere about?"

"Haven't seen him yet, Matriarch. There are plenty of Turtles still coming in, mostly males. If I see him, I'll tell him you've been asking. Ahh! Here's a bunch of young Nematts. I'd best keep an eye on them. Excuse me please."

Letty was content to be alone. Choosing a cosy armchair formed from a massive ammonite fossil, Titanites Giganticus, worn and comfortable through millennia of wear from Leatherback carapaces, she relaxed, sipped her drink and gazed happily around the exotic beauty of the magnificent cavern. Extinct submarine volcanoes had left behind broad billows of puffy pillow lava, great swathes of smooth black basalt which had been hollowed into chairs and tables of a size suitable for Giant Leatherbacks. Scattered about, twinkling like stars among the matt black basalt were more intricately carved tables and chairs adorned with the flashing rosy-red crystals of Balas-Ruby Spinel while others were ornamented with glaucous green Pleonaste Spinel. This iridescence continued in the roof hangings of Turquoise stalactites, whose blue crystalline surface gleamed with diamonds of every variety: white, red, green, yellow, even rare black and blue diamonds were dotted about. Refraction caused these minerals and crystals to change colour so that a kaleidoscope of harlequin prisms chased across the cavern making it a spectrum of ever-changing luminescence. Letty and the Leatherbacks had been brought up among these wondrous rocks and crystals but their beauty and grandeur remained fresh and precious to them. This unknown and untouched natural kingdom deserved and received reverence and respect and the Giant Leatherbacks felt privileged to be both benefactors and stewards of so much matchless and irreplaceable beauty.

Filled with peace and tranquillity, Letty finished her drink, waved to Bertie and glided out into the Great Hall. Better get back to Isabella and see what that young Nematt had on her mind! Barely using her flippers, Letty floated gently towards the Beauty Parlour. A short distance away a large, dark Turtle was holding court to a cluster of young female Nematts who seemed mesmerised by her loud shrill voice.

"And what I always say is ..." she shouted in a strident screech.

Help! It was Matriarch Volubility. She must escape or be cornered and forced to listen to interminable boring rubbish and spiteful gossip in that siren scream! Letty took instant evasive action and darted swiftly into a sandy passageway in the rock. Swimming speedily down this she thankfully spied a narrow fissure invisible from the main hall. Squeezing herself in head-first she drew a sigh of relief. Phew! Old Volly wouldn't find her here! She lay very still and silent, head well tucked into her carapace, trying to look like a large rock. Volly glanced down the sandy alleyway as she passed, talking at the top of her voice to the group of Nematts.

"That's odd. I thought I saw Matriarch Laetitia dodge down here but there's no one there. Well, she's no loss. I sometimes think Great Mother forgot to give her a tongue she's so quiet. Can't get a word out of her! Not a very entertaining Turtle. The males like females who chatter and keep them amused. I well remember ..."

"But – isn't she married to Patriarch George?" interrupted one Nematt, greatly daring.

"Yes, and he has to make up for her silence. He's a most *amusing*

Turtle." Volly fluttered long eyelashes and swished a hefty flipper over her long neck. The Nematts hid giggles at this display of coquetry. No wonder Patriarch George had married sensible Laetitia!

Letty heard the loud abrasive voice fading into the distance and breathed a sigh of relief. Cautiously raising her head a little she listened. Not a sound! Now to get out of this cramped space. Elongating her neck, she peered around, amazed at what she saw. What was this place? A crevice, slightly wider ahead which Letty hadn't noticed before. Yet she'd spent years exploring the Meeting Place, on her own and, she smiled reminiscently, with various suitors before she'd married George. How bizarre! Underwater volcanism resulted in fresh fault lines and structures, new crevices and caves occurring regularly in this vast and ancient geological formation. Usually she was well up to date with changes. How dark and dim it was! No refracted light twinkled and sparkled off brightly coloured crystals. No cosy chairs or comfortable pillow lava existed here. No gaily coloured fish swam busily about. It was deserted, silent, spooky. Letty didn't like it. Slowly and with extreme care she moved further into the cave. Jutting out from the walls, ready to tear and pierce were sword-sharp black glass daggers. Obsidian! A volcanic lava resembling glass but ten times tougher! A nasty trap for unwary Turtles whose soft plastrons could easily be torn. They would bleed to death. Was the Zamorin aware of this cave? It ought to be sealed off. Everything in the Meeting Place was supposed to be safe for Leatherbacks and their invited friends. This cavern certainly wasn't.

Echoing through the cave, reverberating off the glassy walls, causing the chamber to tremble with its intensity, resounded a ghastly noise. Simultaneously its temperature cooled dramatically. Letty's amazing 'counter-current' circulation sprang into action, moving blood away from her flippers towards her body in order to safeguard its heat. What was happening? Alarmed, she lay still, curling herself on the floor, the gleaming chestnut brown carapace providing a natural shield. Unlike her cousins, the Land Tortoises, she was unable to retract her head and this remained revealed and vulnerable. Crouched in sinister silence and deepest gloom Letty's prehistoric warning system vibrated with danger signals, every sense alert. Locating the sound she realised it was coming from further along the narrow chamber and from a lower subterranean level. Stealthily, she edged forward. The deep rhythmical rumbling, like snoring but more stertorous, became louder. Letty slowed down and stopped. Whatever was causing the cacophony must be an enemy. Her defensive reactions had given her ample warning. The 'counter-current' reflex and urge to curl up only sprang into action if danger threatened. There was something very evil nearby.

Isabella! With a start Letty remembered the young Nematt. She was supposed to be meeting her and had booked a Beauty treatment! The Sapphire Team would be waiting. It had gone clean out of her mind. She had to get back. Should she mention this weird cave and its mystery to George and the Zamorin? No – not yet. She would commandeer a sturdy trident from the Armourer, 'Z', and investigate further before saying anything. It would be silly to cause needless anxiety and upset the happiness of the Leatherback Metanoia. The strange sounds could be a trick of oscillating sea currents or a strong breeze echoing down a volcanic pipe. There were all sorts of possible reasons. But Letty couldn't forget the cold and her defensive reflex action. They were a response to danger, not aberrant sea currents!

Thus resolved, Letty began to turn round. But she couldn't! Her size and lack of manoeuvrability required considerable space to turn. The cave was too narrow! She could continue forward – or reverse out backwards, feeling along the razor-sharp sides as she went. She would have to do it, there was no way she was going forward! The safest thing would be if she followed the track she'd made coming in. This was clearly marked by the tractor-like indentations of her plastron and massive sand ridges and furrows thrown up by her flippers. She would have to 'feel' her way out! Just for once Letty wished she were a crab and could scuttle out sideways! Sighing, she drew her head in as much as possible and cautiously placed a flipper behind her, feeling for the ridge. Yes! That was ok. Positioning both flippers accurately within the furrow she pushed forwards and moved backwards. If she remained in her tracks she would be alright! To veer aside from this constricted course could mean death. Obsidian daggers would soon cut and tear flippers or plastron. She was alone, no one knew where she was; without help she would bleed to death. With infinite care Letty gently felt for the next ridge and furrow, then the next … and the next …

Inch by precious inch she retreated through the cave. Gradually her massive body began warming up. The evil presence must be some distance off now! Letty drew a sigh of relief. Patting gently with her flippers, she gingerly placed them in the furrows.

A soft, stealthy slithering came from behind her. Stopping abruptly, she tried to peer round but could see nothing. Crouched in the darkness, Letty waited and listened. There it was again! A muffled rustling, swooshing noise like one of those sideways-travelling water snakes. Oh no! What *now*? She must be quite near the entrance to the cave. A little further and she would be out and safe. But not yet. Panic swept through her, confusion and fear clouding her judgment. Lying absolutely still and quiet, her senses alert to danger, great tears of exhaustion oozed down her beak. She couldn't think, let alone think clearly! In this state of terror, tiredness and frustration a clear, authoritative Voice suddenly spoke; "Letty! Letty! Stay calm! Think quietly, remain calm. You know that sound. Be calm, *think!*"

The Voice! The interior voice of right, reason and good advice. It gave help and showed what action to take. It had helped her many times and little Clementine had already paid heed to the Voice's guidance and saved her life. Letty lay, breathing deeply, trying to obey its command and control her tumultuous thoughts. Listening quietly now, without panic and its resultant despair, she heard the noise again. Soft, stealthy, swooshing, slithering – of course! The sandy ridges caused by her flippers were capsizing! It was no monster set to overpower and kill her, merely coarse sand sliding, glissading towards the ground. But – it meant her guidelines were disintegrating! With no ridges to feel for it would be more difficult locating the furrows. Still, after what her imagination had conjured up, coping with a few low ridges would be easy! She was sure the opening was not far.

Adjusting to the lower banks, Letty continued cautiously backwards. It wouldn't do to injure herself now by carelessness caused by relief. Light was beginning to seep into the cave. The obsidian daggers gave way to smooth rock. With a final mighty push Letty shot out, tail flipper first, into the side alley where she'd taken refuge from Matriarch Volubility. *Phew!!* That was a close-run thing! Now she must take a good breather and have something to eat, she was starved of both! Quickly locating a breathing hole, Letty shot upwards. Reaching the surface she stayed for longer than usual, taking deep, refreshing gulps of air and looking about appreciatively. Down in the cold cave she'd thought she may never see any of this again. How beautiful it was!

Beauty – Isabella! With one more bracing lungful of air she dived, uttered the secret code which opened the breathing hatches and was back in the Great Hall. Swimming purposefully into the 'Jolly Jellyfish Takeaway' she purchased a sea purse full of pelagic tunicates, stuffed it hastily into her capacious mouth and flew through the water to the Beauty Parlour. Would Isabella have waited? And what was she so worried about?

Chapter Nine

FAN-FAN THE FRUIT BOAT MAN

Fan-Fan brought the boat to a gentle stop, cut the engine and let it drift quietly on the glassy water.

"Dere, Missah. Hereyah's Silken Lake. See? No currents and de fish plain fo' yo to see. If you wanna sea bath, dere ain't no danger. Look at dem Parrotfish and Angelfish! Yo have plenny to draw here!"

Penny took out her periscope and dipped it in the crystal clear water. It was fantastic! Fan-Fan was right, she'd have no problem drawing fish. The canvas awning, called 'Joseph's Technicolour Dreamcoat' because of its multi-coloured stripes, was a shady place to settle in and Penny pulled sketch book and camera from her beach bag. The boat rocked gently and a slight draught lifted the rainbow of coloured flags, pennants and streamers that Fan-Fan decorated his boat with. Even the sides were decorated with flower motifs painted in a medley of shades; red, green, blue, mauve, white and shining jet black. The boat gave the impression of a little turreted castle floating merrily in the water. *Everyone* recognised it as Fan-Fan the Fruit Man's boat and he did a good trade. There was shrewd business sense behind the many decorations which fluttered from the mast and almost covered the boat. Not only did they attract custom but kept the fruit cool, fresh and sheltered.

Gathered at dawn, the morning's fruit had been sold and Fan-Fan, like Penny, was having a break from work. Fan-Fan was an old friend and out on the sparkling ocean they were relaxed, chatting happily to each other, Fan-Fan lacing his conversation with picturesque dialect. Penny loved the lilting musical phrases and tried to memorise them. By the time they reached Silken Lake Penny's mind was a jumble of expressions and colloquialisms. It was exhilarating being out in Fan-Fan's boat. Helping with her mother's research was not exactly a bundle of fun. Convincing the authorities about the huge decrease in Giant Leatherback numbers was not easy. What they wanted were *facts* and it was essential to produce statistical evidence. Penny insisted on helping her mother so Gemma had asked her to sort out masses of very boring data. They worked indoors, windows tight shut, jalousies closed against the fierce heat. Air conditioning whirred, electric lights flickered whilst outside the sun glistened in a gleaming sky and the sea lapped softly onto the sand. The staff were under strict instructions not to disturb 'de Professor' but Gran brought them up a drink and snack from time to time. Even so, she knew better than to interrupt her daughter's intense concentration too frequently. Penny had imagined being a Professor was easy; achieving it was the difficult part. Yet her mother never stopped: 'phones rang; emails poured forth; requests for information; interviews; lecture notes; thick files were piled up on her desk. How did she find time to see any marine life for her research? Penny was astonished at the amount of hard slog Gemma had to do and until Penny and Gran had arrived she'd been struggling along on her own. So despite the monotony and tedium of carefully checking the long lists of facts and figures Gemma pushed over to her, a feeling of importance suffused Penny. For the first time since her father died she felt useful and needed.

But today Gemma had decided Penny needed a day off and had arranged a surprise trip with their friend, Fan-Fan. Silken Lake was a long way, further out in the ocean than Penny had been before. Gemma told her to take a sketch book.

"If you go back to school with your project book full of statistics and nothing else, they won't be too happy! You go out with Fan-Fan and enjoy yourself," smiled Gemma.

And Penny had been only too pleased to desert her mother and go. Silken Lake was a wonderful place and Fan-Fan proudly recounted how it had been named.

"Our Queen's sister, Her Royalty Princess Margaret, she name it. Many year ago, she honour dis island and come hereyah. Ma Daddy, he take her out to dis pool one day. She say she see nuthin like it afore. So beautiful and clearyah and smooth. She call it de 'Silken Lake' and dis name, he stick."

Although it was a long way from shore, well out in very deep water, it was a shallow, transparent pool only a mile or so in diameter stretched across an off-shore coral reef. The local fishermen knew precisely where it lay, but visitors only found it by accident. Fan-Fan had no navigational problems and, securing the boat, he lay back comfortably, shading his head with a decrepit straw hat. Carefully placing a spotlessly clean hankie, or 'rag' as he called it, over his face, it was soon rising and falling rhythmically as gentle snores emanated from behind it. Penny sat entranced in the bow, watching and drawing the fish as they emerged to view the boat and its quiet, non-threatening occupants. How inquisitive they were and the resemblance to certain humans was remarkable!

Some fish looked angry, like the Greater Amberjack, and she decorated him with a bristling moustache, small eyes and deeply cunning look. The Spadefish looked spectacularly miserable, so they received drooping whiskers. Next came the Porgies with their high-set eyes, making them look perpetually startled. Gleefully Penny added pencil thin arching eyebrows and embellished the porcine mouths with deep pouts. With a few swift strokes she turned the common Coney, that timid chameleon, into an aggressive predator.

"What'll yo Ma say when she see dis?"

Fan-Fan had quietly woken up and was chuckling over her sketches.

"I'll copy them without the additions for school, Fan-Fan. Anyhow, don't you think they look funny? See the Porgies? Don't they look like models?"

"Yo ketches them all too well Missah!" grinned Fan-Fan appreciatively, "but I doan see dem Parrotfish or Angelfishes."

"They shot off very quickly. I saw a beautiful deep blue fish but it just flashed past."

"Abou' how long?"

"Two feet?"

"Sounds like a Midnight Parrotfish. Yo'll have to learn scuba divin', Missah. Then yo see some real huge fish. De Blue Parrotfish, he four feet. De Tarpon, eight feet, but best of all, de Manta Ray. Dere wings are twenty-two feet wide!"

"Oh Fan-Fan! That's a fish I'd love to see! How old do you have to be to learn scuba diving?"

"Yo can see plenny Mantas near de surface if yo knows where to look. Up near ma village, Caithness Point, we see dem sailin' along in Pirates Bay. It veree quiet there and secret. No one knows how to get to the beach 'cept us." Fan-Fan chuckled conspiratorially.

Caithness Point? She'd heard that name before but it eluded her. What a wonderful place it sounded! Just the sort of remote bay she'd like to visit.

"Com'on Missah. I smell a squall a'commin. We best set sail."

The island people still 'set sail' even though it was the little motor that would take them to shore.

"Do you ever use the sail, Fan-Fan?"

"Sure do Missah. We like de sails. Quiet, better for de fish and marine life too. No fumes nor oil spillage. Is good to float along on de currents and winds. But now, listen. No wind, it veree still, veree placid."

"You said a storm was coming. Shouldn't there be a wind?"

"Not yet. Too soon. It gets gustin' later, very quick, just before she arrive," he smiled.

Phut-phutting gently back to the beach, Penny settled in the stern under the gaily-coloured awning and closed her eyes. As the boat surged softly forward a feeling of peace and tranquillity enfolded her. It was great to know Mum needed her and she had begun to realise why Gemma worked so hard. When David, her father, died, Penny had been young, deeply shocked, heartbroken and desolated. She hadn't been interested in what her mother was going through. Gemma was a grown-up, used to dealing with problems, that was what adults did. They coped with life when it became difficult, protecting their children from harm, leaving them free to grow and develop in security and peace. Now she was older, and beginning to understand how terrible it must have been for her mother. By filling her life with the work her husband would have been doing Gemma must feel a sense of continuity and satisfaction which helped her come to terms with her sad loss. Cocooned in the warm security of the boat Penny suddenly realised her mother's absence from home had nothing to do with her. It was the only way Gemma could keep going, trying to live without her husband. How stupid and selfish she'd been, reflected Penny. With this new understanding she'd ask Mum about Dad's death instead of hiding from it. They could have a proper grown-up discussion!

BUMP!

"Come on Missah, we just landed. No need to wait fer de wave. Is all quiet."

Fan-Fan was standing in shallow water holding out a strong hand to her. The hotel was to the left of them.

"Great! Thanks, Fan-Fan, that was a smashing trip. Can we go again?"

"Sure ting Missah, whenever yo Ma says, providin' de weather hold. Ah've me fruits to see to though, and ah'm jammin' mos' evenin' at de mas camp."

Penny knew enough Island dialect to understand this. It meant Fan-Fan was rehearsing most afternoons with his Carnival Steel Band.

"What do you play, Fan-Fan?"

"Ah beat pan, Missah. We're jammin' fer de Panorama now but we got a big problem. Our new man, he's trouble, ah'm tellin yo! A brabadap fo' sure!"

"What's that mean? A 'maybe dappy'?"

Fan-Fan chortled appreciatively.

"Well – yo is wrong but sounds good to me. A brabadap is a person wit' no manners. He ignore courtesy and good conduct and tink he mighty clever. Pah! Fool! If only he see 'imself in his tawdriness, he soon improve."

Fan-Fan drew a deep sigh, that of a man sorely tried with the burdens of the world on his shoulders. Penny grinned.

"If anyone can sort him out it'll be you. Perhaps you can sack him from the band?"

"He too good, Missah Penny. Dat's de problem. Dat's why he tink he can ignore de courtesies. Maybe he get fed up wit' all de jammin' we have to do in our free time. Or maybe he just grow up," added Fan-Fan, without much conviction.

"Good luck and thanks again, Fan-Fan. See you around," said Penny, and, taking the beach bag from him, she walked slowly up the beach. Turning to wave she caught her breath at the stunning sight. Fan-Fan was standing on the beach securing his boat to one of the palm trees. Overhead the sun gleamed in a diaphanous sky. Waves lapped diffidently onto the chiffon sand. Fan-Fan's flags and streamers drooped listlessly from the mast, a tangled, glowing spectrum of colour. A single magnificent Frigate bird spread its seven foot wings and glided in from nowhere, hoping to find a catch of fish. It was an enchanted moment. Penny knew it was an image she would carry with her throughout life. She turned away, reluctant to leave.

"I thought it was you. Where have you been?" came an aggressive voice.

Jimmy! Why was he always around when she didn't want him! And, as always, adorned in his orange life-jacket. Did he go to bed in it she wondered? Ignoring him, she continued trudging towards the hotel. Jimmy uneasily tagged along behind.

"Where have you been?" came the insistent voice.

"Silken Lake," replied Penny without turning.

"I've been there hundreds of times," he bragged.

"That's quick work!" riposted Penny. She trudged on. There was silence but for the scuffing of Jimmy's feet in the sand.

"It's hard for me. Pa won't let me go anywhere except this beach. He says I'm to stay put and if I don't he'll keep me in the hotel. You're the only other person my age. Can't we talk, at least *sometimes?*"

"But you do go out! You've just said you've been to Silken Lake hundreds of times," Penny shot out.

"Well, perhaps that's an exaggeration," he admitted awkwardly. "When I do go out it's in Pa's yacht. The crew are hand-picked by Pa so he knows they're safe."

"Why shouldn't they be? What does he think they're going to do?

Drown you in mid-ocean?"

This had a surprising effect on Jimmy. Shaking with suppressed emotion – was it anger or fear? – tears filled his eyes. This was very odd, was he about to have a fit or hysterics? Penny looked at him with interest.

"It's nothing to do with me. I can't help it. Anyhow, it's none of your concern."

Penny, remembering how he'd tried to stand up to his father in the restaurant, took pity on him.

"Anyhow, you *do* go out! It must be nice having a posh boat of your own."

"Yep, the crew are always available and I'm a good sailor," he added complacently.

Penny sighed. Whenever she tried to be kind he put his foot in it. Smirking smugly, he appeared blissfully unaware of dropping a clanger.

"Uh, huh! So Fan-Fan's boat would be a doddle for you to sail I suppose?" remarked Penny sarcastically.

"What's a 'doddle'?" Jimmy had never heard the expression.

"Easy, something that's very simple and easy to do."

"That's his boat isn't it? The little decorated one."

"Yes, I've just come off it. I suppose you think that beneath you, it being so small and ordinary, just the fruit man's!"

"Yep. You're right there. It's mighty small and mighty ordinary! Reckon I could sail that ok. No problem," he replied derisively.

"Why don't you then, as it's so easy?" Penny had had enough of his boasting. He wouldn't know how to sail a toy boat on the London Serpentine let alone Fan-Fan's outboard motor. He was far too scared! Jimmy paused, looking speculatively at the boat with an odd expression on his face, almost sadness. Seeing his hesitation Penny jumped in.

"Oh it's alright. Don't bother yourself. You wouldn't be able to steer it anyway." Turning, she marched off towards the hotel.

"STOP!"

It was Jimmy. Taking no notice she strode on.

"STOP!" yelled Jimmy again, stumbling through the soft sand

towards her.

"What do you want *now?*" snapped Penny.

"I'll do it! I WILL!" shouted Jimmy excitedly. "Come on, it's your idea and I'll need help."

"Don't be silly. I was teasing. You're such an insufferable swank."

"Uh, huh! Who's a wimp now then? *You're* the one who's a scaredy cat, not me! Your mother wouldn't let you go." He smirked at turning the tables.

"I am *not*! I've done things you've never done. My mother doesn't worry about where I am or what I do! Your precious pa does! Run along back to him, he'll be sending out a search party soon!"

Hands on hips, red in the face, they glared at each other, their feet sinking into the softly subsiding sand.

"I will! And I'll tell him he needn't worry about buying the beach. If your mother's a coward like you, he'll have no problem."

Penny's face changed from red to white. How *dare* he call her mother a coward! How *dare* he? Clenching her fist she took a step towards him.

"Sorry!" said Jimmy hastily, warding off the blow. "I shouldn't have said that about your ma. Sorry." Turning to go, Penny grabbed his arm.

"Oh no you don't. You're the one who's been swanking about being a brilliant sailor. Ok – prove it. We'll borrow Fan-Fan's boat and you can take me on a trip. Come on! I bet you can't handle it," she sneered.

Holding his arm firmly, Penny frogmarched him down the beach to Fan-Fan's boat.

"Ok. Ok. Let go my arm. I bet I can so! Where do you want to go?"

"Anywhere – Silken Lake. You know the way. You've been there hundreds of times. You won't drown, you've got your life-jacket on," snapped Penny. Still angry, she jumped into the boat leaving Jimmy to cast off. Let him get on with it if he was so clever. She didn't care. Swank. Boaster. Wimp. She'd teach him a lesson!

Surprisingly he cast off and started the boat up quickly and efficiently. Penny sat bolt upright gazing out to sea, her beach bag clasped primly in her hands. Much to her chagrin, they seemed to be going along quite well.

"Do you really know how to find Silken Lake?"

"I know the general direction. That's where I'm heading."

He was far less talkative, concentrating on steering and direction. So be it. The water was dead calm. There was no wind to throw them off course. They chugged along with the bay and village receding into the distance. Abruptly they disappeared and the boat with Jimmy and Penny was the only moving object on the limitless sea. Not even a Brown Booby, which fly further out to sea than the Pelicans and Frigate birds, was to be seen. Penny began to feel apprehensive. It was one thing being on the open sea in a little boat with an experienced mariner like Fan-Fan and another being with a boy her own age. She'd got angry and a bit carried away, but would have to grin and bear it now. Give him his due, Jimmy seemed to be making a reasonable fist at sailing the boat.

"Where did you learn to sail?"

"I've been brought up with boats. I'm used to them."

"Does your father have much time for sailing?"

"No, not now. He used to do a lot."

"Have you lots of different craft?"

"I used to have my own called 'Jimbo's Boat' but since…" Jimmy sighed. "Pa sold them. He bought the yacht especially for this holiday so I could go out on it."

Penny tried to imagine the sort of wealth that could buy a luxury yacht for a holiday! Yet Jimmy and his father always looked miserable. Mr Saxon's laugh was a hollow and artificial 'haw, haw, haw!' and she'd never heard Jimmy laugh.

"You must have pots of money but you don't look very happy with it," she commented curiously, glad Gran and Mum weren't there to tick her off for making 'personal remarks'. They were bad manners!

"Oh sure, Pa's loaded. But I don't agree with his ideas on money and happiness. He says it's because I'm young and don't understand. I 'spect he's right. He usually is." Jimmy looked more mournful than

113

ever.

"Do you know where we are?" asked Penny, hastily changing the subject.

"Er ... mmmh. Maybe. I think we're still heading in the right direction for Silken Lake. It's west-nor'-west, isn't it?"

"I don't know! It's no use asking me. *You're* the expert," replied Penny, her anger rekindled by a flash of fear. Honestly, he'd been sailing along *thinking* Silken Lake was west-north-west when it could be east-south-east for all he knew!

"Jimmy – do you *know* or do you *think* you know where the Lake is? Because if you don't we ought to turn round and head straight back before we really get lost. There's a very big ocean out there called the Atlantic," she added sarcastically.

"Look! There it is. The water's changing colour." Jimmy gave a small sigh of relief.

Sure enough the deep grey was lightening, becoming paler grey, then dark blue, then green. They were passing through shoaling water and soon the white coral sea floor could clearly be seen.

"There!" said Jimmy. "Told you I could do it and I have." He glanced jubilantly at Penny.

"Yes, you did well," she admitted, smiling wryly. "In fact *very* well. I was sure you were just boasting but you proved me wrong."

Jimmy was astonished. It was his first experience of someone admitting a mistake! In his experience people *never* admitted they'd been wrong. It was always someone else's fault. Most often a computer was blamed, so individuals never had to accept responsibility. But here was Penny smiling cheerfully as she apologised! His opinion of her rose.

"Well!" he managed to get out at last, "You sure shocked me there! Most folk wouldn't have admitted that. Thanks."

"Dad and Mum brought me up very strictly about being honest and truthful. Being dishonest is cowardice isn't it? You did handle the boat well so why not say so? We're here now. Let's go for a swim. Do you know what the Islanders call it? A sea bath."

"You're lucky, being able to go out and mix with everyone," Jimmy said enviously. "I s'pect you'll be speaking fluent Creole soon."

"Humph! Shouldn't think so. The Islanders invented their patois so the slave owners and masters couldn't understand what they were talking about. It's a mix of languages. Anyhow, come on!"

Adjusting her snorkel she leapt into the smooth, still water. "Wow! It's beautiful!" exclaimed Penny. "Look, it hardly reaches my neck. Take that life jacket off and come in." Jimmy hesitated, frowning.

"Oh, *come on!*" repeated Penny. Coming to a sudden decision, Jimmy threw off his life jacket and with a mighty yell dive-bombed into the shallow water. Splashing, walking on their hands, heads underwater, Jimmy began to enjoy himself.

"Look!" he shouted, "I'm a Dolphin!" and began plunging in and out of the water with what he hoped was Dolphin-like agility. Penny stood in the water and laughed.

"Poor old Dolphin if it can't do better than that! You'll soon drown, the amount of water you're swallowing!"

He came up spluttering and coughing, water pouring from his mouth. Penny could hear an odd sort of gurgling noise as well. He was laughing. For the first time, he was laughing!

"Here, borrow my snorkel. You'll get a terrific view of the fish and won't drown yourself in the process," she grinned. Watching the shoals of vividly coloured fish darting and flashing about in the water they didn't notice the straight, pencil-thin dark line on the horizon. Slowly it widened to fill the sky as it advanced menacingly towards Fan-Fan's boat, now gently rocked by an unseen force.

Chapter Ten

STORM AT SEA

After the sad leave-taking of Horace and rise of the fiery new Turtle Star, George, Godfrey, Montague and Archibald continued their journey westwards at top speed. Their streamlined bodies and magnificent nine-foot flippers flashed through the water making short work of the distance to the Spacious Sea Meeting Place. Here they would join their beautiful wives and latest batch of Survivors. The Patriarchs wondered if the previous year's laying and hatching had gone satisfactorily and how many Hatchlings had survived. They were so tiny and vulnerable to innumerable predators and accidents. Patriarchs were far too large and heavy to approach shallow water and kept a safe distance out to sea from the laying beaches. It was almost certain death for an adult male to be stranded on a shore. Being so weighty they couldn't move on dry land whereas the slighter females could just about drag themselves up the beach and back again. So it was the Matriarchs who gave news of how the laying and Terror Run had gone, how many Frigate Birds, Pelicans and callous 'Laughing' Gulls had swooped upon the miniature Turtles as they scurried towards the sea and swam frenziedly to the relative safety of deep water. Even there danger was always present. Tar balls, fishing hooks, speed boats, water skis and commonest of all killers, plastic bags and balloons, spelt certain death. Sharks and sea birds ate entire Hantles of Hatchlings as light snacks. A mere five out of every five thousand eggs laid by the brave females would return as Hatchlings and each year this low number decreased even further. The Patriarchs could only wait and hope.

"Look! Look ahead! Meeting Place ahoy!" bawled the irrepressible Monty. "I can see the Portal!"

"Let's have a breather before going in," suggested Godfrey, and the four giants surged towards the surface in a swash of effervescent sea.

116

"What still water!" exclaimed Monty, "Something smells odd though. A disturbance must be on the way," he murmured, sniffing the air like a BloodTurtle.

"Look there! It's a little boat. I hope the Humans know what they're doing," commented George anxiously. The Leatherbacks glanced towards Fan-Fan's tiny boat in the distance, which was cheerfully bobbing about on the quiet waves. Two miniscule Humans could be seen, their shrieks of laughter carrying clearly over the water.

"Everything looks ok," said Godfrey, who understood George's concern for Humans.

"Come on – time to dive," suggested Archie, whose mind was fixed on a gallon cask of Marine Poteen in the 'Archelon'. Down plunged the four, accelerating like Formula One cars as they skidded up to the huge Portal of the Meeting Place, barely avoiding a crash into the majestic pillars.

"OI!" came an indignant shout. "Oi, Oi! What do you think this is then? An 'atchlings' 'oliday playground?" admonished Cerberus, the Portal Steward. He strongly objected to his imposing Portal, with its decorated columns and stately statues of antediluvian Leatherbacks, being irreverently treated.

"'Ere, just get back and pull yourselves together. You can't go in there with the Matriarchs in that state. You've been out on the 'igh seas on your own for too long if you arsk me. Let's 'ave a bit of respect, *h'if* you please! You're in company now and best remember your manners. Orf you go and tidy up a bit."

Keeping the Portal firmly closed, Cerberus stationed himself in front of it, flippers folded. He presented an awesome sight. Of similar build and bulk to George, his gleaming well-oiled carapace was adorned longitudinally with seven magnificent frills, one on each of the keels that streamline Leatherback carapaces, helping them swim faster than any other Turtle. Two further frills formed bands around his huge front flippers. These 'frills' consisted of multicoloured sea anemones which, when touched, shot out tentacles. What appeared to be an innocent, even vain, decoration was in fact a dangerous weapon, for each tentacle contained a venomous sting. Cerberus saw to it that his 'guests' led a comfortable life and, when needed, they reacted instantly in defence of their Host and the Meeting Place.

George and company hastily withdrew, ashamed of themselves. They acknowledged the Portal Steward's primordial right to guard the Portal and ensure courteous behaviour by all who entered. They knew the Leatherback Code of Conduct, none better, yet despite this had behaved in a manner unworthy of their position. As Patriarchs and Members of the Moot they had serious responsibilities and not least of these was to give good example. Disappearing behind a dense clump of sea wrack they commenced a wash and brush-up session. That was the problem of being on your own nearly all the time. Foraging two- to three-thousand feet down in the mysterious oceanic abyss where no light shines, the social niceties were forgotten. You saw no one and no one saw you! But now there were wives to see, female relatives to meet, Nematts to impress and Hatchlings to astound, for this was the first time the Hatchlings would meet their fathers and other truly gigantic Leatherbacks. The selfishness caused by being solitary must give way to consideration and thoughtfulness for others.

"Here, Godfrey, you're good at this. Have a look and see if we're up to flunter will you? We'll go to the Barber's Shop as soon as we're in and fix a proper clean-up."

Godfrey extracted a pince-nez from his plastron pocket, adjusted it carefully and solemnly inspected George, Archie and Monty.

"Mmmh … you do look a bit worse for wear. Hardly surprising under the circumstances. Rescuing Archie was not conducive to pristine carapaces. Rough-looking carapaces and tatty about the flippers. Your guests could do with a brush-down too. Stop flapping about! Fold your flippers in and I'll give you a light dusting."

Godfrey neatly severed a seaweed covered in stiff, bristly hairs and whisked this over his friends' carapaces.

"Here!" came a muffled squeak, "if you're going to put us back in the sea we want due notice. Don't just give us a mighty thwack with your flipper and send us flying," tweeted a tiny Trochus, its shell gleaming with refracted light.

"*Oh!* Sorry dear fellow. I didn't mean to give you such a swipe, but

118

you know how powerful our flippers are," apologised Godfrey.

"Yes, they do us proud, that's why we'd rather stay put," cheeped an exquisite Mother of Pearl shell. "Thousands of my relatives end up as necklaces and buttons, but as long as I'm on George's back I'm safe. Please can I stay, George?" the iridescent, delicate little mollusc pleaded anxiously.

"Gently does it, Godfrey, careful with the little chaps and chapesses. I'm encouraging Trochii onto my back. I want them along my seven keels in rows like other Chief Patriarchs …"

"And Cerberus!" croaked a hermit crab.

"… So I offer them protection. Humans may want them dead but I want them alive and well cared for. Look how beautiful they are and every single one unique!"

At this compliment the Trochii blushed with pleasure and lit up their favourite colour. Blue, indigo, lilac, pink and green suffused their translucent shells until the area surrounding the Turtles was illuminated by a scintillating spectrum of shining incandescence.

"*Ahhh!*" gasped the Turtles, "the Reef of Righteousness must look like this!"

George looked on complacently.

"See? How many other molluscs are iridescent?"

"So you'll be keeping them?" enquired Monty ironically.

"Come along," interposed Godfrey, "it's time we were in the Meeting Place. You'll do, but we must get to the Barber Shop A.S.A.P. Let's approach the Portal with a bit more dignity this time."

"Yes, our rowdy, dishevelled appearance upset old Cerberus. I don't think he recognised us. Let's have some civilised behaviour."

The four reappeared from behind the sea wrack and with masterful precision swam in slow, well modulated breast stroke towards the Portal. In majestic pairs, heads well up, large mobile mouths set in authoritative lines, they presented a very different aspect from their original reckless dashing approach. George's magnificent bulk led with Godfrey, bespectacled and scholarly, beside him.

"*Ahhh!* Good morning to you Sirs," greeted Cerberus, affable and courteous now. "My apologies for not allowing you entry, but there are *rules* which apply to *everyone*," he said firmly.

There was a meaningful pause. Unbending slightly Cerberus continued, "But perhaps you had been avoiding a Serious Threat Sirs, and had to swim for it?"

"Good morning, Cerberus," replied George and the party. "It is we who must apologise for our unseemly behaviour. We have indeed been swimming at all speed away from a scene of great danger and disaster. We're *very* glad to be here." George stopped, gathering himself together.

"We have sad news. Horace, our friend, is dead, gone to the Reef of Righteous Turtles …"

Cerberus groaned in horror. "Oh no! How did it happen? Not them shrimp fishers again?"

"No, a long-line fishing net. You know how enormous they are, ninety miles some of them. We don't stand a chance."

"But I thought them clever Humans had put 'Turtle Escape Devices' in the nets so we can get out?"

George and the other Leatherbacks snorted derisively.

"*If only*! *Some* long-line fishing fleets have them but many don't. If only those 'clever' Humans made sure *every* fishing fleet had them it would help us survive. But they don't. Cost too much and what value is a Leatherback Turtle? Our friends the Dolphins and smaller Whales get caught too. We're called 'by-catch' and left to die. Horace died but at least we managed to save Archie."

Cerberus shook his head in sorrow and anger.

"Another gorn Sir! Our numbers get lower every year. Do you think that's what the Humans *want?* To make us extinct?" He glanced around furtively as if some Human Demon was listening. "They've got rid of lots of our prehistoric friends. We're the only creatures still living who existed in the Jurassic time," he hissed nervously.

"There are some good Humans trying to protect us, I know that. They've left it very late, but we've got to keep calm and optimistic, Cerberus, because if we don't the females will be upset and won't lay. Then Leatherbacks will *definitely* become extinct. So come on, present a cheery face for the Matriarchs. Have our wives arrived yet?"

Like Stewards and Porters throughout the world Cerberus knew everything, which was not to say he repeated everything. Within the Leatherback Clan he enjoyed a good gossip but outside the Clan an amiable wave and civil time of day would do. Cerberus was highly discreet.

"Indeed Sir, I'll soon regain my composure," he replied, unfolding an enormous seaweed hankie and wiping away copious tears. "Your wives have arrived and are in the Beauty Parlour," he confided. "Matriarch Laetitia went looking for you and Miss Isabella is in the Damselfish Café waiting for her to return. They're all safe."

Glancing at the Turtles' noxious carapaces he added, "Pardon me Sirs, I think you ought to book into the Barber's Shop before the rush. There's the Metanoia and Scrimmage Fortnight to be thinking of as well as the Marriages and Egg Laying Vigil. There'll be a terrific rush by the young males wanting to look their best for the females, bless 'em! Ah! We were all young once Sirs!"

George, Godfrey, Monty and Archie nodded solemnly in agreement with this portentous statement. With good relations established on both sides the massive gates swung open. In stately manner George thanked Cerberus and led the others through the Portal and into the Great Hall. Home at last!

But before Cerberus had time to close the Portal there was an immense flurry of activity and another group of Giants swooshed through the gate with reckless speed. Tired, unshaven, trailing strands of seaweed mixed with the debris of broken coral, their guests clinging on to their carapaces for dear life, they signalled to Cerberus to close the Portal quickly and collapsed onto a Mountainous Star Coral.

"What's going on?" demanded George. "Why are you looking so scruffy and exhausted?"

Shaking out his flippers a superb jet-black Leatherback, equal in size and girth to George, replied.

"Are we glad to be here! We didn't think we'd make it! Something strange is going on. A huge wave seems to be building out to sea over Bermuda way."

"Afraid of a wave! Come off it, Simba, Leatherbacks take those in a flip!"

"Underwater volcanic activity you mean?" suggested Godfrey, which could kill by heat.

"No, not volcanic. There were none of the signs. We could sense a huge force nearby. It felt evil. We put a spurt on! You would have thought we were in the Scrimmage Games."

"But what *sort* of force? Can't you tell us anything else?" queried Cerberus, who'd been listening carefully.

"We didn't stay. It was too overpowering."

George and the other Leatherbacks looked puzzled. What 'force' would upset these mature Turtles? Simba and his friends were over twelve feet in length with enormous strength and power. Their strong flippers propelled them through water at scorching speeds. Their carapaces were virtually impregnable; they could dive deeper than any other Turtle and were unafraid of most sea creatures. True, their friend 'Bluey', the colossal Blue Whale, was bigger, a hundred feet long, but he was a placid, beautiful vegetarian who wouldn't knowingly harm anyone. Great White Sharks were the enemy.

"Did this 'force' follow you here?" asked Monty.

"No, it's causing a storm out at sea some distance away. There'll be high seas round here. Anyone for the 'Archelon'?" suggested Simba, ready to forget his fright and down a few gallons of Marine Poteen.

Archie's eyes lit up as he took his first mighty stroke towards the pub, but George gasped and smote him heavily on the flipper.

"Those Humans in the little boat! Simba, did you see any Human boats about?"

"Yes, in that bit where it's too shallow for us."

"Will the sea rise there?" asked George anxiously.

"Yes. But they'll be alright. Humans don't care about us so I'm not going to care about them," said Simba dismissively.

"*Some* Humans *do* care!" shouted George after his retreating barrel shape. "Anyone willing to come up with me and make sure the

Humans are ok?" he called.

Archie, his narrow escape from Human long-line fishing nets fresh in his mind, shook his head.

"No way! They killed Horace and nearly had me too. No more mixing with Human boats for me! I'm for the 'Archelon' with Simba," and without more ado a large party set off for the pub.

"Monty, Godfrey, what about you? It was only a very small boat, not a factory ship. We should be ok. It's not right to leave anyone in danger, even Humans." George had never forgotten his terrible experience in Cornwall.

Godfrey looked thoughtful.

"Unless we are attacked, all creatures should be cared for – except jellyfish, the rats of the sea. They're in no danger of extinction, and we're meant to eat them or they'd take over the seas. I suppose *some* Humans are good?" He looked questioningly at George.

"They can be, Godfrey, good and helpful. You know one of them died saving my life. If I can save a Human life that repays a debt I owe."

"Yes, good point. Ok, George, I'm with you."

"If you feel it's right, I'm game too," added Monty. He wasn't up to philosophy like Godfrey but honourable behaviour was very important to him.

The three rose to the surface and looked about. Simba had been right. The calm, glistening sea of a short time ago had changed into a boiling cauldron of wild waves. In the distance the tiny boat could be seen rocking about dangerously on the rising waves, the sea much higher than before. Whatever the evil 'force' was, it could certainly cause a disturbance! Setting off in the direction of the boat they saw two small figures frantically baling out.

"Look!" exclaimed Monty, "those Human Hatchlings are in trouble."

"Children, Monty. They're called children," advised George.

"They're not very good on water ergonomics," he added in a shocked voice. "I suppose that comes from living on that horrible dry land, they're not born and bred to be efficient in water like us."

"Poor little things," tutted Godfrey, "they're getting in a terrible mess."

"Monty, you go to stern, Godfrey, you take bow and I'll go amidships. We'll position ourselves under the boat and hold it steady using our carapaces as a platform above the water. It's no weight at all. Use steady state, flipper in ten."

Soon the boat was evenly balanced between the three.

"And five, four, three, two, one … and there," called George, as they adapted their flipper rate to a slow, even pull which counteracted the riotous sea.

* * *

Penny and Jimmy had been caught unawares by the abruptly-changed conditions. Sudden storms occurred but they'd been enjoying themselves and not noticed the warning signs. Within seconds the boat had begun bouncing about like a rubber ball on concrete. Penny scrambled hastily aboard.

"Jimmy! What are we to do? Can we get back to shore?"

"Nope," he replied laconically. "It'll be safest to sit it out. The nearer the shore, the worst the turbulence."

"Sit it out?" gasped Penny. "We'll be overturned at any second! Look at those waves out there. They're heading straight this way!"

"Calm down. It's no use panicking," said Jimmy putting on his life jacket with astonishing calmness. "Here's your life-jacket. Put it on and tie it to this lifeline. If you get washed overboard at least you're secured."

Penny did as she was told, wondering at his new quiet competence. If Americans could be so calm in an emergency, so could Brits!

"There," she remarked casually, "all done. Give me that bucket and I'll bail out."

Jimmy looked at her admiringly. These Brits! You had to hand it to them. Just take a look at that! Kneeling in the stern bailing out, cool as a cucumber.

"Now we wait until the storm blows itself out?" queried Penny, trying hard to sound nonchalant.

"Yep. That's what my pa says is best."

Chucking pailfuls of water out of the boat they waited. Penny tried humming a little jig and Jimmy tried whistling but his mouth was too dry.

"You need to wet your whistle! Here's a drop of water," grinned Penny, mischievously offering him the pail.

"Can't get it going somehows. Don't you know – *never* drink seawater?" he admonished sharply.

Penny looked at him. Of course she knew about the dangers of drinking seawater. It had been a joke. Where was his sense of humour, or was he as terrified as she was? The boat jerked and rose in the water.

"AHHHHHH!" screamed Penny.

"HOLD TIGHT! Don't let go!" yelled Jimmy.

With a roar the tiny boat descended, drenching them in spray.

"It's ok," shouted Jimmy. "It'll bounce. Keep tight hold."

Penny could see another wave approaching. She would *not* scream this time. She would be the epitome of British 'phlegm'. To her it sounded like something very nasty but both Gran and Mum set great store by it. "Coolness under adversity" was how Gran defined it and it was apparently a preserve of the British. She would show proper 'British phlegm' despite being terrified. The wave was upon them. Abandoning British phlegm she hurled herself onto the floor of the boat, wrapping her arms around an iron stanchion. She felt a lot safer down there. Jimmy too had flattened himself on the floor. Up, *up, up* went the boat, then down with a roaring rush. Penny and Jimmy slid across the deck together. It was like sliding along a brillo pad as tiny splinters of wood floor pierced their skin. But for the lifelines and lying flat they would have been washed overboard. Spray smashed down on their scantily-clad bodies like hailstones. Penny was frightened, cold, hungry and bruised but determined not to cry. She'd be able to tell Mum and Gran she'd been phlegmatic and they'd be so proud! But – would she ever see them again? The little boat was lifted high in another surge. Eyes tight shut, shivering with cold and fear they braced themselves for the bone-jolting rollercoaster descent.

Chapter Eleven

GEORGE IS VINDICATED

Nothing happened. The crashing vortex of water didn't come. They waited, crouched low, eyes still closed. The boat remained quietly poised, rocking very slightly.

"Jimmy," whispered Penny, "what's happened? Why are we still? Has the storm passed?"

"I don't know," he whispered back, "I've got my eyes shut."

"One of us should take a peep," suggested Penny.

"Yep," agreed Jimmy helpfully.

They remained where they were. The boat stayed quiet, hardly moving, although they could hear the sea lashing about them.

"JIMMY!"

"Yep?"

"Open your eyes and see what's going on!" demanded Penny.

Girls, thought Jimmy. Weren't they supposed to be equal these days? Cautiously opening an eye he peered carefully about.

Nothing had changed. Waves thundered around, yet the boat remained almost unmoved, bobbing cheerfully as it had been before the storm. And there was something else strange too, thought Jimmy. What was it?

"Jimmy! Can you see anything?"

"Open your eyes and tell me what *you* see," answered Jimmy.

In her guise as a woman of unflinching British phlegm, Penny reluctantly raised her head, bumping it in the process, and quickly opened her eyes.

"OUCH! What's going on? The boat's not moving! The storm's in full swing but we're sitting here calm and quiet. Are we grounded?"

Holding tight to the sides of the boat they carefully rose to their knees and peered over the side. There was silence.

Sinking back into the boat they looked at each other in disbelief. At one accord they heaved themselves up and looked over the side again. Blinking like disturbed owls they stared, dumbfounded, at one another. Penny reflectively rubbed her head where she'd bumped it.

"Did you see errrm … anything?" asked Jimmy in a wobbly voice.

"What did you see?" replied Penny, still massaging her head.

"Rocks?" he suggested.

"I wouldn't like to say. I think I've got concussion," Penny craftily avoided the question.

Jimmy looked over the side again, this time staying there for some time.

"Penny," he began in a determined tone, "there are three Giant Leatherback Turtles down there and they're supporting the boat. Come on, look again," he demanded in awe.

Balanced on her forearms, Penny stuck her head over the side and gazed, gaping, into the water.

"I'm right, aren't I?"

There was no reply. Seeing the Leatherbacks brought back a searing flash of memory to Penny. As clear as yesterday she recalled the Cornish Leatherback, 'George' she'd called him. She remembered every detail of him: his immense size; majestic flippers; expressive face; his long curly mouth which seemed to be always smiling happily. She'd thrown water over him and talked to him and he'd laughed, or made a sort of wheezing chuckle anyhow – and killed her father. Here were another three huge amiable-looking Turtles, their faces wreathed in smiles, their wonderful flippers paddling rhythmically in strict unison to maintain the boat on an even keel. But the one directly beneath her in the middle of the boat had something else, something she recognised. Across his leathery carapace ran a number of deep, jagged scars. Through her binoculars on that dreadful day in Cornwall she'd seen George slash himself badly as he turned back through Razor Rocks to kill her father. *He* was the killer Turtle! Yet here he was saving her life!

"Can you see them?" rejoiced Jimmy. "Aren't they *great*? Aren't they *bootiful*? I bet you've never seen anything like this before. Why are they holding us up? Is it accidental or – *Wow!* Do you think they *know* what they're doing?"

Penny didn't hear. She was hanging perilously over the side talking to George.

"I know you," she muttered. "It was *my* father you killed out by Razor Rocks. You turned so fast you gashed yourself on the sharp rocks. I can see part of the scars across your back. They're the same shape as the rocks. Why did you kill him, you horrible thing! He'd *saved* you! I *hate* you!" Penny's voice shook with anger and sorrow. She was no longer the epitome of British phlegm. She was a fatherless girl.

Jimmy's elated voice cut across her sad thoughts. "Are you talking to the Turtles?" he asked, amused and interested. "What are you saying?"

"Look, Jimmy. See those deep, strange-looking scars on this Turtle's back. I know how he got those, by killing my father!"

Jimmy gasped.

"*Nooo!* No way. That can't be. Turtles don't kill human beings. They're as gentle as their cousins, land tortoises. They eat jellyfish and plankton. They can't bite; they haven't got any teeth, only eating spines."

He was horrified at her suggestion.

"How did he die? C'mon, give. I don't believe a Leatherback killed him!"

Safely cradled in the gently rocking platform of the Turtles' carapaces, they'd forgotten the storm.

"This Leatherback, I called him George, was stranded on our beach in Cornwall. My dad organised a rescue party and got him out to sea again. He swam with him, escorting George to the safety of deep water. George was through Razor Rocks when he suddenly turned round, gashing himself on the rocks. The next thing water was flying everywhere, as if a terrific fight was going on. Then George was holding Dad up on his flipper, like a … like a *trophy!* He was dead," sobbed Penny.

Jimmy sighed, shaking his head. None of it made sense.

"Why did the Leatherback turn round? They don't behave like that. They strike out to deep water A.S.A.P. They don't turn round and go back to danger. There must be a reason."

"*Yes*! To kill my dad! I keep telling you!"

"So why are they helping us now? We're Humans, they know we're in danger and they're *saving* our lives." Jimmy paused. He'd an idea.

"Perhaps your father was in danger. You couldn't see it but someone in the water could. Perhaps George was trying to *help* him?"

George had been listening to this with great sadness and wished so hard he could speak Human language. He wanted to tell Jimmy he was right. That the deadly Portuguese Man-of-War jellyfish had attacked and bitten the Human and George had turned round to defend him. After killing the giant jellyfish George had seen Penny's father sinking into the water. He knew Humans needed air, so held him up on his flipper, above the water. Then some large and very angry men had chased him away. It had been terrible and he'd felt bad about it ever since. Now here he was saving the daughter of that Human! If *only* the Human child could know the truth.

Penny looked mutinous. She didn't know the answers and didn't like admitting she may be wrong. Her beloved father was dead, that was all that mattered. Yet – *could* there have been an unseen danger out by Razor Rocks? Her father had always told her not to swim there, but apart from the rocks what other dangers lurked? Strong currents, deep water, these wouldn't have bothered her father. Anyhow, no cuts had been found on his body, only long, peculiar whip-like bruises resembling scorch marks had covered his back, chest and shoulders.

"Your ma can't agree with you." Jimmy's comment cut across her thoughts. "She wouldn't have specialised in the conservation of Leatherbacks if she thought they'd killed her husband. Does she ever talk about your pa's death?"

"No … She spends a lot of her time out here doing research and leaves me in England. We don't see much of each other – and *that's* all down to Leatherbacks too!" Penny stopped, remembering a conversation she'd had with her mother. "She did tell me that Dad had strange bruising on his body. She said it was typical of being stung by a ... oh, I can't remember ... a 'War' jellyfish! Jellyfish sting but don't kill. Not in England anyway. Mum said this type was usually found in the tropics, so what was it doing in Cornwall? Sounds daft."

George was agog. So the Lady Matriarch *did* know what had happened and had tried to tell her Hatchling! But she hadn't believed her – like most Hatchlings! And the Matriarch was a specialist in Leatherbacks and tried to protect them! How glad he was to be saving her Hatchling's life! If only he could speak to them! A thought occurred to him. Humans not only spoke, they used signals. He'd seen it many times, especially underwater. They nodded their heads, sideways for 'No' and up and down for 'Yes'. He could try nodding at these Hatchlings!

"A Man-of-War jellyfish!" exclaimed Jimmy triumphantly. "Their stings kill. They and other sea creatures move around a lot following food. Wherever there are sardine shoals or plankton blooms they'll be around. Sometimes they're swept along by strong sea currents, like the North Atlantic Drift, or storms take them to places where they'd never normally be. Perhaps it had been caught in a storm and got stuck in your bay. After all, if a Giant Leatherback had got into it, so could an exotic jellyfish," reasoned Jimmy. "He'd be feeling real mean and bitten anything. Can you remember – had there been a storm?"

In the water, George nodded enthusiastic agreement. *YES, YES,* he wanted to shout, that's what *did* happen. He, George, had been following a massive jellyfish bloom. Huge, luscious and juicy, they'd all been caught up in the storm and tumbled through the Rocks into the horrible little cove. Come on, pleaded George silently, *Look* at me, see me nodding up and down! Yes! Yes! But no one did.

Penny looked thoughtful. She didn't want to think about that awful day. It was the first time she'd talked about it to anyone, but seeing George had released her pent-up anger.

"I *do* remember a terrific storm," she responded slowly. "We couldn't go out all day. Then we went down to the beach and found George. He'd been washed up, lying on the shore stranded with a whole load of other rubbish. Being so huge and heavy he couldn't drag himself to the water."

"So – what other rubbish was there? Any jellyfish?"

In her mind Penny saw again the debris-strewn beach and the nasty, strange-looking jellyfish she'd carefully avoided.

"Jimmy! There *were* a lot of big, horrible slimy-looking jellyfish! Yuck!"

The boat jumped up and down a few times.

"Is that the storm again? No, the Turtles are still steadying us. Yes, there were plenty of jellyfish, not ones I'd seen before."

"Well – there you go. Your ma's probably right. Your pa was stung by the Man-of-War."

"Maybe you're right," admitted Penny in a low voice. A quiet voice inside her said how nice it would be to love Leatherbacks again, as she had George. And he was right there, under the boat. And she couldn't ask him. Leaning precipitously over the side, secure in the knowledge that the Leatherbacks held them safe, she spoke to George.

George was on the look-out for an opportunity like this. It was his chance to put things straight and he was determined to take advantage of it.

"You *are* George, aren't you?" began Penny, and stopped, shocked, for George had given her a slow, solemn and very definite nod. Sliding back into the boat she whispered, "Jimmy! I think this Turtle, George, understands what I'm saying!"

Jimmy looked at her in alarm. Perhaps that knock on the head had affected her.

"You feeling ok, Penny?" he asked solicitously.

"Yes, course I am! Come over here. See for yourself."

Placing his knees carefully on the bench, he too hung over the side. George alertly greeted him with an enormous grin and cheerful nod of the head, as clear as anything saying 'Hello!' Jimmy nearly took a header into the sea with shock. Penny chuckled.

"Ok. Go on then. Talk to him," challenged Jimmy.

"Ahem!" began Penny. Was there a special mode of address she should use?

"Er, George," she said, as inspiration came to her. "If you understand me, please nod," she asked politely.

George nodded.

"*There*! What did I say? He *knows* what we're saying! Don't you?" she asked George.

Once again he nodded carefully, his large mouth upturned in a great smile of joy and relief.

"WOWEEE! This beats everything!" exulted Jimmy. "Now you can find out what really happened to your pa."

"How will I know if it's true?" asked Penny in a low voice.

"Ask him questions and see if his answers are the same as your ma's."

"Good idea!" Leaning over the boat again she asked, "Did you kill my dad?"

The boat rocked violently as George shook his head energetically from side to side.

"No! Who did?"

"That's no good, Pen, he can't *talk*, only nod. You've got to stick to yes/no questions."

Penny thought for a minute.

"Did a jellyfish kill him?"

George nodded vigorously.

"There!" whooped Jimmy. "Told you so!"

"Was it a big, nasty slimy one with great long tentacles?"

This puzzled George. All jellyfish were tasty food, not at all nasty or slimy. He paused, trying to think like a Human.

"He doesn't know after all," said Penny sadly.

"Leatherbacks *eat* jellyfish and think they're good food, not nasty. You've got to ask him a different way."

"Was it a big, tempting, juicy jellyfish?" Penny asked tentatively.

George nodded eagerly, a large grin spreading over his face.

"You love jellyfish, don't you?" queried Jimmy.

Again a huge nod and grin.

"There! We've got to remember we're talking to a Giant Leatherback Turtle, not a human being. He sees things differently to us."

"Let's get more info out of him!" said Penny. "Did this lovely big jellyfish sting my dad?"

George nodded, the wide grin vanishing.

"Was he badly stung?"

Sadly, George nodded again.

"Did you come back through Razor Rocks to rescue him?"

George gave a sigh of relief. *At last*, after all these years, the truth would be known. He nodded his head until it nearly fell off.

"You killed the jellyfish but it was too late?"

Another sad nod.

"Why did you hold him on your flipper? It looked as if you'd killed him!"

George wondered how he could explain about needing air. Of course! Breathing in deeply, he slowly expelled the air. Taking another exaggerated breath he repeated the pantomime.

"What's he *doing?*" asked Jimmy.

"I know!" exclaimed Penny, pleased with herself. "He's trying to show us Dad needed *air*, he needed to breathe. George held him up so he could *breathe!* I'm right, aren't I George?"

George nodded so enthusiastically the boat started to rock. From his station at the bow Godfrey called, "I say, George, easy does it. They'll be in the sea if you're not careful."

George was too happy to care. *Almost* too happy to care. They knew the *truth*, that was what mattered. He wanted to take a quick skim across the Atlantic and back, break the Deep Sea Dive Record, do Dolphin impressions, win the Conch Shell Chariot Race, tell Laetitia – *Laetitia*!

What with saving the children and the joy and relief of putting the record straight about the Human who'd died to save him, George had forgotten about Laetitia waiting for him. They couldn't leave yet. The storm was abating but not over. All must be safe before they left. As a Matriarch, Laetitia would understand, especially when he told her who they'd been saving!

The little Humans weren't worried now. Gazing with rapt attention and awe at George, the girl was drawing him.

"I'm going to show this to my mother." She showed George her sketch. "She'll recognise your scars because they're the same shape as Razor Rocks, jagged, like teeth. Pity I can't see more of your carapace."

George nodded, overwhelmed with happiness. Very cautiously, he edged a bit more carapace out from under the boat so Penny could sketch more accurately.

"George!" Monty called from the stern. "How much longer should we stay? Our wives will be getting anxious."

"Not long now, Monty. We think these waves are tiddlers but these Human Hatchlings ..."

"Children, George, Human *children!*" Monty butted in with a mischievous grin.

"... Can't cope with them," continued George. "I'll send one down to keep you company. If they talk to you, nod or shake your head. It's great fun!"

By jerking his head left and right George indicated that Jimmy and Penny should go and meet his friends. Delighted they cautiously moved off, Jimmy to the stern to meet Monty and Penny to the bow to meet Godfrey. Sensing some special effort was required, they both bowed gravely to the two wide-eyed Giants. Godfrey and Monty responded gleefully. What a day! What a story to tell in the 'Archelon'! How their Hatchlings would lap it up, 'The day Pa talked to Humans'!

Chapter Twelve

LAETITIA GOES VISITING

Letty pushed aside the Black Laminaria curtain and burst into the Beauty Parlour.

"Madam Laetitia! You've just missed Miss Isabella! She left this note for you." The Reception Wrasse swished the note over to Letty. 'Back soon,' read Letty. Great Sea Snakes! Were they never going to meet?

"Would Madam like to begin her treatment? The Sapphire Team are free now," asked the Reception Wrasse in a soothing tone.

"Yes – and if Isabella returns, bring her to me, please."

"Certainly Madam. This way."

Soon Letty was supine on a smooth, low bed carved from sparkling mica with the efficient Sapphire Team of Cleaner Wrasse massaging Solanaceae Anti-Ageing Oil onto her carapace with gentle wafts of their fins.

"A touch more round my eyes please. They're dry after all that time in salt water."

She closed her large, almond-shaped eyes with a sigh of pleasure. Immediately an image of the sinister cave sprang to mind. Had it always been there, undiscovered and undisturbed, or was it a more recent feature caused by earth movements? Did anyone else know of it? Perhaps, after all, it would be wiser to consult with George or the Zamorin before taking action. But no, they were far too large to explore such a narrow chasm and she'd feel a right fool if the 'heavy breathing' turned out to be air currents reverberating round an empty cave! No, she'd stick to her original plan of finding out more herself. She'd see her friend, 'Z' the Armourer, and pick up a Trident, perhaps a Plastron Shield and Helmet too. Letty suddenly remembered the bottleneck shape of the tunnel. It had been a tight squeeze in and out, how would she cope encumbered with weaponry? Shuddering, Letty thought of the slow, backward progress out of the cave.

The Chief Beautician, or Pivotal, stopped rubbing oil into Letty's flippers and gasped. Peering through half-moon glasses she commented, "You ought to take more care, Madam. You make very long round the world journeys and your flippers aren't in good condition. You must have been in cold water very recently. The oil content is low and they are below temperature," she sniffed disapprovingly. "Miss Peacock! More Special Lignum Vitae Flipper Restorative please."

Letty grinned – clever old Pivotal! She never missed a trick! Miss Peacock reappeared, staggering under the weight of a large cornucopia of Lignum Vitae. Giggling, she whispered to the Pivotal, who took the urn and waved her aside. Pouring more oil over Letty's flipper she confided, "Miss Isabella's here. You can retire to the Damselfish Café shortly. That will give the oil time to soak in. Miss Isabella's waiting there."

Isabella! Of course! In a flash Letty knew the answer to her problem. Slightly built, agile and intelligent, she would be just the person to help Letty reconnoitre. If she held the weapons, Letty could get through the funnel without them and put them on when the tunnel opened out! Isabella could wait for her there.

The Pivotal wafted a final layer of oil onto Letty's flippers and carapace. Miss Peacock was delegated to escort her to the café, where the young Wrasse comfortably ensconced her on a large sofa cushioned with the bubbly green seaweed, Vesiculosis. Isabella swooshed over from the Zoanthus coral table she'd been sitting at.

"Matriarch Laetitia – am I glad to see you!"

"Isabella dear, I'm pleased to see you too!"

"I've got loads I want to ask you about," began Bella in a rush, ending in a sob.

Letty smiled comfortingly but not too broadly in case her Solanaceae Anti-Ageing Mask cracked.

"Shush, there, there. Calm down, Bella, one thing at a time."

"Oh Matriarch," sobbed Bella, "Cerberus told me that Patriarch Horace, my father, has been killed. He was caught by a long-line fishing net as 'By-catch'."

136

Letty sighed deeply.

"Come here, dear." Bella was enfolded by Letty's huge flippers, and, resting her head on Letty's substantial shoulder, wept. Some things were far more important than Anti-Ageing Masks, thought Letty.

"Cerberus said Patriarch George and the others saw his Turtle Star rise, so he's in the Reef of Righteous Turtles ok," stammered Bella. "But oh, Matriarch, no one's seen my mother, Cassandra, either. Simba says there's been a strange disturbance at sea. Perhaps she's been caught in that? And that big white Turtle, Azazel, is following me everywhere and I don't know what to do. It's so sad about Pa but Cerberus said he died happy eating a huge jellyfish, but where's Ma and how can I get rid of Azazel?"

Bella paused, large, pear-drop tears coursing down her beak. Holding on to one of Letty's massive flippers, she settled herself on the sandy floor beside the sofa and howled loudly.

"Bella, when Patriarch George appears he can take you to see Patriarch Horace's Star in the Celestial Luminescence. You can make your formal farewell. Perhaps Zozimus would like to escort you," added Letty guilelessly. "As regards your ma, Turtles are arriving all the time. Many natural forces could have slowed her down. That must wait until later. Now, I want you to join me in a little adventure. You'll be perfectly safe from Azazel because you'll be with me. What do you say?"

Bella mopped her eyes and brightened up a fraction. Being with Laetitia could mean being with Zozimus! It sounded promising. "Yes, I'll help," she responded enthusiastically. "What's it about?"

Letty told her of the eerie cavern, its coldness and sense of danger and evil, and how she wanted to return with armour and find out more.

"I've never seen or heard of it before and I listen to everything. You never know when a snippet of information may be useful in these dangerous times."

It sounded exciting to Bella. She'd be with Laetitia; there was no chance of real danger.

"What do you want me to do?" she asked.

"I need someone small and supple who can twist and turn easily. You're ideal."

"But Madam, I've no experience of Trident hurling and flipper to flipper combat! I'm still a Nematt!"

"I'll do any fighting – but it won't be necessary. This is an exercise in observation. We need to know if anything unusual is happening so near the Spacious Sea. It could be just the echo of waves or a peculiar rock structure. It *could* be some threat. But whatever it is, we must *know*. Leatherbacks must be protected and the Spacious Sea kept safe."

Reclining on her luxury sofa, flippers and carapace covered in expensive oil, Letty made an odd warrior. Yet never before had Isabella seen her so fiercely determined and proud of her Giant Leatherback ancestry and traditions. Suddenly Isabella understood how much the Turtles relied on the courage and tenacity of Letty and the other Matriarchs. They were the ones who surmounted numerous dangers to go up onto dry land and lay the eggs essential for the preservation of the species. Using their instincts and experience they shielded the young Turtles as much as possible and passed on their vast knowledge. And Isabella shared the same unique history and distinguished ancestry as Letty. She too was a direct descendent of the first Marine Turtle, the Archelon, who lived with Dinosaurs. There were barely any creatures alive now who could claim that lineage!

Isabella's anxiety faded away. Squaring her carapace and shaking out her flippers, she looked purposeful.

"*Yes!* We must find out. It'll be an honour to accompany you, Matriarch. Tell me what to do and I'll do my best to do it."

Letty grinned. "That's the spirit! Up and at 'em," she approved. "My ma was 180 when she went to Great Mother Turtle. There weren't so many dangers about then so they lived long lives. She always used to say, 'Never swim around complaining about things. There's always something you can *do*.' She was right. We'll try to find out more about this mysterious cave and if we can't do it we'll call in others."

They smiled cheerfully at one another, co-conspirators.

"Matriarch Laetitia, you're done!" warbled Miss Peacock. "I've come to collect you."

"Wait for me here," hissed Letty, "Don't go *anywhere*! Have a nice mug of Mippsy Juice. It's very good for you."

Mippsy Juice – yuck! Isabella remembered it all too well. A mixture of phyto-plankton syrup, high in nutrients and sea of stillness water. The grey, gluey drink was supposed to be good for females. It tasted of 'Velella, Velella', a jellyfish eaten by plankton and had a disgusting flavour. No thanks, she'd go into this adventure on a jeroboam of chocolate flavoured coconut juice, mmhh!

Just as she was finishing the delicious jeroboam, Laetitia hastened into the café. Her rich mahogany carapace gleamed lustrously, each streamlined keel shining like jet. Her beak was polished, her large eyes clear and wise with no trace of salt. The powerful flippers glistened, each segment flashing and twinkling and smelling strongly of Parfum d'Apocynaceae a la Nerium Oleander, a much sought-after essence.

"Wow! Matriarch, you look terrific!" enthused Isabella. If she looked like that at Letty's age she'd be very pleased!

Letty bowed in acknowledgement of the compliment.

"Thank you dear. Did you enjoy the strengthening Mippsy Juice? Good!" Letty hurried on, much to Isabella's relief.

"Come along. We mustn't waste any more time. Let's butterfly to 'Z' and she can kit us out."

Moving swiftly through the Beauty Parlour, where Letty was showered with compliments, into the Great Hall, they butterflied speedily towards 'Z's' Headquarters.

"Won't she tell others we've been?" asked Isabella.

"She doesn't tell anyone, except the Zamorin if he asks. And she only deals with authorised Zacans."

Bella thought of Letty as a Matriarch, the mother of Hatchlings, Nematts – and Zozimus. She never thought of her as a Zacan, a doughty and experienced fighter, expert in methods of defence and, if necessary, attack. It was known that she defended her Hatchlings from Sharks and predatory birds. And wasn't her name on the Trident Marks'Turtle Trophy as well as the Chelonian Cup? Speeding along in Letty's wake, Bella thought what a very talented Turtle she was, even if she was getting on a bit now.

"Madam Laetitia! Please – could I have a rest? I need air too."

"Dear me, yes, of course. I'd forgotten how small your lungs are compared to mine, and your capillary vascularisation system is still incomplete. We'll both pop up. There's a breathing exit just ahead."

They shot upwards, poked their beaks out of the water, barely breaking the surface, took a few deep breaths and shot down again. Letty was off again like a Tuna fish, making Bella look like a slow-moving Grouper. Within the vast Meeting Place Bella would have lost her bearings, but Letty led the way without hesitation. They rose into shallow water and dropped into Deeps, dodged and darted round extinct volcanoes, passed 'smokers' and kelp forests until at last they stopped before an enormous plume of Black Coral.

"Wait here," commanded Letty, "until I've given the secret code."

She floated silently behind the Black Coral and Bella heard her knocking confidently on something solid. As she tapped there was a strange echo. It seemed altogether different to Letty's code. This is a clever system, thought Bella. It was similar to the Turtles' emergency Chelonian Auditory Wavelength, used only in the most extreme circumstances. She waited quietly, staring at the coral's fantastic weblike design as it moved slightly in the current. Suddenly she became aware of a beady green eye watching her. It glared through the intricate coral curtain, neither blinking nor moving. Bella jumped backwards, breathing quickly. About to call Letty, she stopped. She wasn't being threatened, no one was attacking her, let them stare. Moving towards the appraising eye, she held her ground, returning the stare in a calm, dignified manner.

"Good!" came a brisk, authoritative voice. "She's got some courage. Let her in."

The entire magnificent fan of plumes moved slowly aside revealing itself as a door. Inside, Letty and a smaller Leatherback with a flipper missing, were smiling at her.

"Bella, meet my old friend, 'Z' the Armourer. We were at Turtle Academy together."

Bella showed 'Z' the greatest deference she could by giving a low flipper curtsy. She was a very revered Turtle who rarely emerged from this well camouflaged cave. Bella knew she was highly honoured and kept respectfully silent, although she was bursting with curiosity.

"I expect you're wondering about my missing flipper," said 'Z' unexpectedly. "Marine Turtles rarely live with only one flipper, yet here I am, alive and well."

Yes, thought a startled Bella, that's exactly what I was thinking. Like air to Humans, the Giant Leatherback imperative was to swim great distances. This could only be achieved with two working flippers. Losing one was usually fatal. The loss of blood could kill but in Leatherbacks the loss of mobility also killed. 'Z' smiled, nodding her head at Bella's reaction.

"It's a story of great unselfishness and courage," began 'Z'.

"On a night with a beautiful full moon, I went up our beach to lay. Laetitia and other Matriarchs were there too. We heaved ourselves onto that dreadful dry land, onto the sand above tidal range and started the Laying Ritual. It's very exhausting my dear, and you need to drink plenty of Mippsy Juice to give you strength. I was in the Laying Trance when I realised that Human poachers were about. The trouble is, once you're in the Trance, nothing will stop you laying. Whilst I was still laying, they cut my flipper off. Humans like Turtle Soup you know. I would have bled to death, but Laetitia saw what had happened and came to my rescue. She bound the wound with sea wrack lying on the beach, dragged me back to the sea and helped me home. If I'd been as heavy as most Leatherbacks, she'd never have managed it. But she was determined and resourceful and got me back to the Spacious Sea. Dr Aesculapius treated me and wrapped his Salubrious Sea Wrack Plaster around my wound. I can't swim very fast but I can make myself useful in other ways and I do. As I'm in the Meeting Place nearly all the year, I've time to invent weaponry.

"With our natural size, speed and impregnable carapace, Leatherbacks rarely need additional weapons, but sometimes they do. Then I'm here, ready with my inventions. And it's all due to Letty," she concluded, turning to her. "Thank you again, m'dear. I owe everything to you."

Strange, thought Bella, before hearing 'Z's story, she'd been thinking along the same lines!

"Madam 'Z' – thank you for telling me that inspiring story! ... Do you get lonely here?"

141

'Z' chuckled.

"I've more visitors than you'd expect! Not for weapons, for conversation and gossip. I enjoy all the news. As my friends swim in from faraway seas they call in with ingredients for my special Manatee Grass Wine and a chat."

Bella looked hopeful at the mention of this exotic wine, but neither Matriarch took the slightest notice.

"Now, Letty, what's this about? What're you up to?"

"I need a sturdy Trident, 'Z'. Your reinforced 'Elkhorn Bespoke' would do nicely. A plastron shield, no, better make that two, and two helmets as well. That's all."

"What is this? Some early practise for the Scrimmage Games?"

Letty placed a large flipper over her wide mouth.

"Shush! Tell you later," she replied.

"If you won't tell me what's going on, I won't authorise the weaponry," replied 'Z' sternly.

The two determined Matriarchs looked at one another.

"Oh – alright then," said Letty. "I heard funny noises in a cave. We're going to investigate them. Ok?"

'Z' stared at her. There was a lot more to this than met the eye. Letty didn't usually requisition armour for an exploratory tour of the Meeting Place.

"Where is this cave?"

"Near Manatee Reserve there's a slip fault like a bottleneck. It's marked by a big Basket Sponge I put there earlier on. After a narrow funnel, it widens out. We'll manage to squeeze through but mature males like George would never make it. That's where we're going. It's to listen and spy out the sea, that's all." Letty grinned reassuringly, "Nothing dangerous at all but I'm not taking any risks."

"Humph! Take care. Return your armour within an hour – any longer and I'll inform the Zamorin."

"Two hours," snapped Letty. "It'll take an hour to make the return journey."

Before 'Z' could argue any more, Letty had whisked out of the cave taking Bella and the armour with her. 'Z' shook her head resignedly. Letty! If it hadn't been for the same courage and determination she was showing, she, 'Z', wouldn't be here.

Glancing at the Armorial Clock beside the camouflaged door, she carefully noted the time. Two hours from now.

Bella had never moved so fast in her life.

"Madam," she puffed, "can we slow down? My flippers are only half the size of yours. I can't keep up."

Letty stopped. In her anxiety she'd forgotten Bella was still a Nematt.

"Sorry, but please swim as fast as you can. In two hours 'Z' will inform the Zamorin. She'll stick to her word."

"Yes, I'm doing my best," gasped Bella. This was a serious challenge and she must try to deserve Letty's trust. They swam briskly on. At Manatee Reserve Letty slowed.

"There's the Basket Sponge," she pointed out, adding, "Bella, you don't have to come with me. You can leave if you want to." Letty waited silently. Bella drew a deep breath.

"Matriarch Laetitia, I'm proud you asked me. It's for the good of all the Leatherbacks and I want to help you. But you'll have to tell me what to do."

Letty embraced her affectionately. She must keep her safe.

"Here, put this plastron shield and helmet on." Bella struggled into the strange protective garments. Letty adjusted the helmet and stood back, viewing the effect.

"If your mother, Cassandra, could see you now, she wouldn't recognise you!" she laughed.

Donning the plastron shield, she gave her helmet to Bella.

"Hold on tight to that until I ask for it," instructed Letty.

"Right, follow me, do *exactly* what I say and *keep quiet!* Watch out for obsidian daggers. Further in, the temperature will drop. Our counter-current circulation will balance that. Listen and look. If you want me to stop, tug the Trident."

Tucking the long Trident firmly under a flipper, Letty edged her way cautiously into the narrow opening. Bella followed, the helmet in her flipper.

Darkness. Silence.

Leatherbacks were accustomed to both and swam slowly onwards.

Obsidian daggers gleamed menacingly and Bella stretched out a flipper and touched the Trident. Letty stopped at once, turning her head.

"Ok?" she whispered.

"Yes, just checking," breathed Bella. They moved on and the tunnel began to open out.

"AAARRRGGGGHHHHH!"

A long drawn-out rumble reverberated around the cave.

"LE … TTY!" stammered Bella, too frightened to remember her manners or keep quiet.

"QUIET! Be quiet!" ordered Letty peremptorily. "Listen!" she hissed. "Where is that noise coming from?"

Bella tried to focus on the dreadful noise.

"PPPHHHEEUUUGGGHH!"

The cave shook with the force of a mighty draught. Gripping the end of the Trident to stop herself screaming, Bella concentrated.

"We must move further in," murmured Letty. "Look, it's widening out and there's a faint light ahead. Come on."

Letty surged silently forward, Bella following more slowly. Louder and more insistent the raucous rumble was repeated.

"Where from?" queried Letty.

"East-nor'-east and below us," whispered Bella.

"Yes, that's what I think too. We'll have to move right down the cave if we're to see."

Bella didn't want to see anything very much, especially what might be in the inner regions of the cave. She longed for the safety and merry hum of the Great Hall. But – she mustn't let Letty and the Leatherbacks down. Letty glided softly forward, her head moving from side to side, aware and alert to any danger. Bella followed stealthily.

"AAARRRGGGGHHHH!"

They stopped, frozen. The ghastly sound surrounded them but nothing could be seen. Letty took her helmet from Bella, put it on and adjusted the Trident ready for hurling. It was time for action.

Chapter Thirteen

THE MYSTERY MONSTER

The passage widened, they could see more light. There must be a blowhole, thought Letty. Now their way was obstructed by a sloping wall of dense black basalt, which extended left and right as far as they could see. It was the outer ridge of an immense crater formed by an extinct submarine volcano which had collapsed in on itself – a caldera. There would be a huge depression inside the caldera, a perfect refuge for anything sinister. To see inside they would have to scale the steep slope and look over. There was no way Letty could manage it, being far too big and cumbersome – but Bella wasn't …

"Do you know what that ridge is, Bella?" she asked.

"Yes," replied Bella. "It's part of a caldera. The collapsed cone of a volcano. We learned about them in Basic Geology at Turtle Academy."

"Well … do you think you could scuttle up there and peep over? Nothing more, just a cautious look? We need to know what's in the crater, if anything. The noise is probably just a trick of the waves swashing about."

Bella swallowed and, forgetting Letty couldn't see through her helmet, tried smiling bravely.

"PPPHHEEUUGGGHHHH!"

The colossal exhalation created minor tsunamis, bouncing Letty and Bella onto their carapaces.

"Er – maybe not waves then," murmured Letty as the Turtles righted themselves. But Bella had vanished. Taking advantage of the wave's surge she was halfway up the ridge.

"Bella – LOOK OUT!" shouted Letty unguardedly, as she saw the wave break and begin to pound back down the ridge. Bella knew what to do. Ducking under the wave she disappeared.

"Good girl!" sighed Letty in relief. If Bella continued to utilise water so cleverly to advance up the slope, it shouldn't take long. 'Z' would be counting the minutes, of that Letty was sure. Looking up she spied Bella perched on top of the ridge, hanging on precariously with her flippers. The smooth basalt didn't provide a purchase and Bella was struggling to get a firm grip with the crampons on the plastron shield. Her helmet went flying into the tumultuous water and she instantly reacted by tucking her head well in. Another wave threatened to wash her over into the crater itself, but she hung grimly on. Then the hooks in her plastron shield caught and gripped the shiny surface like claws. She was secure. The water quietened. Bella seized her chance. Extending her neck she peered over the edge and stared down into the massive basin-shaped abyss.

Surrounded on all sides by smooth slopes of black basalt, the crater's surface was broken by small volcanic cones dotted around. Little puffs and gasps of smoke emerged from these as the ancient, extinct volcano still continued spewing out hot lava and noxious gases from the depths of the earth. Cracks and fissures shot out columns of steam. The foetid, nauseous atmosphere was ghastly. To the right a glimmer of light penetrated the murky gloom where a wide tunnel had been eroded through a weakness in the rock. Bella pressed further forward. The remains of many wrecks – ships, boats, even planes – littered the pit. There was a fuselage with 'A A' on it in large letters and a smashed wing with a big red leaf drawn on it. Among the rotting wood and rusting ironwork, ships' names were visible; 'Persephone – Ber ...', 'Calypso 2 – Be ...', 'Jimbo's Boat – Berm ...' Bella shuddered. Never had she seen so many wrecks in one area. They were usually scattered widely over the vast sea bed, thousands of miles apart. Why were they all here in this gruesome cavern? Something must be responsible for these doom-laden relics and she didn't want to find out what it was! She'd seen enough of this terrifying place. Time to return to Letty.

Moving to turn round, Bella paused. What were those vaguely familiar objects piled up in a mound at the side of the pit? She'd take a closer look. Carefully easing her body over the ridge's edge, she leaned forward, looking in puzzlement at the strange, discarded heap of rubbish. What was it? Why did it look familiar? Furrowing her beak, she edged nearer. NO! ... NOOOO! ... It couldn't be! Blinded with horror, she stumbled against a rock, dislodging it. With an echoing roar it crashed into the crater. Bella barely noticed. Choking, gasping for breath, she blinked, clearing her eyes and bravely refocused on the gruesome mound. Don't scream, don't scream, she commanded herself, stuffing a flipper into her mouth.

Recognition of the grisly sight had suddenly dawned and she cowered back, frozen with horror. Smashed, crushed, sliced through by gargantuan teeth, the heap was barely recognisable as Leatherback carapaces. Bella sobbed, sickened at such a diabolical sight. Some very large and beautifully coloured carapaces hung on the sides of the pit like trophies. A particularly radiant one, of gleaming amber with twinkling keels like diamond necklaces, was whole and untouched. It had the place of honour, high on its own rock. A fearful awareness coursed through Bella. Tears rolled down her beak. This was no longer an adventure or a challenge. This was a nightmare, far worse than anything she'd had to face. She *must* get back and tell Letty and the Zamorin. Wiping away her tears with a shaking flipper, she looked again. The carapace was that of her mother, Cassandra.

"AAARRRGGGGGHHHHHH!"

Bella jumped out of her carapace with fright and ducked swiftly behind two solid volcanic pyroclasts. That petrifying sound! The Thing, whatever it was, must have been alerted by the tumbling rocks. Something big and very, very evil was down there in the abyss. Should she try to catch a glimpse in order to tell Letty and the Moot? Such terrible murderous danger so near the Spacious Sea must be eliminated. The Sea *must* be safe for Giant Leatherbacks. Bella didn't want to stay a second longer. Terrified and sickened at the ghoulish sights and scenes she had witnessed, she wanted to reach the reassuring bulk of Letty and the security of the Meeting Place. She must get out – *fast!* A stealthy slithering sound came from the pit. Wedging herself more securely behind the rock pyroclasts, she kept completely still. Nothing could be seen. Nothing happened. If the Thing went past she could lever herself over the caldera's rim and make a dash for Letty. With infinite slowness

147

she shifted position for a better view into the caldera. An enormous, grotesquely elongated and narrow head was emerging from behind a bubbling, viscous cone. Fearsome, sharply pointed fangs, huge, uneven and overlapping, the better to crunch and tear with, lined the massive jaws, which must be at least nine feet long, thought Bella in revulsion. Stifling a scream and strong urge to flee, Bella shrank back into the crevice formed by the rocks. What on sea was it? With its long thin head swaying cumbersomely from side to side it resembled a snake. She'd never seen anything like this in her school text books, and there were some very ancient, strange creatures in them! Curiosity overcame fear. Clinging onto the rocks, with flippers fully extended, Bella peered out. She could see huge globular green eyes set well back and very wide apart on the long snake-like head. Unusually round for a marine creature, the eyes appeared to stare straight ahead. Bella knew differently. Eyes like these, set on either side of a creature's head, meant its lateral vision would be incredible. Its soft, slow, serpentine movement continued. To her horror a massive pair of flippers came into sight. She didn't want this ghastly, creepy, macabre creature to be related to Marine Turtles. Yet, however far back in geological time, possessing flippers indicated that it *was* related! A wide, solid body glided by, much longer than even the biggest Leatherback, with a second set of gigantic flippers and a long powerful tail that effortlessly swished the wreckage to one side. It used its flippers in a strange way, the front ones going upwards while the back flippers went down. It looked uncoordinated and clumsy to Bella, whose flippers worked in unison so that she 'flew' through water. This creature's movement was similar to Whales or Dolphins, who didn't have flippers. It must be at least seventy-five feet long, reckoned Bella, the biggest creature she'd ever seen, apart from the Turtles' gigantic, beautiful and peace-loving friend, Bluey, the harmless and gentle Blue Whale.

It stopped. Bella shrank further into the rocky pyroclasts. How strong was its sense of smell? Would the sulphurous fumes from the volcanic cones mask her scent? Its nostrils were in a strange place, on the top of its head. A good thing Letty wasn't here covered in her pungent perfume!

"AAAAHHHHH-HHHAAAAA! Not ship nor sail nor plane but another silly little Leatherback. Not much of a snack but you'll do for starters, like the others. I can smell you! Your fear, your horror, your revulsion. HHHAAA-HHHHAAAA-HHHHHAAAAA! Let's play a game. You hide and I'll seek."

The monster turned its massive long snout in Bella's direction and sniffed. So that's what nostrils on the top of the head mean, she sighed. A strong sense of smell! What an idiot she'd been. Curiosity had got her into this fix, how was she going to get out now? Hemmed in by rocks with no space to manoeuvre her bulky body in, she was trapped. The grotesque, bulging eyes were watching her. Could she retreat backwards over the edge? Flicking her short, stubby tail left and right, it encountered only rock. She'd slid too far over the rim. Moving towards those voracious nine-foot jaws and dagger-shaped fangs was the only way she could go. Opening her mouth to scream for Letty, Bella closed it again. *Think!* She told herself. You've already made one drastic mistake, don't make any more. The monster knew she was there and would kill her. All her discoveries would be wasted. Letty would try to find her and be killed. Nothing would be gained. She must make it look as if she was exploring on her own. Thank goodness her protective helmet had been washed away! Surreptitiously she set about removing her plastron shield and hid it behind the rocks. If only she could tell Letty what she'd seen! Cassandra and the other Turtles must be avenged, but how? Think! *Think*, she commanded herself. Putting her horror and grief aside, she concentrated.

The C.A.W.! The Chelonian Auditory Wavelength, the Mayday code used only in the direst emergencies. That was it! It was taught at Turtle Academy but so rarely used it was often forgotten. Could she remember enough to alert Letty? She *must!* And quickly! The monster was directly below, its massive head swaying towards her hiding place, not quite reaching. Come on Bella – *do it!* Gathering every bit of courage she possessed, she retreated as far back into the pyroclastic crevice as she could. The monster's head suddenly jabbed viciously upwards towards her, dislodging an avalanche of rocks as it did so. With a snort of irritation it backed off, shaking the scree and debris from its head and blinking volcanic dust from its huge, spherical eyes. *Now!* While the monster was distracted. Get on the C.A.W.!

Turning her head sideways to increase Letty's chances of hearing, Bella began vibrating the eating spines in her throat at tremendous speed. The result was a high-pitched screeching which she interspersed with twanging noises. This was the 'DON'T RESPOND' warning. Good! That sounded ok. She struggled on. Now for the coded message. Still using the backward pointing eating filaments in her mouth and throat, she began. Warning of immediate and mortal peril, Bella emphasised that Letty was *not*, repeat *not*, to take action. It would be useless and she was pretending to be on her own. The apparently panicky screeching continued as Bella briefly described the pit and its horrific contents. Then she described its devilish occupant and her own situation. Forgetting bits of the code, Bella pressed bravely on. Clever and experienced Letty would sort it out.

"Warn Zamorin and Moot *immediately* – also Humans if possible."

She was finished. The monster had stopped shaking its head and was glaring up at her.

"Tell Zozimus I'd like to be his wife, but he must find another," she hastily added with a sob.

Whatever fate awaited her, the Leatherbacks had been warned.

She would join her parents in the Reef of Righteous Turtles with a clear conscience. She'd done her best. Glancing down, she saw the horrible eyes focused menacingly on her. With a frustrated snarl of cruelty it swerved its immense body, reaching out a gigantic flipper covered in putrefying green slime. It smelt and looked like rotting jellyfish. The stink of mouldering ships, the monster's rancid breath and the decomposing Leatherback carapaces filled Bella with hate and loathing. At last she screamed and screamed. Abruptly, the faint glimmer of light from the tunnel went out and the cave was left in inky blackness.

Chapter Fourteen

TROUBLE AT TURTLE BEACH

The tumultuous sea had calmed. Gently refloated and sent safely on their way by the Leatherbacks, an elated Penny and Jimmy sat silently in the boat, reliving their astounding experience and thinking over what they had seen and learned. Penny was in a reverie. Her mother was right. George had done no harm. He had tried to save her father, but horror and distress had confused everything. From the Cornish beach his actions had been distorted and misinterpreted. What a tale to tell Mum! Penny glanced at the sketches she'd done, clutched protectively to her chest. They were a reasonable likeness of George and she'd drawn his scars very carefully. They looked like the jagged edges of Razor Rocks. Mum would be bound to recognise them. But would she believe such a strange and wonderful story?

It was *unbelievable*! Jimmy was trying to concentrate on steering the boat safely back home but was lost in a dream. He'd *seen* Giant Leatherback Turtles! He'd *talked* to them! He'd done a school project on Leatherbacks when he was ten and ever since had been fanatical about these superb creatures. They were the most ancient Turtle, with ancestors going back to the Jurassic period of Dinosaurs! There had been a *massive* one called 'Archelon' at that time and, despite being smaller now, Leatherbacks still held the title 'Godzillas of the Turtle World' with good reason. No other Turtle was as large, could dive as deep or swim faster or further. Why – Leatherbacks had been recorded feeding 3,100 miles from their nesting grounds! They were built for speed with streamlined well-oiled carapaces and keels enabling them to track swiftly through water. The powerful front flippers projected them along without the slowing effect of claws, Leatherbacks being the only Turtles without them. They were gentle, harmless, eating only plankton and jellyfish, and with their huge, upturned mouths

151

appeared to be constantly smiling. Jimmy knew they were on the point of extinction. His school project four years ago had been for Conservation Studies and their numbers had been very low. Since then their extermination had continued at a faster pace. It was the most serious source of disagreement between his father and himself. If Pa would give up his idea of developing the Turtle Beach, Jimmy could put up with being constantly supervised and guarded and kept 'safe.'

But Pa's project was a *calamity!* If only he could *see* a Leatherback he might change his attitude. Jimmy's mind was full of plans to ensure his father saw the Turtles coming up the beach, and yep! sure, the best way would be to give him a good description of how they'd saved Pen and him from danger and take Pa out in the boat. With any luck he'd see the Turtles in their own environment – he'd *never* build on their beach then, Jimmy was confident. Explaining this plan to Penny she agreed energetically. They'd have to confess to taking Fan-Fan's boat and going off on their own. Oh boy – there'd be big, *big* trouble! They'd have to face it.

To the pensive pair it seemed no time at all before the boat was in the shallows, sand grating beneath the keel. About to jump out and secure it, Jimmy heard a loud shout and looked up.

"Dere dey be! Prof. Heffernan, Mr Saxon sir, down hereyah. All is safe!"

Jolted out of their thoughts and plans the children saw Fan-Fan, Jomo, Livingston, Tyrone, Merlyn, a large group of holidaymakers and … their parents and Granny Fairweather running helter-skelter down the beach towards them.

"Take a deep breath!" said Penny quietly, trying to force a smile.

Jimmy jumped out of the boat, which was drawn up the beach by Fan-Fan and willing helpers.

"Where yo bin in ma boat?" demanded Fan-Fan crossly. "Crapaud smoke yo pipe! Yo Ma and Pa dey blame me fo' yo takin' ma boat! Yo pair o' frizzle-fowl! Yo …" but before he could really get launched Andy Saxon took over.

"JAMES!" he began in a voice of thunder, his face puce with rage.

"How *DARE* you disobey my orders and go jaunting off on your own! You borrowed Fan-Fan's boat without his permission, he says ..."

"That's true, Pa," Jimmy put in quietly. He wasn't going to let Fan-Fan get into trouble.

"Don't interrupt me son! You disobeyed orders to stay near the hotel. You *stole* a boat and took it out with this ... girl. We'd been told an unexpected storm was taking place out at sea. The hotel staff, visitors, police, even a helicopter have been searching for you. That's the end of your holiday, Jimbo! No chance of seeing your precious Turtles now. You're for home. Go and pack."

"But Pa ..."

"AT ONCE, do you hear? Go and pack!"

Mr Saxon was shaking with anger. There was no way he was going to listen to stories about Leatherbacks, reflected Jimmy.

"I'm ashamed of you, Penny!" Now it was Gemma's turn. "What were you thinking of, taking Fan-Fan's boat and going out without telling us? What a stupid, irresponsible thing to do! We've been worried out of our minds. I thought you had more sense."

Gemma was practically sobbing with wrath and relief in equal proportions. Compared to Mr Saxon's outburst Gemma's was mild, but the realisation of the terrifying anxiety she'd caused hit Penny for the first time.

"Mum! Gran! It was stupid, we shouldn't have taken the boat without asking Fan-Fan first and we're very sorry, we really are. But we've had a terrific time..."

"How selfish is that! Only thinking of yourselves and how *you* had a 'terrific time'! What about all the people who were anxious for your safety? Actions have consequences and *you* have to take responsibility for *your* decisions! What if you'd drowned? What if Fan-Fan's boat had been damaged? It's his livelihood, remember. What if you'd got lost? What ..."

"My son knows how to navigate a boat, Ma'am!" Mr Saxon butted in quickly. "He may be foolish and disobedient but he's a reliable sailor."

Jimmy was trailing disconsolately down the beach to his hotel.

Penny smiled wryly. Pity he couldn't hear his dad defending his sailing skills!

It was useless talking to either parent. Best to go quietly and wait until they had simmered down. Now that Fan-Fan had his boat back safe and sound, he was beginning to feel sorry for the pair.

"Look Ma'am," he spoke in a conciliatory manner, "Look at ma boat. See? Everytink safe. No holes nor gaps nor scratch. Dey must've bin mos' careful sailors."

"Good. At least that's one less worry. I'm so sorry for my daughter's stupidity, Fan-Fan. She didn't *intend* any harm I'm sure."

"Pickneys will be pickneys, Ma'am! She only young. She larn." Penny couldn't stand being spoken about as if she wasn't there.

"I *am* sorry Fan-Fan," she reiterated, "Jimmy and I were dar … playing a … game. We, er, we wanted to go sailing and your boat was handy. We didn't think…"

"No, you didn't think," snapped Gemma. "After this terrifying escapade, let's hope you'll learn consideration for others. Come on, back to the hotel. I want to know exactly what happened. Good afternoon Mr Saxon," Gemma added frostily.

"Would yo like some tea brought Ma'am? Is too hot day for de horrors," said Merlyn placatingly.

Granny Fairweather replied quickly, "Yes please Merlyn. That would be a good idea after all the anxiety and chasing round. I expect Penny would like a double freshly squeezed orange."

Gran belonged to the generation that believed implicitly in the restorative qualities of a cup of tea. It cheered, refreshed and calmed under any circumstances and she relied on its magical properties now. Merlyn and Livingston set a brisk pace back to the hotel, the visitors dispersed, Fan-Fan jumped into his boat to collect some fruit and Jomo and his friends ambled away talking animatedly. What a story for the village! Gran, Gemma and Penny returned in miserable silence to their rooms, Penny holding tight to the precious sketches.

Three showers were turned on and the women stood under them, pondering the situation. Gran was upset because Penny had lacked respect for another's property and not shown any common sense.

Going out in a frail boat with a young lad! It was a miracle they'd both returned safe and sound. She should never have touched Fan-Fan's boat, let alone gone sailing in it! If only the child had asked permission and had someone, Fan-Fan or Jomo, with them! She could then regard the escapade in a more tolerant light. Adventures had been acceptable when she was young and taught many valuable lessons. Children weren't allowed to do *anything* nowadays: no camping in proper bivvies with cows trying to eat through the guylines; none of the strange shrieking, hooting, rustling sounds of the rural night; no campfires in case they got out of hand. When she was eleven she was taught by an adult how to correctly set and light a fire in the open with complete safety. Surely young people today weren't so different inside? Were they really as lacking in common sense and as stupid as all the painfully puerile 'child guidelines' suggested? Exploration, adventure, fun, these Gran understood very well. But *not* 'borrowing' other people's property, nor venturing into the Atlantic Ocean with only a young boy for company! It was not like Penny, she was a sensible girl, well aware of the dangers at sea. I bet they were daring one another, thought Gran, with a flash of insight born of much experience. Yes, that would be it. They would have dared one another to sail the boat and wouldn't have been able to wriggle out of it without looking cowardly. She'd find out.

Gemma was sobbing with relief. For what seemed like an eternity she thought Penny must have drowned. After leaving Fan-Fan, no one had seen her or knew where she was. Then that ghastly man Saxon had turned up in a tizz looking for his son, Jimmy.

Putting two and two together they decided the children had gone off exploring. At Mr Saxon's insistence Mr MacRobert, the Hotel Manager, had asked for volunteers from his staff and visitors to form a search party. Gemma thought he was making a fuss about nothing and it was not until Fan-Fan came careering down the beach shouting his boat had been stolen that she began to worry. They'd gone out in the boat together! Out into the limitless Atlantic in what amounted to little more than a raft! A Police helicopter had been sent out and the search intensified. It had been a nightmare, second only to her husband's death. Now here she was, thank God, safe and sound, sunburned and hungry, clutching some sheets of paper. A wave of interest rose – what were they? Penny had tried to show her but she'd been too angry. She'd have a look over tea.

Carefully placing her sketches on the bed, Penny washed all the sand and salt from her hair and body. Mmmh, that felt better, although the bath looked like a sandy beach! About to put on an old tee shirt, she threw it aside in favour of a light blue funky style dress, cool and pretty. Gran and Mum liked her in dresses. Wow! Her hair was a mass of curls, was it the salt? It didn't matter how much she combed, it bounced back like a boomerang! Mum had hair like that too, it must be – what was the word? Genetic! Pleased with herself, she rummaged round and found the pale blue cross-over sandals that matched the dress and viewed herself in the long mirror. You look a bit like Anne of Green Gables she muttered at her reflection. Now came the tricky bit. Gran and Mum would want every single detail of the boat trip and were quick to notice any gaps in a story. How could she play down the storm's ferocity yet still bring in the Leatherbacks? Have tea first, she planned, then I'll show them my sketches. Mum will be so interested she *may* forget about the storm.

Penny sighed – Gran wouldn't, nothing would distract her! Gathering them up, she went through into the sitting room. It was cool and shady. Merlyn had drawn the curtains against the brilliant light, switched on the ceiling fan and left the usual scrumptious tea: home made cherry jam and scones, nutty banana bread, little almond cakes and … brilliant! Crab back and toast, which Merlyn must have done especially for her, knowing how hungry she'd be. The smell was delicious, tempting Penny to tuck in at once but no – that would be *the end* to begin eating before Gran and Mum arrived. A swig of orange juice would be ok though. But Gran and Mum soon came in from their respective showers.

"You may begin, Penny," said Gemma, pouring out tea for Gran and herself.

"Do you want any crab back?" Penny asked politely.

"No, help yourself. You must be starving." Gran sounded quite reasonable. Penny tucked in to the delicious dish with relish. Food was always much tastier when you were *really* hungry! Gran and Mum drank their tea slowly, nibbling nutty bread. The quiet dimness was refreshing after the blinding sun, panic-stricken searching, shouting and yelling on the beach. Penny worked her way through the crab back, two scones, a piece of banana bread and fresh paw-paw slices and began to feel better. Gran and Mum were on their third cup of tea and had slowed down too, noticed Penny apprehensively. The reckoning was rapidly approaching. She was right.

"Penny, Gran and I had a terrible fright. We thought you'd drowned – like your father." Gemma paused, controlling her emotions. "Tell us what happened."

Penny was only too pleased.

"Mum, Gran, I'm terribly sorry I gave you such a fright. It didn't cross my mind. After Fan-Fan dropped me on the beach, he went off for his sleep. Jimmy came sidling up and we had an argument. We always argue. He's a swank and was banging on about how he could sail boats and that Fan-Fan's would be easy." She stopped. Now came the difficult bit.

"Yes – go on."

"Well … I, er, sort of, er …"

"You dared Jimmy to sail the boat, didn't you?" chipped in Gran.

Penny stared, taken aback.

"How did you know?"

"I've not always been old, Penny dear, and I've a very good memory. It's what I'd have done, but *not,*" she added hastily, "gone sailing out into the Atlantic Ocean! That was stupid!"

"But we were only going to Silken Lake, that's not the Atlantic!"

"Yes, and what if Jimmy had been a useless navigator and you'd got lost? *You* didn't know when you dared him how competent he'd turn out to be."

There was nothing Penny could say, it was true. She'd dared him in a flash of temper and jumped into the boat still furious and wanting to 'show him up'. It would have been a disaster if she *had* 'shown him up'. She wouldn't be here now!

"Look, don't *ever* do anything like that again. You're growing up, Penny, and wanting to explore is fine. But you've got to be sensible about it. We've many good friends here who watch out for you on land but wandering around on sea in a tiny boat is seriously dangerous. Then there's the chance of sudden storms. We heard you had one. Fan-Fan told us there was an odd feeling in the air. He didn't like it but had no idea you'd put to sea on your own. Jimmy must be a *very* good sailor to have negotiated it."

Penny drew a deep breath – *now* was her chance!

"Yes, he is, I was surprised. Mum, Gran, I *promise* not to be so thoughtless in the future but we *must* go out again – *all* of us," she emphasised, her eyes shining.

"Why must we *all* go out? What's the attraction?"

"It *is* an attraction! Wait till I tell you, you won't believe me!"

She'd caught their attention. Gemma and Dorothy looked intrigued. What had Penny seen, or thought she'd seen? Mermaids? Mermen? Sea Monsters?

"Come on then! A bit of light relief will do us good!" smiled Gran.

"Promise you'll listen? Promise you won't laugh? It's *amazing* – but *true*!" Penny picked up her sketches. "There, that's what it's about – Giant Leatherback Turtles!"

Gemma gasped. "*What*? You saw one in the sea? It came up for a breather? You lucky, lucky girl! I've never seen one out at sea – apart from George." She glanced quickly at Penny, not wanting to upset her.

"*It was George*!!! Mum, I'm sure it was! Look at the sketch. See, I've drawn the scars especially carefully. Don't they look like Razor Rocks?"

Gran leaned over to get a better view as Gemma scrutinised them.

"This is a remarkable drawing Penny. How did you get so close? Usually they hardly leave a ripple when they come up to breathe and unless you're incredibly fortunate there's no way you'd see them. It almost looks as if he's *talking* to you!"

Gran and Gemma smiled at this weird and wonderful idea.

"He *did* talk to me! What happened was …"

Gran interrupted, "Penny, did you get a knock on the head during the storm?"

"Just a little one, nothing to worry about," replied Penny, rushing on. "What happened was the boat was rolling and pitching. We were really fright … frozen. Then it stopped. The storm carried on but the boat only rocked gently. We looked over the side and there were three Giant Leatherbacks holding us up! We couldn't believe our eyes! They seemed to be smiling at us. I noticed the one in the middle was *huge*, like George had been. Then I noticed he had scars across his carapace. George turned back through Razor Rocks so swiftly he cut himself – remember? So I knew he was George and when I asked him he said 'Yes'! Isn't it exciting?"

"We'd better get Dr Gumbs in," said Gran quietly to Gemma.

"She's suffering from concussion. Have you got a headache dear, do you feel sick at all?"

"NO! Gran honestly, I'm *fine*, I haven't got concussion. Look, could I have drawn those sketches if I was feeling ill?"

Gemma and Gran looked at her carefully. She appeared alright; no sign of bruises, eyes a bit over-bright but not feverishly so, speaking lucidly. They bent over the drawings again. Nothing to worry them there. Neatly and carefully drawn, properly annotated, they showed the head and front part of a Giant Leatherback, grinning up at the artist. A separate sketch showed a large section of the carapace in close-up, the scars meticulously marked and even a rough scale, 'longitudinal zig-zag slash approx. eighteen inches / two feet.' Gemma was impressed with the accuracy and detail.

Penny was becoming increasingly anxious. If they didn't believe her they wouldn't go out to try and find the Turtles. Jimmy's father wouldn't see a Leatherback and the beach would be built on. It was *essential* they believed her!

"They didn't talk to me using words you know, they nodded or shook their heads when we asked them questions. They talked among themselves in a grunting, whistling, croaking sort of language. We didn't understand it – but they understood us."

"Ah! That makes a bit more sense," said Gemma cautiously. "What questions did you ask?"

Penny was relieved. Mum seemed to have forgotten the storm in her excitement about the Turtles.

"I asked him if he was George and he nodded his head and smiled. Then I asked about … Dad, and what happened. You were right. It was a big jellyfish that stung him. George came back to kill the jellyfish, then held Dad up to get air. But it was too late."

Penny could see tears rolling down her mother's face and looked anxiously at Gran who was smiling gently.

"It's alright, Penny, just relief that you know and understand at last. Your mother recognised the sting marks left by the jellyfish, a Portuguese Man-of-War, and realised what had happened. You were convinced the Turtle had killed David. We knew that was impossible but you were in terrible shock and wouldn't believe us. That's one reason your mum's got you out here now, during the laying season. She hoped you'd see a Turtle laying and understand there's no way they could have killed your father. Anyhow, it seems you've learnt about it from George himself!"

Penny went over and hugged Gemma.

"Mum – I know now. George really did tell me. He seemed very pleased to as well. Perhaps *he's* been worrying about it. Those brawny bikers who helped us …"

"Oh yes!" butted in Gran dreamily, "With the marvellous Yamahas R 1s, 1,000 ccs! … The Gospel Makers," she concluded happily.

"Yes, Gran! Anyhow, they chased George away, so he knew we thought he'd killed Dad. I think they're sensitive creatures and it upset him. Mum, Gran, *please* come out in the boat and see if we can find George and his friends again. He'd be so pleased to see you!"

"Yes, I think I'll have to," agreed Gemma.

"And … please will you ask Mr Saxon too?"

"NO! Dreadful man. Why should we invite him to meet Leatherbacks when he's planning to destroy their beach?"

"Well, Mum, perhaps if he *saw* Leatherbacks he'd realise how wonderful they are and *not* develop the beach. That's what Jimmy and

I thought."

"So you've been plotting have you? What else did you plan?"

"We asked George if he and his friends would come up to the boat if they saw us out and they said yes! We would have to be in deep water. Silken Lake is too shallow normally but the sea was so high during the storm…"

"The storm! Let's hear more about that. It seems to have been overlooked," remarked Gran shrewdly.

Wouldn't you know it! Just as she thought they'd got away from the subject! Gran's memory was a bit too good. Fancy remembering the Gospel Makers!

"It came from nowhere. It was peaceful, hardly a ripple, and we were swimming and watching the fish when the sea went wild. It was amazing!"

"What did you do?"

"Jimmy made me put on a life-jacket and attach it to the lifeline. Then we sat tight and baled out until the Turtles came. There was nothing to it. We were whistling and singing quite happily when they arrived." Crossing her fingers, Penny hoped the white lie would pass undetected.

"You've been a lucky girl! You and Jimmy could easily have drowned. I see your point about taking Mr Saxon. If he knows this story he *may* look on the beach development with different eyes. Yes, ok, we *will* ask him, but he must know about Jimmy's rescue first. Whether he'll believe him is going to be interesting!"

Heaving a huge sigh of relief, Penny gave her mother another big hug.

"I'm glad I know the truth about Dad and George. I had a plan to tell the poachers where the Turtle eggs were in revenge for Dad, but I won't do that now."

"OH! Oh Penny, I *am* glad! Destroying the eggs would have been a *terrible* thing to do. Very few of the Hatchlings survive anyhow, only four or five out of 5,000. Nowhere near replacement level."

Helping herself to another slice of nutty banana bread, Penny spoke thoughtfully, "I've had nightmares about it. I thought if I only destroyed eggs it wasn't the same as killing Turtles. Then I thought, when does an egg become a Turtle? I couldn't work it out."

"Eggs *develop* into Turtles just like unborn babies *develop* into girls and boys, then women and men. There's no sudden change. It's a question of size. *You* are still growing and will do until you're seventeen or eighteen, sometimes even longer. Everything you've got now you've had since day one when you were a gleam in Dad's eye! It's called …"

"Genetic inheritance!" grinned Penny, "like my hair going curly when it's wet, just like yours!"

Gran burst out laughing. "It's not just your mother, I'm the same!" she grinned. Penny stared at Gran's short, silvery-blonde hair. It was difficult to visualise her with mops of bouncy, auburn wire wool but yeeees, she had seen photos and could just about imagine it.

"Look," continued Gran, "I've a cunning plan. Don't jump on me. How about ringing Mr Saxon and inviting him here for dinner? We can say we're pleased Jimmy and Penny are back safely and thought it would be pleasant to have a meal together for Jimmy's last night. We'll ask Jimmy what happened – you keep quiet, Penny – and Mr Saxon will have to listen out of courtesy. How about that for craft and guile?"

After a bit of arguing on Gemma's side – "Don't expect me to be a gracious hostess, I'll lose my temper" – Gran's idea was carried.

"Go on then," challenged Gemma, "you ring him, Mum. I'm keeping out of it as much as possible. Penny, let's leave wily old dogs to exercise their wiles," and off they skipped to the beach. Dorothy rang the grand-sounding Carapuse Bay Beach Resort and spoke to Mr Saxon. Charming and persuasive, she eventually managed to talk him into allowing Jimmy an outing. Dancing out onto the balcony she waved her arms triumphantly at the pair on the beach.

"Yippee!" she called, "I've done it! Scramble, Scramble! They're coming tonight! Quite soon, come and tidy," and disappearing indoors they heard her singing 'O Island in de Sun' in a gleeful contralto.

162

Chapter Fifteen

AN EVIL ALLIANCE

Jammed behind the jagged corrugations of volcanic pyroclasts, Bella froze. Why the sudden darkness? Something must be coming down the tunnel blocking out the light. Here was a slim chance to scramble back over the caldera's edge. She must act quickly. Turning round caused another avalanche of rocks to bounce down on the monster's head. She heard his angry snarl but didn't pause. She must get to the other side of the caldera! The dimness decreased and she heard his infuriated scream.

"YOU! You stupid little creature! I told you not to use this tunnel except for emergencies! You'll pay for this! I'm feeling like a light snack!"

With his attention distracted, Bella was able to move nearer the edge. Spreading her flippers like wings, she was about to haul herself over when another voice, one which she knew, replied unctuously, "Then you'll miss the treat I've come to tell you about! Would you rather eat me, small and tough, or take your choice from 2,000 tasty Humans just right for the appetite of such an eminent Dinosaur as Liopleurodon?"

Bella couldn't believe her ears. Liopleurodon! A Jurassic Dinosaur thought extinct! He must have been lying dormant within the volcano for thousands of years. Desperately wanting to get away, she was riveted by that voice. Cautiously, she took cover behind a lava bubble and peered over.

It was as she thought. In a day of horrific and ghastly revelations this was one of the worst. In the swirling misty gloom she could see part of a Turtle, a very large one, with familiar keels down its back. Talking to Liopleurodon and making himself quite at home with the furious monster was a Leatherback! Here was the betrayer of her

163

mother, Cassandra! Bella shook her head in disbelief. There were some unpleasant Turtles, selfish, thoughtless stupid bullies who enjoyed frightening Nematts and Hatchlings, but that was nothing compared to this terrible murderous treachery. She *had* to be sure about that grating voice. She must get a closer look. With flippers slipping on the smooth, wet sides of the caldera, Bella used the bubble like a revolving door, sliding round it and landing with a dull thump on the other side. More debris and stones fell into the crater with a clatter. Bella hardly noticed. There was no mistaking that pale white, almost luminous carapace and the mouth that sneered instead of smiled. It was Azazel.

"HAAA!" came a roar from the cave, "Thought I'd forgotten you, you silly little Turtle? Not at all, just enjoying a conversation with one of your kin."

Azazel looked up, startled by Liopleurodon's sudden movement as he stretched out a gargantuan flipper towards Bella.

"Bella!" he exclaimed in horror. The monster slowly swung his massive head closer to Azazel until his gobstopper eyes gazed at him from a few inches away.

"A friend of yours? What a pity. I can't have her swimming the oceans telling everyone about me. You'd better say goodbye."

With amazing speed Azazel regained his composure.

"Oh leave her! She's not worth bothering about. Merely a Nematt. Don't you want to hear about my treat?"

"I'm expecting a friend soon, a very special friend," sneered the monster. "We're going fishing," he continued with a ghastly widening of horrific jaws. "We don't want you slowing us down," he added disparagingly.

Azazel's white translucent carapace flushed deep purple in anger and embarrassment. He was one of the swiftest swimmers in the sea but not being seventy-five feet long, of course he couldn't keep up! Who was the friend, he wondered?

He didn't have long to wonder. Fizzing down the tunnel came another shadowy figure shaped like a torpedo and going at the same speed. Hastily, Azazel backed away behind the monster's head. He knew and had an 'understanding' with Liopleurodon but his friend would attack him immediately. The long, white, muscle-packed body shot into the cave like a bullet. It was a Great White Shark.

"What's that hiding behind you, my tea?" snarled the Shark, opening his mouth to show his razor-sharp teeth.

"Not much of a mouthful for a friend," he complained, swerving round Liopleurodon to get a better view.

"Leave him," snapped Liopleurodon. "He's a useful acquaintance, that's all. I don't want him dead – yet."

"He's not hunting with us? We don't want a weakling like a Leatherback tagging along," sneered the White Shark.

"No, he can clear off. But he's about to tell me something of interest. Come on, out with it!"

Azazel had been mocked and insulted. Boiling with fury he wanted revenge, yet was helpless. The only way to keep both the monsters at bay was to flatter, be respectful and make a show of humility. He had an idea. Drawing a deep breath, he loosened up the eating spines in his throat.

"Of course I know I can't keep pace with you, the fastest swimmers the oceans have ever seen," he grovelled. "I didn't intend to, I know what great swimmers and hunters you are." These ingratiating words were accompanied by a loud, nervous humming.

"Why are you making that silly sound?" queried the White Shark suspiciously.

"It's a sign of respect, Sir," replied Azazel. "Haven't you heard other Turtles hum when you're around?"

The White Shark laughed contemptuously.

"I have, but they didn't have long to hum, ho, ho!"

Liopleurodon joined in the sinister laughter.

"Never mind that. Tell us about this treat."

"It's a cruise ship, Sirs. A nice, big cruise ship with at least 2,000 fat Humans on board. It's coming from Bermuda and will be in the Triangle at dawn."

All the time Azazel was humming and making nervous whistling and rattling noises in his throat.

"Ha! With such good news there's no need for you to be afraid! I love destroying cruise ships! My favourite occupation. All those tasty, juicy Humans that fall out of them! Come, tell us more."

Liopleurodon and the White Shark bared the fearsome batteries of their scimitar-shaped fangs in abominable anticipation. Azazel cowered back, bowing low.

* * *

When the White Shark shot down the tunnel, Bella had been petrified. Liopleurodon *and* a White Shark, the Leatherbacks' worst enemy! What chance had she now? At the moment they were enjoying themselves, scoffing and sniggering at Azazel. She felt almost sorry for him. What would happen when they tired of that pastime? She preferred not to think about it. But – what was that? Bella pinned her ears back. Apparently humming and rattling with fear, Azazel was furtively making the emergency call up signal on the Chelonian Auditory Wavelength! What was he saying? Bella strained every nerve to decipher Azazel's disguised message.

"Stay still! Be quiet! I'll distract them. Go *at once* when I say. Only chance."

Could this offer of help from the evil Turtle be genuine? What should she do? There was no alternative. Preparing to fling herself back over the rim, Bella puzzled at Azazel's behaviour.

"Stop that rattling and drumming! We're not going to eat you."

The White Shark squinted sideways at Liopleurodon – weren't they indeed?

"Tell me more about this treat. I like anticipating fear and horror, especially in Humans. How they scream as they tumble into the sea! Ah, ha, ha! How they scream!" continued Liopleurodon sadistically.

"Get ready," signalled Azazel, apparently clearing his throat.

"It's one of those big cruise ships called Luxury Caribbean Cultural Tours. Lots of rich fat Humans." Pausing, he let the monsters savour this. Yes, their attention was caught, their eyes glaring greedily at him. "GO!" he signalled on the C.A.W.

"And lots of other Humans looking after them. Big store cupboards full of meat, fruit, ground provisions…" (but not a jellyfish in sight, thought Azazel).

Soundlessly, Bella lunged over the rim into the whirling vortex of water below and swam for dear life towards the funnel-shaped tunnel leading to the Meeting Place. Whatever happened, she was not going back to that caldera of carnage!

"Go on, go on!" Liopleurodon's gooseberry eyes goggled with expectation. As he gnashed his teeth with gloating joy the stink of putrefaction wafted from the glutinous saliva streaming down his massive incisors. Even the Great White looked at him in distaste.

"What time is the ship coming? I don't want to cause a freak wave too early – and I don't want anyone seeing me. Freak waves are more fun when they're unexpected and no one knows what causes them."

"Dawn," replied Azazel, with a surreptitious glance at the rock where Bella had been. She'd gone! He must cover for her a little longer. "With your permission Sirs, I'll withdraw and keep watch beyond the cave. I'll let you know when it's near enough. You wait secretly in here and emerge when I warn you. A Dinosaur of your immense size and strength can cause a freak wave in minutes!" Azazel bowed respectfully.

Liopleurodon smirked, the less impressionable White Shark snorted.

"In seconds," corrected the monster proudly. "I can create a 100-foot freak wave with one crashing dive and thrash of my tail. It takes longer to build up and travel through water, so warn me as soon as you see this ship approaching."

Liopleurodon began prowling up and down the cave, his globular eyes rounder, wider, madder than ever, his colossal tail smacking up and down as he rehearsed the freak wave he was about to launch. Barely moving, the White Shark watched, floating warily to one side, well clear of the monster, a flick of whose tail could kill him. He had seen these killing frenzies before and knew better than to get in the way. Bowing low, Azazel backed deferentially into the tunnel.

Once there, he swam his fastest to the relative safety of the open sea. He did not enjoy interviews with the bloodthirsty Liopleurodon and was concerned about Bella. She was a pretty little thing and he'd been thinking about taking a second wife.

Positioning himself where he would see the cruise liner coming over the horizon, Azazel thought of his first wife, Ermina, who had been killed, horribly, brutally, by Humans some years ago. Against these cruel, murderous creatures he bore an implacable hatred. His beautiful Ermina, pale, like himself, placid and kind, had been on her first laying expedition up the beach. With the other husbands he'd escorted and guided her as far as he dared towards their traditional Laying Beach. Worried and anxious but unable to continue further into shallower water, the husbands settled down to wait, catching and storing jellyfish delicacies under their flippers for when their exhausted wives returned. Smiling lovingly at Azazel, Ermina had waved her flippers energetically and plunged bravely into the shallower water. More experienced Matriarchs patrolled the beach from the safety of the sea, watching for anything suspicious: hidden Humans; lurking Dogs; unnatural lights and new buildings on their age-old laying sites. Ermina, excited and eager, had emerged first from the sea. Instantly Humans had sprung up holding brilliant lamps. After a year in the ocean's dark depths she was completely blinded and followed the lights into the sea grape and scrub. There the merciless Humans had slashed and severed her silvery, sparkling, radiant carapace from her defenceless innocent body. She was alive when the flaying took place and her agonised groans had been heard by an older Matriarch hidden in the shallows. When the evil Humans had ripped off the entire carapace, they turned Ermina onto her naked back and left her, helpless, to bleed and bake slowly to death throughout the following scorching day.

The older Matriarch had crept out and stayed by her. The sun rose, the sand became too hot to touch and all the time Ermina's unshielded body lay exposed to its sweltering rays. Ermina died at the height of this terrible torture and the Matriarch, herself exhausted after a ten-hour vigil, was barely able to move. She had crawled down the beach into water and remained there for some hours, slowly recovering.

Eventually she set off to find the young Azazel and tell him of the savage barbarity of Ermina's death. From that day Azazel's spirit died. Humans, any Human, every Human, were to be pursued and killed. But Leatherbacks, the gentle Giants of the oceans, are not equipped to kill. Despite their immense size their only prey is jellyfish, the acknowledged rats of the sea. This problem prevented Azazel carrying out his revenge and thinking and planning ways and means to effect it, he rejected the kindness and sympathy of his own kind and left the Spacious Sea, wandering inconsolably wherever ocean currents wafted him. How could he terrify and kill Humans? He needed an accomplice. A killer – but one who would not eat him on sight. During these wild tormented travels Azazel had accidentally discovered Liopleurodon's cave and, in return for his life, had reached an agreement with him. Azazel would keep him informed of approaching ships and other prey and Liopleurodon would create storms and freak waves.

Using this malevolent carnivorous monster as an instrument of vengeance, he seized the opportunity to wreak terrible reprisals on Humans. The loss of ships, planes, fishing boats, yachts, swimmers and surfers in the Bermuda Triangle became an alarming and macabre mystery. At the heart of this was Azazel and his executioner, Liopleurodon. Realising how close Liopleurodon's lair was to the Meeting Place, he returned to the Leatherback community. The Zamorin, Moot, Patriarch George and his like tried to console him and preached toleration towards Humans, some of whom were good, like those who saved George. Such noble sentiments and largeness of mind and spirit were not for Azazel. He didn't care. Humans deserved to die; young or old, Azazel made no exceptions. Encouraged by Liopleurodon he became used to viciousness and killing. Bitter and morose, he caused malicious damage and enjoyed spiteful mischief-making until he was shunned by other Leatherbacks. Choosing to attribute this to his unusual colour rather than his own ill nature, he conveniently forgot that pale Ermina had been one of the best-loved Leatherbacks.

Ermina! Tortured and helpless, left in the baking sun for ten hours to die! Why did Humans do these diabolical deeds? Azazel had spent years uncovering the reason for such cruelty. Ermina's beautiful carapace, whole and entire, would be polished and stuffed then sold to another Human for money. This Human would be a foreigner, a visitor to the country, who bought it as a travel trophy to decorate the wall of his distant home. Even Azazel couldn't understand the idea of decorating walls with dead Turtles. After a short time the 'shell', as Humans called carapaces, would be thrown away. Thrown away, without a thought for the Turtle whose carapace it had been and who had died slowly and horribly to provide an ornament of momentary interest. If only they knew, groaned Azazel, each 'shell' had belonged to a live Matriarch about to lay. No wonder Turtle numbers decreased so rapidly. Large tears flowed down Azazel's beak. Humans deserved the havoc and brutal deaths he initiated.

Chapter Sixteen

PLANS ARE HATCHED

Laetitia waited below the crater keeping watch as Bella balanced precariously on its rim, leaning over in an unstable and dangerous position. Letty opened her mouth to shout a warning, then thought better of it. Safer to stay silent and hope Bella hurried up. Time was getting on and 'Z' would stick to her word. Letty looked back down the funnel-shaped tunnel but could neither see nor hear anything. She'd signal Bella to come back on C.A.W., the Chelonian Auditory Wavelength. Would she recognise the warning? How much C.A.W. code did they teach at Turtle Academy these days? Surely the emergency warning anyway! Letty loosened her throat spines in preparation for sending the message and looked up. Bella had vanished! Where was she? What had happened? She'd heard no cry of alarm, no sound of any sort. What had occurred so silently and stealthily? Letty was in a quandary. Should she try to follow Bella into the crater? Should she stay where she was and wait for 'Z' and reinforcements? Or should she go and find 'Z' immediately?

Pondering these things, Letty caught a strange screeching and twanging sound coming from within the caldera. The C.A.W. warning signal! Bella was sounding the alarm! Letty listened, every sense alert to the message Bella was trying to send.

"Mortal peril! Don't respond: repeat, *don't respond*. Letty – listen carefully. *All true*. Vital you remember. Tell the Zamorin *at once*. Warn Humans – if possible."

Letty was listening so strenuously her ears were in danger of never recovering their normal size. Resisting a strong urge to shout, "I can hear you!" she remained silent as Bella had instructed.

The message continued. Sometimes Bella's code was wrong but Letty understood the meaning. Monster; description (ahh! reflected

Letty); the caldera and its terrible contents (no! oh, no! Letty wept silently); the outside tunnel; Bella's own terrifying situation. Letty was on the point of swimming for dear life to find 'Z' and the Zamorin when a short piece of wobbly message was added, "Tell Zozimus, I like his wife. Get another."

This ended on a little sob and despite its quaint code, Letty understood its real meaning. She must get her out! Turning to go, the silent, stifling air was suddenly rent by a hideous scream. Bella! Abandoning her armour for more speed, Letty turned and flew towards the tunnel, tucking the trident under her flipper. That she would keep.

Halfway down the tunnel, before it started narrowing, she heard noises and hid swiftly in a crevice. Whose voices were they? They ought to be Leatherbacks, they *had* to be Leatherbacks! Sure enough, swimming swiftly through the tunnel at great speed surged a group of fully-armoured female Zacans. Assisted by two swift moving, slim Nematts, 'Z' accompanied them.

"Letty! Your two hours were up. I'd already told the Zamorin and gathered a group of Zacans. Trouble is, the males are too large to squeeze through the tunnel. They're waiting for news at the entrance. What's happened? Where's Bella?"

"Missing. We must go back to the Meeting Place. We need the big males. I'll explain there."

Without question or argument the female Zacans immediately turned round. Being in the wider section of the tunnel, this didn't present the problem Letty had experienced. Soon they were all streaming out of the entrance again to be greeted anxiously by the Zamorin, George, Godfrey, Archie, Monty and the assembled Zacans, big, tough males, and the smaller Apprentice Zacans.

"Here's Letty," barked 'Z' abruptly, "Bella is missing." From among the younger Apprentice Zacans, Zozimus gave a stunned gasp.

"Stay calm," commanded 'Z'. "Matriarch Laetitia will tell us the whole story."

Briefly, but omitting nothing, Letty told the strange story. Beginning with hiding in a narrow slit-like cave to avoid 'someone' and continuing with the abrupt drop in temperature and freakish, unaccountable sounds, Letty recounted the entire adventure.

"I didn't report to you Sir," she bowed respectfully to the Zamorin, "because I didn't have sufficient information. To say I'd heard odd noises would not be unusual with all the Hatchlings and Nematts playing tricks and practising for the Scrimmage Games. I had to be sure there was something seriously amiss. I shouldn't have involved young Bella, a sensible, courageous and most magnanimous girl, asking us to warn the Humans after what they've done to her father – and so many of us. We must rescue her," she added fiercely. Everyone present knew the chances of Bella still being alive were negligible, but all agreed they must try.

"You did the right thing, Matriarch Laetitia. Try not to feel too bad about Isabella. Poor girl, both parents killed in dreadful circumstances. The best revenge we can take is to use the valuable knowledge she's given us to rid ourselves of this monster. He sounds like a very early and most unpleasant ancestor, Liopleurodon. He's supposed to be extinct but as we ancient sea creatures know, sometimes this is not so. They are merely sleeping. Geological or climatic changes can awaken them. It looks as though Liopleurodon has broken through his dormancy and is up to his prehistoric tricks, catching and killing for fun. Not an ancestor to be proud of."

"What can we do, Sir? How can we catch him and rescue Bella? We must be quick!" pleaded Zozimus.

"We've got to be careful as well as quick, young Zozimus. All the Moot and most of the Zacans are here, we can agree on a plan now. One thing is clear; we've got to get into that caldera. The males are too large for this entrance. Bella mentioned a tunnel that led to the outside. That's our only hope. We must send out search parties and find it. We can surprise Liopleurodon that way."

"That'll take ages!" protested Zozimus. "There are hundreds, thousands, of tunnels and caves in the Deeps! Is there a quicker way of finding it than sending out search parties?"

Everyone looked pityingly at Zozimus. Wasn't it obvious that Bella must be dead and devoured by now? Letty put a flipper round him but he gently shrugged it away.

"I'm grown-up now, Ma," he said solemnly and sadly. "I've got to face responsibilities like you and Pa. There must be a quicker way of finding Bella!" he repeated obstinately.

It was George, with his wide experience and knowledge, who had the idea.

"The Humans have something called sonar they use on their ships. It maps the sea and everything in it very accurately. It's how fishing trawlers locate huge shoals of fish and catch them – with a 'by-catch' of Turtles, Dolphins, Mantas and others!"

"Do we want to ask such Humans for help?" queried the Zamorin coldly.

"Some Humans use sonar to preserve marine life, coral reefs, fish and all sea creatures. They would be glad to help us."

"How can we ask them? They don't understand our ancient language!"

"Perhaps those Humans you helped, the Hatchlings ('children', corrected Letty) will come back. They have a boat. You can make them understand," pleaded Zozimus.

George considered. That could take even longer than search parties! He had no idea when or *if* they would return. Were there other, faster ways of contacting Humans?

"I can contact Humans," came a quiet, determined voice. All the Turtles looked round – Letty! Volunteering for another dangerous mission!

"NO!" bellowed George. "I say no. I'm your husband, Letty, you mean too much to your family, the Turtle community – and me! – to risk your life again."

"But George dear, I can do it easily. You haven't heard my plan yet."

"Do you speak Human?" interposed the Zamorin interestedly.

"No Sir, I don't, but I've a good friend who does."

There was a murmur of excited speculation. Who did Letty know and speak with in the Human community?

"When I go up our traditional Laying Beach, I've met and spoken to a Parrot. He's called Chico. He sometimes sits and watches us laying."

"Yes," interrupted George furiously, "so he can either eat the eggs or our young Hatchlings as they emerge from the nest."

"No, George, he doesn't. He's an unusual bird. Chico's proud of us and guards the nests. I saw him swoop down on Dogs digging up one of my nests for the eggs and he pecked and pecked until they ran off. That's how I got to know him. I said 'Thank you' and he understood me. He speaks lots of languages and understands lots more but pretends he's just an ordinary Parrot. He could easily take a message."

"If he pretends to be an 'ordinary' Parrot, how will he make the Humans understand?" asked the Zamorin shrewdly.

"His Master, Mr MacRobert, understands him. They talk to each other when they're alone. Chico warned Mr MacRobert that Hurricane Flora was on the way. Mr MacRobert took safety precautions just in case Chico was right. No one was hurt and his hotel suffered less than any other. Since then Mr MacRobert has listened to Chico."

"Won't he think it's a joke if Chico tells him about Bella's discovery?"

"We've got to take that risk."

"Let's have a vote. Who agrees with Laetitia's idea?"

Nearly every flipper was reluctantly raised except for 'Z', George and dear old Godfrey who kept their flippers firmly at their sides.

"That is passed," sighed the Zamorin, who never voted in case he caused 'undue influence'.

"Good," cried Letty. "I'll set off to the beach at once."

"LETTY!" thundered George, "I will not have you going up that beach! It's daylight on land. The hot sand will roast your plastron and flippers, all sorts of animals will see you and Humans too! It's far too dangerous. It's suicidal!"

"George dear, I must go *at once*. You know why." Letty glared at him meaningfully. Yes, he knew why. She'd got Bella into the terrible situation, she must try to get her out. And if there was any hope at all of rescuing her, she must go immediately.

"Can't you wait until it's dark? At least the sand won't be so hot and fewer creatures will see you."

"Chico is taken inside at night. He steals food from the Humans.

Sometimes they forget and leave him out, but we can't take that chance. I've got to go while it's light and he's still on the loose. If I don't leave soon, it will be dark anyhow. Here, 'Z', take this, I need to move fast."

Whisking round, Letty tossed her trident to 'Z' but George caught it, stowing it under his vast flipper along with his own.

"I'll take that. Two don't bother me. I'm coming with you. I know I can't get up the beach, but I can keep you safe in the water."

Letty gave George a grateful look. They touched flippers briefly, then, saluting the Zamorin and Zacans, swam swiftly to a nearby breathing exit.

"Great Mother Turtle go with you," said the Zamorin solemnly as they shot through the porthole into the open sea.

"We must plan what to do if the Humans agree to search for the caldera. How best to deal with a pliosaur?" queried the Zamorin, turning away from the breathing exit.

"Kill it!" replied Zozimus immediately.

"Easier said than done! Did you see seaweed oleographs of them at Turtle Academy?"

"Er – no. We did Archelon and Ichthyosaurs. I can't remember Liopleurodon."

"They used to eat Ichthyosaurs for breakfast," commented Godfrey. "That gives you some idea of their size!"

The Apprentice Zacans opened their eyes wide. Long-spined sea urchins! Ichthyosaurs were giants, twenty feet or more!

"Sir, how big was Liopleurodon?" gasped an Apprentice excitedly.

"Huge, sixty to seventy-five feet with a massive long head and gargantuan teeth. But we've no time for lessons now. We must think of a plan. That includes you, Apprentices. You've got duties now. Think hard, how do we get into that tunnel?"

All the Zacans, female, male and Apprentices pondered deeply. Ideas flowed thick and fast and were quickly dismissed as impracticable.

"What if we lured Liopleurodon *out* of his cave?" suggested Zozimus hesitatingly. "It may be easier than trying to get in."

"Good! Good! Yes, that's a point. If we get him out we won't be trapped in the cave. Well done Zozimus!"

The young Turtle glowed with pride at the Zamorin's praise.

"How do we do that?" queried Archie anxiously.

"Send a decoy. When he emerges, we seize him," replied 'Z' quickly.

"What decoy? *Not* another Leatherback. I refuse permission for that!" said the Zamorin firmly.

"The Human children! Humans have useful machines as well as evil ones. Perhaps their parents would know of a false decoy? They've a boat! We've *got* to ask them!" snapped an inspired Monty.

"CHICO!" came a shout of realisation from the Turtles. Chico was the only creature who could make the children understand and Laetitia had already left on her terrible mission to speak to him. She must be told there was a second request! Archie shot past the Zamorin like quicksilver and was halfway to the breathing exit when a female Zacan caught up with him.

"You may need me if Letty is already on the beach. You can't go up Archie, I can," and so saying they disappeared together. The female streaked away so fast the Turtles hardly had time to realise who she was – vain, silly Tasha, Letty's rival for Speed Swimming! The Matriarch who was terrified of going up the beach.

Flying through the water as close to the surface as they could, George and Laetitia kept pace. The dreaded Frigate birds and Pelicans watched them skimming through the water but left well alone. Mature Leatherbacks were no good; they wanted tasty bite-size Hatchlings struggling through the waves.

"Not far now, George. I can smell it and sense it. Our beach! Keep your eyes open for those terrible motor boats. I don't want you slashed in half."

"I'm fine, Letty. Stop fussing. Save your breath."

They swam on, Letty at her topmost speed, George easily keeping up.

"Look! There's our beach. I'll be first one up this season even though I won't lay. George, stay here," she added peremptorily, "and keep your eyes open! Whatever happens when I go up, *don't* try to follow me! Do you hear?"

"Yes dear," answered George patiently, understanding how worried and upset she was about Bella. "I'll stay here in the deep water. Off you go – good luck!"

The sun was setting in a flaming arc of incandescent scarlet as Letty flung herself forward from the foam onto the familiar beach. It had a very special meaning for her. She'd been hatched here, safely negotiated the Terror Run, and, after twenty-two years, had unerringly found her way back to nest and lay her own eggs. This was the twenty-fifth time she'd come up. It was a Leatherback beach and had been for many thousands of years. Females like herself had crawled up this beach, gone through the long, protracted ritual of nesting and laying and returned to the sea countless times. It was *their* beach. They knew every inch and inlet: where the sand was right for nests and where it collapsed; where the Dogs ran and played and where it was safe; where the Humans gathered to swim and where it was quiet. It was Leatherback Turtle Beach.

Pausing to orientate herself, Letty heard Chico cadging food and the Humans laughing at him. Heaving her heavy body a few more feet up the cooling beach she called out, "Chico! Chico! It's me, Letty. Can you come here?"

"Letty! Wait a minute. I'm just about to get some luscious pineapple."

"It's important, Chico!"

"Ok, ok," came a pineapple-muffled reply. A loud clatter of wings announced his arrival in a Hibiscus shrub.

"You're early, Letty. What's so important?"

"Chico, we've got to get an urgent message to the Humans. We know why their ships and planes disappear. We can tell them but need their help and knowledge."

"Are you sure about this? I always tell Mr MacRobert the truth. He'd stop listening to me if I didn't. How do I know you're not playing a trick?" Chico was very serious. He wouldn't do anything to make Mr MacRobert distrust him.

"No Chico, I'm *not* joking. Struggling up the beach just to talk to you is no joke! I'm not even laying! Everything I'm going to say is true, even if it does sound far-fetched."

Letty was desperate. Chico had to be convinced she was serious.

"Just *listen* to me. Then *you* decide whether to tell Mr MacRobert or not. It'll be your choice."

"Fair enough. So long as you understand I may decide not to say anything."

Letty breathed a sigh of relief and launched into the story. How Isabella had seen and described the monster Liopleurodon; the evil cavern and its dreadful contents, both Human and Leatherback; a tunnel leading to the outside. She explained why the Humans were needed to find the tunnel quickly with their sonar and the decision the Zamorin and Zacans had taken when she'd said Chico could be relied upon to bear their vital message to the Humans. (Letty laid it on a bit thick, and Chico shivered his plumage proudly.) How she'd come straight from the Meeting Place to find him, although it wasn't time to lay. How George was waiting for her off shore and how she must return with Chico's answer.

Letty could see the story was having an effect on Chico.

"It's *true!*" she emphasised. "Chico, I wouldn't pull your claws over something as ghastly as this. We've *got* to try and rescue Bella, although there's little hope of that now. But the Meeting Place must be kept safe, and the Humans will benefit too."

Chico put his head on one side and reflected on the tale. Letty was an honest creature. He'd met her several times. Polite and courteous, she always had a brief word with him before settling down to nesting and laying. She'd even taken the trouble to return and thank him after he'd saved her nest from those pesky Dogs. No, she wouldn't play a nasty, horrible trick like this. He gave a quiet squawk as he reached a decision.

"Ok, Letty. I believe you. I'd better get back. Mr MacRobert will be putting me inside for the evening soon. You need sonar to search for this tunnel and huge caldera, right? I'll find out. Come up again in an hour or so. If Mr MacRobert agrees I'll be waiting with him here."

"I'll be here Chico. Thank yo…"

Letty stopped, interrupted by a loud groaning and slapping noise. It sounded like another Leatherback coming up the beach!

"Letty, Letty!" called a weak, frightened voice. "Where are you?"

"Over here, near the Hibiscus. Who is it? What's the matter?"

"Don't let the Parrot go! There's another request."

Chico let out a small groan. He'd be up all night talking to Mr MacRobert at this rate!

Darting terrified glances around the beach, the second Leatherback struggled up to Letty and Chico. Tasha! Letty hurriedly hid her amazement.

"You look all in, Tasha. What is it? Tell us quickly. Chico has to go."

"The decoy, Letty! The decoy! We must have one!"

"Calm down, Tasha. It's alright. There's only Chico here."

Tasha took a few deep breaths and started again.

"We need Human sonar to find the tunnel. We also need a decoy to lure Liopleurodon out of his lair. The Zamorin refuses to use a Leatherback. I came to ask the Humans. They have machines and strange instruments. They may think of a decoy."

Letty and Chico gasped.

"That's expecting a lot!" rasped Chico.

"You can ask!" snapped Tasha. She had swum her fastest and was exhausted and angry.

Letty stepped in quickly to correct this breach of good manners.

"Could you possibly mention it to Mr MacRobert, *please*, Chico? I know it'll be difficult. It's not an easy thing to ask anyone!" Chico glanced at both the Leatherbacks, one so fearful and one so brave. Yet the scared one, Tasha, had come up the beach to catch him! It was definitely a serious matter.

"Yes, I'll ask," replied Chico amiably. "I'll tell him the whole story as convincingly as I can. Whether he'll believe me is another matter. I'll try. I like Leatherbacks. I don't want to see your safe place ruined. Now I must go."

Chico rustled off into the shrubs and a few minutes later they heard him shriek, "Wotcha! Who's a pretty Parrot then? Cor blimey and stone the crows mate, where did you get that hat? …"

Despite the perilous circumstances the generous mouths of both Leatherbacks curled up in wide grins – Chico!

"Come on Tasha, time to get back. Were you escorted?"

"Archie was coming on his own. I realised if you were already on the beach he wouldn't be able to follow. I'm the fastest swimmer, apart from you, so I came too."

Letty looked at her admiringly. Ever since Tasha's eggs had been stolen from under her and her flippers nearly cut off, she'd been terrified of beaches, yet she'd volunteered for this dangerous mission!

"Well done, Tash," said Letty simply, patting her well-groomed carapace and half expecting a brusque response. But Tasha turned a bright mauve and gave a shy smile.

"Thanks, Letty," she breathed, and held out a flipper. The two Matriarchs embraced and sighed contentedly. It was much nicer being friends!

"Letty, would you show me the beach a little? So I feel more familiar with it again. I'm going to try and nest this year," she said, her eyes wide with fright at the thought.

"Of course, Tash, but we mustn't be long. George and Archie will be anxious, as will the Zamorin."

Letty really wanted to get back but didn't want to be unhelpful. Besides, Chico couldn't give them the vital answers for some time. A recce of the beach would make no difference. Tasha desperately needed reassuring or she'd never lay again. The Leatherbacks couldn't afford that. There were already too few females laying. Moving knowledgeably along the beach, *their* beach, Letty pointed out the places best avoided: shadowy shrubberies where poachers might lurk; posts hammered in by beach traders which impeded the Leatherbacks' progress and nest building; the brightly lit areas which disorientated the Turtles

"Aren't there *any* safe nesting sites?" wailed Tasha.

"We have to be more careful than in the old days, Tash. It's best to have a good look at the beach from the sea to spot possible dangers. I swim along the beach in the shallower water until I see a clear run up and back. Come on – I'll show you."

The two Leatherbacks shuffled down the beach into the shallows where they progressed gently along, causing soft ripples in the surf. Letty paused now and then to point out safe, clear, open spaces.

"It's different from a few years ago when we could dash up our beach anywhere, lay and dash back again. There seem to be dangers everywhere," remarked Tasha apprehensively as they left the water to investigate a wide stretch of untouched sand.

"We'd better go now. Let's hope Chico has good news soon."

The Leatherbacks set off down the beach again, puffing and grunting at the effort of moving on dry land, leaving a meandering trail. A rustle in the undergrowth startled Letty.

"Stop!" she whispered. "Listen! What was that noise?"

But Tasha could hear nothing.

"You carry on. Go! Quickly! I'll deal with it. It's probably those nice Turtle Custodians keeping an eye on us," added Letty reassuringly.

Tasha nodded and continued down the beach as fast as she could. Quietly purling waves welcomed her into the shallows – deep water – lovely! Raising her head she looked back at the beach.

Large male Humans completely surrounded Letty, moonlight glistening on their cruelly curved cutlasses. One held a bright light, which he shone directly into Letty's eyes. She'd be blinded! Now he was walking back up the beach and Letty – Letty was following the light! No, no Letty, it's not the moon, Tasha tried to convey. It's false light! Letty, still blinded by the artificial brightness of the lamp, continued following the Humans. Looking on from the relative safety of deep water Tasha was paralysed with indecision. What could she do? Not return to the beach – two Turtles could be killed as easily as one. Gazing out to sea she wondered how far away George and Archie were. But they couldn't help! As soon as they reached shallow water they'd be stranded, far too big and heavy to go anywhere or do anything. Just two more targets for the Humans to kill! Tasha heard a harsh laugh. A big Human raised his cutlass. Letty was being murdered before her eyes!

Chapter Seventeen

A DIPLOMATIC DINNER

Gemma, Dorothy and Penny had decided they must put Jimmy's father, Andy Saxon, in a good mood at Jimmy's last dinner on the island that evening. They'd had a confab about how best to do it and decided on a 'Plan of Action'.

"American gentlemen like slightly 'old-fashioned' clothes and well-brought up girls are expected to look pretty, like 'English Roses', Penny," said Gemma in an assured tone. "We've got to rummage round our wardrobes and see what's suitable." Rummaging around their wardrobes had not produced many 'pretty' things so with great glee they had gone on a swift shopping expedition to Shepherd's Cave, the biggest store in town. Now was the moment of truth as each retired to their rooms and prepared to impress Mr Saxon. Penny's part of 'The Plan' was simple – 'Look good and *keep quiet!*' She repeated these words over in her head as she slipped on a cream linen tunic dress and plain white sandals. Ferociously brushing her hair and dragging it back into two bunches, she tied them up with blue silk ribbons borrowed from Merlyn's little girl. The bunches were agony but Penny was determined to play along and give Jimmy the chance of a reprieve. Fortunately, as soon as Gemma saw the bunches, she said there was no need to overdo her 'Anne of Green Gables' look and had taken the ribbons off. Shaking her hair out with relief, Penny pirouetted before Mum and Gran.

"Do I still look the part?" she asked anxiously.

"You look remarkable!" exclaimed Granny Fairweather. "I don't expect your friend, Jimmy, will recognise you."

"He won't," added Gemma, "especially if you remember 'The Plan'!"

"Look pretty and keep quiet," responded Penny promptly.

Gemma too had dressed very carefully for the evening and was almost unrecognisable. A silk chiffon dress of rainbow colours – red, orange, yellow, green, blue, indigo and violet – rustled and shimmered as she moved. Against her glowing tan and coppery hair the colours were luminous. High heeled shoes of pale mauve and jewellery – long amethyst earrings and a matching pendant – completed the outfit. Gran gave a wolf-whistle and Gemma laughed.

"Mum! You're not supposed to do things like that today. They're politically incorrect."

"Stuff and nonsense! What rubbish! It's nice to know you're appreciated. I was constantly whistled after by the R.A.F. boys. I loved it!" she added wickedly, grinning reminiscently.

"Wow! You look different, Mum!" exclaimed Penny. Gemma rarely wore anything other than shirts and frayed shorts with bare feet and the transformation was dramatic. "You look ..." Penny hesitated, struggling to find the right words. "You look ... beautiful," she stammered.

Gemma put an arm round Penny and gave her a big hug. It was the first compliment she'd had from her since David's death.

"We mustn't leave out Gran. She's not bad for a golden oldie is she?" laughed Gemma.

"I've done my best, dear, especially as you tell me I'm to be hostess," said Dorothy as she adjusted the amber necklace at her throat. The chic, hand-printed Indian cotton kaftan in subtle shades of bronze, terracotta and gold suited her perfectly. As usual, her little gold Spitfire brooch was pinned on.

"Gran – your Spitfire brooch looks funny on that dress. Couldn't you wear the amber one matching your necklace?"

"No dear, I could not. I always wear my Spitfire, you know that. It's far too precious to be left off."

There was no arguing. Gran's tone of voice said it all. But Penny knew the brooch wasn't precious at all. She'd had it a long time, since the War, Mum had told Penny, but it wasn't worth much. One day she'd find out why it was so important to Gran. Right now, other important events loomed.

"Are we ready? Deep breaths and don't forget everyone, calm, charm and patience!" and so saying Gran led forth her troops to do battle.

Wafting down the winding path the exotic perfumes of many tropical shrubs and flowers contended with those worn by the women. Chico the Parrot was still on the loose and let out a shriek of surprise and mischievous joy on seeing the party of elegant ladies.

"Wotcha! Who's a pretty Parrot then? Cor blimey and stone the crows mate, where did you get that hat? Hello, 'ello there, say 'ello, silly old duffer!"

"Hello, silly old duffer yourself!" replied Granny Fairweather spiritedly. "Where did you pick up that false cockney accent mate?" she imitated, laughing.

"OOHHH!" screeched an indignant Parrot, "Wouldn't you like to know! Chico's a clever Parrot. Chico's a *very* clever Parrot! Give us a pineapple, go on, go on, give us a pineapple," he wheedled.

"I sometimes think that bird's human," commented Gemma in a resigned tone. "He seems to understand everything you say. I wouldn't talk about anything confidential in front of him!"

A loud, derisive and prolonged screeching interspersed with a hiccupping scream met this observation and Chico, ruffling all his magnificent feathers, sent them flying over the immaculately dressed ladies.

"CHICO!" a voice bellowed. Chico hiccupped to a halt, sat very upright on his perch, stowed his colourful wings swiftly and neatly away and commenced a little genteel preening. He was the epitome of a well trained domestic Parrot when Mr MacRobert, the Hotel Manager and Chico's owner, came into view.

"'Ello Guv, Mr MacRobert Sir. Nice day innit? Pretty Chi ..." The last word was muffled as Mr MacRobert threw an old, much torn sack over him, firmly wrapping it round his powerful beak and rapier-like claws.

"Sorry about that, Gemma, Mrs Fairweather, Penny. He should have been taken indoors by now. He's always begging food from the diners or stealing it! Livingston must be busy."

Gemma and Dorothy exchanged glances. If Andy Saxon had arrived, Livingston probably was busy! Seizing hold of the squawking sack-swathed bundle, Mr MacRobert bore it away. Shrill, indignant skirls and muffled screams could still be heard.

"Be warned! I'm serious about Chico. Don't have a private conversation if he's in earshot. He's a memory like an elephant and repeats everything sooner or later," Gemma reiterated.

"He's certainly a remarkably clever character! Anyhow, come along my squad, forward," commanded Gran. Together they walked into the Motmot Restaurant.

"Dr Prof. Ma'am, Mrs Fairweather Ma'am and Penny! Welcome. Ma word! Yo is all veree fashionable dis evenin'! And yo Miss Penny! De fruit sure doh fall far from de tree Ma'am! Ah've reserved de best table. Yo guests are hereyah," he added discreetly, giving no sign of his previous run-in with Mr Saxon. "Dis way if yo please."

"Livingston, what does that mean? About fruit and trees?" asked Penny.

"It means yo is like yo Ma," replied Livingston benignly.

Penny preened. Her mother looked fantastic tonight!

"Come on, Penny. Don't get too carried away," smiled Gemma, pleased at the compliment. Following Livingston through the restaurant they received quite a few smiles and admiring glances. Livingston himself was immaculate in his white tie and tails, every inch the imposing Maître d'Hôtel. His broad, friendly smile and easy manner disguised an authority and expertise respected by his staff, who stood aside with beaming faces to allow them through. Livingston had selected the same table tucked away on the balcony they'd had on the first night.

"Ah thought yo maybe wishin' for a piece of privacy, Ma'am," Livingston whispered. "This hereyah a good quiet spot, no over hearin' hereyah."

The table was lavishly decorated with orchids, the cutlery sparkled, the table napkins looked new and the glasses glistened. Livingston, forewarned by Gemma, was taking no chances! The only dampener on the scene of pleasant conviviality and good cheer was Andy Saxon himself. He had politely stood up as the women came into view but had a hard, unforgiving look about him. Seated at the table, Jimmy glanced up as they arrived. His blond hair, usually resembling an ill-thatched hay rick, was slicked back. He wore a suit complete with tie and kept running his hand round the inside of his tight collar to loosen it. He was the picture of abject misery.

"Jimbo!" admonished his father, "How many times must I tell you! Stand up when ladies join you."

Jimmy jumped swiftly to his feet, knocking over two glasses and a salt cellar. Andy Saxon looked about to explode, but with a practised snap of his fingers Livingston had conjured up two waitresses from behind the screen. Within seconds, order was restored. Oh dear! thought Gemma, not a good start to the evening!

Granny Fairweather saved the situation. Surging forward she grasped Andy's hand in both of hers.

"Good evening, Mr Saxon!" she greeted him with an expansive smile, "How very lovely to see you. And your son too," she added, as if he was an afterthought. "Isn't the table just too beautiful! Of course I expect you're used to exotic flowers like orchids, but to us English they're a real treat! What exquisite colours and the blooms so different! Do they grow where you live or are you too far north?" she chattered on. Penny listened, her mouth falling open in surprise. This was unlike Gran; gushing, smiling, practically flirting with Mr Saxon! Usually she was quite brusque and didn't enjoy 'small' talk, yet here she was gabbling on nineteen to the dozen. It must be part of 'The Plan' and seemed to be working. A faint relaxation of the mouth indicated that Andy Saxon was trying to smile.

"Waall – thank you Mrs Fairweather. It's a great pleasure to meet you formally. Our previous meetings have been a little informal."

He gave a tight smile in recognition of the 'informal' meetings: his demand for their dining table, and fury at Jimmy's unauthorised boat expedition.

"These things happen." Gran swept them aside with a gracious smile. "Boys will be boys and sadly girls don't seem to be much better today." Modestly lowering her eyes Gran turned away slightly. Penny,

187

opening her mouth indignantly to challenge this comment, caught Gran's eye just in time. Winking, she mouthed *"Quiet!"* at her before turning back to Mr Saxon.

"That's mighty charitable, Ma'am, considering Jimmy led your little girl (Penny opened her mouth again and quickly closed it) into very real danger. He should never have stolen that boat. I've made Mr Fan-Fan some recompense for misuse of his property. He seemed pleased and said Jimmy was welcome to borrow it any time. My son's a good sailor, Ma'am, but that's not the point. Borrowing with permission's one thing, without permission is just plain stealing."

Andy was getting worked up again. Dorothy decided on some carefully considered deflecting tactics.

"But how very ill-mannered of me, you've not been properly introduced to my daughter," she paused fractionally. "Allow me to introduce Professor Doctor Gemma Heffernan." Each word was clearly pronounced.

Andy gave a visible start. Whether it was caused by the unexpectedness of this vision of loveliness, the impact of her academic status or the combination of them both was open to question.

"Ah! Erm, how do you do, Ma'am. And what would your subject be, Professor?"

Gemma resembled a beautiful tigress about to pounce. She pounced.

"That would be Marine Biology, specialising in rare species, especially Marine Turtles, which are nearly extinct. This beach," she added with a tigerish smile, "is one of the few existing beaches where Giant Leatherback Turtles, *Dermochelys Coriacea*, still nest."

Gemma smiled broadly, menacingly. Andy raised an eyebrow, gave a small, choking sort of cough, and muttered something which sounded like, "Indeed?"

"And you've met Penelope Heffernan of course," Dorothy rushed to the rescue again, "Gemma's daughter."

"Yes, the girl who went out in Mr Fan-Fan's boat with my son. You were very foolish to allow him to talk you into going. You had no idea what sort of sailor he was. He may have been useless, talking big to impress you. You could have drowned."

Andy Saxon paused, his mouth tightening. A strange expression flitted over his face.

"You must never do that again," he said emphatically. "I sure hope you've learned your lesson."

Penny was too puzzled to feel furious with this additional ticking off. What had Jimmy told his father? It didn't sound right. *She* was the one who had egged him on, not the other way round. Sneaking a look at Jimmy who had been morosely munching coconut crisps she saw he was glowering meaningfully at her and shaking his head almost imperceptibly. Ok, ok, I've got the message, she signalled back; *keep quiet!*

"Let's sit down and order, shall we?" suggested Dorothy, "I'm sure the children are starving. All this delicious fresh air and sea swimming makes you so hungry!" she twittered on happily.

Callaloo soup with crab; ackee and salt fish; okra stew with shrimps; fried flying fish; lobster; christophene salad and fresh Johnny bakes made way for delicious mango and banana pudding, rich chocolate fruit cake, rum omelettes and a choice of ice cream: guava; maple; pecan; almond; pineapple; cherry; paw-paw; rum and raisin. The choice was endless. Penny and Jimmy sat silently, doing their best to enjoy the food whilst keeping anxious ears open listening to what their relatives were talking about. It had been polite, social stuff with Dorothy Fairweather leading the way in light, easy topics: the heat; the food; the luxurious Carapuse Bay Hotel; places of interest to visit and so on. No mention had been made of their sailing expedition or of Jimmy staying on – or of Gemma's work. A number of Planter's Punches had disappeared down throats and Andy Saxon had been persuaded to try a Rum-Rum Cocktail. The conversation flowed more freely and Andy even managed a few laughs.

But Jimmy and Penny were growing restive. Wasn't it time someone said something? Right on cue Gran delicately led the subject of boat tours round the island to their own boat tour.

"What a pair of young monkeys they are!" trilled Gran. "Going off on their own like that. Dear me!" she added, turning almost absentmindedly to Penny. "You haven't told us yet where you went or what you saw, Penny. We've all been too upset and cross to ask. Has Jimmy told you, Mr Saxon?" she enquired. A negative shake of the head. "Perhaps Jimmy can tell us the story then. Being a boy and navigating he will know more about it, much more than Penny. Girls are so unobservant aren't they?"

Penny gasped, opening her eyes wide at this bit of blarney, but Gran swiftly gave Penny the 'keep quiet' look and, remembering 'The Plan', she remained silent.

"Would you permit Jimmy to tell us about the trip, Mr Saxon? Or may I call you Andy?" she asked coyly.

"Waall certainly, Mrs Fairweather. May I call you Dorothy, Ma'am? Jimmy will surely have a most complete record of his journey which he can recount. He's a good memory and, as you happily witnessed, he's a good sailor too," replied Andy, with a hint of pride in his voice.

"My goodness yes, excellent. What an accomplishment! And in one so young!" gushed Gran.

Penny had cottoned on to her tactics by now and nearly laughed but kept her head down and silently ate the ice cream. Gran was wasted, she should have been on the stage!

"Come on then, Jimbo, now's your chance. The ladies would be interested in hearing about your escapade. And I would too, so let's be hearing from you. A good, straightforward account and nothing left out."

Andy Saxon rocked back on his chair, relaxed and content. These Limeys weren't too bad. A bit scatty, sure, but then what could you expect? One Grandma in her eighties if she was a day, one Professor of some weirdo subject, and one schoolgirl.

Remarkably handsome women though. That Professor was quite a looker, and she must be fifty-ish – mid-forties he politely amended in his head. It would be interesting to hear Jimmy's story. He'd wanted to ask but fear and anger had stopped him.

"Pa, are you sure you want to hear it *all*? It'll take some time and it'll be boring."

Dorothy could have wept. She'd worked her socks off getting Andy to this state of tranquil acceptance and now the wretched boy was going to thwart their careful plans! She looked at Penny for inspiration.

"I think we owe it to our parents to let them know *all* about *everything*," said Penny virtuously, giving him a meaningful glare.

"Yeah, come on, Jimbo. Out with it. Let's hear the full story," commented Andy lazily. Dorothy hastily thrust a second Rum-Rum Cocktail into his hand. A soft, cooling evening breeze wafted in from the sea as he sat back in his comfortable chair, relaxed and content.

Jimmy hesitatingly began the tale of how *he* had decided to borrow Fan-Fan's boat and persuaded Penny to go with him. (This time *he* gave Penny a meaningful glare.) How they had uneventfully reached Silken Lake, watched the fish, gone for a swim, etc. Mr Saxon appeared to be dozing off. Jimmy continued more confidently, thinking it was only Granny Fairweather and Gemma he was talking to.

"We had a fantastic experience when the storm blew up."

Careful Jimmy, it was only a *little* storm, Penny tried to telegraph.

"It was really dangerous," he continued, blissfully unaware of Penny's black looks.

"The boat was pitching and rocking and we thought we'd be thrown overboard."

"Goodness, what happened then?" exclaimed Dorothy loudly. Andy gave a slight jerk and took a sip of his drink.

"It was great, Mrs Fairweather. Gee – unbelievable! The boat suddenly righted itself and stayed quiet. Waves were still thrashing around and we were perfectly still! We couldn't understand it. Looking over the side we saw three huge Leatherback Turtles steadying us on their backs! We thought we must be dreaming. Penny recognised one of them. It had scars on its carapace. We talked to them and were as safe as houses! They told us all …"

Andy gave a jump. "Whaaat?? What's that you're saying, Jimbo? Some sea creatures rescued you and you 'talked' to them? Now please, don't insult these ladies' intelligence and stretch my patience. People do not talk to animals!"

"Oh but, Andy, what an entertaining story! Do please let him finish. How did you 'talk' to the Turtles, Jimmy? Gemma, they only grunt don't they?"

Dorothy turned appealingly to her daughter.

"No, Mum, they can make a variety of sounds, like Whales and Dolphins. But how did you communicate with them, Jimmy?"

Jimmy sensed they already knew but wanted him to tell the tale. Looking across at Penny she was surreptitiously nodding at him, her eyes shining. Ok, he'd go for it. He told the whole story of the Leatherbacks, from when they first appeared during the storm to their leaving when it had died down, and how they hoped to see them again.

Andy Saxon listened attentively. When Jimmy told about Penny's father being killed and how it happened, he lowered his head, his eyes glistening. Jimmy came to a halt. Gemma turned to Penny and said very sternly, "Is this true?" as if she'd never heard it before. This was Penny's cue in 'The Plan'.

"Yes," she replied firmly. "Every word. I sketched the Leatherback we called George. You can see it (again!) if you want. You said all along he wouldn't have killed Dad and he didn't. The Turtles said they'd come up again if we went further out into deep water. Oh Mum, Mr Saxon, *please* let us go and see them!" she pleaded.

Andy Saxon looked confused and bemused by the astonishing tale. Dorothy rushed in again.

"Why, Andy! What a wonderful opportunity! Of course we must *all* go! Then you, er, we, will see if it's true. I'd just *love* to go!"

"We must discuss this further, Dorothy Ma'am. Ah, here's coffee. Perhaps the children could go for a walk while we talk about it."

"Yes, don't go too far away, children. Stay in the hotel grounds," added Gemma with an exaggerated show of maternal solicitude.

Penny darted her a dark look but dutifully answered, "Yes, Mama. Thank you, Mama. Come along, James," pondering if a small curtsy would be in order. She heard Gran coughing into her hankie and decided that 'Mama' was probably sufficient.

Jimmy rose carefully from his seat.

"Good night, Mrs Fairweather. Good night, Professor Heffernan.

Thank you so much for a delightful evening. When do you want me back, Father?" he asked punctiliously.

"Say, half an hour, son. We'll see you in the lobby here."

Jimmy and Penny walked decorously out of the dining room and down onto the beach.

"Yeoow-eee!" yelled Jimmy, tearing off his tie and jacket and throwing them onto a nearby boat. Two pairs of shoes followed as they ran barefoot down to the water's edge.

"It's going to work! Jimmy, we had a plan and I know it's going to work!" exclaimed Penny, as they raced along the soft sand.

Their relief at getting out of the hotel and being able to run, chatter and enjoy themselves was wonderful!

"Phew! Some dinner! So what's this plan then? Hadn't you told your ma and gran about the Turtles?"

"Yes. They decided your dad had to hear about them. The dinner was a way of forcing him to listen. Gran nearly went spare when you tried to wriggle out of it!"

Jimmy flushed.

"Pa would think I was making it up. He'd have been furious."

"You did make some of it up! What about you persuading *me* to go on the boat? You know it was me who dared you."

"Pa wouldn't have believed me. He'd have thought I was telling lies to wriggle out of blame. He hates lying and dishonesty. So I said it was my fault."

"Oh, right. I thought you were being brave, taking the blame away from me," muttered Penny disappointedly.

"Waall, I did too," began Jimmy, when Penny put a finger over her mouth.

"Look," she breathed.

A small group of men loomed out of the gloom ahead. One of them was holding up a lamp and walking slowly backwards up the beach towards the thicket of sea grape, mango and palm trees which led to the road. A soft swooshing sound followed him. By the flickering light they could see others carrying machetes, the long curved knives used

193

for harvesting sugar cane. Penny and Jimmy stopped.

"I don't like this," murmured Jimmy. "Let's hide in that sea grape," he pointed to a large, dense bush nearby. Quietly they crept the few feet and crouched down behind the shrub.

"What are they doing?" whispered Penny. Three or four men had gathered round something and were looking down at it.

"She make a good cook out, Kafele," said one. "Big, not too old, and man – look at those flippers!"

The man called Kafele nodded, holding the lamp closer to the object on the sand.

"Sure ting, Flint. I see de old girl. She be good foh we in de pacro water, heh, heh, heh! Yuh two take de flippers, ah'll take de head."

Realisation dawned on Penny and she gave a gasp of horror.

"Jimmy! They've got a Turtle! They're going to kill her! We've got to stop it!"

"They've got knives, Penny! Can't we run back and get help?"

"*No!* It'll be too late. She's already disorientated by that lamp. They'll have cut off her flippers by the time help arrives. *We've* got to do something."

Without stopping to think she seized a fallen palm branch and rushed down the beach, yelling loudly and brandishing the cudgel threateningly. Jimmy hesitated for a second then grabbed a hefty stick and followed, whooping and hollering like crazy. Startled, the men turned away from the Turtle to see what the commotion was.

"You're breaking the law! Leave that Turtle alone! They're a protected species!"

Penny dashed in front of the Leatherback, cutting off the light from the Turtle's eyes and stopping anyone reaching her.

"My father will hear about this and you'll be prosecuted!" shouted Jimmy, with more assurance than he felt, joining Penny in front of the Turtle to form a protective barrier. The men paused, then sniggered.

"Dey is only likkle pickneys! Hereyah, grab de girl. Yuh take de boy."

"Don't you dare touch us!" Penny and Jimmy fought like lions, kicking and biting, but were easily overpowered, their arms firmly held by two of the men.

"Seein' yuh likes de Tortoise so much, yuh can watch us make Turtle fillets," sneered the man with the lamp, Kafele.

From behind Penny came a mournful, sad sigh. Knowing Turtles could understand Human speech, Penny turned and said, "Don't you worry. We'll get you out of here, come what may!" The Turtle responded with a gentle grunt like a cow lowing.

"Ho, ho – harken at de pickney talkin' to de Turtle," scoffed the men.

"You can laugh as much as you like," responded Jimmy angrily, "you're breaking the law. You'll be caught and go to gaol."

"Yes, and what's this Turtle done to you? She's not harming anyone!" Penny added.

"Foh centuries we eat de Turtle meat. Now is Harvest Festival. Is our tradition hereyah dat we eat de Turtle meat at de Festival. We keep up de old tradition. Ev'ry home in our village, he eat de Turtle meat foh celebration. We don' need no interference from outsiders like yuh an' yuh kin," came the menacing reply. "See dis cutlass? It foh no decoration. Yuh ease up yuh mout'. Doan vex me no more or mebbe I use it on yuh."

Coming close to Penny he placed his machete across her throat. Jimmy and Penny stopped wriggling and stood very still.

"Tha's good pickneys. Yuh stay tha' way. Hey, Agouti, yuh do de flippers dis side man, an' Flint, yuh take de other. I'll take de head when yuh is done. Here, Jevaun, hold de pickneys."

Jimmy and Penny looked on aghast. It couldn't be happening! It wasn't going to happen! This beautiful innocent Leatherback was going to be slaughtered and carved up before their horrified eyes! Despite the danger there was only one thing they could do. Exchanging a glance, they nodded and, opening their mouths wide, screamed and screamed, the noise undulating along the beach, filling the languorous air with the clamour of clangourous cries.

Chapter Eighteen

CHICO REPLIES

Drinking their coffee on the wide airy terrace, neither Gemma nor Dorothy had mentioned the subject of Jimmy staying on. Another Rum-Rum Cocktail and the time would be ripe to raise the subject, calculated Dorothy. Gemma was turning on the charm and making polite conversation with Andy.

"I do lecture, but most of my time is spent in research. I'm researching the Giant Leatherback Sea Turtle, the least known and most mysterious of all sea creatures, so it's not easy getting the relevant data," she smiled. "Have you had the great privilege of seeing one of these wonderful creatures, Andy?" she murmured in dulcet tones.

"Waall, no Professor, I can't say that I have. Young Jimbo, he's crazy for them." Andy paused.

Dorothy recognised her cue. "What a shame he's going! They're due up any minute now, aren't they, Gemma dear? He'd probably see quite a few."

"Yes, it's nearly time for the egg laying to start. It's a fascinating procedure which very few people ever witness. Would you consider …"

A series of piercing, terrified screams rent the calm serenity of the evening air. A shocked, startled quiet fell on the dining room. Gemma, Dorothy and Andy leapt to their feet. Again – more screams and shrieks followed by a sudden and even more alarming silence.

"This way!" shouted Andy, sprinting towards the beach with incredible speed. Kicking off her high heeled shoes, Gemma followed, her beautiful dress billowing like a gauzy sail. Dorothy rushed into the dining room.

"Livingston! Quickly! Any able bodied men down to the beach *now*! Something terrible is happening!"

A number of men instantly rushed out and hurtled down the beach, including Livingston and other staff members. It was tough going. The soft powdery sand crumpled at each step, their feet sinking into the porous potholes. Undeterred, they struggled on as fast as possible. Andy was well in the lead with Gemma not far behind. Both had recognised those desperate cries – their children, Penny and Jimmy! What was happening to them? Would they be in time to save them from whatever threatened? Stumbling, panting, unarmed but never pausing they ran on to where they could see a flickering light partly obscured by sea grape and wide fan palms.

Bursting onto the scene like a pair of avenging furies, Gemma and Andy skidded to a halt. It was a scene from hell. A large Leatherback Turtle was surrounded by four men. One held a machete poised to cut off a flipper he'd wrested into the air. Another held the lamp. His eyes huge with horror, Jimmy was helpless, gagged and immobilised by a third man. The biggest man held Penny hostage, a machete pressed to her throat. About to rush forward, Gemma was kept back by Andy.

"Don't move," he cautioned. "Leave this to me."

Startled, the men paused, looking up from their grisly work.

"Ho! Yuh stay where yuh are," commanded the man who held Penny. "We don' want no unpleasantness. Hereyah, yuh take de pickneys, we keep de Turtle. Is ours. Jest yuh leave our traditions alone man."

"Kafele! Flint! Agouti! And who's that?"

The other man didn't wait to be recognised by Gemma. Releasing Jimmy, he dashed headlong into the scrub. Before Jimmy could move, Kafele had snatched him too.

"Yuh'd best be quick, Mister," he growled. "Now yuh dou-dou know de block we from, we doan want no pressure."

Kafele had hardly finished speaking when a large group of people led by Livingston and Jomo erupted onto the scene. Jomo hurled himself straight at Kafele in a perfectly executed rugby tackle, knocking him down and disarming him. Massaging her throat Penny ran to her mother. Andy seized the man threatening the Turtle, wrenching the machete from his hand. Trying to escape, the man with the lamp was neatly tripped up by Livingston, who promptly sat on him.

"Ok, ok, man! I can…not … breathe!" he gasped. Livingston sat on him harder.

"Yo is a disgrace to de community! Yo evil, wutless saga boy! I know yo Ma an' Tanty! Wait 'til dey hear 'bout dis! Dey give yo de horrors man! Dey sure will!"

A scuffling in the sea grape followed by a crash and a curse heralded the entrance of more men. Dressed in the black uniform of Turtle Custodians, they had a firm grip on the man who'd run away. One of them stepped forward.

"Well done, Jomo, Livingston and thank you, Sir," he nodded to Andy. "I'll take over now."

The Turtle Custodians snapped handcuffs round the poachers.

Gemma was puzzled. Turtle Custodians were able to make arrests but they didn't usually carry handcuffs. Grasping hold of the lamp, she stepped forward, suspecting a trick.

"Who are you? Show your identification!"

Shaking his head free from its black knitted rasta hat the leader held out his ID card and grinned. He was very tall with a wonderful warm smile and a mass of soft, woolly dreadlocks forming a halo around his head. It was Adrian Kanhai, the journalist from 'Modern Nature'! What was he doing here?

"Mr Kanhai! I thought you were a reporter?"

"That's my disguise, Professor. I work undercover for Customs to prevent illegal trade in threatened species souvenirs: Turtle shells, stuffed Hatchlings, tortoiseshell jewellery…"

"Yes, I'm well aware of that evil trade. But why pretend to *me* you were a journalist?"

"We wanted to be sure you weren't involved."

Gemma's eyes flashed.

"How *dare* you?" she stuttered, choking with fury. But before she could unleash more tongue-lashing, Penny interrupted.

"Mum, it doesn't matter. We're all safe. I've met Mr Kanhai too, on the plane. Are you still eating peppermints?" she asked, adding,

"Your accent's changed!"

"Yes," he smiled broadly. "Sorry we didn't arrive earlier. We've been watching Back Bay. There's been bad goings on there and we're out to catch the villains. We heard the tan-ta-na and drove fast over the headland. Let's get these criminals outta here. You want to look after that Turtle Prof., she don't look too good."

Gemma took a deep breath. How dare he tell her what to do!

"Yes, thank you. You do your job and I'll do mine," she said frostily.

Adrian turned to Penny and smiled.

"My accent comes and goes. It's part of my undercover disguise like my dreadlocks."

Turning away, he rounded up the villains and the manacled men were just being led off by the Custodians when Dorothy arrived. Barefoot, hair awry, panting, she clutched her tennis racket, grim determination written over her face.

"It's ok, Mum. Everyone's safe," said Gemma quickly.

"Who caused my granddaughter to scream like that? I'll have his guts for garters!" replied Dorothy grimly. Spying the poachers she darted after them, swinging her racket purposefully. Whack! Whack! Whack! Backhand followed forehand as she thwacked the hapless men through the scrub.

"Take that you beastly coward! And here's one for you, you mingy villain! How dare you frighten my granddaughter and daughter! And peaceful little Turtles too! You want to be ashamed of yourselves! What will your Greatmas think? I'll find out who they are and tell them!"

The belaboured men picked up their feet and hastily scurried towards the waiting police van. Anything was preferable to the wrath of infuriated Greatmas! The terrible tension was broken and everyone laughed.

"Well done, Mum!" smiled Gemma, her arm round Penny.

"Did you take those villains on by yourselves?" asked Dorothy. Penny nodded.

"We had to. There was no one else around. They were going to kill the Turtle," she added defiantly.

"You're a very brave pair with lungs of brass! Just as well too!" Gemma smiled.

Andy Saxon shook Jimmy's hand.

"Well done, son, well done. I'm proud of you."

Jimmy pounced.

"Pa, please can I stay on here? I'd like to see more Leatherbacks."

Andy had been shocked and sickened by the ferocious attack on Penny and Jimmy, and the unthinking brutality to the amazing Turtle lying exhausted and panting before him. It was the first Leatherback he'd seen and he could hardly believe his eyes as he took in its immense size, wonderfully streamlined carapace and powerful flippers.

"Waall, I reckon so. Now I've seen this here beautiful creature I'd like to see more of them too."

"Yippeeee!" shouted Jimmy, doing a little dance. His joy was cut short by Gemma.

"That Turtle hasn't moved. She ought to be back in the sea where she belongs," she commented worriedly.

Everyone gathered round Letty.

"Are you alright?" asked Penny, forgetting Letty couldn't speak. Letty raised her head slowly, heavily, sighed deeply and let it drop again.

"She's completely exhausted!" snapped Gemma. "We'll have to carry her down to the sea!"

A number of men had remained, gazing in admiration at the magnificent Leatherback. Gemma quickly estimated that at least six large, strong men were needed to carry Letty safely, perhaps more. Could they do it? They must try.

"Livingston, you're used to carrying heavy things. Come this side please. Jomo, you're immensely strong. You go the other side. Now I need more *strong* volunteers to carry this beautiful but very heavy Turtle down to the sea. She'll weigh nearly a ton, so if you've a bad back, please don't volunteer."

A number of large men sprang forward eagerly, including Andy.

"Ah've bin champion weightlifter Ma'am," stated a huge, brawny fellow. "Ah'd take it an honour to carry this lovely lady back to her home."

200

"Eh, Missus, I'm a builder. I lug heavy weights round all't time. I'd like t'help," volunteered a man with a strong Lancashire accent.

A short, square Japanese gentleman bowed courteously.

"I Sumo wrestler, Madam. I very strong."

Quickly the two teams were assembled.

"It's like when Dad rescued George," whispered Penny to Jimmy. Andy Saxon ousted a stalwart American from one side and prepared to lift. Gemma looked doubtfully at him. Under her questioning stare Andy hesitantly explained, "I know how to lift. I help look after quadriplegics," he muttered reluctantly. "Sometimes my folks weigh twenty-five stone." He looked furious at having to speak of his personal and private life.

Gemma's estimation of his character rose. Someone who didn't boast about his good works! Wonder of wonders! Jimmy looked amazed.

"Pa! I didn't know you did voluntary work! You never said!"

"Let's get this Turtle back to water, huh? Right now that's all that matters."

Remembering George's rescue, Penny organised water carriers to keep Letty's head and eyes moist. Dorothy had abandoned her trusty Maxply Fort tennis racket and found empty bottles on the beach. Amidst much tut-tutting about dangerous litter she handed them out for people to fill.

"Glass bottles on beaches! Tut-tut-tut! Whatever next! Cut feet, blood poisoning, to say nothing of Turtles having their soft plastrons torn and bleeding to death! Dear me...!"

Another loud shriek made the busy party leap around.

"'Ello, 'ello folks. Here's Chico. Clever Chico! Very clever Chico!" the Parrot announced himself in no modest manner. Mr MacRobert was running alongside the Parrot trying to keep up with him.

"Gemma! Chico's just given me an important message. I heard about the poachers and came straight here hoping to catch you and the Turtle – if she's still alive," he panted. "You must listen."

"We've got to get this Turtle back to sea at once," Gemma insisted. "Tell me the message later."

"Rubbish!" shrieked Chico, "Naughty lady! Harken to boss man!" Swooping down, Chico settled himself comfortably on Mr MacRobert's shoulder and nibbled his ear encouragingly. Drawing Gemma aside Mr MacRobert whispered, "The message is *for* the Turtle! You know Chico can understand their language and ours. He's been acting as go-between. I can't say this in front of everyone, they'd think I'd gone barmy. But this Turtle came up the beach with important information for us and needs an answer."

Knowing Mr MacRobert, Chico and the Leatherbacks, Gemma took this on board quickly and didn't argue.

"Let's get the Turtle back to sea first. Chico can give her the message then, as soon as she's able to remember it. She'll die if we don't move her into water quickly."

Nodding in agreement, Chico flew to Letty.

"It's alright m'dear. Relax. Tell you when you're in the sea."

Letty raised her weary head and blinked.

"Thanks, Chico," she stumbled out. Her eyes, usually large and clear, twinkling and gleaming like stars, looked glazed and milky. Chico flew back to Gemma.

"You move darn fast, lady," he commanded. "That Turtle, she's about to die."

Fed up with people – and now birds! – telling her what she already knew, Gemma ran back to the teams.

"Get ready to lift and hold her steady. Her plastron is soft and must not be damaged or she'll bleed to death. Brace yourselves for her weight."

The men nodded and, amidst much stripping-off of jackets, ties and shirts, they flexed their muscles ready for the daunting task. Black, white, yellow, brown, all the marvellous variety of human skin shades glistened and shone in the pale light. It seemed like the United Nations had come to Letty's aid.

"Penny, Jimmy, your party keep throwing water over her but don't get in the way. Now, are we ready? Walk slowly, bearer party, I'll count. If anyone has to drop out, call 'Stop' and lower her gently. *Don't* just stop carrying her. Ok? Three, two, one and LIFT!"

A few of the men staggered, unprepared for the dead weight of the massive Turtle. Others had grasped her so gently their hands slipped. But keeping hold, they managed to adjust their balance and grip and nodded to Gemma.

"AND – one, two, one, two," called Gemma from the front. Penny, Jimmy and others ran alongside the bearers splashing refreshing water over Letty. Penny was murmuring urgently to the Turtle, "Stay alive! Don't die! We're near water; we're nearly there; we've arrived!"

By unspoken agreement the men trudged on until they were waist-high in water, their elegant evening clothes ruined and the short Sumo wrestler nearly drowning.

"…one, two. Gently now, let her go," instructed Gemma. Wet and bedraggled, the gorgeous chiffon dress drooping limply round her, she remained in the water stroking Letty's head as the men carefully lowered the Turtle. Straightening up, they eased their aching muscles, grinning cheerfully at one another in a satisfied way as they watched Letty flap her flippers and show some sign of life.

"Ye did a reet good job there, Jomo," said the Lancastrian builder, slapping Jomo on his back with a hand like a ham, "I'll 'ave t'add thee t'workforce, lad!"

"Livingston," called Mr MacRobert, "take your suit to the cleaners and have the rest of the evening off."

"You all deserve a drink after that. Come back to the hotel. Drinks on me," grinned a transformed Andy.

"No, no, Mr Saxon, drinks on the hotel," corrected Mr MacRobert quickly. "Visitors from all over the world come to my hotel for one reason – its unique natural heritage, the Leatherback Turtle. If it hadn't been for these brave young people," he put his arms round Jimmy and Penny, "we'd have lost a precious part of that heritage." Penny and Jimmy grinned and blushed as everyone clapped and cheered. "Come on, drinks on me."

The bearer group hoisted Penny and Jimmy into the air and carried them in triumph to the Bar, exchanging cheerful comments as they went.

"Bah gum lass, ye weigh nowt compared t'other lady! She were a hefty lass!"

"Ah've more weight liftin' trainin' to do afore ah can manage a Leatherback on mi own!"

"Most excellent excursion. Most heavy sea serpent," chimed in the Sumo wrestler, sighing contentedly.

* * *

Letty felt life-giving water close over her parched body and breathed deeply. Never had the sea been so beautiful! Lying quietly, the water lapping softly over her and guarded by Gemma she felt safe. How on sea did these Humans manage to live on that horrible hard, dry land? Ugh!

There was a soft rustling of feathers as Chico alighted on her carapace. He squawked in Turtle language.

"How are you, old girl? Can you hear me?"

"A bit better, Chico. What's the answer? Tell me quickly."

"Everything's organised. Mr MacRobert part-owns a boat with sonar. He's going out to locate the cavern. And Letty – he's volunteered to be the decoy himself."

Letty's eyes filled with tears.

"Oh Chico," she gulped, "to think there are such good, brave Humans and such evil, vicious ones. Please thank him from all the Leatherbacks."

"I will. He says he'll sail right by the cave and tempt Liopleurodon out. You Turtles will have to keep track of him and when he stops, be ready to deal with the monster."

"When's he going?"

"First light. You said there was no time to waste."

"I must fly. The Zamorin must be warned and a Zacan vanguard sent to Mr MacRobert's boat."

"Are you ok, Letty?"

"I'm hungry. Not to worry. Jellyfish will turn up where it gets deeper. Bye, Chico – and a million thanks."

Chico gave her a soft peck of farewell and flew back to Mr

MacRobert's shoulder. Letty languidly turned towards home. Gemma patted her gently, watched to make sure she headed in the right direction, then swam back to the beach.

Letty was exhausted, swimming an effort, not a joy. She limped on. A disturbance in the water ahead caused her to look up. Not a Shark, she prayed. Dear Great Mother Turtle, send some jellyfish, not a Shark! As if by magic in front of her appeared a school of small Pelagia jellyfish, just the right size for an easily-digestible snack! Letty gratefully seized a large mouthful. Another and another, ahh, that was better! A huge black shadow with gaping jaws appeared above and behind the jellyfish and below it another, smaller wraith. Letty cursed – sand and tsunamis, what now? The two shapes floated unswervingly straight for Letty. Drawing her head back protectively she waited. Would she ever succeed in getting the message back to the Meeting Place?

"Letty!" called a familiar voice. "Letty! It's us, Tasha and Minnie."

Letty gave a huge sigh of relief.

"Am I glad to see you! We must get back to the Meeting Place at once! Where did that Pelagia school come from?"

"I knew you'd be hungry and luckily met Minnie. We went on a shopping expedition. She rounded up the entire school and stored it in her mouth. Then we came back and waited. When we saw you she opened her mouth and out they came. Humans call it a ready meal."

For the first time in what seemed aeons, Letty laughed.

"What a brilliant idea! Many thanks to you both. Yes, I was a bit peckish! But we must get to the Meeting Place," she repeated anxiously.

"Did you get the answer, Letty?" asked Tasha worriedly.

"Yes, sonar and decoy, all correct. Come on, I'll tell you as we go. Thanks again, Minnie, see you soon."

"I'm coming with you," said Minnie determinedly. "You need a bit of extra protection."

Gazing up at the twenty-foot wingspan of her friend, Letty felt reassured. Yes, another large friend would be welcome.

"Let's go!" she urged, and, hastily swallowing a few leftover

Pelagia, starting swimming for home. Quite soon, George and Archie could be seen heading towards them.

"What happened? We've been frantic!" remonstrated George.

"Did you pass on the second message? Why's Minnie with you?" asked Archie.

"Tell you as we go. Quick, we must reach the Meeting Place. No more questions," replied Letty abruptly. "We must swim all out. Give me a helping flipper please, George, I'm rather tired."

George tucked his nine-foot flipper securely under hers, as in the three-flipper race during the Scrimmage Games, and off they set at full speed to the Meeting Place. Letty recounted the remarkable tale in between gasps for breath with Minnie and the Turtles hanging on every word.

Amazed at what she'd been through, Tasha whispered, "Letty – you knew they weren't Turtle Custodians, yet you sent me home?"

"We've no defence against Human poachers, Tash, you know that. Better one Turtle killed than two. I hope you've marked that dangerous bit of sea grape where the Humans hid."

Nearing the Meeting Place, George felt a dead-weight on his flipper.

"LETTY!" he shouted, "Letty! Come *on*. We're nearly there!"

"George dear, I'm so tired. I can't keep going, must rest. You go on, I'll catch up."

"No way! We'll go slower."

Minnie had been waiting to help and saw her chance.

"I'll carry Letty on my wing."

"That's kind, Minnie, but you know how heavy we are."

"I couldn't carry you, George, but I can manage Letty. Let's try. The three of you manoeuvre her onto my wing. Stand by in case she slides off."

Tasha, George and Archie followed Minnie's instructions until Letty was safely ensconced between Minnie's wide wings.

"Ok, Letty?" they asked.

"Mmmh, fine," she replied drowsily.

"You have a refreshing sleep, dear," Minnie suggested. "When we reach the Meeting Place you'll feel better."

But Letty, safe and relaxed, was already asleep, her head resting peacefully on Minnie's wings.

"Right, full speed ahead. We'll try and keep up with you, Minnie."

It was a magical sight, one which Humans never see. Her graceful streamlined wings outstretched, Minnie glided smoothly, sinuously, through the sea, causing only the smallest susurrus on the ocean's surface. The three Leatherbacks kept pace, flying through the limpid water, their magnificent flippers rising and falling in unison.

"Breathing hole ahead!" called George. The party slowed down. Minnie gracefully dipped her wings and Letty slid gently off, bump! onto George and Archie's outstretched flippers.

"We've arrived, Letty."

Opening her eyes, they were relieved to see them clear and sparkling again.

"Thank you, Minnie. That's a good way to travel!"

"The Humans call it Concorde!" smiled George. "Although I haven't seen many of those lately," he reflected sadly.

"You'll need someone enormous to deal with that Lioplo-what's-it's-name," cried Minnie. "I'll rope in Bluey the Blue Whale if I can find him. Jeté's Pod will spread the news."

"Yes please! Meet here, nearest exit to the monster's cavern, at dawn. THANKS!"

The Leatherbacks turned turtle and dived swiftly into the breathing hole. With their speedy and efficient communication system, Minnie and the Dolphins would soon tell all their allies.

Chapter Nineteen

'LOLLYPOP' LURE

George, Letty, Tasha and Archie thankfully slipped through the breathing hole to find it buzzing below. A short distance away, the Zamorin and Zacans were surrounded by excited Nematts and Hatchlings pulling at their relatives' flippers.

"What's happening, Matriarch? Why are all the Zacans assembled?"

"Oo-er, look at that Zacan with the jet black carapace! Isn't he gorgeous! Look at his eyelashes," commented one young female.

"That's Simba," replied another knowledgeably. "He's won lots of Tridents and stuff at the Scrimmage Games."

The young females gazed admiringly.

"What about the Games? Nothing's organised that I know of," complained a male Nematt crossly.

"Ask the Zamorin. He'll know," replied another cheekily.

But no one dared ask Kenronishe. Looking magnificent in full armour, with well-polished plastron shield held casually in one flipper and his majestic helmet crowned with waving sea plumes thrown back on his neck, he looked every inch the leader and Chieftain he was. 'Z', supported by Godfrey and Monty, were close by him, looking anxious, Monty's usual cheerfulness nowhere to be seen.

"Hey Ziggy! Ask your Uncle Archie's friend, Patriarch Montague, about the Games."

But Ziggy remembered disturbing his Uncle Archie and friends in their pursuit of a Man-of-War jellyfish and thought better of it. Uncle Archie had only just arrived and was talking to the Chieftain.

"He's too busy. Look at the Moot and Zacans in full armour, and who's that Matriarch with only one flipper? I've never seen her before.

How has she survived? Something really serious is going on. We'll be told soon enough about the Games. They're not likely to forget a billion-year tradition!"

Letty, George and party had stopped in front of the Zamorin and 'Z'.

"Sir – good news! Letty's dangerous mission was a success. She's tired so I'll tell you the story. Chico, the Parrot, took our message and his master, Mr MacRobert, has agreed to use his boat, which has sonar, and has volunteered to be the lure for the Liopleurodon himself."

A gasp went up from the throng of Leatherbacks. A Human who was risking life and limb for them! It was amazing! Unselfish, brave, and *very* unusual!

"You're sure of this?" the Zamorin asked the question everyone was thinking. "He's sincere? Can the Parrot be trusted?"

"I can vouch for them both," came a low voice. Leaning on George's flipper, Letty spoke firmly.

"I've known Chico for years and seen his devotion to our kind. Mr MacRobert, his master, has always seemed a kindly Human. He's tried to clear Dogs from our Laying Beach and orders all the lights to be put out when he knows one of us is coming up the beach. He's even stopped parties when a Matriarch comes up close to the Humans' drinking place. I think we can believe them both and their astonishing offer."

A burst of speculation and chatter greeted this speech. Letty had many years' experience as a Matriarch and was deeply respected in the Leatherback community. Her opinion was important.

The Zamorin gave a dignified nod.

"So be it. We go ahead," he announced. "We congratulate you, Matriarch Laetitia, on your courage and dedication to the good of our community. But more of that later. Time is of the essence. Laetitia – are you able to give us more detail?"

"Yes Sir. Mr MacRobert's boat will leave just before dawn. It's moored in the bay next to our Laying Beach, south of L'Anse Crag. An advance Zacan patrol must meet him in deep water near there. He'll pick us up on the sonar. Wherever he goes, we follow. The main party of Zacans must wait in readiness for the advance patrol's call on C.A.W., when Liopleurodon's lair is located. Once the monster emerges and is diverted away from the caldera, a rescue party must get into the tunnel and find Bella. But Sir, when Liopleurodon comes out, what do we do? None of us are large enough to overcome him!"

Kenronishe had already thought of this. Large as he was, fifteen feet, he was no match for a seventy-five foot rampaging Dinosaur.

"I will take that responsibility," he replied calmly. "Others must try to incapacitate this monster and render him powerless with dormancy drugs. He must be taken away, far, far away, from our Spacious Sea."

He paused, then soberly warned, "We may have to kill him."

Good natured, friendly Leatherback faces looked solemn at this terrible thought. None of them killed. Yes, Turtles ate jellyfish, but they were deadly predators and multiplied at an incredible speed. It gave them their nickname, 'rats'. Humans didn't like jellyfish, yet had caused Marine Turtles, especially Leatherbacks who kept jellyfish numbers down, to become almost extinct. Once extinction occurred the jellyfish population would explode and take over the sea, causing plagues, like the rats they resembled. Apart from this jellyfish diet, Turtles were kindly, shy creatures, innocuously roaming the world's oceans until it was time to return to the Spacious Sea. How could they kill this heavyweight Dinosaur?

'Z' put an end to further discussion.

"Time to go," she commanded. "Is everyone fully kitted out? Who has the sand and venom bombs, dormancy drugs and extra long tridents?"

"My patrol has those," replied Simba, the large, powerful jet black Turtle.

"Apprentice Zacans will find and escort Mr MacRobert's boat. We will wait for the C.A.W. signal and be ready to attack and divert Liopleurodon when he comes out. Is everyone ready and prepared for action?" asked Kenronishe.

There was an excited rustling as armour was adjusted and the Zacans checked their equipment.

"Hatchlings, please leave now," commanded Letty. "Matriarch

Anastasia will escort you to the Nursery. Whilst your Matriarchs and Patriarchs are away fighting for our security and safety, you will be under her care. Young Nematts, kindly help the Matriarch and stay with the Hatchlings in the Nursery."

Tasha bustled happily forward, deeply honoured that Letty had chosen her for the vital job of caring for the little ones. She bore no resemblance to her former vain, glamorous self. The mad scramble up and down the beach head, the horror of seeing Letty and the Human Hatchlings threatened, and the sprint back to the Meeting Place had taken their toll. Gone was the gleaming, immaculately polished and perfumed carapace. Now it was festooned with seaweed and trailed streamers of kelp and laminaria. The artificially-enhanced elongated eyelashes had been snatched away by the speed of her fastest swim ever. She looked wiser and more kindly; a Matriarch who'd experienced sadness and suffering and learnt from both.

"Come along, Hatchlings," she called confidently, "follow me. We'll have a great time in the Nursery and your parents will be back soon. Here, you tiny new ones, climb up on my carapace and I'll give you a ride."

Waving goodbye and chattering boisterously the Hatchlings swam off at their best speed, some clambering up onto Tasha's broad carapace. Their parents waved them off, determined to make the Meeting Place safe for their families.

"Zacans," called the Zamorin, "you know what to do – rescue Bella and drug the Dinosaur. I have news that Lord Bluey is making a special excursion to these waters to help us take this monster away from our Spacious Sea. Apprentices, you must find Mr MacRobert's boat and stay with him. When he locates the caldera give the C.A.W. signal *immediately*. On *no* account involve yourselves with the monster. I want no heroic dead Nematts."

He looked piercingly at Zozimus who lowered his eyes and fiddled with his trident. No, he didn't want to die, but he might just rush into the cave and find Bella.

"Let Great Mother Turtle guide and guard us in this dangerous battle. Let Choirs of Angel Fish welcome Zacans who die into the

Reef of Righteous Turtles. Let no one dishonour the name of Giant Leatherback."

So saying, the Zamorin led the advance patrol of Apprentice Zacans to the breathing hole and ushered them through, naming each as they went: "Good luck, Ginger. Good luck, Boadicea. Good luck, Zozimus," and so on until the whole party had disappeared through the hole. Returning, he found George and Letty in heated argument.

"I *am* going!" Letty was saying. "I'm a Senior Zacan and you're not going to stop me!"

"But Letty, dear, you've just got back from a highly dangerous and exhausting mission. You must rest. No one will think any less of you."

"I'm not the slightest bit interested in what others think. I've *got* to go. I'm responsible for Bella being stuck in that cave, and I must help to get her out ... if she's still alive."

"Go – but promise me you'll turn back if you get too tired?"

Letty looked mutinous. George persisted.

"Promise. Ah! Here's Kenronishe as a witness."

"Oh ... alright. I promise. But I won't get too tired."

George and Kenronishe breathed sighs of relief. Letty was a very determined Turtle!

* * *

In the hotel Mr MacRobert handed drinks to the Leatherback rescue party and beamed at their happy contentment.

"A good job well done," he murmured to Gemma.

"Yes, and look at Penny and Jimmy! Quite the heroes!"

The entire hotel had turned out to congratulate them. As they told the story there were whistles of horror and amazement and applause for their defiant courage.

"They were very brave," commented Gemma proudly. Mr MacRobert nodded in agreement.

"They were," he said quietly, "and I must tell you what the Turtle message was."

"There really is a message?" asked Gemma thoughtfully.

"Yes. They used Chico as go-between. That Turtle was a messenger. If Penny and Jimmy hadn't rescued her my answer wouldn't have gone back to the Leatherbacks. It's vital they find a submarine caldera. According to Chico it's the lair of a massive Dinosaur called ... Lollypop is it? It kills Leatherbacks and its caldera is near the Turtle Meeting Place. They've reliable information that it's also the cause of those freak waves and earth movements which have been creating havoc in the Bermuda Triangle, causing ships to sink and sometimes planes to crash too."

Gemma listened to this in amazement.

"It's a good thing we're old friends, Alistair," she remarked, "or I'd think you're as tight as a tick. I know Chico talks to you and since Hurricane Flora you've paid attention to him. He's not having you on is he? Can you trust him?"

Alistair MacRobert shrugged.

"Chico's careful when he speaks to me. If he tells one lie or exaggerates a story I'll never believe him again. He acts the greedy, silly Parrot in public but with me he's sensible and very clever, as he keeps reminding us! I've promised to do what the Leatherbacks requested."

"You can't go back on your promise. It'll be interesting finding out how much of this is true! What do they want?"

"I'm taking the boat out at dawn to locate Lollypop's subterranean lair with my sonar. I've volunteered to be Lollypop Lure too! Sounds a bit of a laugh to me but I love those Turtles, the beauts. It's the least I can do, the success of my hotel is entirely due to them."

"Right, so we meet at the boatyard at five?"

"Oi, oi! Who's 'we'? I said I'm going."

"You can't go on your own. It could be dangerous. I've got to go with you."

"Sure thing, that goes for me too," a quiet drawl chipped in. Andy Saxon, standing close by, had overheard the conversation.

"No, Mr Saxon, I can't take that responsibility," replied Alistair firmly. "It might be dangerous or could be a waste of your valuable time. Professor Heffernan here, she's prepared to do anything to help Leatherbacks but you've no such interest."

"Stop right there. I sure do have an interest. Turtles and Parrots talking? Extinct Dinosaurs skulking in the ocean deeps? The answer to the Bermuda Triangle Mystery? That's more than enough interest." Andy turned pale and spoke passionately, his voice shaking with emotion.

"My wife was drowned near Bermuda. She took out a catamaran, 'Jimbo's Boat' we called it. It was well equipped. The weather was calm. She was a first class yachtswoman yet disappeared and was never seen again. It's one of the Bermuda Triangle's mysteries and if I can find out what's causing these deaths and prevent others being killed, it will be some consolation."

He paused, took a deep breath, then continued.

"Those Giant Leatherbacks, they sure are something else. I'd like to help. How about taking my yacht out? It's bigger, better equipped than your boat and has state of the art sonar."

Gemma and Alistair stared in amazement. Andy Saxon's yacht was a beautiful ship. Its polished brasswork, sparkling white paint and luxurious equipment were pointed out wherever she docked and admired by everyone.

"I'm sorry, I can't accept your kind offer, Mr Saxon. What if the Leatherbacks are right and there is some monster of the deep waiting to sink us? We must face that possibility. Apart from lives being lost, that yacht of yours costs millions! No, I can't risk that."

"Call me Andy and forget the money. Human lives are more important than cash in the bank. If the Leatherbacks and that cunning Parrot are correct, it would be safer to use my yacht. It can contact emergency services faster and will withstand more buffeting and rougher seas than your little cockleshell. It makes sense."

It did, and Gemma and Alistair eventually agreed to his plan.

"Ok. Thank you. We'll meet at your private mooring…"

"What are you planning, Mum?"

Unnoticed by the intent adults, Penny and Jimmy had come up. They'd had enough of the limelight and everyone asking questions. It was a relief to be back with their parents.

"Is it Turtle Watch? When are we meeting? Is Pa coming too? Great!" enthused Jimmy. "You'll love it, Pa," he added condescendingly.

The grown-ups glanced at one another in dismay.

"We're not planning anything, Penny," stammered Gemma, going pink.

"But I heard you arranging to meet. Anyhow, you're lying. I can tell because you're blushing," said Penny candidly.

"Ok yes, we're arranging to meet. It's not for you two, it's too dangerous."

"What's dangerous?" Jimmy broke in, his eyes gleaming. He was still feeling heroically brave. "Is it about the Turtles?"

"Yes, Leatherbacks come into it. It's probably a lot of fuss about nothing. Much better if you went quietly to bed after your exciting evening. Leave it to us, son."

Both rebelled at this idea.

"*We* saved the Turtle! It's not fair if you don't tell us what's going on!" Penny was furious.

"You young people should be asleep by now, not arguing with us," replied Gemma crossly. "Go along now."

"But Gran's still up enjoying herself. Look at her!" Arms held wide, Dorothy was pretending to be a plane. Every so often she tilted her 'wings' and let rip with strange staccato sounds. An admiring group of men surrounded her, taking in every word and action. Penny watched, totally puzzled. Why were those men gazing at Gran with such rapt attention and admiration?

"Mum, what's Gran *doing*?" she asked.

Gemma glanced at her mother and smiled.

"She's flying her Spitfire," said Gemma, grinning like a mischievous schoolgirl. "Jimmy and you are today's heroes. Gran was a heroine many years ago during the War."

Seeing the looks of interest, she continued.

"Gran was in the mainly women Air Transport Auxiliary, the A.T.A. She flew Spitfires, Hurricanes and many other planes from factories to R.A.F. airfields, and from base to base, wherever they were needed.

She was shot at, more than once and an A.T.A. friend was killed."

Penny and the listening group gasped, goggling at Mrs Fairweather with new eyes. She had 'landed' her plane amidst a burst of applause. Penny tried to imagine what she must have been through, but it was impossible. The sudden transition from scatty, arthritic, gentle old lady into a daring and courageous Spitfire pilot was too much to take in. She remembered the 'Gospel Makers' and Gran's mania for fast machines. This explained it! It could also explain something else.

"Mum! Is that why all the pilots and airport officials fussed over us so much?"

"Did they? Yes, not many A.T.A. 'girls' are still alive. Her little Spitfire brooch was given to A.T.A. members. She wears it in memory of them and all the young R.A.F. pilots who were killed. After the War Gran broke various flying records, then became a flying instructor. She's a living legend!"

There was silence. Respect and awe mixed with gratitude flooded through the older people present. Amazement and determination to get Gran reminiscing, gripped Penny and Jimmy. She would be *fascinating!*

"Anyhow, you won't divert me any longer! Off to bed with you!"

The 'Living Legend' strode across to the group.

"What's going on? Our heroes look mutinous."

"Gran – Mum's plotting something about the Leatherbacks. She won't tell us what's going on and is trying to pack us off to bed. That's not fair is it?"

"We've told you – it's too dangerous!"

Dorothy looked at Gemma. It wasn't for her to interfere, yet Gemma was always honest and straightforward with Penny. What *was* going on?

"Perhaps you could tell the children why it's so dangerous. Then they'll be happy to leave you to it," she suggested.

Penny and Jimmy nodded in agreement.

"Yes, tell us – then we'll go to bed."

There was no help for it. Gemma and Alistair MacRobert told the whole strange story, beginning with Chico's message and ending with Andy Saxon's yacht. Penny and Jimmy's eyes grew round with incredulous interest.

"We've *got* to come, Mum! The Turtle wouldn't have taken the message back if we hadn't rescued her! She's *our* Turtle now."

"We could all be killed. We can't risk that happening to you. Stay here with Gran where it's safe."

"I'm coming too!" Gran was indignant. "I'm not a child and I've come through more dangerous situations than any of you. So that's settled."

"If that Lollypop monster killed Ma, I've a right to go. Come on Pa, you understand," Jimmy appealed to Andy.

Andy nodded slowly.

"Everyone's going but me! I'm the only one who can talk to Turtles! That huge one with the scars will be around. He looked like a Leatherback Leader and knows me," complained Penny. Gemma sighed. They'd be here all night arguing, she knew how determined Penny could be.

"Alright, come. You'd better do as you're told mind! Now will you go to bed? It won't be worth it if you don't go soon!"

Dorothy waved goodnight to her admirers, grasped Penny's hand and bolted out of the bar. She wanted some sleep even if no one else did!

Andy Saxon turned to Jimmy.

"Come on, Jimbo, we'll sleep on board tonight and be ready for everyone at dawn. The ship's fully equipped and the crew on standby."

Jimmy sighed happily. He wasn't being packed off home but going in search of further adventure with his father!

"Let's go!" he grinned. Andy smiled back.

"S'cuse me, Sir." Livingston, showered and spruce in fresh evening clothes, stood with a tray of drinks.

"Hello Livingston! I said you could take the evening off."

"Yes Sir an' tank yo, but I overhear some excitin' tings a gwan. Wid yuh permission, ah'd wish to be a part o' dat Sir."

"Are you sure, Livingston? I don't want you getting into trouble with your neighbours by helping the Leatherbacks."

Livingston's dark eyes flashed fire.

"Ok, we have some bad johns round de block, but don' tar us wit' de same brush. All ma frens, dey respect de Leatherback, she part of our hist'ry. Is de sprangers man. Dey bring bad name to de island. We wish to come and keep yo an' de Turtles safe," he added with great dignity.

Alistair MacRobert looked questioningly at Andy Saxon and Gemma. They nodded affirmatively.

"Ok, Livingston, you win. We meet at Mr Saxon's mooring at dawn," smiled Gemma.

A huge grin spread over Livingston's face.

"Tank yo Prof. Dr Ma'am! Is ok if I bring some of ma frens?"

Andy looked worried. This was turning into a real party and what if the risks were real? All those lives would be in peril!

"Say, Livingston, it could be a very dangerous business. How many friends were you thinking of?" he asked anxiously. Livingston gave him a calm look.

"Don' yo worry, Sir," he replied, "Only good frens who love de Turtles is comin'."

Andy gave up. Let it be a party. They'd all drown together.

Chapter Twenty

A PERILOUS VOYAGE

Daybreak. Wisps of indigo and pink broke the muffled greyness of night. A cock crowed piercingly; a dog yawned loud and long. Soon the breeze would veer from land to sea but now was the pre-dawn hush when all was still. Pink turned to gold and the light increased. The first cook fires were lit and the aromatic woodsmoke wafted straight to the sky through tranquil air.

Pitter-patter, pitter-patter, like rain on trees, the fan palms began to rustle, quietly at first then more loudly as the daily onshore wind began to blow. Two weary figures patrolling the beach sniffed the air and called to one another.

"Hey! Time we got along to dat yacht. We don' want dem leavin' witout us!"

"Jus as yo say, man, jus as yo say. Livingston pickin' us hup eh?"

"Yep, he be goin' by de fort any minute. Let's go!"

Stripping off their black Turtle Custodian uniforms, they made swift tracks up the beach to the old fort and sat on the crumbling wall.

"Ah'm hungry, man. Yo bring provision?"

"No. Mebbe we get food on board."

A gleaming, well-kept old Ford car drew up and Livingston opened the door.

"Quick, hop in. Ah sure hope Mr Saxon permit yo on board his sumptuous ship lookin' like a pair o' frizzle-fowl!"

Hopping in with alacrity the pair tried to smarten themselves up.

Aboard his yacht, Andy Saxon woke Jimmy.

"Come on son. Time for breakfast. I bet none of our Dinosaur hunters have eaten so I've a dozen places laid and Chef is standing by."

Jimmy fell reluctantly out of bed into the shower trying to put his mind in gear. Yeah, they were going to get rid of the monster who had drowned his mom. They'd be helping the Turtles too. In the middle of pulling a jumper over his head Jimmy paused. Could it be true? It sounded like Chico having a laugh. Anyhow, it was too late to worry now and soon loads of people would be on board. It would be a great party even if it was a hoax! Heaving the jumper into shape he scampered off to investigate the mouth-watering smell of frying food drifting from the galley.

"Good morning, good morning, good morning!" came a loud, harsh screech from the gangway. "How are we all this morning?"

"Good morning, Mrs Fairweather Ma'am, Gemma, Alistair, Penny – and Chico!" Andy looked less than pleased to see the rowdy Parrot perched on Alistair's shoulder.

"He's the only one who understands Human and Leatherback, Andy. He had to come. We may need an interpreter."

Chico gave a complacent snicker of satisfaction and shook out his wings, sending colourful blue and green feathers flying in all directions.

"Chico! Stop that. Mr Saxon won't give you breakfast if you behave badly."

The Parrot immediately hopped across to Penny, digging his large scaly claws into her padded anorak and walked, crablike, up her arm until he settled on her shoulder. Smirking, he gave a final shimmer of his wings and sat bolt upright, looking the picture of injured innocence. As he'd expected, Penny stroked him fondly.

"He's alright here, Mr Saxon, I'll look after him," she said protectively.

"Ok. Fine. You stay right there until Penny says otherwise. Traditional English breakfast in the galley. Jimmy's already started."

Andy led the way down a carpeted gangway and opened a thick door. Jimmy, just beginning a plate piled high with delicious fried bacon, eggs, sizzling sausages, tomatoes and hash browns, jumped politely to his feet.

"G'mornin," he mumbled, his mouth full of food.

"Good morning, Jimmy. Please sit down and finish your food," smiled Dorothy.

Andy indicated a large side table filled with several massive covered hot plates. Mounds of melons, mango, papaya, pineapple, oranges, pink grapefruit and bananas were piled high on a huge dish. Shining silver urns, an automatic toast maker and bins full of crusty fresh bread, rolls and pastries completed the spread.

"Coffee, tea, orange, mango, milk – help yourselves. If there's anything you want, ring that bell and a steward'll come."

He rushed off with some trepidation to greet Livingston's party who were coming up the gangplank.

"Hi Mr Saxon! Dis a mighty fine ship! Hereyah ma frens, Cora and Jomo, dey both veree strong. Sorry dey look sich a fright. Dey just come from dawn Turtle watch on de beach. Fan-Fan you know. He clever wit' de winds and currents and kno' de sea. Yo don' need sonar wit' Fan-Fan! An' dis 'ere is Adrian Kanhai, a government man. He's goin' to keep de record straight 'bout Turtles an' Dinosaurs and suchlike tings."

Livingston spoke casually, as if searching for Dinosaurs was an everyday event.

Andy looked at Cora and Jomo. He'd already seen Jomo in action and Cora looked as muscle-bound as he was! He'd admired Fan-Fan's boat after Jimmy and Penny had been out in it, and Adrian Kanhai he'd met briefly on the beach. Andy breathed a sigh of relief. Not the entire village as he'd half expected!

"Ah 'spect yo thought ah'd bring de whole block?" Livingston easily read his thoughts. "Ah've more sense than that, man," he remonstrated gently with a wide smile.

"You're all very welcome," replied Andy. "Breakfast in the galley if anyone's hungry. Can you find your way? I must go to the bridge. We're leaving right now."

Fan-Fan unerringly wove his way along the corridor and into the immaculate galley. In a corner, on a wrought iron Parrot cage, was perched Chico, his mouth full of papaya, a large melon grasped securely in his talons. Beneath him a pristine white tablecloth had been laid on the floor with further supplies of nourishment. Although well away from the food tables he kept up a flow of banter and commentary with the hungry

Dinosaur hunters and greeted the new arrivals with enthusiasm.

"'Ello, 'ello, 'ello," he spluttered. "We all frens 'ere. Sidown and 'elp yerself. Plenny good food 'ere."

But Livingston insisted on introducing everyone properly. Gemma gave Adrian Kanhai a cool "good morning" and Jimmy and Penny were startled to recognise Cora as the large Security Officer who'd arrested two men at the airport. Acting on Gemma's suggestion, Jomo had roped Cora in for Turtle Watch and she'd turned up after Letty's rescue to share the dawn patrol. She was tired, hungry and frazzled. Dorothy Fairweather brought her a mug of strong coffee and large platter of hot food and the two ladies settled down companionably, eating and chattering happily. With plates piled high, Livingston, Jomo and Fan-Fan plumped down next to Jimmy and Penny. Alistair MacRobert took pity on Adrian Kanhai and sat by him, whilst Gemma picked at a roll and studied a complicated nautical map. At her side was a formidable looking tome, *Dinosaurs of the Mesozoic Era*, by D. Brachi, G. de Boer and J. Appleton. A red sticker marked her place. As the yacht glided smoothly out of harbour the 'Lollypop Lure' breakfast party was in full swing.

"I've found the Dinosaur. It must be Liopleurodon, a Jurassic pliosaur. It's a vicious carnivore and would easily be able to kill our present-day Orcinus – the Killer Whale. It's huge, the largest skeleton pieced together was over sixty feet long, so it could be even bigger, massive jaws, enormous overlapping teeth, terrific sense of smell. Look, here's a reconstruction."

Gemma opened the book and passed it round. People gasped or grinned:

"Hey man, I doan like de looks o' dose teeth!"

"That's a mean looking crittur. Just the type to eat Leatherbacks! We'll have him though!"

"Yeah – how?" added the thoughtful voice of Adrian Kanhai. Ignoring this remark, Gemma spoke to Andy as he entered the galley.

"I've been searching this map, Andy. It's covered in offshore 'deeps', submerged valleys and caves. How are we to know when we've found Liopleurodon's?"

"He'll show up on sonar. We can make out the shapes of small fish, we'll have no problem making him out or the…"

The Captain's voice on the tannoy interrupted him.

"Mr Saxon, Mr Saxon. We've picked up a large group of Leatherback Turtles. You told me to watch out for such a gathering."

There was an excited murmur. The Leatherbacks had found them!

"Life-jackets on! No one permitted on deck without a jacket." There was a rush to the cupboard and a mad scramble to adjust the clumsy gear.

"You've done a Granny knot, Penny!" said Jimmy, who already had his life-jacket on.

"Clever clogs! We don't all have a private yacht and crew to teach us Reef knots!"

"We learnt 'Knots' when I was a Girl Guide," Dorothy chipped in cheerily. "Our uniform tie had to be tied with a reef knot at the back of our necks! Captain used to inspect us to make sure they were done properly."

Crumbs, Penny thought, you learnt some funny things in those days! Or perhaps useful things?

"Everyone ready?" checked Andy and the entire company rushed on deck to see the amazing sight of a Leatherback convoy.

* * *

Kenronishe, the Zamorin, heaved a sigh of relief. The message on the C.A.W. was reassuring.

"The Apprentices have located the yacht and are swimming alongside. Now we wait for a further signal," he announced to the waiting Zacans. Finding the yacht had not been too dangerous, but life was always hazardous for Turtles and Kenronishe had been anxious. The Apprentice Zacans had done well. So far, so good. The Zacans, including 'Z', Letty, George, Godfrey, Archie and Monty, were waiting patiently when Ziggy floated up, looking embarrassed. Too young to be an Apprentice Zacan, too old to be with the Hatchlings, Tasha had sent him on an errand. From both of his already large flippers a string of bulky Mermaid Purse shopping bags trailed in the sea. An immense and very dead Man-of-War jellyfish was secured to his rear flippers. Closely observed by the assembled experts, Ziggy tried to untangle himself from the Man-of-War's trailing glutinous tentacles, no longer strong and deadly poisonous but limp and supine. He knew how he was *supposed* to deal with eighty-foot-long tentacles, Madame Louisa had taught him, but being watched by such eminent Turtles made him clumsy and inept. Growing mauver and mauver by the minute, he fumbled and bungled. The Zacans hid their mirth as best they could. They'd had the same problems at Ziggy's age!

With a sigh of relief he eventually managed to extricate himself from the clinging, wavering embrace of the sticky tentacles and handed everything into the competent flippers of Letty and George.

"Matriarch Tasha sent these," he muttered in embarrassment.

"She did some bulk-buying of assorted jellies at the Supermarina and caught the Man-of-War. She said you'd be getting peckish."

Mounds of fresh jellyfish tumbled out of the Mermaid Purse shopping bags and were quickly snaffled by the females whilst the male Zacans made short work of the Man-of-War.

"Thanks, Ziggy. Tell Matriarch Tasha we feel fighting fit." Gathering up the empty Mermaid Purses, Ziggy bowed to the Zamorin and shot away. Fancy having to lug shopping bags around when Nematts not much older than himself were out fighting! As soon as his body grew in proportion to his over-large flippers he'd apply to be an Apprentice! It wouldn't be long, he consoled himself.

* * *

The Lollypop Lure party were on deck watching the Leatherbacks swimming easily and purposefully either side of the yacht.

"Woweeee!" Jimmy jumped up and down in delight. "See them go! Aren't they great! Look Pa, look, they're beautiful!"

Gemma, Penny, Dorothy and Cora gazed with wondering respect at the large Turtles. They could see their streamlined silhouettes shimmering as they swooped through the crystal clear susurrus of wave and water, flexible flippers flicking aside the sea so efficiently they appeared to fly. Why would anyone want to hurt or kill these amazing and harmless creatures?

"How are they going to overcome de monster?" repeated Adrian sceptically. "They're too small and docile."

"These aren't the largest," replied Penny defensively. "We've met much bigger ones, haven't we Jimmy?"

"That one you called George was enormous. Not seventy-five feet though. That's what the book says Lollypop can grow to. Or bigger. Mary Anning would know," he added reflectively.

"Who's she?" whispered Penny, glancing around.

"Some old bird. She was an expert on fossils and found out about Dinosaurs."

"Is she here? I haven't seen anyone I don't know."

Gemma laughed.

"She died in 1847. Jimmy's been reading my book."

But this was no time for teasing Jimmy about his newly acquired knowledge. With a strong headwind blowing in their faces and water soaking their clothes, the Dinosaur seekers watched entranced as the Turtles kept pace with the yacht.

Blip, blip, BLIP – the sonar!

"Gemma! Alistair! To the bridge!" Andy led the way, moving fast on the slippery deck.

"What is it? What have you spotted?" he asked the Captain.

"There's a vast cave down there. Two huge creatures are swimming about, one much larger than the other. Here, take a look."

Andy, Gemma and Alistair scanned the screen where the Captain pointed. Yes! *Two* creatures, their shapes ill-defined but gradually becoming clearer as the yacht drew nearer.

"Can it be Liopleurodon's *calf*?" Gemma was horrified.

"Whatever it is, we must warn the Leatherbacks *now*!"

Andy took the bearing and Alistair ran to tell the indispensable Chico, who'd refused to come on deck, preferring to remain in the galley near the food supply.

"'Ello Guv. What's happened? Have you located the cave?"

"Yes, come on Chico. We need you to talk to the Leatherbacks and tell them where it is. Hop on my shoulder and hang on tight. It's blowing a gale on deck."

Chico hopped smartly onto Alistair's shoulder and wound his claws securely into the old woolly jumper he was wearing. There was no brash cockiness about him now. Perfectly sober, with every nerve alert, Chico showed he was made in the best tradition of loyal, courageous Parrots.

"Give me the details Guv and lead on."

* * *

"Quiet everyone," commanded the Zamorin, "there's a message coming through from the Apprentices!"

There was an immediate hush. Familiar twanging, whistling sounds resonated through the water.

"Cave located: Longitude sixty West; Latitude twenty-three-and-a-half North. *Two* creatures, one approx. seventy-five feet, second approx. twelve feet. Yacht will cut engine and await events. Apprentices guarding ship until you arrive. Proceed with *extreme* caution."

"Action stations!" shouted 'Z'. With only one flipper there was no way she could swim properly let alone fight, but she could and did organise.

"Is everyone clear on strategy?" called the Zamorin.

Confident nods greeted this. George snapped his helmet closed over his beak and moved the trident to 'fast swim' position. Simba adjusted his plastron shield and gave out the dormancy drugs to the Zacans under his command. Godfrey and Monty tightened their grip on the leading edges of an enormously thick and weighty Laminaria net and checked it was evenly distributed throughout the Carrying Platoon. Raising his ancient trident surmounted by the Archelon cypher high in the water, the Zamorin brought it down in a great flashing, gleaming arc, propelling himself forward through the breathing hole and out into the open sea. Amidst spouts of spume and a maelstrom of swash the formidable Giant Leatherbacks followed.

* * *

From his lookout position in the sea, Azazel saw Andy's yacht approaching Liopleurodon's lair. The cruise ship remained beyond the horizon and Azazel guessed they'd slowed down to watch the 'Dolphin Display', which those silly creatures put on for the Humans. He'd tell the Dinosaur about the yacht. There'd be 'starters' as well as a 'main course', thought Azazel with a merciless laugh.

Azazel set off for the cave but was soon overwhelmed by the familiar scent of Leatherback. There was no sign of any, yet they must be close by. Had Liopleurodon already snacked on Turtle? Azazel sniffed the sea. No. *Live* Leatherback coming from the direction of the yacht. He swam cautiously towards it. Yes! There were young Zacans moving warily but deliberately alongside the yacht. What were they doing there? Turtles avoided boats. Fishing nets or lines could be thrown out. Propellers could cut off flippers and kill. Azazel was mystified. Deciding to brazen it out, he swam boldly towards the leader, Zozimus.

"Well met, young Turtle! And what may you be doing escorting this yacht? Does the Zamorin know you're all out on sentry go?"

Zozimus was puzzled. Azazel was a highly accomplished Zacan and Zozimus's first reaction had been relief. He'd been sent ahead to help them. But he seemed to have no idea what was going on! Perhaps he was joking. Zozimus didn't like or trust Azazel, yet he was still a Leatherback and a Zacan. He gave a straightforward reply.

"We've been sent by the Zamorin to guard this yacht. The Humans on it are helping us find the Dinosaur monster."

Azazel was totally taken aback. What did this scruffy little Nematt know about Liopleurodon? Why were they so close to his caldera? How had the Zamorin found out? Bella! Bella must have got back and told him. What were the Humans up to? His mind buzzing like an electric eel Azazel feigned nonchalance.

"You're very brave, young Turtle. Have you located the monster?"

"Yes. We're very close. We've sent a message to the Zamorin. I thought that's why you'd come?" answered Zozimus artlessly.

"Yes, yes. Naturally. I was checking the course. Well done." With a brief nod, he was gone, leaving Zozimus perplexed. There had been something odd about Azazel. Something *very* odd. What was it? Puzzle as he may he couldn't work it out, and put it down to his own dislike of the Turtle.

"The yacht's slowing down. Stay well clear," he reminded the other Apprentices, who all knew the deadly dangers of ships' propellers.

The Zacans were speeding through the water, churning up a magnificent wake of frothy foam. This was the part they loved. Vast miles of uninterrupted sea to swim in, ocean deeps to dive in, strange upside-down jellyfish and other delicacies to eat and huge underground caverns which never see the light of day to explore. This was their world for most of the year and they loved it. Now their enjoyment of flying easily through water on strong, wide flippers was diluted by the seriousness of the task. Some may be injured, some may die. But the Spacious Sea Meeting Place, their unique home and safe shelter, must be protected.

"STOP!" called the Zamorin. He could see the yacht and smell the young Zacans. "Proceed with all due care." No need to tell the Zacans about possible dangers – they knew. Floating gently, silently, cautiously, the Zacans surrounded the yacht. Like a warm welcoming wind a rapturous sigh of wonder came from the Humans on deck. No one spoke. The magical experience of being surrounded by these massive and mysterious creatures, living Dinosaurs, silenced even Chico.

Listening to the low gruntings and hummings and replies in higher pitched warbles and chirrups the Humans had no doubt that the bigger, older Turtles were greeting the smaller ones.

"Come on Chico," Penny broke the awed silence on deck, "Time to do your bit again." Chico had reattached himself to Penny's anorak and, grasping a fold of material securely between his talons, lent overboard.

"Er … 'ello there," he called in Leatherback. "Sorry to interrupt. You've got the position ok?"

The Zamorin replied. There was an excited rush to that side of the ship. Unless a male Leatherback becomes stranded, like George, they were rarely seen by Humans and everyone crowded round to share the marvellous sight of this magnificent specimen of adult male Leatherback.

"Yes, thank you. You're Chico I take it?"

"Yes, that's me. Who're you?"

It was Letty who replied.

"Hello Chico. This is Zamorin Kenronishe. He's our Chief."

Chico, well aware of the etiquette attached to pecking order in animal communities, hastened to apologise.

"Oh! Sorry Sir, I didn't know ..."

"We owe you a great deal, Chico. Laetitia has told us of your care for our Matriarchs on their dangerous journeys up the beach. And now this. We're in your debt."

Chico coughed in embarrassed fashion.

"May I ask – what are your plans? The Humans need to know."

"Can the yacht move very, very slowly towards the cave? We need to draw Liopleurodon and his friend into the open sea. We're setting a trap. It's extremely dangerous. *We* will engage the monster, *not* the Humans. They don't understand him as we do. As soon as he emerges their ship must back off and return to shore. They must *not* get involved."

"What's he saying, Chico?" Penny was agog, as were the others. Gemma had a firm hold on her as she leant overboard with Chico gripping her shoulder, Andy had an arm round Jimmy who'd nearly fallen into the sea with excitement at seeing more Turtles. Dorothy and Cora, shorter and rounder than the others, were balanced precariously on deckside benches watched over by Fan-Fan, Livingston and Jomo.

Chico translated the message. "And you Humans – keep out of it. Return to shore. The Chief says – far too dangerous for Humans." Chico smirked slightly.

"Now see here ..." began Andy crossly, but Gemma butted in.

"We must do as they ask. We have no practical knowledge of Marine Dinosaurs and their behaviour patterns. The Leatherbacks have. They're Dinosaurs themselves."

The men muttered angrily.

"Dat all veree well, Ma'am but say dey get inta trouble? Wha' we goin' do den? Sit by an' watch?"

Jomo had a point.

"I've got deep water fishing gear on board, strong nylon line attached to a winch. That could be useful?" suggested Andy hopefully.

"If their Chief wants us to stay out of it, we must respect his wishes," repeated Gemma. "Animals, fish, reptiles, they have very strong instincts about such matters."

Fan-Fan nodded his head in agreement.

"Dat sure right, Missy. Me see dis many times on de land and de sea. Missy Prof, she right. But we doan wan' dem to perish!"

"Chico, ask if we can help," suggested Penny.

"These Humans," said Chico to Kenronishe, "this little Hatchling girl," he wheedled, "they want to help. Is there anything they can do?"

"The Human children must be kept safe," replied the Zamorin sternly. "Humans located the cave and provided bait. They've done their part. We are grateful to them. Better to keep away from our feuds. We fight alone."

Chico translated and, thwarted and angry, the men looked at each other. Secretly, they were making plans.

* * *

Azazel swam thoughtfully towards Liopleurodon's cave. When little Isabella had escaped, she must have reported straight to the Zamorin. He didn't want to sacrifice so many Leatherbacks. It was Humans he hated. Yet how could he separate them from the yacht? The Dinosaur wouldn't discriminate between Humans and Turtles! And where was that cruise liner? Surely it should be over the horizon by now? Looking towards where it would appear, Azazel saw a plume of smoke. *Ah,* here it was! Good – he'd inform Liopleurodon about the cruise liner and keep quiet about the yacht. They were approaching from different directions and the smell of many hundreds of people on board the liner would overpower the scent of a few aboard the yacht. Azazel dived into the tunnel leading to the caldera.

*   *   *

Andy's yacht glided silently closer to the caldera. The young Apprentices had been relegated to swimming well to stern of the ship. Objections had been made but discipline prevailed and they reluctantly obeyed orders. Zozimus paddled thoughtfully along, his mind seething with plans to rescue Bella. Would she still be alive? He mustn't think like that but stay alert, ready to act as soon as an opportunity came. But what *was* it about Azazel that kept niggling him?

Ahead of the yacht, dispersed over a wide expanse of ocean, Kenronishe and the Zacans swam stealthily along in full fighting order. They knew the keenness of the Dinosaur's sense of smell. It should draw him out of his lair before the yacht came into the danger zone. Passing fish gazed in awe at the slow moving, armed convoy. Some nodded knowingly. From inaccessible rocky retreats and crevices these fish had seen the monster and guessed what the Leatherbacks' mission must be.

With startling suddenness a huge black cloud erupted, spreading wraithlike throughout the sea, blocking out all subterranean light and stinging the Turtles' sensitive eyes.

"Adjust helmets! Adjust helmets!" The urgent cry echoed down the line through the murky water.

"Black gusher eruption from sea floor. Usual gases. Archie – warn Apprentices!"

The Zamorin, George and Letty looked anxious. This was the sort of trick a Dinosaur could play to confuse his prey and make an attack easier.

"Could be a diversionary tactic! Stay alert! Do not break formation!" shouted the Zamorin. Accustomed to dark water the unexpected gloom did little to upset the Turtles but the noxious gas was dangerous. With helmets adjusted over their beaks to exclude poison they swam steadily on.

"AAARRGGGHHHHHH!"

A terrifying booming bellow reverberated through the water. The Zamorin halted and the Zacans stopped swimming, floating silently. The Apprentices heard it and turned mauve. The 'Lollypop Lure' Humans heard it and shivered.

"What was *that?*" whispered Penny.

"The monster, Missah. The 'orrible monster from the deep," Chico cried, trying to bury his head under Penny's anorak.

"Hey, Pen," Jimmy stuttered, "I'm not sure I'm enjoying this adventure any more."

"LOOK!" screamed Penny.

Heading towards the yacht at phenomenal speed was a dense black wave.

"It's probably octopus ink," Gemma suggested in a shaky voice. "No need to worry."

But Penny, Jimmy and Chico had fled. On the bridge Andy was advising the Captain, "Back off! Back away! That disturbance in the sea may be submarine volcanic activity or other, er – dangerous activity." Staying only long enough to see his command obeyed, Andy sprinted to the stern where a powerful telescope was bolted to the deck. With its magnification it might help uncover the mystery of the black water. But the telescope was already in use. Fan-Fan was peering through it with Jomo, Adrian and Livingston huddled round.

"Hi Mr Saxon, sir. Sorry meh has to shout. De wind, she blow. Meh left Mr MacRobert wit' de ladies. Doan yo worry 'bout dat black sea. She a 'smoker' from de bottom o' de ocean. Meh see her afore," commented Fan-Fan casually.

"We doan like de looks o' dat dinosewer an' we make de boat safe," added Jomo. "No need to inform de ladies," he winked conspiratorially. "See dis here?" he pointed to a neat mound of tough nylon fishing line. "We use dis."

Andy nodded approvingly.

"Yep, that was my thought too. We'd better be ready for some action."

The men gathered round Andy. They didn't notice Penny, Jimmy and an amazingly silent Chico crouched behind a tarpaulin.

Chapter Twenty-One

AZAZEL MAKES A DECISION

Liopleurodon's nostrils stretched wide, savouring the heady aroma of food, gobstopper eyes glistening with greedy anticipation. He could smell Humans, lots of Humans! Mouth stretched wide he bellowed a welcome.

"AAAAHHRRRGGGGHHHH!" he roared. "Smell them, White Shark? Enough for both of us!"

"What happened to that 'friend' of yours, the white Leatherback? He was supposed to warn us!"

"HHHAAAAHHHAAA!" screeched the Dinosaur. "My nose tells me what's approaching faster than any Leatherback! He keeps me in touch with oceanic activity – a useful idiot … and here he comes! Late as usual, Leatherback!" The Dinosaur greeted Azazel contemptuously.

"The cruise ship slowed to watch those stupid Dolphins showing off," replied Azazel. "It's in the Bermuda Triangle area now. Time for your Freak Wave. An extra huge one," he added placatingly.

Liopleurodon flicked his massive tail flippers, throwing Azazel and the White Shark off balance.

"HA, HA, HO, HO!" he cackled malevolently, watching them flounder. "Just practising! My wave will be much bigger than that! And you, Leatherback," the round evil eyes came close to Azazel's, "keep away. I can smell your kind out there and want no interference," he snarled.

Glaring fixedly, his convex eyes reflected the Leatherback like a mirror. But Azazel saw something else reflected in them. Behind him, in the tunnel, a small Turtle slipped furtively into a fissure. Was it an advance scout?

* * *

Zozimus had been fed up hanging around, waiting for orders. What had happened to Bella? He'd passed on Archie's commands and the Apprentices had adjusted their helmets. Further away from the smoker's epicentre the poison gases dispersed and were less dangerous. The young Zacans were safe. Zozimus had watched the miasma of black water approaching and had a brainwave. They were near the caldera, the site of an ancient volcano, and the smoky stream originated from it. If he followed the 'gusher' he would find the monster's cave! Diving into the darkest part of the smoke he had slipped away, swimming strongly against the current. Whenever the misty shape of another Zacan swam near, Zozimus kept still and quiet, remaining in the dark heart of the gusher. Then, in the murky gloom below, he'd seen a wide chasm in the sea bed from which the thick black cloud flowed. He'd found the caldera! Heading straight for it Zozimus had stopped abruptly. A loud bloodcurdling laugh reverberated through the chasm. Then another voice echoed down the tunnel. It sounded like Azazel! Maybe he was negotiating with the monster! Perhaps he needed help in releasing Bella! Keeping close to the wall, Zozimus had plunged down the tunnel.

* * *

"I'm frightened."

"Me too."

Seeing the sinister black wave approaching, Penny and Jimmy had fled to the stern of the ship. Taking cover behind a safety barrier, they crouched low.

"Have you got your life-jacket on?" fussed Jimmy.

Penny had become used to his safety mania and patiently replied, "Yes."

"Here … grab this and pull. It'll keep us dry." Jimmy heaved a large tarpaulin over them. Chico was almost speechless with fear, his plumage pale.

"Don't like water," he complained, his beak chattering. "Don't know why mariners took Parrots on board ship. Me – I'm a Land Parrot."

Penny snuggled him up firmly against the life-jacket.

"Keep tight hold, Chico. We'll look after you."

"Look! Here come the men. Be quiet!"

Jomo, Livingston, Fan-Fan and Adrian lurched into view.

"We need han emergency plan," stated Livingston.

"Sure ting man. Meh agrees wit' yo dere," said Jomo. "Dem Turtles, dey need help! We help dem."

"Yup, an' kep de boat upside too!" added Fan-Fan thoughtfully.

"But what can we do? If there is a Dinosaur we need guns and stuff," said Adrian. "Leatherbacks with tridents, what use are they?"

Adrian looked gloomily at the dense, inky water. Why had he come on this wild goose – or rather Dinosaur – chase? Was there really a prehistoric monster out there causing havoc?

"Pheweee! Am I glad you're all here!" A windblown Andy appeared clutching the safety rail.

"We're gonna need to make plans. And quick!" he stated peremptorily.

The massive coil of strong nylon fishing line would help, everyone agreed. Liopleurodon could be tied up with it and attached to the winch if the Leatherbacks needed help. But they mustn't interfere unless it was essential.

"Ok. But doan tell de ladies nor pickneys, dey mus' be kep' safe. An' doan tell dat dratted wutless bird!" shouted Livingston above the wind.

About to give vent to a protesting squawk, Jimmy wrapped his fingers firmly round Chico's long curved beak and kept it shut. Chico blinked angrily. Worthless bird was he? He'd show them!

* * *

As Zozimus swam along the tunnel the dark gusher dispersed. He could see the open caldera with its grisly wreckage, bones and carapaces scattered about. There was no sign of Bella. Some yards away a White Shark and massive monster with large powerful flippers faced him, their eyes fixed on a pale Leatherback. Azazel! Realisation dawned on Zozimus. That's what had been wrong with Azazel – he wasn't wearing armour! He couldn't be negotiating! And the monster with flippers must be an ancestor! Darting swiftly into a nearby fissure, Zozimus thought things over. Azazel was talking to two hated enemies. They weren't attacking him. Why not? There had been something odd about the monster too. What was it? Very cautiously he peered round the rocky fissure. While the monster concentrated on Azazel, Zozimus concentrated on the monster. Yuck – what an ugly specimen! It looked like a Pliosaur – that was it! Liopleurodon, the Zamorin had said. Drooling foul-smelling saliva from his jaws, the protuberant wide-set eyes above the dagger-sharp teeth glittered malignantly. Zozimus gasped and jumped back into the fissure in horrified recognition. The monster had three eyes! Above and between the two yellow orbs, a third eye had momentarily glared. Protected by a portcullis of fine bones, it was difficult to see. But Zozimus knew about this third eye, the Argos Eye. He and all Leatherbacks had a similar 'eye', a soft spot of thin delicate tissue, which provided additional sensory knowledge. It acted as a compass and also regulated temperature, it was useful in many other ways too. Without it Leatherbacks would lose their amazing sense of direction, freeze to death, forget how to swim. It was a hidden but vital asset. And the monster had one. Zozimus shuddered. It linked the monster inexorably to the Marine Turtle dynasty.

Azazel sensed increasing animosity towards him and foresaw the outcome. White Sharks hated Leatherbacks and were very short-tempered. So was Liopleurodon. He made a swift decision.

"The black gusher's done its work. The exit's camouflaged," he remarked casually. "I'll go ahead." Before either creature could move or reply Azazel flew towards the exit tunnel. Globular luminescent eyes followed him angrily, the White Shark lashing his tail in frustration. Azazel reached the tunnel and started down it, humming loudly as he went. Amazed, Zozimus listened carefully to Azazel's C.A.W. message.

"*Get out*! Warn about White Shark."

Azazel came closer to the fissure.

"GO! GO!" he urged on the secret Chelonian Wavelength.

Zozimus shot out of the fissure and flung himself along the tunnel taking advantage of the black smoker's final surge of power.

"HA!" yelled the White Shark triumphantly, "Look what he's flushed out! A little Leatherback soldier in hiding. What's he up to?"

"GET HIM!" screeched Liopleurodon to the faster-moving White Shark. "Don't let him escape!"

Without hesitation the White Shark rocketed down the tunnel.

"Get out of my way, you stupid, interfering Leatherback!" he barked at the stationary Azazel, who was floating diagonally across the tunnel blocking the exit. Azazel didn't move.

"Get out of my way!" shouted the Shark angrily, "or it will be the worse for you!"

Still Azazel didn't move. With a roar of fury the White Shark threw himself at the Turtle, mouth open, jagged-edged teeth exposed. Azazel waited. As the jaws were about to close over him, he moved with the incredible speed of Marine Turtles. The Shark's teeth snapped shut on empty water. Bawling in indignation he prepared to attack Azazel from below. With every ounce of his two tons behind it, Azazel threw a huge flipper left hook across the White Shark's sensitive jaw. Howling in pain and indignation the Shark fell back. Azazel made no move to escape. With his massive carapace turned towards the White Shark he remained blocking the exit.

"OH! HO, HO, HO!" roared the White Shark. "Quite the hero! I knew you were stupid."

Silently, stubbornly, Azazel stayed in position, his decision unchanged. Recovering from the blow, the White Shark closed for an attack on Azazel's soft plastron. They were a well-matched pair. Both twelve feet long, superbly muscled, wonderfully adapted to their watery environment, Azazel's impregnable leathery carapace provided a natural shield – but the White Shark's teeth were his advantage. Unable to retract his head like his land cousins, Tortoises, Azazel knew that a bite in the neck or soft plastron would kill him.

Near the ocean end of the tunnel Zozimus heard a gurgling, croaking cry and looked back. The White Shark had Azazel by the throat, sinking his long, rapier-like, teeth into the exposed flesh.

"NOOOOO!" cried Zozimus.

"Ggggooooo ..." croaked Azazel. Looking up, Zozimus saw Liopleurodon on the move, heading straight for him. Turning, he swam for his life.

* * *

The diminishing black wave was approaching the yacht when Andy hurriedly returned to the bridge.

"Steady and slow ahead. Steer into the wave," he commanded.

"Aye aye, Sir," agreed the Captain. "Sea's very murky. Can't see the Turtles."

"Don't worry about them. They're excellent swimmers," replied Gemma, attempting cheerfulness.

"Yes Ma'am," replied the Captain worriedly.

"Stop immediately when I give the word," instructed Andy.

In the stern, Livingston, Jomo, Fan-Fan and Adrian had been joined by Alistair, determined not to be left out of the action.

"See dat wave?" Fan-Fan pointed to the smooth black wall of the approaching gusher. "She need firm handlin'. Ah tink ah go aid de Capt'n sail de boat."

With a rolling gait he walked steadily along the deck, the others crowding close behind. Penny and Jimmy peered out cautiously.

"They've gone! We can come out. Be careful, the deck's slippy."

"Phew!" gasped Penny crawling out from under the tarpaulin, "That was stifling."

"Careful! Keep hold of the rail," instructed Jimmy.

Chico let out a squawk of horror.

"No Missah Penny! Stay here. Safe," he pleaded.

"Come on you silly Parrot! Hold tight to me."

Digging his talons into her life-jacket Chico closed his eyes and set up a low moan.

"Shut up, Chico!"

Grasping the safety barrier, Jimmy and Penny lurched unsteadily to their feet. SMACK! Over the side they flew, together with something large smelling strongly of brine and seaweed.

SSSPLASSSH! A boiling, effervescent vortex of black water, full of fragmented seaweed, dust, broken shells and small fish, poured over them. Chico clung frantically to Penny, his teeth chattering. Thrashing about in the water they hit a piece of thick, rubbery detritus and clung to it. The detritus emitted a loud hoarse sound like a strangulated 'YEOOOWWW!'

"Penny! It's a Leatherback!" gasped Jimmy.

"Wha … ss happened?" spluttered Penny, holding on to the leathery carapace and spitting out seaweed.

"Turtle … hit us when wave came. Washed overboard … Wh … why . . ssss he making tha noise …?"

Zozimus, caught up in the black gusher's surge, had been thrown across the yacht just as Jimmy and Penny emerged from their hiding place and had carried them into the sea with him. He must warn them about the Shark and Liopleurodon, he must make them understand the danger! Whistling and grunting, his flippers waving about like windmills, he pointed at the submerged entrance to the caldera.

"Wha? What's he saying," Penny appealed to Chico, now swaying about on Zozimus, his ferocious talons firmly dug into the Turtle's tough carapace.

"Hhhe's wwwarning us," stuttered Chico. "A dinosewer and a … OOWW! … OHHH! … White Shark are coming! Oooww! That's big trouble." Chico attempted a swift take-off but his water-logged feathers stopped him.

"No you don't!" Penny grabbed him. "The Leatherbacks and our parents must be warned. You're the only one who can do it."

"Not a sea bird!" Chico said angrily. "Me, I'm a *Land Parrot*. I'm for dry land!"

"Livingston was right. You're a worthless bird, a coward," taunted Penny. "Ok, we'll all be killed and it'll be *your* fault."

His eyes flashing pure hate, Chico screeched at Zozimus and with a series of grunts and clicks the Leatherback replied.

"Ok!" said Chico. "This guy's called Zozimus. I'm going to warn the Leatherbacks then the Humans. Zozimus says hang on to him, one each side, and you'll be safe. The Humans will soon rescue you. Must fly!" and he was off, soaring out to sea where the Zacans were congregated.

* * *

Zamorin Kenronishe, George and Laetitia had seen Zozimus whizzing by in the air. There was no time to wonder at his extraordinary appearance, flying along on the crest of the black gusher when he should have been safely tucked away at the stern of the yacht. Action was imminent, and the Zamorin was deploying his troops when out of the sky hurtled a javelin of brilliant coloured feathers.

"Sir, Sir," shrieked Chico, "the youth Zozimus says to warn you. A dinosewer, Liopleurodon, and a White Shark are coming down the tunnel!" He paused for breath, pointing towards the tunnel entrance with a wing. "I must alert the Humans!"

Chico took off with a spectacular display of spread wings. He was beginning to enjoy his role as saviour of the world.

"Don't move 'til I say," commanded Kenronishe. "Godfrey, is the net ready?"

"It is Sir," responded Godfrey calmly.

"Simba, are the dormancy drugs to flipper?"

"They are, Sir," replied Simba.

They watched, alert and prepared, as the turbulent sea frothed and boiled.

"Steady. Steady," commanded Kenronishe as the Zacans grasped their tridents, ready to attack.

Seething, hissing blood-red water erupted from the cave and spread over the surrounding sea. In its midst the torpedo shape of the White Shark stood out clear and stark, revealing a hideous scene. Impaled on his razor-sharp teeth were the mauled remnants of Azazel's white body, which he shook viciously. A sibilant hissing and growling of shock and loathing came from the Zacans. Instinctively they moved towards their enemy.

"STEADY!" admonished Kenronishe sternly. "Steady!"
Unwillingly they fell back, held the line and waited for orders.

* * *

"We're through it, Sir!" shouted the relieved Captain. "The gusher's behind us. There's a terrific commotion to port." Everyone rushed to port. The rampaging sea threw up great gobs of glutinous red matter. One landed on deck. Jomo picked it up and recoiled.

"Is flesh, Mr Saxon, from de fish. See hereyah, big teeth marks, Shark's foh suh. Dem Turtles, dey attack now."

"STOP all engines! Go astern! Gemma, get below. The children, Mrs Fairweather and Cora are there."

"No way! I'm staying here. I've got to see this!"

"It's too dangerous! If that Dinosaur shows up …"

"LOOK!" screamed Livingston.

A long, gruesome snake-like head set with round staring eyes and gigantic overlapping teeth was slowly emerging from the seething, bloodied, frenzied welter of water. Liopleurodon had arrived.

Chapter Twenty-Two

Chico's Finest Hour

Penny and Jimmy clung onto Zozimus, one arm twined round a flipper, the other flung over his carapace.

"Penny – are you ok? Is your life-jacket whistle working?" Penny sighed. Jimmy and his safety mania! As if she'd be blowing whistles now!

"Yes, yes, I'm alright. But we're drifting away from the yacht, from Mum and Gran and everyone. We'll ask Zozimus to swim nearer to them."

Giving his flipper a tug she asked the Turtle to swim closer to the yacht. But the Leatherback paid no attention. He was watching a monstrous head emerging from the water.

Chico skimmed over the water above the rearing head of Liopleurodon and hastily warned the Humans about the Dinosaur and the White Shark. With wings widespread he pointed to where Penny and Jimmy were floating on Zozimus's back, not far from the monster. There were screams of horror as Gemma, Andy and the others spotted them among the turbulent water.

"I thought they were in the galley with Dorothy and Cora!" wailed Gemma.

"We must fetch them in at once," declared Andy.

"But Ma'am, Sir, you'll be heading straight towards the Dinosaur!" exclaimed the Captain.

"It's the only possible way of saving the children. They're what matter most. Full speed ahead Captain, straight for the Dinosaur."

"Aye aye, Sir!" he responded glumly.

"Hereyah brother! Doan yo fret. Me and ma frens, we help yo. I kno' dese waters." Fan-Fan clapped the Captain reassuringly on the back. "Man – we do dis ting together an' rescue dem pickneys."

In the galley the abrupt change from slow to full speed threw Dorothy and Cora across the table where they'd been sitting chatting.

"Eh Dotty! What's to do? Let's go upstairs and discover." The ladies recovered their balance and tottered up on deck.

"Hey, Jomo, what's goin' on hereyah?"

"Look! See dat head over dere? Dat's a Dinosaur!"

Cora and Dorothy gazed, white with horror at the nightmare head with its malignant stare.

"It looks like the Loch Ness monster!" stammered Dorothy.

"Ah see some strange tings in mah work and hear plenny lackeray 'bout jumbies and suchlike. Is all pappy talk. But dis Dinosaur, man, ah'm seein' he good!" quavered Cora.

"Jomo – who's that in the sea?" whispered Dorothy.

"Is Penny and Jimmy, Ma'am, we is goin' to rescue dem right now."

"We thought they were safe with Gemma, Andy and you men! Were they washed overboard?"

"It suh seem so, Ma'am. No one kno' how dey come to be sittin' in de sea." Jomo shook his head in bewilderment.

Chico was not happy. He'd delivered his messages and proved he wasn't a 'worthless bird' but there in the sea were Penny, Jimmy and Zozimus in the most deadly danger. He felt in his feathers he ought to be *doing* something to help them. What could *he* do? A bird whose only weapons were a sharp beak and claws like talons? They wouldn't harm a Dinosaur! AH! There was one thing he could do that no one else could. Shaking out his feathers he swooped off towards them.

He was greeted with cries of relief.

"Chico! Thank goodness you've come!"

Jimmy and Penny would have hugged him, but clinging on to the Leatherback's broad carapace stopped them. Mesmerised and terrified by the gigantic head that had appeared from the depths, they couldn't understand Zozimus's strange reaction. He had stopped swimming and lay still, quietly floating, humming and twanging loudly. *What* was he doing? Only Chico could translate for them.

"What's Zozimus doing? What's he saying? We don't understand!

He ought to be swimming away as fast as he can!"

With his eyes fixed nervously on Liopleurodon, Chico had a brisk exchange with Zozimus.

"He's on the emergency Chelonian Auditory Wavelength sending out an S.O.S. Every Leatherback, Marine Turtle, Dolphin, Whale, Manta Ray and other friendly species will know exactly where he is and what's happening. If he remains still and disturbs the water as little as possible there's a better chance of the Dinosaur and White Shark ignoring him. He says will you keep still too and stop thrashing about, drawing attention to yourselves."

Jimmy and Penny obeyed as best they could.

"Chico," whispered Penny, "Please don't leave us. We need you." Chico's heart swelled with pride. He was no longer a 'worthless bird'! He was *needed*!

It was very quiet in the sea as all four of them watched the gargantuan Liopleurodon rising from the sea bed. Away to their left, boiling, effervescent water followed by a flurry of activity heralded that the Zacans were engaged in battle. Alone against the fully armed, alert Zacans the Shark wasn't a problem. The Dinosaur would be.

As Liopleurodon rose slowly and majestically from the vastness of his gory caldera, the lamp-like eyes swivelled from side to side surveying the scene. Emerging near Zozimus and his passengers he ignored them. Tasty-looking little yacht to his left, small Turtle with two tiny Humans attached in front, possibly dead already so no fun there, and away to his right – AAAHH HHAA HAAA! Here were better pickings! A mêlée of huge Leatherbacks, that fool the White Shark and, on the horizon, a tasty-looking cruise boat! Which prey would he take? Easing himself around he focused his flaring eyes on the Zacans and cruise ship and listened carefully to their sonar vibrations. Many Humans, many Leatherbacks close together. Yes, he'd take them. Decision made, he smiled widely, displaying his nauseating teeth as he prepared for his famous tidal wave and anticipated the chaos it would cause.

"Look at those teeth! Can't we go any faster?" Gemma strained over the rail towards her daughter.

"GEMMA!" cried Dorothy sharply, moving forward. "Get away from that rail! We don't want you overboard as well as the children."

Reluctantly, Gemma joined the older woman.

"We're catching up with the Leatherback. We'll soon have the children on board," said Dorothy, trying to sound reassuring.

"Everything's ready. Lifeboat and scaling nets are in position. The men have gone aft to prepare fending off the Dinosaur with stun guns. We'll save them, don't you worry," shouted Andy confidently, his eyes diamantine with determination.

Penny's eyes were shut tight. She was sure her arms would never recover. It was as if they'd been wrapped round Zozimus's flipper, then frozen.

"Jimmy," she murmured quietly, "what's happening? Is the Dinosaur very close?"

But it was Zozimus who replied, mutedly clicking his beak.

"He says the Dinosaur is looking away from us," translated Chico out of the side of his mouth. "Lie absolutely still. He thinks we're dead. He only likes live prey."

Chico was lying flat as a pancake on Zozimus's carapace, his rainbow-coloured wings tucked well in to his sides, his claws adhering like glue to the leathery back.

CRRAASSSSSSHHH!!!

Penny, Jimmy, Zozimus and Chico were smothered by a waterspout, a vortex of sound, spiralling swash and frothy foam. Something very large and heavy smashed into the sea right in front of Liopleurodon. The monster turned lazily and looked down. More Humans! Dear, dear, they were all over the sea these days! Like the others they would drown in the wave. Its mind full of dreadful deeds, Liopleurodon returned to surveying the slowly-approaching cruise liner.

"MUM!!! GRAN! CORA! What are you DOING?"

Penny gave an anguished scream as the three ladies crashed into the water.

"Jimmy, Chico, Zozimus – *do* something! They'll all be killed and *eaten*!"

Zozimus had his eyes closed, pretending to be dead but really thinking of Bella. That horrible Dinosaur must have eaten her! He wanted revenge! Just as Penny screamed her appeal, Zozimus had a brainwave. His eyes shot open, gleaming with hope. Gabbling as fast as he could, he told Chico of the sensitive spot, the Argos Eye, in Liopleurodon's forehead. If the children could reach and destroy that, Liopleurodon would be paralysed.

"Can't you do it?" gasped Chico.

"No. Leatherbacks don't go in for flying except in water. Anyhow, we couldn't get our large flippers through the portcullis that protects the membrane. You need fingers, Human fingers which separate."

"I'll ask Cora! She can look after herself," replied Chico desperately.

"No! – It's *got* to be the children! They're the only ones with small hands and thin, narrow fingers. Adult fingers will be too big. Quick, oh, quickly, Chico, do as I ask!"

"Mum! Over here. Get close to us! Don't drift away!" Penny was sobbing in horror as the women drifted nearer the Dinosaur.

Chico stopped arguing with Zozimus. Swiftly he explained about the Argos Eye to Penny and Jimmy. Abruptly Penny ceased yowling.

"We've *got* to save Mum and Gran and Cora! And the others too. Jimmy, come on. It's our only chance!"

"Yep, right," he stammered. Gazing up at the Dinosaur's massive head, he added, "How are we supposed to get up there? Right now I don't feel full of bright ideas. Is Chico going to fly us?"

"Get on Zozimus's flippers, one on each," called Chico. "He's going to try and throw you up. Catch hold of Liopleurodon's neck when you're there!"

"*No!*" shouted Jimmy. "No way!" We've been holding onto Zozimus and Humans shouldn't touch Turtles. It can damage and distress them."

Penny nodded energetically in agreement.

"*Sometimes* you may have to to help them, but not unless you've *got* to," she added.

Zozimus gave a loud grunt followed by a string of sharp clicks.

"He says just do it," interpreted Chico. "We've *all* got to take risks if we're to defeat Liopleurodon."

Jimmy and Penny looked up at the drooling, glowering monster towering above them. Without further argument they climbed carefully onto Zozimus's outstretched flippers.

Sweeping his flippers underwater to get a good powerful throw, Jimmy fell into the water while Penny slipped sideways, half off, half on. Zozimus gave an exasperated grunt.

"Keep tight hold until the flipper is out of the water and don't fall off again. You're very heavy and Zozimus will run out of energy," translated Chico.

Jimmy clambered back into position.

"Ok. GO!" With the children clinging on like limpet 'guests', Zozimus submerged his flippers. Halfway out of the water he stopped, unable to raise them any further.

"Come on, Zoz! You can do it!" urged Chico.

Zozimus emitted a plaintive wheeze followed by a groan.

"You're too heavy! … Get those life-jackets off!" squawked Chico.

Penny quickly threw off the cumbersome box-like jacket but Jimmy took no action.

"QUICK! Mum's drifting further and further away! Jimmy – take it off!"

"I can't! I CAN'T!" he wailed. "I'm too frightened. I've *got* to have my life-jacket!"

"We're too heavy for Zoz to throw. It's our only chance. *Everyone's* depending on us!"

With a deep sigh, Jimmy threw off his life-jacket.

"Zoz will catapult you onto Liopleurodon's back. *Hold on* when you're there. You know what to do. *Good luck!*" encouraged Chico.

Submerging his flippers slowly, Zozimus quickly drew them up clear of the water. There was a sickening scrunching, tearing sound and a peculiar yelp. Penny and Jimmy went flying through the air, plummeting into the water not far from where Gemma, Dorothy and Cora were floundering. Chico anxiously hovered over them.

"You're too heavy for Zozimus! He's only a young Leatherback. We'll have to think again."

Trying bravely not to squawk in panic he rounded all the Humans up like a Sheep-Parrot and herded them back towards the broad Turtle carapace rising above the waves like a small island of safety.

"Here – climb aboard. You ok?"

As Jimmy and Penny climbed onto the outstretched flippers they were aware of a difference – bigger, stronger flippers, a broader carapace. Had Zozimus grown? Chico too looked startled as he took in the size of the Turtle, who grunted urgently to him.

"I'm Laetitia, Zozimus's mother. I heard his distress signal and came at once. His flippers have cracked. They're bleeding. Liopleurodon will smell blood. Tell those Human Matriarchs his only chance is if they lean over his carapace and support his flippers. Hold them firmly against his sides. That should staunch the blood flow and keep the Matriarchs afloat. He can bear them leaning on him *in water*. I'll take over here."

Chico translated to the three ladies, leading them the short distance to Zozimus, lying helpless in a spreading pool of blood. Chico arranged the ladies to his satisfaction; Gemma and Dorothy supporting one flipper and Cora the other. They murmured soothing words of solace and appreciation to the vulnerable young Leatherback and he, seeing the reassuring size of Cora, instantly felt better.

"Now hold on tight m'dears. We don't want you to drown or attract the Dinosaur's attention. The children are safe with Matriarch Laetitia," added Chico confidently, before taking off back to them. What a busy day! His wings would be worn out!

Jimmy and Penny readied themselves on Letty's broad muscular flippers and with one mighty throw she swiftly and unerringly landed them on the monster's back, a short distance from the Argos Eye. There they sat, their arms clinging onto Liopleurodon's neck. They'd made it!

* * *

When the Zamorin gave the order to attack the White Shark, the Zacans knew exactly what to do and the part each would play. They had moved rapidly and purposefully, some distracting by weaving to and fro across his eyes and vicious jaws, others ready with poison, snare and rope. Skimming into a favourable position, Simba had lobbed a dormancy drug into the gaping jaws. Defeated and immobile, the White Shark was securely trussed and fettered in a net carried by Godfrey's team. Later he would be towed away by Bluey, the massive Blue Whale who had promised his help and was on his way towards them.

"Good work, Zacans! Now for Liopleurodon. George, gather the teams together. Monty's team will guard the White Shark. Are there any casualties?"

"Yes Sir, the females who distracted the Shark, but thank Great Mother Turtle nothing too serious. A few flipper scratches and plastron bruises. 'Z' is looking after them."

The Zamorin looked around.

"Where's Laetitia?"

George paled. Being in the thick of it, he'd not noticed what she'd been doing. Strong, swift and clever, he didn't worry too much about her. Then he remembered – Zozimus's S.O.S. call! She would have responded instantly to her son's call for help. They were in terrible danger!

"She must be with Zozimus near Liopleurodon. You heard his S.O.S. Quickly Sir, we must go!"

"We *are* going! Monty, stay here. Guard the Shark well. Zacans – all speed to help Zozimus and Laetitia!"

* * *

Clasping Liopleurodon's neck, Penny and Jimmy exchanged petrified looks. What next?

"We've got to get a closer look at this Argos Eye thing."

"What'll we do when we've located it?" Penny breathed.

"Zozimus said stick our fingers through the portcullis and break the fragile bones. Once we've made a gap we must pierce the membrane beneath."

"How strong is it?"

"Let's find out," hissed Jimmy.

Cautiously they slid along the head until the monster's 'third eye' could be seen pulsating through an intricate fretwork of delicate interwoven bones.

"*Wow*! Even Mum couldn't get her finger through that mesh! It's so fine! Zozimus was right. Let's hope our hands are small enough. The bones cover it like a spider's web."

"One of us must stab the 'eye'... Our fingers won't be strong enough. It's a thick membrane. What can we use?"

Carefully unzipping a capacious pocket in his sailing shorts, Jimmy gave a subdued yelp of triumph.

"Look!" He gave the merest flicker of a grin. "It's the Swiss Army Penknife Pa gave me for sailing. This'll help!"

"Right – we'll break through the portcullis together, then sink the knife into the Argos Eye. Ok?"

"Yep." Jimmy had forgotten his fear in the thrill of action.

"Let's do it!"

"One, two, three!"

Reaching out, each grabbed a handful of brittle bony portcullis and pulled with all their strength. There was a snapping, cracking noise and a roar of fury as Liopleurodon realised what was happening. Jimmy and Penny clung on as it shook its massive head angrily.

"I'm falling off!"

Jimmy had slipped sideways almost off the head.

"Hold on to the portcullis! Don't let go!" shouted Penny.

Jimmy clung precariously onto the Dinosaur's fragile bones. A creaking noise like rusty door hinges came from the portcullis. The whole structure was coming away in his hand!

"JIMMY! Use the penknife!" screamed Penny.

Jimmy lunged at the 'Eye', jabbing into thin air.

"AGAIN!" yelled Penny. But swinging away from the 'Eye', Jimmy missed.

"Pass me the knife!" instructed Penny. "NOW!" she screamed, as Jimmy swung towards her.

Taking careful aim he reached out and thrust the knife into her outstretched hand just as the portcullis shattered. Quickly Penny grabbed it, catching it by the blade and cutting her fingers. Reversing it, she stabbed frantically at Liopleurodon's weak spot, the Argos Eye. How deeply entrenched under the skin was the gland? Would one blow be enough to damage it? The monster continued thrashing about, howling in anger. Penny clung on to the Dinosaur and again thrust the knife deep into the 'Eye'. Still nothing happened. Reaching over to remove the knife for a third attempt Penny gasped with horror. She couldn't get the knife out! It was stuck fast in the 'Eye'! Releasing her grip on Liopleurodon, she used both hands to pull and tug at the knife. It wouldn't budge. Now, like Jimmy, she was slipping, slipping, unable to hold on any longer. Shrieking, she fell into space…

* * *

Aboard the cruise liner, people lining the decks were marvelling at the magnificent balletic display put on by Jeté and his Pod of Dolphins. Suddenly, as if on a word of command, the Dolphins ceased leaping and curvetting and shot away into the distance with incredible precision and speed. Binoculars were adjusted to watch them go. It was then the crew and holidaymakers became aware of the horrific events being played out on the horizon. They could make out an enormous creature rearing from the sea, small shapes floundering and a nearby yacht. Everyone on the ship and in the yacht saw Penny and Jimmy falling into the pulsating water. But the four mothers in the water couldn't see.

"Chico!" grunted Letty, who had swum to help Gemma, Dorothy and Cora with Zozimus,

"What was that big splash? Go and see." But Chico was tired and didn't want to go anywhere. He felt safe curled up on Letty's wide carapace.

"Go *on*!" urged Letty. "We need to know."

Chico took off with as little disturbance of his brightly coloured feathers as possible and wearily circled over the area where ever-increasing circles indicated something had smashed into the sea. There was nothing to be seen. Penny and Jimmy had lost consciousness as they plunged into the sea. Chico flew back to Letty.

"Can't see anybody Madam," he miserably reported.

Letty frowned. This was bad. It must be the Human Hatchlings who had fallen and they weren't good swimmers or deep sea divers. She would have to look for them.

"Ma, I'm all right now. They're my friends. I'll find them." Zozimus had read her intention and without waiting for a response turned turtle and disappeared.

* * *

A loud shout went up from the yacht.

"LOOK!"

Liopleurodon was jerking disjointedly in the water, its globular eyes glazed, its horrific jaw twitching convulsively. Writhing and teetering it made one final attempt to advance on the astonished group in the water. Letty moved quickly.

Enfolding the three ladies and Chico with her flippers she dived, leaving the quivering, floundering monster behind. As Letty descended, not too deeply for she knew Humans couldn't cope with a real dive, she met George in the vanguard of the Zacans.

"Letty! Zozimus and the Human Hatchlings are ok. We're on our way to net Liopleurodon. Can't stop. He's still dangerous." With that George and the other Zacans sped away.

As soon as they'd gone, Letty gently surfaced, much to the relief of Gemma, Dorothy and Cora who were gasping for breath.

"Phew!" gurgled Dorothy. "As a famous Duke once said – that was a close run thing!"

Chico shook out his bedraggled feathers and sighed. Oh for his quiet perch outside the Motmot Restaurant! There was more splashing and panting nearby and, turning, Letty and the women saw Zozimus towing Jimmy and Penny.

"Penny! Jimmy!" shrieked the women. "What happened?"

"Hold onto me!" said Letty urgently, afraid that Zozimus's flippers would start bleeding afresh.

"What's she saying, Chico?"

Chico roused himself to translate and the children quickly transferred their weight to Letty, who was beginning to resemble a lifeboat.

"Here we are, Ma!" said Zozimus. "Pen and Jim are ok. I picked them up almost at once. They need air and food. They don't like jellyfish."

"Mum, Gran, Cora, are we glad to see you!" exclaimed Penny, her eyes shining. "We fell off Liopleurodon's neck. But we pierced the Argos Eye. Look – he's staggering about all over the place. Zoz picked us up. Then his dad and a whole lot of *huge* Leatherbacks came along. Mum, it was *amazing*! They were armed with tridents and nets and stuff."

"Yep," interrupted Jimmy. "Zoz here told them what we'd done and they swam off at a terrific pace. Wow, did they go!" he enthused.

The Matriarchs smiled, Letty at her son being called 'Zoz' and the women with the idea of Penny and Jimmy eating jellyfish.

But Zozimus, his flippers and carapace still stained with blood, looked tired and sad.

"Did you go down the tunnel?" Letty asked cautiously.

"Yes."

"What did you see?"

"Terrible things. Horrible! I don't want …"

Great tears welled up in Zozimus's eyes.

"And Bella?" asked Letty gently.

"No sign."

Letty put a flipper round his carapace.

"You did your best, we all did. She was a very brave Nematt. I've got a message for you." Softly, Letty told Zozimus of Bella's last words.

"Look," whispered Penny, "Zozimus is crying. Chico, what's happened? What's he upset about? Tell him we all love him and want to help."

The tired Parrot hopped onto the young Zacan and nuzzled his neck. "The Humans want to know what's happened. They're dotty 'bout you, Zoz and can they help?"

Zozimus was comforted, if surprised. Humans usually *caused* dreadful things to happen! But not these. They valued and respected the ancient Clan of Giant Leatherbacks. Haltingly he recounted what had happened in the tunnel.

"Azazel saved my life. He could have got away but blocked the tunnel and fought the White Shark to give me time."

"Poor Azazel!" commented Letty. "It was a tragedy Ermina was killed so brutally and deliberately by Humans. He never forgave them. He was trying to make up for his treachery to us by saving you. I'll tell the Zamorin of this."

Recounting the dreadful story calmed Zozimus. He had lost his brave and beautiful Bella but was determined not to become bitter and vicious like Azazel. Leatherbacks were brought up living with danger. From the moment they were laid in the nests so lovingly built by their courageous Matriarchs the Turtles were threatened. Dogs and Humans ate the eggs, Humans drove cars over the sand, compacting it so the Hatchlings couldn't crawl out and suffocated. The Terror Run loomed large with Humans stepping on them, Birds eating them, Fish too. Then longline fishing nets, filthy oil-saturated water, building projects on their nesting beaches, the 'false-food' of plastic bags and balloons abounded in the seas and all killed. Human 'souvenir hunters' carried off Turtle carapaces and stuffed eggs without a thought for the live Turtles they once were – or would have become. Leatherback numbers dropped horrifically year after year and friends failed to return to the safety of the Spacious Sea. Yet here were Humans prepared to risk *their* lives for the Leatherbacks! Perhaps Humans were learning that the unique and wonderful creatures who shared their planet should be treated with respect and be protected, not killed?

"Chico," he whispered, "please thank those Humans who helped us. The Zamorin and Moot will thank them too when this is safely over."

"Yes, indeed Zozimus, I can vouch for that," added Letty, smiling mysteriously.

"Here comes the lifeboat!" exclaimed Dorothy.

"At last!" commented Cora wryly.

Fan-Fan skillfully manoeuvred the boat until it lay alongside Letty and her human burden. Livingston and Jomo clutched fearsome-looking boathooks and stun guns, which they kept pointed at Liopleurodon.

"Ahoy dere yo mermaids! Jump aboard," shouted Jomo.

Gemma, Penny and Jimmy jumped aboard but Cora and Dorothy were neither so young nor as agile.

"Zozimus, be a good son and give the smaller lady a bunk up. I'll help the more traditionally built one."

Cora found herself being raised gently out of the water on Letty's massive flipper as if on a lift. Beside her, Dorothy too rose composedly from the sea on Zozimus's flipper. Livingston and Jomo settled them in the boat and both ladies thanked their 'lifts'.

"Right – let's go!"

"No – wait!" shouted Penny. "Chico's not aboard. Come on, you daft Parrot, it's not far," she urged.

Chico lay utterly exhausted on Zozimus's broad head, his curved beak resting on the tough carapace.

"Chico! Come on!" everyone encouraged.

"Dat bird! He always big trouble!" tutted Livingston exasperatedly.

"Chico's a hero, Livingston! He flew about taking messages and translating. He told us about the Argos Eye. We'd be dead and George and the Leatherbacks still fighting that Dinosaur if it weren't for Chico," reproached Penny.

The others nodded in support. Chico shivered his feathers and blinked. He wasn't a worthless bird, he was a hero! He'd better behave like one. Shaking out his iridescent but very damp feathers he spread his rainbow-hued wings wide and flew straight to Penny, pecking her appreciatively and affectionately grasping a beakful of hair. Letty and Zozimus gave the boat a helpful shove and waved farewell. Everyone waved back. It was sad to leave their amazing new friends, the Leatherbacks, but they were chilly and very hungry and it was hard to get excited about a diet of jellyfish.

Chapter Twenty-Three

AN ILLUSTRIOUS VISITOR

Lumbering around clumsily, Liopleurodon knew his Argos Eye had been pierced. Twisting and turning he staggered and splashed around, his sense of direction and balance lost. The Zamorin observed him with a cautious eye. He was not prepared to take chances with his group of highly-trained Zacan Turtles. With his enormous size and weight the Dinosaur remained dangerous.

"Keep out of his way!" he warned. "If he treads on you, you're dead! Simba – follow me. The rest of you stay clear 'til I call. Godfrey, have the biggest and strongest net ready to throw."

Checking his dormancy drugs were secure, the gleaming black Turtle swam swiftly after Kenronishe. They would need a powerful inertia dose to immobilise this monster!

* * *

The Cruise Director on board the liner couldn't believe his luck. First a large Dolphin Pod had kept the passengers entertained. Then a tremendous commotion had broken out on the horizon. Disney Films doing a stunt for filming he reckoned. Now the decks were crowded to capacity watching a magnificent flotilla of gigantic Manta Rays. In Red Arrow formation they swept majestically by, their wings widespread. Like the Dolphins, they too were heading towards the aqueous disturbance. Videos whirred, cameras clicked, the passengers watched in fascination and the Cruise Director boasted that these things happened all the time on a Caribbean Luxury Cruise.

* * *

Minnie had kept her word. Sea creatures many miles away had heard both Minnie's rallying cry and Zozimus's emergency call and were swimming at all speed to the Leatherbacks' aid.

* * *

"Hereyah, wrap dese round yo."

In the galley of Andy's yacht the crew handed out warm woolly Witney blankets to the 'Mermaids' and 'Mermen'. A large selection of fresh fruit had accompanied Chico to the boiler room where he was drying out. Hot showers had been taken, dry clothes donned and freshly baked Island scones hastily eaten before everyone scampered up on deck. The Chef looked at the large tray laden with mugs of steaming hot cocoa and sighed, "Yo boy. Take dis hereyah tray up. Ladies first remember! And watch dem steps!"

"Yassuh! Tank yo Suh!" exclaimed Walcott, the young cabin boy. Here was his chance to shine! Expertly balancing the heavy tray on an outspread hand he headed nimbly for the door.

* * *

"Simba, throw the drug into his mouth. We want him completely paralysed before Godfrey's Platoon net him."

Simba was fast bowler for the Leatherback 1st Cricket XI and to lob the pouch into the huge lolling mouth of Liopleurodon was no problem. Retreating quickly from the noxious stench of the Dinosaur's breath, he waited with Kenronishe. Soon the uncoordinated movements of the monster stopped. With a gargantuan 'SSSPPLAAASSSH!' he slowly toppled over into the sea. Simba moved forward.

"STOP!" commanded Kenronishe. With his great experience he knew the last thing Liopleurodon had thought about would be imprinted on his mind and he would still try to carry it out.

Simba halted immediately.

Liopleurodon's massive tail and rear flippers began to rise out of the water.

"Prepare to ride wave!" shouted Kenronishe.

The tidal wave programmed into Liopleurodon's brain was about to occur.

"CCRRAACKK!"

Liopleurodon's tail smacked into the water just as Walcott arrived on deck with the hot cocoa. The yacht juddered. Walcott shuddered. Chef would be furious if he dropped the tray! He hung on tightly. The yacht swayed, righted itself and remained calm. The tidal wave had been a failure. Simba had knocked out Liopleurodon in the nick of time. Walcott continued on his way.

"Cocoa milady," he announced unperturbed to Dorothy. Bowing slightly, as he had seen Livingston do, he proffered her a steaming mug.

*   *   *

Letty and Zozimus swam to where George and the other Zacans were grouped.

"Are the Apprentices still at the stern of the yacht?" asked George.

"Yes, Patriarch. When the Gusher began I told them not to move. They're probably still wearing their gas masks," Zozimus said reflectively.

"Humph! They should be safe enough there." George couldn't resist a smile at the thought of earnest young Zacans still floating around in gas masks! "Stay close you two! I don't want any flying off," he instructed sternly.

"Yes Patriarch," said Zozimus tiredly.

"Yes George dear," said Letty demurely.

"Godfrey! Bring up the Net Platoon. Throw it over him quickly." The Zacans soon had the massive moribund monster semi encircled with the net. Collapsed in the water, Liopleurodon resembled a partially submerged tower block. But the Zacans couldn't throw the net right over him. He was too high out of the water. Neither could they get it under him. He was too heavy. They waited for orders from

Kenronishe who was frowning impatiently. Diving, he listened to the sounds and conversations that carried far and clear under water. Ah! It was all right! Help was fast approaching. A sibilant susurrus in the sea and the gleaming curves of a large number of leaping, fast swimming Dolphins drew appreciative smiles from Kenronishe and the Zacans as Jeté and his Pod plus two other Pods swooped into sight.

"Zamorin Sir, we are here to help," announced Jeté. "What can we do?"

"Jeté! You are welcome indeed. The monster has been drugged. We need to net him for Bluey to tow away but can't get the net over his body. See the height?"

Jeté glanced at the motionless mass of Liopleurodon and chuckled.

"You Leatherbacks are magnificent swimmers and divers, none better, but this is a job for us. If you would withdraw a little?"

Godfrey and his Platoon handed the net over to the Dolphins. Smiling in anticipation they backed away to give the Pod space.

*   *   *

Dry and warm on the yacht, Gemma, Andy, Jimmy, Penny and the others sipped hot cocoa and watched the unfolding drama in amazement. A massive Dolphin Pod had arrived and, judging from the assonant whistles and other sibilant sounds, were talking to the Turtles. The Dolphins gathered round the Chief Leatherback, easily distinguished by his magnificent helmet decorated with sea plumes … there was George with the zig-zag scar down his carapace … and wasn't that Letty nearby? Zozimus and a gleaming jet black Turtle as big as George was with them.

Underwater, a long line of the biggest Leatherbacks were lying on something. Now the Dolphins dived, picking up a long strand of green, twisted rope in their mouths, and spread out along the sides of the recumbent Dinosaur. What was happening?

*   *   *

259

Jeté checked the unbroken line of Dolphins. Amused glittering eyes met his. This was going to be fun! He gave a high-pitched whistle. In perfect unison the Dolphins leaped high into the air over the body of the Dinosaur, the tough leading edge of the net held in their long laughing mouths. Landing with a single enormous 'SPLASH!' the net was now stretched tightly over Liopleurodon and was quickly secured on the sea bed by the Zacans.

"Magnificent! What a display of synchronised leaping! Thank you!" the Zamorin and Leatherbacks applauded. "Now we need Bluey to give him a shove and get the net underneath so he can be moved!"

"AHEM!" A dignified yet indignant cough interrupted. "*We* can do that. There are enough of us here!"

Minnie and the Manta Ray Muster had been watching the aerial display and now glided sliently up to Kenronishe.

"Minnie!" exclaimed Letty joyfully. "Oh it's good to see you again!"

"Excuse me ..." Kenronishe didn't want the two friends to get chatting. "How are you going to ease the net under Liopleurodon, Madam Minnie?"

"Easy – just watch," smiled Minnie, taking in a casual mouthful of plankton. "Would you tell Godfrey and his Zacans to stop lying on the net and hold it up, so we can get to the Dinosaur? Come along Muster. We'll show them."

On the yacht and in the sea everyone watched, agog with interest. Grasping the net firmly in their flippers, Godfrey and the Net Platoon rose in the water, allowing enough space for Minnie and her Muster to float in underneath. Submerging, each Manta Ray fanned its wings out checking that they overlapped. A strong raft-like structure resulted.

"All together now – PUSH!" instructed Minnie. The Muster pushed and pushed at the Dinosaur until he began to topple over into the net. Godfrey and the Net Platoon swam swiftly under the rolling monster. The Mantas swam out and the two edges were closed with stout Laminaria cord. Liopleurodon was well and truly 'netted'.

"Well done! We couldn't have managed on our own. Many thanks, friends!"

The Zamorin gave a satisfied sigh. What teamwork! What courage! What loyalty everyone had shown! An idea came into his mind. With a majestic flipper he beckoned Jeté, Minnie and Letty to his side where they briefly bent their heads together. Then Letty shot away at top speed.

"How are they going to move Liopleurodon?" asked Jimmy. "He's far too heavy!"

"Like me! Like me!" Chico chattered cheerfully. He'd flown up on deck and was now perched on Alistair. "Good food 'ere. Make anyone heavy, hee, hee, hee!"

No one told him to shut up. No one told him not to be so greedy. Through the united efforts of Chico, the Leatherbacks and the children, Liopleurodon had been rendered harmless. Made secure by the innovative teamwork of sea creatures, everyone had used their different abilities to best advantage. Now it seemed as if Humans would have to step in to remove the Dinosaur.

The sun was well up in the cerulean sky and everyone basked in its warmth. A profound silence had fallen. Liopleurodon lay inert and helpless. In his net, guarded by the vigilant Monty and his Platoon, the White Shark remained unconscious. Zacans, Dolphins and Mantas floated serenely, content with their endeavours. Small subdued waves splashed apologetically against the yacht. It was as if the sea and every living creature in it was holding its breath, waiting for the final act of this amazing drama to begin. Even the Humans were affected. The Cruise Director had stopped gabbling, the passengers had ceased videoing and the Liner was at 'slow ahead'. The Chef and crew of Andy's yacht had come up on deck and were looking out to sea with the 'Lollypop Lurers'. Something momentous was about to occur.

Low-pitched yet intense, a plangent, vibrant, resonant song reverberated through the water. Gradually it changed, becoming higher and more soulful, recalling the sibilation and swish of shallow seas. Now it was a sonorous bass again, like a deep-toned gong. The sea creatures waited respectfully. To them every harmonious cadence bore a distinct message.

"He'll be here very soon. He's made fantastic time. Good old Bluey!

Never lets you down," commented the Zamorin.

"Now we'll see some really elegant and dignified swimming!" enthused Jeté.

Minnie cast him a dirty sideways glance. Bluey was very special. They all knew that. But Manta Rays were pretty accomplished swimmers too! And Jeté's Pod were renowned for their grace. But she didn't argue, Bluey was such a sweetie.

The Humans couldn't hear Bluey's lyrical song. Never as sensitive to sound as sea creatures, Human hearing had deteriorated and nearly been destroyed through the enduring deafening discordance of their land-bound environment. Bluey's mellifluous melodies were wasted on them. Without their high-tech listening equipment they were deaf. But Penny and Jimmy's youthful hearing was not yet coarsened and Gemma, long attuned to the sea and all its inhabitants, caught an echo of the exquisite and unique Song of the Blue Whale, its elegant phrases and ethereal rhythms.

Subdued and soft as a spring zephyr, a sigh rippled through the ship. Lingering over the quiet, still water it was echoed on the yacht. A colossal blue streamlined shape – bigger than a submarine, bigger than a Boeing 737 – had materialised in the ocean. Barely a splash marked its majestic course as it cruised languidly through the placid water. No one moved. An awed silence prevailed. Keeping well clear of the Cruise Liner its prodigious tail fluke rose slowly, gracefully from the water and glided under again. A scintillating geyser of water erupted from its massive head, arched high into the aquamarine sky above and fell in a myriad motes of rainbow-coloured slivers. In its stately grandeur and sublime grace it created a hallowed moment rarely experienced in Human existence. Bluey the Blue Whale had arrived.

Bluey had sent a message when he was still many miles away so the other sea dwellers were not surprised at his arrival. He was the gentle giant of the oceans who lived entirely on krill and wasn't interested in killing. Everyone was pleased to see him and crowded round, patting and gently scratching whatever bits of him were closest.

"My Lord Bluey! Many thanks indeed for coming all this way. Out of season too! We're *very honoured* and pleased to see you."

The Zamorin bowed low, speaking for all the sea creatures present.

"No problem!" boomed Bluey good-naturedly. "I hear you've got a Liopleurodon for me to remove. My ancestors were familiar with that Dinosaur but I've never seen one. That him over there?"

"Yes. He's been drugged and will remain that way for many eras. There's a White Shark too. Can you manage both?" asked the Zamorin courteously.

A carillon of bass chimes bounced merrily over the water. Even the Humans heard them. Bluey was laughing.

"Kenronishe – polite as always! Yes, I can cope with both. I'll tow them to the Sea of Ill Repute – brrrr! I hope that White Shark is well secured? One of them tried to take a bite out of my tail fluke once! The cheek of it! I showed him! Brought it down right on his head, smack, and into the depths he tumbled with a splitting headache! I don't trust them."

"Neither do we, Bluey, they're big trouble. But they're in danger of extinction too. We'll have to hope they learn their lesson in that faraway, freezing Sea. I've a little favour to ask …" continued the Zamorin, whispering.

From beneath them a noisy chattering and squeaking interspersed with sharp Matriarchial rebukes could be heard.

"Sebastian! Put that clown fish down at once!"

"Clementine, I've told you before, *no* riding underwater currents 'til you've passed your map reading and navigation exams!"

"Keep *up*, Hatchlings. Ziggy, give that Hatchling a helping flipper."

"It's the Hatchlings come to see you, Bluey. I sent Letty for them."

Kenronishe's explanation was unnecessary as Letty and Tasha emerged from the Deeps, leading a large Hantle of Hatchlings and many other young Leatherbacks of assorted ages. Letty made a dignified curtsy. Behind her …

"BELLA!" shouted Zozimus. For the first time since leaving the Spacious Sea he smiled. With one flick of his flippers he was at her side.

"Bella! We all thought ..." he stopped.

"I know you did. Letty's told me everything. Azazel saved me too when I was in the caldera. We must remember that."

The tough Zacans looked on, broad grins wreathing their mouths. A few of the female Zacans wept large oval tears.

"Well now, well now ..." Even the Zamorin was overcome. "This is a happy occasion indeed. Miss Isabella, it is a great joy to see you. I think we can safely leave you in the care of Zozimus who has shown great courage and fortitude during this dangerous time. He is now a fully-fledged Zacan."

Everyone clapped and cheered, even the Apprentices whom Zozimus had left languishing at the stern of the yacht. Hearing the goings-on clearly through the water they had swiftly swum and joined the others.

"I have another announcement," continued the Zamorin, when the applause had died down. "The Lord Bluey has given permission for sky-riding – if anyone is interested?"

There was an outburst of gleeful excitement. Bluey looked down at the tiny, delighted Hatchlings.

"Just one minute while I get ready," he said, submerging quietly.

"Ok! Let's get started! Form an orderly queue," instructed Bluey as he reappeared.

Instantly the Hatchlings swam up onto his head.

"Sebastian! Stop pushing!" admonished Tasha. "Lord Blue Whale said an orderly queue!"

As if by accident the Apprentice Zacans, Dolphins and even Mantas floated furtively into the queue for sky-riding. The Zamorin, George and Simba looked on longingly. Letty had no such qualms and instantly joined the queue with Bella and Tasha. The males huffed and puffed to no avail. They were far too big and heavy.

"Right, first Hatchling group please," called Bluey.

Ten little Leatherbacks moved forward and positioned themselves in the middle of his head, warbling and prattling in shrill staccato whistles to each other.

* * *

Penny saw them first and broke the awed entranced silence that had greeted Bluey's appearance.

"Look at that, Mum!" she exclaimed. "Lots of little Leatherbacks are climbing onto the Blue Whale!"

Clutching their cocoa, warmed by the sun's noon-day rays, safe and content, the entire yacht watched the sky-riding in a state of euphoric wonder.

* * *

With an enthusiastic expulsion of air from his lungs Bluey shot the Hatchlings high into the air on a powerful waterspout.

Squealing with laughter the Hatchlings flew upwards into the sky then rode the waterfall down to the sea – SPLASH!

"Oh, oh, oh! More, more!" they pleaded. But it was the next group's turn. The Manta Rays floated down on graceful wings and performed flowing butterfly dives into the water. The Dolphins, used to aerial displays, waited until last.

"Bluey – are you ok for our performance?" asked Jeté, who had planned this with the Zamorin earlier. Bluey assured him he was, he was looking forward to it. The smallest Dolphins were shot into the air and began the show with a demonstration of easy acrobatics. Just simple leaps and twists they did for Humans who were easily impressed. Then came the older Dolphins, shooting skywards in a single column then breaking outwards in a series of spiral curvets resembling a beautiful, living flower opening its petals. Entering the water with backward dives, sea creatures and Humans cheered, clapped and shouted.

"Bravo! Bravo! Magnificent!" congratulated Kenronishe. The Mantas looked a bit put out. Letty swam towards them.

"Bewitching!" she applauded. "But nothing is more exquisite than the sun sparkling on your spangled, luminescent wings." The compliment restored the Mantas' good spirits, just as Letty had intended.

"Look," she continued, "Jeté is going to perform a solo."

The Dolphin leader rarely did this, preferring to perform with his Pod, but this was a very special occasion and he'd agreed to Kenronishe's request. Serene and perfectly balanced on Bluey's head, he waited for the Whale's call to commence.

"Now!"

An enormous geyser of water rose hundreds of feet skywards.

Like an arrow, Jeté shot upwards with it, performing perfect pirouettes as he flew. The waterspout slowly subsided and Jeté was alone, dancing in the scintillating rainbow motes of effervescent air. Like an acrobat or ballet dancer he curvetted and coruscated in Arabesques and Cabrioles, his eyes twinkling with joy, his mouth smiling with pleasure. He was superbly confident, perfectly at ease in his natural environment. Lower and lower he flew until, just above the glistening water, he ended with a superb round of Jeté en Tournant. Everyone watched awestruck at this electrifying display. So skilful was Jeté's entry into the water he scarcely caused a ripple.

"That Dolphin reminds me of Rudolf Nureyev at his best," whispered Granny Fairweather.

He was greeted with total, awed silence. Then tumultuous applause broke out in the water and from the yacht. Cascading over the water in billows, it could be heard from the Cruise Liner. Bluey was making thunderous bass noises in his cavernous throat and had to be very politely asked not to clap as he might upset the yacht.

"Wonderful! Superb! I wish I was a Dolphin!"

"No, no Bluey. You stay a Blue Whale. There are far too few of your kind left," replied Jeté patting him affectionately. "*You* are unique."

"Hemm, hmm, there's something in that," admitted Bluey, blushing a deeper blue. He was a very modest Whale.

The sea creatures crowded round Jeté thanking him. The younger Leatherbacks held out bits of chalk rock and solid pieces of lettuce seaweed for him to autograph. His own Pod looked on proudly. Kenronishe, Minnie, Letty, George and the older Zacans looked on approvingly. The games and displays had been planned to dispel the tension and anxiety of hunting the White Shark and Liopleurodon. Now everyone was happy and relaxed, the fear and horror forgotten.

The Zamorin swam over to the massive Whale and patted his nose gratefully.

"Thanks so much, Bluey. We've had a wonderful time, especially the Hatchlings! We couldn't have done it without you. Are you ok, towing that pair of villains to the Sea of Ill Repute?"

"I'm a bit peckish, old man," Bluey admitted. "Those youngsters take it out of you! I'll find a snack ..."

But Minnie had heard and motioned her team into action. Before he finished speaking a huge cluster of krill had been ushered towards him by the efficient Manta team. Bluey opened his gargantuan jaws halfway so as not to accidentally swallow any friends and the krill disappeared. Another cluster and another soon followed. Contented swishings as of a large boat gliding through reeds issued from Bluey as the krill was digested.

"Ahh!" he sighed contentedly. "That's better! Right, time to go. Give me the tow rope."

Godfrey gathered up the ropes and secured them in Bluey's mouth. They swam over to where Monty and his Platoon were still patiently guarding the White Shark and Monty did the same thing.

"All ok, Bluey? I'm going to send a party with you as far as we can go. They will make sure you're properly fed. Liopleurodon's swallowed plenty of dormancy drugs and his Argos Eye is out of action too, he'll be no trouble. Once again – many thanks."

Archie, one of the fastest male swimmers, stationed his Platoon on either side of Bluey, and Simba went to his head. Just about to set off, Minnie and her Mantas flew along.

"Wait for us," she gasped, hastily swallowing the remnants of krill she'd caught. "We're coming too!"

"And us!" announced Jeté, who'd escaped from the autograph hunters. "We're not going to miss out on this!"

Resembling both Queen Mary liners put together, Bluey grasped the tow ropes firmly and set off, accompanied by a flotilla of Leatherbacks, Mantas and Dolphins. They were cheered to the skies as they sailed serenely past the Caribbean Cruise Liner whose occupants still lined the decks. The Cruise Director fainted with delight and had to be taken to the Medical Centre. What a cruise! What a story! What a lot of tips!

Chapter Twenty-Four

Honoured Guests

The Zamorin, George, Letty and other Leatherbacks waved their marine friends off. Except for Bluey, they would return soon. The Metanoia was underway and the Zacans must get back to their wives and families.

"Sir," Letty turned to the Zamorin, "what's happening about the Scrimmage Games? There's no time to include all the necessary preparations, practising, eliminating rounds and performances now. It'll be a disappointment for the Nematts and Hatchlings."

"I know, Letty. It's the sacrifice we've made to ensure the safety of the Spacious Sea Meeting Place. I arranged Bluey's sky-riding treat and the Dolphin Performance in compensation. Everyone understands the safety of the Meeting Place comes before recreations like the Scrimmage Games."

"Of course Sir, even the little ones know that. Perhaps next year's could be an especially big event?"

The Zamorin grinned, looking a bit like a Nematt himself. "Good idea! I'll emphasise that – and arrange coaching from former Champions. Let's hope Simba, Archie and the others return quickly!"

Letty beamed happily. Taking the Zamorin by the flipper she drew him aside, whispering persuasively. He nodded once or twice and Letty flapped off in a great hurry. George, Zozimus and Bella looked after her. What was she up to *now?*

Reluctantly, Andy's crew returned to their duties and the yacht moved slowly away from the scene of so much danger and excitement. Carrying the tray of empty mugs down to the galley, Walcott was in Seventh Heaven. Just *wait* 'til he told his brothers, Worrall and Weekes, about what he'd seen! They'd want to pack up waiting on in hotels and go to sea like him! Their pa was a fisherman so it seemed right.

"Yuh no slack boy, Walcott! Hereyah's de cook-out pot. Enjoy man!" Walcott blushed at the Chef's highest compliment. He'd never forget today, never!

Spellbound by all they'd done and seen, Penny, Jimmy and the grown-ups remained on deck. With binoculars and the telescope they watched Bluey and his amazing entourage until they disappeared over the horizon into the incandescent glow of the sun. No one spoke or moved. The sorcery of the mysterious sea and its mythological inhabitants held them in thrall. Penny gave a long sigh and, glancing at her mother, saw tears slowly sliding down her cheeks.

"I can't believe it all happened! We'll wake up soon and find it's a dream."

"No we won't, Mum. Sitting on top of that Dinosaur's head and you clinging on to Letty was no dream!"

They both laughed. What a day!

Sitting solitary in a sun lounger Jimmy thought about the day's incredible events. He'd helped revenge his mother's cruel death. His father had seen more of the marvellous Giant Leatherbacks, their awesome friends too, and had witnessed their immense courage. He'd seen breathtaking displays of acrobatics by the Dolphins and the magnificent Blue Whale. Jumping up, he ran to Andy.

"Pa, you won't be buying the Turtle Beach now, will you?" smiled Jimmy confidently.

"I have every intention of so doing, son."

"PA! You can't! Not after what you've seen! You just *can't*!"

"It's *because* of what I've seen I'm determined to buy it. I'm off to negotiate for it right now."

Andy sped off to his cabin, which bristled with electronic equipment, and closed the door firmly. Jimmy slouched off to his favourite hiding place, an isolated lifeboat. Angry and deeply upset by his father's money-grabbing scheme, he couldn't understand his sudden change of attitude. Pa had been brilliant about lending his yacht and seemed proud and pleased with Jimmy's handling of Liopleurodon when he'd returned, bedraggled and soaking wet, to the yacht. What had gone wrong? Jimmy hoped Penny wouldn't see him curled up in the lifeboat. He was too deeply ashamed of his father to speak to anyone, especially Penny!

"Hey! Gemma, Penny, everyone. We seem to have a Leatherback escort too!" shouted Dorothy excitedly.

Cora came to join her and very gingerly they leaned over the rail. They'd had enough wetting for one day.

"Come and look Dr. Prof.," called Cora, "We tink we see an interestin' ting hereyah!" she grinned broadly. "Where's dat Chico? It may be an urgent message," she chortled gleefully. Gemma gazed fondly down at the large Turtle swimming alongside, banging a flipper loudly into the water to attract attention. It was Letty, the big female who'd rescued them! Gemma grinned at her and waved. Letty grinned back and winked. All was well – but what did she want? There was only one way to find out.

"CHICO!" everyone shouted.

*   *   *

Back in his usual position outside the Motmot Restaurant Chico grinned complacently. After his heroism of yesterday he was being spoiled. Pineapples, bananas, pawpaws, mangoes, even peaches were piled around him. Best of all – he had a secret. Letty had given him a message. It was a surprise for the Humans and he was to keep quiet until later that day. Chico had been enjoying himself, winding everyone up with mysterious hints, winks and nods. Chomping contentedly, he looked around for someone else to tease. And here they were! Jimmy and Penny coming along the path straight towards him! Chico stopped eating and speedily changed his expression into the nearest he could get to a sinister cloak and dagger one.

"'Ello, ello," he whispered in a sepulchral squawk. "I've a secret message I have," he added, winking conspiratorially.

"Chico! Are you ill? Have you got stomach-ache? I'm not surprised the way you've been guzzling!" exclaimed Penny crossly. Chico opened his eyes wide in surprise and disgust that his Secret Agent look could

271

be interpreted as stomach-ache! Taking careful aim he spat out a string of grape seeds at the pair.

"That's downright rude! Here Pen, help me take his fruit."

Jimmy and Penny swept together the luscious fruit left for the Parrot.

"STOP!" he shrieked, "STOP! THIEVES! VILLAINS! *My* fruit. I'll *starve*," he added plaintively.

"Tell us your secret message and we'll leave it," said Penny sternly.

"Never!" cackled Chico. "Pull my feathers out, tickle my talons, I'll never split!" he declaimed dramatically, drawing himself up proudly. "I'm a hero, I'll never crack!"

Chico's droll performance dispelled sternness. Penny and Jimmy dropped the fruit.

"Chico, you're a hoot! We won't tickle your talons today, thanks; we've other important things to do. See you later," they called, and started to walk away.

Chico looked after them, furious at losing his audience.

"OI! OI!" he called. "You come back 'ere."

"Only if you tell us the secret message."

The Parrot fluffed out his feathers, scratching his ear thoughtfully with a talon.

"Mmmh," he conceded.

"Is that yes?" insisted Jimmy.

"Ok, ok. But Letty said *I* was to deliver the message, not *you*, so *keep quiet*," he commanded imperiously.

"You've earned that privilege, Chico. We agree not to say one word."

Chico leaned towards them and hissed excitedly. Penny and Jimmy turned to each other, their eyes glowing.

"Tell people *now*, Chico. Arrangements have to be made." Chico gave an appreciative croak.

"Yep, you're right. I'll tell Mr MacRobert."

"I'll fetch Pa!" shouted Jimmy and went flying back towards his hotel. Here was one last chance to save the Turtle Beach!

"I'll bring Mum and Gran!" screamed Penny. "Be quick, Jimmy, and tell Fan-Fan! He'll be in his hut," and she too ran off at full speed.

* * *

Cerberus, Portal Steward to the Spacious Sea, was tired and longing for a hearty meal of jellyfish – Lion's Mane for preference. He'd been on Guard Duty for many long hours. His stomach was rumbling, his flippers aching. As soon as 'Z's Special Messenger warned him of danger he had securely locked and bolted the massive gates to the Spacious Sea. Donning full Zacan armour he had patrolled the Portal without eating or sleeping. No one was permitted through the Portal now until the Zamorin himself arrived to reopen it. He would return to the impressive gates and officially declare them open and the Meeting Place safe. Cerberus's eyelids drooped. Stay awake, he chided himself. The Grand Patriarchs and Matriarchs, young Matriarchs and Hatchlings are depending on you to keep them safe! His eyelids drooped again, his flippers twitched with fatigue, his endurance stretched to the limit. Only his immense sense of duty and responsibility kept him awake. Blinking rapidly to clear his eyes he stoically about-turned and started swimming slowly along the wide gates. But hark! Echoing clearly through the water he could hear Leatherback voices, male and female, mixed with the Apprentices' excited barks and – yes! – the authoritative voice of the Zamorin! His weary vigil was almost over.

"Cerberus, I command you – open the Portal!" called the Zamorin, Kenronishe, in a clear, powerful voice.

Cerberus swam quickly to a spy hole camouflaged in the solid, barricaded gates. Keeping his helmet closed and raising his trident he peered through it and challenged, "Who makes this demand? Let me see you clear."

The Zamorin slid back his magnificent helmet, placed his trident on the sandy floor and floated forward.

"It is your Zamorin, Kenronishe, who makes this request. Peace, safety and tranquillity have been restored. The Spacious Sea Meeting Place is no longer threatened, the Giant Leatherbacks are safe. Open the Portal!"

With great joy Cerberus obeyed, throwing wide the huge gates. Alone, Kenronishe swept through, pausing to shake flippers with Cerberus and thank him for his long vigil.

"Oh Sir, it's been worth it to know our Meeting Place is secure and the little 'uns safe. Well done Sir and all you brave Leatherbacks," applauded Cerberus as they crowded through the Portal. "Oh, I see we've a new Zacan! Congratulations Sir!"

Zozimus gasped in astonishment and pride. A short time ago Cerberus addressed him as "Oi you! You 'orrible Nematt." Now he was a fully fledged Zacan entitled to be called 'Sir'!

* * *

Chico knew Mr MacRobert was working in his office some distance away. He must be summoned and told. The Parrot pondered how to attract his attention. At last, in a winning but penetrating impersonation of Gemma's voice, he called loudly, "Alistair! Alistair, are you there dear?"

Chico waited. Nothing happened.

"ALISTAIR!" he screeched, "ALISTAIR! I need to talk to you!" The door of the Motmot Restaurant flew open. Out shot an irate Livingston closely followed by Mr MacRobert and Adrian Kanhai, who thought poachers must be about.

"Yo listen, good man! Yo may be an 'ero but dat don' make yo boss man! Jest yo cease dat screechin'!"

"Who's a clever Parrot? Who's got a secret message? It's for Boss man MacRobert, not you," cackled Chico cheekily.

Livingston looked daggers at the Parrot. But before this traditional rivalry could progress further Mr MacRobert butted in.

"What is it, Chico? Be quick. I've a lot of work to get through."

Chico told him. Mr MacRobert gasped. Adrian looked sceptical. Livingston's face lit up.

"Yo not envigglen' we? Yo sure o' dis?"

Chico looked hurt.

"It's what Letty told me."

"An' who's Letty? Yo dou dou?" Livingston burst out laughing at his own wit.

"It's ok, Livingston. Letty's the Giant Leatherback who rescued the ladies."

"Yo believin' dis Parrot, Sir?"

"Yes, Livingston. It brightens up his day to tease you but he wouldn't try it on me."

"No Sir! No Mr Boss Man Sir! Chico always honest with you," chirped the Parrot ingratiatingly.

"Ok, Sir. Ah'll get Merlyn an' de others to spread de word." Livingston vanished speedily through the doors of the Motmot Restaurant as Penny came sprinting up the path followed by Gemma and Dorothy.

"Chico! Tell them," urged Penny.

Alistair MacRobert stepped forward to greet the group.

"An amazing…"

"STOP!" shouted Penny. "Sorry, Mr MacRobert, but Letty the Leatherback told *Chico* to tell us!"

"Ahh! I understand. It's his privilege after all he's done." Alistair gestured politely to Chico to tell his secret. Gemma and Dorothy listened intently.

"This is unbelievable!" exclaimed Gemma. "Are you sure, Chico?"

"Yes Dr Prof. Letty's Chief, he's called the Zamorin, wants to thank all the Humans properly. Letty had the idea and he gave the ok."

"We'd better round everyone up, there's not much time," Gemma said excitedly.

"Livingston's gone to tell the staff. We'll spread out and tell the guests. Lots of them helped Letty when she was stranded. They'll love it."

"Mum, what about Mr Saxon? Do you think he'll come?"

"After what Jimmy told you, he'd better!" replied Gemma, her eyes flashing dangerously.

Penny and Dorothy looked at one another. Wow! More feathers

than Chico's would fly!

* * *

"Is everyone ready?" shouted Letty hoarsely.

The amount of noise was terrific. In the Great Hall, Giant Leatherbacks of all ages and sizes had gathered. First year baby Hatchlings clutched their Matriarchs' carapaces and clung on, chattering and gabbling in high-pitched squeaks. Directed by Madame Louisa and Dr Laurence the older Hatchlings from Turtle Academy floated in neat lines close to their families and near to a helping flipper should they need one, their colourful scarves wafting gently in the underwater current. The Nematts were in their element. Old enough to swim solo, they gathered in carefree chattering cohorts, splashing and laughing. With no family responsibilities they were free to do as they wished. Zozimus gleefully swashed over to join them.

"Zozimus!" called George from the ranks of the mature Turtles. Zozimus floated back to him.

"Yes, Patriarch?"

"You're a Zacan now, Zozimus," George reminded him in a low serious voice, "and engaged to Bella. You have to join the mature Turtles."

Cerberus calling him 'Sir' and now this! Being a Zacan was great but Zozimus was fast learning that his new status brought a whole lot of new responsibilities.

"Is everyone ready?" shouted Letty again. "Sir, I think you'd better take over. They're so excited. No one's listening, not even the Great Patriarchs and Matriarchs!"

With a single flip of his flippers Kenronishe rose to the top of a Mountainous Star Coral and held up a massive flipper for silence.

"Shush!"

"Be quiet!"

"Stop that giggling, young Clementine!"

"Ziggy! Control your cohort!"

At last, silence fell. The Zamorin smiled proudly as he looked around his wonderful Bale. What a privilege it was to serve them! He would give everything, everything, life itself, to protect and serve them and secure the Leatherback dynasty for another few million years.

"Giant Leatherbacks!" he began. Some Turtles glanced at the tiny new Hatchlings and grinned.

"We are safe. The Spacious Sea Meeting Place is secure again. I thank and congratulate you all. Hatchlings – you were obedient and did as you were told without question. Nematts – you helped with the little ones and in many other necessary but unobtrusive ways. Each little job was done well." (Everyone looked at Ziggy who went bright purple.)

"Apprentice Zacans and Zacans – your discipline, courage and determination were outstanding. Guarding our home was Cerberus who showed his enormous strength, stamina and devotion to duty."

The Zamorin paused and everyone clapped their flippers for Cerberus. Then he put out a massive flipper and drew Bella to his side.

"Our beautiful young Nematt, Bella, lost both parents in horrific circumstances. She controlled her sorrow and showed great heroism and daring in a highly dangerous situation. I am proud to call Bella – my daughter!"

There was more clapping and shouting at the Zamorin's announcement, except from Zozimus. As the Zamorin's adopted daughter, Bella would not be free to marry him!

"Bella will marry the Zacan of my choosing …"

Jumping jellyfish, thought Zozimus, that's me out.

"… who is our newest fully-fledged Zacan – Zozimus, son of Grand Patriarch George and Grand Matriarch Laetitia."

Zozimus's capacious mouth fell open in relief. He'd forgotten he *was* a proper Zacan! Raising both flippers above his head he clapped them joyfully together with such a terrific 'THWACK!' some of the baby Hatchlings were washed off their Matriarchs' carapaces.

"Sorry, sorry," cried Zozimus, hurrying to replace them, but, squeaking and chortling, the little Hatchlings were turning somersaults in the water.

"Matriarch Laetitia discovered the threat to our security," continued the Zamorin, "and thanks to her instant response and cleverness we are safe."

There was more clapping. 'Z' looked at her timepiece and sighed impatiently. Why did males like making speeches? Even the Zamorin couldn't resist an opportunity!

"Always remember there are *good* Humans. Not all of them want to kill us and cause our extinction. Some of them risked *their* lives to help save ours. To show our thanks we're going to venture as near the coast as possible and give them a surprise. Hatchlings, Students and Nematts, you know what to do?"

A great cacophony of sound echoed round the vast Hall, the high pitched squeaks of Hatchlings mingling with Student bawls and Nematt bellows.

"YES!!!" came the response.

"Time to go!" grinned the Zamorin, and, raising his trident, led the whole Bale out of the Portal in joyful exuberance.

* * *

The Humans were hurrying excitedly towards the wide, sandy nesting beach where Turtle Custodians were hastily forming a line to stop people getting too close to the sea and compacting the soft sand. Many carried binoculars and all were dressed in dark clothes. Cora and Jomo stood at the front, and it would be a foolhardy person who tried to get past them! Gemma, Penny and Dorothy stood a little aside, making room for others who had not seen the Leatherbacks at such amazing proximity as they had. Alistair MacRobert was with them, whilst Chico perched in a nearby banana palm. Adrian Kanhai stood a short distance away.

"Can you see Mr Saxon?" asked Penny anxiously.

"He'll be over the other side with Jimmy. I can't see that far," replied Gemma.

The full moon shone its ghostly light on the scene, turning the sand into silvery snow and the shrubs to sable. The sea gleamed ebony, its miniature wavelets breaking serenely onto the translucent beach. An occasional subdued cough or whisper were the only sounds breaking the reverent silence.

Used to Turtle-watching it was Gemma who saw it first.

"There!" she whispered. "There's the ripples in the surf. A Turtle swimming sideways along the coast, coming towards us."

Everyone nearby craned their necks but saw nothing.

"Watch for the ripples when she pokes her head out. She's trying to locate us!"

Like a wraith, barely breaking the surface, the Leatherback's familiar beak appeared.

"I can see her!" exclaimed Penny.

Low, delighted murmurs spread along the beach. The Turtle turned towards them, paused and disappeared from view.

"She's gone!"

"Perhaps they changed their minds?"

"Trust you to cough just as she started to come up!"

The Humans shuffled their feet, not sure what to do next.

"It's ok," reassured Gemma. "That was a preliminary scouting party. They know where we are now. Keep watching," she encouraged.

Mr MacRobert looked through his binoculars.

"That's funny! A lot of Humpback Whales are out there in a long line. There's a great deal of disturbance and splashing going on yet the sea's as flat as a pancake." He sounded puzzled.

There were murmurs of astonishment and speculation.

"The message said the Leatherbacks had a surprise for us," someone commented.

All eyes turned towards the horizon, now clearly illuminated by the full moon.

* * *

"Tasha's sent the message, Matriarch. We're in the right position," reported Bella, who was proudly helping Letty.

"Good! Now – is everyone ready? Hold tight, Hatchlings!"

"Yes, Matriarch Laetitia," came an assortment of eager squeaks.

"One, two, three and – UP!" commanded Letty.

The long line of massive Leatherbacks surfaced gently, the Hatchlings clinging onto their broad carapaces. Some fell off and enjoyed a brief splash before being hustled back up by the Nematts.

"KEEP HOLD, will you! Don't you Hatchlings *ever* do as you're told?" exclaimed an exasperated Zozimus, quite forgetting that he had been one of the world's worst Hatchlings not many years ago.

Letty swam anxiously along the line, checking everyone was alright.

"One, two, three and – UP MESSAGE!" she shouted.

The watching Humans saw a wavering line of letters emerge from the sea. Each letter appeared to be stuck on the hump of a Whale. But as the scene became clearer they realised it was Leatherback carapaces they were looking at, not Whales. The large clear letters were carved on big sheets of white, opalescent seaweed, held tight in the little flippers of small Turtles!

'THUMAN YOU SANK! YOU AVEDS LOR UIVES!'

Abruptly, amidst much frothing and swashing of water, they disappeared. The smiles, laughter and cries of puzzlement stopped. Now what? The letters reappeared again.

'THANK YOU UMANS! YOU SAVED OUR LIVES!'

"REALLY!" expostulated Letty, hastily lifting up a splashing Hatchling holding the letter 'H'. "Humans will think we can't spell! Stay put Hatchlings, give them time to read it."

'Z' glanced at her stopwatch.

"DOWN!" she called. The seaweed message descended and the Hatchlings made much of massaging their flippers and saying how *hard* it was to hold seaweed script and how they'd nearly dropped the letters and weren't they incredible Hatchlings!! But they had little time to preen themselves.

"Next message ready!" called Letty, and the Nematts gave out new seaweed letters and hoisted the little Turtles back onto the carapaces. This time everything went perfectly.

'STAY ON SAND FOR DISPLAY,' read the cryptic message.

"Is Mr Saxon watching?" Penny again asked her mother.

"I'll walk round and find out," responded Gemma.

The Turtle message disappeared and the Humans waited expectantly. Without warning the silky night sky was lit up by great arcs of shooting stars flashing across the horizon like a rainbow: red, orange, yellow, green, blue, indigo and violet. "Ooohhhh! Aahhhh!" exclaimed the Humans. "How can Leatherbacks do that?" they exclaimed in wonder.

The amazing show continued. Dazzling cones of twinkling light shot into the air illuminating the shadowy sea; smaller round catherine wheels trailed delicate tendrils of brilliant stars; phosphorescent patterns glittered and gleamed on the Turtles' broad carapaces, constantly changing colour, shape and size like St Elmo's Fire. The sea was incandescent with sparkling light and colour. The people on the beach gazed in rapturous wonder, lost in the beauty and magic of the Leatherbacks' genius. Every eye was on the wonderful 'Thank you' they were privileged to watch.

"Ahhh! LOOK!" gasped Penny.

A row of Turtle heads appeared in shallow water close to the beach which the Custodians had kept empty and unsullied. Laboriously, the female Leatherbacks hauled themselves up the soft sand. Clearing the waterline they began digging, their enormous flippers scattering sand in all directions.

"*Wow*! They said a 'display' but who included Egg Laying? Letty I bet!" gasped Dorothy, her eyes wide with awe and respect for the superb creatures. In total silence everyone watched the Matriarchs. Out of their natural element they groaned and sighed as they excavated their carefully constructed nests, shaping the sides and forming a deep hollow for the eggs. After the eggs were laid, sand was delicately patted round the precious cargo. Not too hard or the Hatchlings wouldn't be able to climb out, yet not too soft or the sand would collapse on them. Each nest was a miracle of precision engineering.

Circling away from the nest the Turtles proceeded to the next stage, digging a false nest to lure Humans and Dogs away from the real one. That completed, they could return to the sea. Exhausted, hungry and desperate to return to water they headed for home. Huge trails like tractor tyres marked their weary route. Greeted by the soft susurrus of the sea, sighs turned to smiles. HOME! Graceful and sleek once more, they swam a short way then, turning, waved to the watchers on the shore. People waved back, applauding, hugging one another in joyous rapture, sighing, smiling, gazing in awe at the massive marks leading down to the sea. Many people searched the ocean through night glasses, hoping to get one more glimpse of the beautiful Leatherbacks.

Into this enchanted circle strode Andy Saxon. The group stared at him as he spoke in a clear, determined voice.

"I know you'll agree with me when I say we've been greatly honoured this evening. Those Giant Leatherback Turtles are magnificent."

He was interrupted by more applause and murmurs of agreement.

"Totally unique, Andy. It's a tragedy they're so close to extinction," sighed Dorothy.

"Waall, I've got news for you." Andy paused, looking round the intent faces. "I'm going to buy this beach ..."

There was a scream of anger from Penny.

"NO! You CAN'T!" she yelled. "It's the Leatherbacks' beach. They've only got a few beaches left that aren't built on. Go and buy some other beach!"

The bemused, happy crowd changed. Anger and fury replaced joy and wonder. Andy saw a lynch mob closing in on him.

"HEY! Hey – hold it right there," he exclaimed quickly. "Yep, I'm buying the beach – but I intend to turn it into an International Site of Special Scientific Interest and have it fully protected as a Leatherback nesting site. *No one* will be able to build on it – however much money they've got," he added grimly.

A delighted Gemma appeared at his side.

"Let's hear it for Mr Saxon!" she cried and the crowd went wild with relief and happiness.

"Back to the hotel!" called Andy Saxon. "Drinks on me!"

Jimmy scuffed his way through the rejoicing throng until he

reached Penny.

"*You* said he'd bought the beach!" she accused.

"He *had* bought it! He didn't tell me what he was going to *do* with it! He likes doing things on the quiet. Look at those paralysed folk he helps! I knew nothing about them!" exclaimed Jimmy, immense admiration in his voice.

"He's much nicer than he appears," grinned Penny. "But, Jimmy – what about the Leatherbacks? They should know their beach is safe."

"Pa told Chico on the yacht and he told Letty. Remember she swam with us part of the way back?"

Penny heaved a sigh of relief.

"*That's* ok then. Phew! What a *lot* I've got to write up for my project! I'll have to tell Mum I'm too busy to help her, and I don't know *how* she'll manage without me," she mused.

Jimmy looked at her thoughtfully. Not long ago she was attached to her mother like a limpet. Yes – and a short time ago he'd thought his pa a money-grabbing over-protective prune! It took challenge and adventure to show a person's true colours and reveal their hidden talents.

* * *

"Well done, Hatchlings! Well done *everyone*! Flying Fish, Wrasse, Mother of Pearl Guests, you did us proud. I bet the Humans didn't know what the 'fireworks' were!" exclaimed Letty mischievously.

"Time to get on with the Egg Laying, Laetitia," said 'Z', consulting her oceanic timepiece. "Only one group of Matriarchs went up the beach, we must press ahead."

"And we can press ahead on our *own* beach again," commented the Zamorin, "with no fear of being harassed or killed. It's wonderful news." He sighed contentedly. "How generous of that Human to buy the beach for us! I thought Humans were a selfish, greedy, irresponsible species, but not all of them are like that. We're lucky to have our beach, but what about the other Turtle Beaches which are being built on by hotels and roads? Where will they go to lay?"

'Z' interrupted this sad and worrying thought.

"Sir, if we don't get the next batch of Matriarchs up the beach soon, we won't be increasing Turtle numbers or taking advantage of *our* Humans' wonderful help."

"Quite right, quite right 'Z'! What a wonderful practical mind you have!"

"Being short of a flipper doesn't mean anything's wrong with my brain," rejoined 'Z', rather brusquely. "Although," she added, turning to Letty, "if it wasn't for good friends I wouldn't be here at all."

Wiping away a joyful tear, Letty busied herself with the Primagravidas, the first-time Matriarchs.

"Come along dears, follow your instincts and you'll be fine. We'll make a recce along the beach. When you see a spot you like, peel off, float in as close as possible, take a deep breath and move up the sand fast. We're lucky, no nasty Humans, Dogs or other predators will be a threat. Good luck girls!" And with that she was away, swimming strongly, leading her group towards the wide stretch of soft sand. The Zamorin, George, Bella and Zozimus watched with love and respect.

"My turn next year, Zoz," said Bella, affectionately flapping her flipper over Zozimus's shining carapace.

"When I was in Liopleurodon's cave I didn't think either of us would be around next year." She shivered recalling the terrible experience. "But here's to it and to its Special Metanoia and Scrimmage Games!"

"And to all our brave and generous Human friends!" added the Zamorin.

Chapter Twenty-Five

BREAKFAST ON THE BEACH

Sparkling slits of glittering light shimmered through the jalousies of the east-facing room. Penny rolled over in bed and opened her eyes. It must have gone six o'clock, she reckoned, and she was still in bed on the last day of her holiday! Later, Granny Fairweather and herself would board the plane bound for England for the long overnight flight. What wonderful events had happened during her stay! Or were they all a figment of her imagination? No, the terror and revulsion she'd felt when Liopleurodon reared up from the sea hadn't been imagined! She could still smell its stale, stinking breath! In the days following the stupendous 'Thank you' display put on by the Leatherbacks, she and Jimmy, accompanied by their interpreter, Chico, had been up almost every night with the Turtle Custodians. They'd kept the beach clear of rubbish, especially deathly plastic bags, chased away Dogs and helped guard the female Leatherbacks as they came up the beach to lay. Letty had reappeared about five times, the usual number for an adult Turtle, Chico grandly informed them. They'd met other females too. Letty asked them to stay with a female called Tasha throughout the entire laying, making sure she and her eggs were safe. Another night they'd met Volly, who'd grunted and sighed and chuffed and chuntered from the moment she came out of the water until re-entering it. Chico said she was a well-known gossip in Leatherback circles! It had been an enchanted time: ensuring the Leatherbacks' safety; listening to their soft, satisfied gruntings as the sand went flying in all directions; drinking fresh coconut juice from the shell and trying to learn the local patois with the help of Jomo, Cora and the other Custodians.

Now it had come to an end. Penny sighed regretfully. Gemma had insisted she went to bed and had some sleep the night before the long flight. How many Turtles had she missed? Who had come up in the night? Jumping quickly out of bed, she pulled on shirt and shorts and ran down to the beach. Yes! There were the familiar tractor trails on the sand. Looking fondly at them she wondered to whom they belonged. There was a massive trail coming from and going to the sea in almost straight lines. This showed an older, experienced female. Despite the huge tracks, it certainly wouldn't be a male – George or Zoz for example. They knew better than to come anywhere near the shoreline, especially George! Here was a smaller, more erratic, trail indicating a young, inexperienced female meandering along the beach. Walking slowly along with her eyes down, she'd counted up to five trails before realising Jimmy was approaching from the opposite direction. He appeared very different from the boy she'd first met. Slimmer and more athletic looking, possibly because he'd jettisoned his bright orange life-jacket! He was sauntering along confidently with his eyes fixed on the sand. Suddenly, he disappeared, slipping out of sight down a steep sandbank into the murky, viscous stream that flowed turgidly across the beach. She grinned reminiscently and waited for an anguished shout of "Help!" but none came. After a muttered "darn it," he reappeared, heaving himself out of the glutinous sand, and continued unperturbed towards her, eyes still fixed on the ground.

"Hey, Jimmy! I see you don't need any help getting out of Black Rock Gully now!" laughed Penny.

"Are you looking for Leatherback trails too?"

"Yep. I've got three. What about you?"

"Only five so far."

"That's eight, Penny, could be worse."

"*If* they are eight *different* Turtles. They could all be repeat layers who have been up before."

"Pa says we've got to stay positive. At least they know their beach is safe. He's going to see the Prime Minister this morning about his plans."

"So's Mum and Mr Kanhai. We've got the morning to ourselves!" exclaimed Penny gleefully.

"Come on – let's go to Pelican Retreat and cadge some breakfast from Fan-Fan!"

Smoke from the cook fire was curling up from Fan-Fan's brightly coloured chattel house and the smell of delicious, freshly-baked salt bread cutters drifted across the beach. The Pelicans, after which the hut was named, sat in a row on Fan-Fan's boat looking disapproving, their glistening eyes closely following his every move.

"Just wait 'til he throws the fish heads away. They'll move like greased lightning!" smiled Penny.

"Ahoy dere pickneys! Yo lookin' fer de bread cutters?" asked Fan-Fan, appearing round the side of the hut. "What yo want in dem – ham, cheese, de flying fish?"

"Don't feel like eating flying fish after that terrific exhibition they put on for the Leatherbacks," said Penny. "I feel as if I might be eating one of the acrobats!"

"Me too," agreed Jimmy.

"Sure ting, sure ting, bu' dere's lots of dem. Cheese ok?"

Penny and Jimmy nodded.

"An' a dish o' good strong corfee or mabbe guava? Hereyah's some nutty banana bread wit' cherry jam and johnny bakes to fill in de gaps. Ah knows how famished yo pickneys get."

Fan-Fan bustled about, preparing the tasty meal, happy to share breakfast with his guests.

"Yo leavin' us?" he queried.

"I am, not Jimmy," replied Penny. "It's been a great holiday. I don't want to go."

"Yo return nex' yeara an' guard de Turtles. Firs' day – yo come sailin' wit' me an' help sell ma fruit. De nex' day, we get down to Turtle protectin'. Ok?"

"Sure ting man," teased Penny, "Ah sure look forward to dat time. But ah *still* don' want to leave!"

Fan-Fan rocked with mirth at her attempt to speak the island patois, but Penny lowered her head, her eyes full of tears. Nothing was going to replace this very special place. Adrian Kanhai had been right. It was an island where unique and wonderful plants and creatures existed, but he'd forgotten to mention the extra special people. Fan-Fan turned to Jimmy.

"When yo goin', man?" he asked.

"After Pa's fixed the legalities for the beach to become an International Site of Special Scientific Interest," replied Jimmy. "He's got appointments with Adrian Kanhai and the Prime Minister this morning to start sorting it out. He says there's no way he's leaving until it's all tied up to his satisfaction. It's really complicated. International Wildlife Treaties and Widecast and Fishing Rights and ecologists and lawyers and beach traders are involved. It'll take time."

Putting his arm affectionately round Penny's shoulder, Fan-Fan offered her a plate of tangy bread cutters.

"Hereyah, help yoself an' tink o' nex' time yo visit. Yo speak de patois good den!"

Penny sniffed, smiled and stuffed a cutter into her mouth with relish. The fan palms rustled softly as the onshore wind began, a large land crab scuttled sideways across the beach, reminding her of Jimmy's 'rescue' on that first day and the Pelicans took off in one synchronised swoop as Fan-Fan threw fish remnants to them. Breakfast on the beach was Heaven!

The entire day was Heaven. Granny Fairweather had told them some hilarious stories about her A.T.A. days. On one hot day she'd flown a Spitfire to Duxford wearing her tennis shorts. She was greeted by a group of scantily clad R.A.F. pilots who'd been sun-bathing. Their amazement at seeing a pair of shapely legs followed by a vivacious red-head emerging from the cockpit had been total! Then they'd been joined by Walcott, the cabin boy from the yacht, and his two brothers Worrall and Weekes, and sisters, Faith and Charity. Granny had shooed them down to the beach, and they'd plunged straightaway into the crystalline water and swum and body-surfed. Jimmy had shown them how to kayak and Walcott showed them how to shin up a coconut palm and cut down fruit, but even his brothers had difficulty doing this. Thumps, shouts and yells resounded along the beach as the children crashed onto the crackling palm branches lying on the ground. After a picnic, which the family had brought, they organised a cricket match. Holidaymakers from the hotel joined in and two teams formed. The brothers' innings was good, but it was beaten by their sisters, who hit the ball to the boundary, the sea, time after time. They were all brilliant players and proudly informed the others that they had relatives who'd played for the West Indies and been world class sportsmen. Even now, they said, they were "veree revered in de West Indies an' in de cricketen' world".

At last, exhausted, they had stretched out under the shady mango trees and Merlyn had brought them a delicious island tea. She knew the family as they lived in the same village, Caithness Point on Pirates Bay. They promised Penny that next time she came to the island they'd explore the ancient Pirate Paths down the cliffside and try to find the caves where treasure used to be hidden. Far too quickly it was time for Penny to say goodbye, go up to the hotel and prepare for departure.

"Listen good ladies!" commanded the irrepressible Chico from his perch on Penny's arm. "Yo wanna come back 'ere pretty darn quick! Them Turtles needs yo. If anything happens to dem, it'll be *your* fault," he added accusingly, a long tear oozing from his beady eye.

"We'll come back, Chico. Don't you go eating too many paw-paws! You know what they do to you!" Granny Fairweather patted Chico affectionately on the scimitar-shaped beak. Another long tear oozed from the other eye.

"Come on Penny, time to go."

Swaying in the Bacanoo tree, the Cocrico birds made their usual discordant din as they watched Jomo load the taxi with luggage. Undetected, Chico stealthily swooped from his perch, over the low roof and into the tree. He had an idea. As Jomo went into the cool lobby to collect the family, he quickly flew into the open back of the car and hid behind the mounds of cases, chortling gleefully to himself.

"Hee, hee, hee! Who's a clever Parrot? Hee, hee, hee!"

From the hotel came Jomo, Gemma, Granny Fairweather, Penny, Alistair MacRobert and … Livingston, his old enemy!

"Dere! Dere he is boss! Ah knew that dratted bird was trouble!" exclaimed Livingston, immediately spying Chico's brightly-hued plumage. From behind the luggage Chico squawked in dismay.

"CHICO! Come out of there! You can't go to the airport. Cora will impound you as highly dangerous wildlife and put you in quarantine for six months. You silly bird!" tutted Alistair crossly, holding out his arm. The others laughed as a crestfallen Chico reluctantly climbed onto it, his plan foiled.

"I'm back to silly bird, am I boss?" he asked mournfully. But there was a chorus of denial.

"No, Chico, you're still a hero. You always will be after what you did. You'll see us again soon."

Even Livingston joined in and promised some fresh banana if he came quietly. Transferring himself to Livingston, Chico was transported back to his usual perch outside the Motmot Restaurant. As the party climbed into the taxi and waved goodbye they heard a piercingly loud screech. Chico was nailing an innocent new visitor.

"'Ello, 'ello! Who're you? I'm Chico. I'm a clever Parrot, *very clever*. I'm an 'ero, I am!"

THE END

WANT TO KNOW MORE? WANT TO HELP PRESERVE THE GIANT LEATHERBACK? HERE ARE SOME USEFUL CONTACTS:

BBC Wildlife Magazine
44 (0) 1179 279009
www.bbcwildlifemagazine.com

Earthwatch
44 (0) 1865 318838, fax 44 (0) 1865 311383
www.earthwatch.org

Florida Wildlife Magazine
1 850 410 4944
www.floridawildlifemagazine.com

International Reptile Conservation
www.ircf.org
(San José, U.S.A.) Foundation

International Reptile Foundation.org   National Reptile Foundation;
P.O. Box 2533; Fort Bragg; Calif.; 95437: U.S.A.
fax 1 408 270 50 06
www.nationalreptilefoundation.org/

Marine Conservation Society
44 (0) 1989 566017, fax 44 (0) 1989 567815
www.mcsuk.org
(Ross-on-Wye, UK)

Marine Conservation Volunteer
www.frontier.ac.uk

National Geographic
www.nationalgeographic.com

National Wildlife Magazine
1 850 822 9919
www.nwf.org/nationalwildlife

New Scientist Magazine
www.newscientist.com

Oceana
www.oceana.org

Programmes
www.earthwatch.org
www.watamuturtles.com

Save Our Sea Turtles
www.sos-tobago.org

Sea Turtle Survival League
4424 N.W. 13th St; Suite B-11; Gainesville; FL 32609; U.S.A.
www.cccturtle.org

The Society For Environmental Exploration
44 (0) 207 6132422, fax 44 (0) 207 6132992
www.frontier.ac.uk

Surfers Against Sewage
44 (0) 1872 555950
www.sas.org.uk

Wildlife Extra
44 (0) 1432 760367
www.wildlifeextra.com